THE TREE AND THE TABLET

The St. James Chronicles
Book 1

Kathryn O'Brien

The Tree and the Tablet
Book 1 of the St. James Chronicles
Text copyright © 2018 - 2020 by Kathryn O'Brien.
All Rights Reserved.

Edited by Jessica Gibson
Interior Design and formatting by Kody Boye Publishing Services
Cover Design by Maria Spada Book Cover Design

No part of this book, or any part thereof, may be reproduced or transmitted in any form or by any means, electronic or mechanical, including photocopying, recording, or by any information storage and retrieval system, or by any other means without written permission of Kathryn O'Brien.

Any reference to books, authors, products, or name brands is in no way an endorsement by Kathryn O'Brien, and she has never received payment for any mention of such.

Any mention of individual names was purely intentional, and that's what happens when you are part of my life.

In Loving Memory of Sherri Lowder
Thank you for being my best friend.
Patiently, I await the day when we will meet again.

And a Special Thank you to:

To David, my rock and my world, who stood by and listened to my rambling and nodded in silence.

To John, who patiently contributed to my discoveries and who always helped me be better by encouraging me and loving me for who I am.

To Daddy, I love you. Thank you for always being there and supporting me no matter what.

And to Two very special women...
(You know who you are).
I can't wait to go to Greece with you.

CHAPTER 1

Glancing out of the windows nearby, the rain fell in dark, thick sheets, landing heavily on the tarmac at SeaTac airport, making it difficult to see the lights of the landing planes. Though heavy rain was usual in November, this seemed a bit extreme. It was only two days before Thanksgiving. What a terrible time to have to travel.

My beautiful niece was sitting across from me, her long blonde hair in braids. Piercing blue eyes, framed with lashes that most women dream of having, were filled with tears as she looked off into the darkness. Clutched to her chest, was a somewhat ragged looking teddy bear that had been passed down to her from her mother. Her beautiful spirit seemed crushed and subdued under the weight of her sadness and her small, fragile, five-year-old shoulders sagged in heart wrenching but subdued crying. My soul wept at the sight of her, at the thought of the unbearable burden such a young and vibrant child had to endure.

Kelsey was such a happy child who always seemed to have a ready smile, a funny joke and a warm hug. She was always giggling at things, or even just laughing at her own thoughts, as if she just heard the funniest story. This is a transformation I would have preferred to never see. So young, so beautiful, and so sad.

She was only supposed to be with me for the holiday so my sister, Andrea, and her husband, Jaxon, could prepare for the arrival of their new baby boy, which they had decided to name Dylon. Now, we had to travel to Denver to attend a funeral and reading of the will.

Andrea and Jaxon, on their way to the hospital to have Dylon, were T-Boned at an intersection by a beer delivery truck. The police officer who called to tell me about the accident, said the coroner had found evidence of the driver having had a seizure. His foot was discovered pressed firmly against the gas pedal, which was why the truck traveled so far through the intersection. It went straight through the intersection and right into Andrea's side of the car, carrying it up into an embankment and a steel light post which pinned in Jaxon as well. They all died on impact. The emergency medical personnel tried to save Dylon. He was in the birth canal at impact and there was some speculation by the officer that Jaxon may have been distracted by the events in the car, but there was really no way to know for sure. It really didn't matter because it turned out the impact was too much for him and he died shortly after they extracted him.

A tear slipped down my cheek. The airport seemed to be closing in on me and I just wanted to run far away or wake up from this nightmare. Kelsey was all I had left now.

My parents were gone as were Jaxon's. I missed my mom. She was always the one I could talk to when I was struggling. After her disappearance, I stayed in Allyn, Washington at our childhood home and 'Drea and Jaxon moved into his parent's home in Cherry Hills, outside of Denver, Colorado.

Lost in my own thoughts, I failed to notice Kelsey's approach or register her soft voice as she spoke. Her lips moved again as I watched her tiny fingers extend toward me in a haze to tap me on the arm, "Auntie?"

Even though I had just watched her actions, for some reason, I jumped, slightly startled by her touch. Staring at her swollen red eyes, I smiled gently as I pushed a stray lock of hair out of her face. "I'm so sorry, Kells. Do you need something?"

She pointed at the ticket counter and said, "That lady talked on the speaker thingy and said that it's time to get on the plane." Having travelled a lot between me and my sister, she knew about the ins and outs of airports and intercoms so I wasn't really surprised by her revelation.

It was true. The few people who were there this late, slowly ambled in the general direction of the stewardess assigned to check tickets and were collecting in a line near the gate. Glancing back to her, I smiled and tried to sound as cheerful as I could, "Well, then, I guess we better gather our things and get in line."

Kelsey nodded. Leaning over, I grabbed the small carry-on kennel with my four-pound Yorkshire terrier, Peanut, and my backpack that had the necessities. Kelsey only had her small rolling carry on, her pink bedazzled backpack with snacks inside, and her teddy. She slipped her hand into mine and we proceeded to the gate.

We quickly boarded the plane to get situated. It was difficult not to notice the extremely handsome man sitting in the same row with us. Feeling the pull of the distraction offered by the view, I sighed softly. He sat in the window seat and as I looked at him, I felt an instant connection like someone had tied an invisible string around us and we were being drawn together. There was a photo of what looked like a beautiful woman in his hand and he quickly slipped the picture into some obscure place that I failed to see, as if he was a street magician. Wondering how I could be thinking of a man at a time like this, I tried to focus on other things but just couldn't stop staring at him.

When he looked up at me, his expression was guarded but I couldn't help feeling that he knew me somehow. The connection was electric, as if a lightning bolt pierced my soul which set every limb in my body into shock, filling me with a tingling sensation. Dark hair, silky and black, shone softly in the muted light and was loosely combed back from his face. The

The Tree and the Tablet

minimal lighting in the plane glinted off his hair, making it look almost blue which made me think of a raven's wings in the sun.

Thick, black lashes surrounded deep, but bright green eyes, the color of the clearest Columbian emeralds. However, the light danced in his eyes and made them look different colors of green with every movement. The dark outline of his thick lashes enhanced the effect. Small crow's feet spread out from the sides of his eyes, as if he spent hours smiling and laughing. His lips were soft, yet strong looking. He smiled at us, showing perfect white teeth, one dimple on his left cheek and small wrinkles at the corner of his mouth, confirming the suspicion that he spent a good amount of time enjoying life. They were totally kissable lips, but those eyes were amazing. My breath caught in my throat.

His face was ruggedly handsome, chiseled like a statue but soft around the edges. His golden tan skin made me wonder what he did for a living as it was obvious he worked outdoors. Looking at him reminded me of coming across a deep, green pool in a forest haven that you just wanted to strip naked and jump into.

He looked away as if he'd read my mind and turning, he asked Kelsey, "Would you like to sit by the window?" I just about melted right there. My knees felt like jello and I struggled to keep my balance. His voice, strong and deep timbered, but not so deep as to be scary sounding, was heaven to my ears. Standing there, I openly stared at him like some lovesick puppy desperate for his attention and wanting him to say so much more. I was thirty-two years old dammit! What was wrong with me? *Snap out of it,*

Maggie!

He looked at me with a puzzled expression, asking, "What did you just say?"

Oh, God! I said that out loud? The blush raged all the way from my toes up to the roots of my hair. My face was on fire and my blonde hair could have been turned red from my embarrassment. The extreme shyness I always struggled with took over and I stammered and stumbled over myself as I quickly said, "What? I didn't say anything." Just then, Kelsey spoke up and said, "Yes, please."

Her perfectly timed response distracted him enough to get his focus off of me. Gingerly, he stood up, as much as he could in the cramped quarters, to assist Kelsey to her seat. So close to me now, I could feel the vibration from the soft and gentle words he was saying to Kelsey yet I wasn't able to make out the exact words because he was talking so softly, but she giggled and said, "Thank you," in her sweetest voice. Dehydration struck me and I nervously licked my lips. Oh, good lord, he almost caught me staring at his butt.

As he returned to his semi-upright position and turned to face me again, I was struck by a sense of height. Hard to tell when you're on a plane, but I presumed he was just over six feet tall. Even though he had on loose fitting blue jeans and a soft green t-shirt that somehow made his eyes seem brighter, I could tell he had a muscular build. The tightness of his shirt outlined his perfectly chiseled torso and the short sleeves of the t-shirt revealed bulging biceps that rippled when he gripped the back of the seat in front of him. However, he wasn't like Mr. Universe or any of those bodybuilder types.

Just then, a person coming down the aisle bumped into me from behind and with almost nowhere to go, I fell into his arms. He caught me and kept us from falling over together, I couldn't help but notice how large and tan his hands looked framed against the lightness of my upper arms. The touch caused a tingling sensation to shoot through me. He held onto me for just a little longer than necessary and it felt so good. A sigh escaped my lips before I could stop it. Was it hot on this plane? It felt like I was burning from the inside out. Fire licked at my open heart and sent magma racing through my veins instead of blood.

Attempting to recover from the momentary weakness, I took a deep breath in through my nose. Nope, that wasn't helping. Oh, good lord help me, he smelled amazing; like Chai-tea and the forest after it rained, with a hint of lavender. It was very soothing but also exciting. A vision of using him as a blanket entered my mind. My thoughts were suddenly interrupted by his sensual voice.

"I got this." he said jovially, as if he had read my mind. He wrapped his arms around me and lifted me up, spinning around with me in his arms. The contact was exhilarating and soothing all at once. It seemed effortless for him to move around in such a small space. My heart raced and the pulsing of blood pounding in my brain, combined with the other more extreme sensations throughout my entire body were driving me crazy but left me wanting more. Could he feel that? Did he know what he was doing to me? Closing my eyes, I offered up a little thank you to whatever force guided this man's arms to encircle me.

My blood was pumping through me in a pulsating pattern like fire followed by the waves of the ocean. The sensation was everywhere. Even my virgin parts ached with some unknown feeling. Holding my breath in anticipation, I knew I would die if he didn't let go of me but it felt so good I didn't want it to end. For just a split second, I wondered who the woman in the picture was. Just then, I was set on my feet in front of the middle seat and he stated matter-of-factly with a cheeky grin, "There you go."

Aching emptiness immediately replaced the pure bliss I'd been privy to only moments before. A small sound escaped me like a grunt from being punched in the stomach. The sensations were replaced with a longing that was so intense it was painful, but not like anything I'd ever felt before. Why was I acting like this? Was I really that lonely or desperate for attention, or was it the ache of my losses seeking comfort in the arms of a stranger? There were so many years I'd spent putting off getting involved with men but none ever made me feel like this stranger had in only this short of a time. Maybe my internal clock was telling me it was time to start dating. Again, I thought about the time I spent so wrapped up in my work and being lost after Mom, that I hadn't spent much time on the dating circuit in the past five years. It wasn't that I didn't want to get involved with someone, it was just the few men I'd dated had never turned into anything serious. Somehow, I always figured that it would happen when it was meant to happen. When I was younger and yearned for someone to share my time with, I was frustrated that I just couldn't seem to make a connection. There was one time in college I got close to giving up my virginity, but an intense feeling of nausea stopped that before it came to fruition. Mom always said that there was a time and place for everything, and that my match was waiting for the perfect time. However, I felt about this stranger, it just wasn't good timing. It never was. Ugh!

The small intimacy of our connection had me so frazzled, I quickly looked down to compose myself and discovered that Kelsey had settled into her seat. She was looking out the window into the darkness.

Reaching down into the isle, he handed me Peanut and then motioned to the upper compartment with Kelsey's small carry-on in his hand. Nodding in unspoken communication with a faint smile of appreciation, I checked on Peanut. Placing her carrier under the seat in front of me, I was still contemplating my feelings about the recent encounter.

Exasperated with myself and my inability to overcome my social anxiety to talk to this baffling enigma beside me, I hurriedly buckled my seatbelt. Hearing a faint sniffle from Kelsey, I turned toward her, placed my hand on her arm and looked out the window with her in silence. There wasn't much to see, but it didn't really matter.

Flying always made me nervous and I chewed my lower lip, worried about the take-off, but soon we were in the air. Suddenly, I remembered why we were making this trip. It was like a hammer on my heart, pounding in the pain like it was a nail with every beat. What was going to happen? Glancing down at Kelsey. She was sleeping peacefully in the seat next to me. At this moment, she seemed untroubled, and I found myself wondering if she'd have the nightmares on the plane that she'd been riddled with since coming to stay with me. Andrea had assured me it was due to a movie she'd watched, but I couldn't shake the feeling that it was something more than what she made it out to be. Watching her for signs of distress, the stain from her past tears streaked her face. Carefully, I leaned over and placed a soft kiss on her little blonde head whispering, "It'll be ok, Kells. Sweet dreams, sweetie." How do kids do that? They just sleep wherever they want, no matter what's going on. So utterly exhausted, I closed my eyes and drifted in and out of consciousness for the next ten minutes.

Surfacing through a haze of incoherent thoughts, my pillow seemed remarkably firm but also warm. There was the distinct impression that my face was resting on a rock of some sort rather than a pillow, but it wasn't uncomfortable. A deep rumble of thunder that distinctly sounded like words was saying, "Good Morning!" My mind instantly snapped awake with the realization that I'd fallen asleep on the arm of the god-like male passenger sitting next to me. Fully awake now, I sat straight up in my seat and would have flown completely out of the seat if it weren't for the seatbelt holding me in place. Kelsey was awake next to me and was smiling for the first time in days. Evidently, we'd landed in Denver safe and sound. Judging by the people moving past us in the aisle, I'd say we were parked safely at the terminal. Kelsey said softly with a slight giggle, "You were snoring."

The stranger stood up and handed us Kelsey's bag from the overhead compartment. Mortified, I grasped the bag and set it in front of his now vacant seat. When I looked up to thank him, he was gone. No goodbye. Nothing! A tiny feeling of emptiness flitted through me. It was a little deflating to know I wasn't worth another thought to him, however, it was probably for the best. There certainly wasn't time to deal with a love interest in the midst of my current problems. He may not have even been real. Maybe he was just a dream. Just an imaginary angel to comfort my anguished heart for a moment in time. Looking around one last time to try and find my elusive stranger, he was simply not there. Shrugging, I unbuckled myself, gathered our belongings and with Peanut snuggled safely in her carrier, we exited the plane.

On our way out to the rental car agency, we decided to go to the restroom. Upon entering the large bathroom, there was a floor to ceiling mirror. Glancing up from my pondering, I came across a hideous site. No wonder everyone we passed in the airport was looking at me strangely. The view that presented itself to me in the mirror was a bedraggled mess of a woman. Standing in at five foot six inches tall and weighing a whopping one hundred and twenty pounds was this puffy faced urchin with blonde hair and blue eyes. Makeup was not something I regularly wore but I could've used some right then. My eyes had dark circles under them and were puffy and red from crying so much. Unfortunately, my face was a little gaunt from lack of sleep and not eating. Disheveled and wrinkled clothing hung loosely around my slight frame. Half of my long hair had escaped the bun it was in and there were hair pins sticking out of my head. No wonder he ran away. Yikes!

Kelsey finished using the restroom and after washing her hands, she stopped in front of the mirror. Looking up at my image, she shook her head and said, "You're a mess, Auntie."

As I glanced down at her solemn face, I smiled in resignation and said, "Yes, it appears I am."

We both laughed hysterically. Making an effort to fix my hair, I also straightened my clothes as best I could and we headed out to pick up our rental car.

CHAPTER 2

Walking out into the brilliant morning sun, I wished I'd arranged for a car to pick us up at the airport rather than having to drive a rental. Oh, well! Too late for that. Besides, it would distract me from feeling for a bit. Driving always kept me focused on the task at hand and helped me to forget my worries, especially in Denver. The traffic just got worse and worse every time I came back. Just then, my stomach rumbled loudly, and I wondered how my miniature companion felt. "Well, Kelsey, after we get the rental car and let Peanut out, what do you say we get some grub?"

Keeping pace beside me and lost in thought with a sullen expression on her face, she seemed to perk up a bit. "That sounds awesome! I'm starving! I could eat everything on the whole planet right now!" she exclaimed exuberantly, rubbing her tummy.

"Okey, dokey, then," I added exuberantly, trying to sound happier than I was as we walked across the four lanes of traffic to the rental agency pickup spot. Peanut whimpered in her kennel. "I know, baby. Not much longer and you can empty your bladder." Peanut was a great travel companion, she did remarkably well on all the trips I'd taken in the past. If she hadn't, I would've found someone to watch her. Maybe I should've left her with my best friend, Sherri, back in Allyn. Her and her three grandbabies loved Peanut. I felt like I was being selfish by wanting everyone and everything that was dear to me to be close.

The discount rental car transporter pulled up with an elderly, kind-faced gentleman behind the wheel. The guy exited the bus. Looking pointedly at me and Kelsey, he asked, "Margaret St. James?"

"Yes, that's me," I said, feeling a little tired still from the trip. I stepped up and held out my phone with the e-ticket on it for the rental car reservation.

He nodded as he looked us over and stated, "Truth is, you're it." Bending at the waist to make eye contact with Kelsey, solemnly he asked, "Princess, can I please take your bag for you?"

Kelsey giggled and stepped back saying regally in her best princess voice, "Yes, sir. You may." She waved her hand toward her bag. This was followed by another little chuckle as she glanced at him sideways suddenly shy.

Smiling softly, he bowed as he took the small bag and said, "If you'd like to follow me, I'll just place your bags on the bus for you." Turning and waving toward the open doors of the transporter, he continued, "The softest seats are close to the front." Taking my bag from me, he continued, "Let me take that for you, M'lady."

"Thank you, kind sir," I responded, playing along as I followed him onto the bus.

Kelsey was seated in the front and wiggling around, she giggled, "Auntie, this seat really is the softest." She hopped up and down, "I know, I tried them."

The bus driver chuckled as he scooted past me to settle in the driver's seat. "See, I told you. Fit for a princess."

She giggled again as I sat next to her, placing Peanut on the floor in front of me. My eyes wide, I looked at her with mock excitement, "Geez, I think we should ask them to put these in every plane. What do you think?"

She nodded her head. "Oh, yes. Those seats were very hard." We laughed for a bit and then sat quiet staring out the windows toward the sweeping views in front of us.

I couldn't help noticing how bright and sunny it was. Denver never ceased to amaze me. It could be seventy-five and sunny in the middle of winter, and the very next day, it would be sub-zero and snowing.

The ride to the rental agency was short. We took Peanut out

to do her queenly duties.

"Hey, Kelsey, what do you think about going to The Breakfast Palace in Greenwood Village on our way to the house?"

"Oh, that sounds so yummy," she said jumping around in a circle. "I can't wait. Do you think they'll be open?"

Glancing down at my phone to see what time it was, I recalled that they were open around the clock. "Yes, definitely."

Kelsey did another jig, and Peanut, seeming to sense her mood, started yipping and spinning in a circle as well. Kelsey laughed at her and kneeling to pat her on the head, asked, "Did you hear that, Peanut?" She paused briefly as if she expected an answer. "We're going to have pancakes!" She jumped up and clapped her hands excitedly. Peanut echoed her excitement by barking and jumping on her hind legs in response. We both laughed.

"It's settled then." Placing Peanut back into her crate, we were soon on our way. The traffic was mild given it was a weekday, but there were always those wonderful drivers out there that made me wish that I couldn't drive so I wouldn't have to deal with them. You know, the ones who cut you off at the last minute diving across four lanes of traffic and then giving you the sign language that depicts that they are unhappy that you were in their way? Yeah, those ones.

Arriving at The Breakfast Palace, I was flooded with memories of the many times we had all gone out to eat there. The food was always good, down home type breakfast and it was

The Tree and the Tablet

one of our favorite places to go when I'd visit. Kelsey grabbed Peanut's kennel and we took her inside. Once we were seated in a booth and Peanut was safely stowed under the table, we began discussing what we would eat for breakfast. As Kelsey sort of bounced up and down in her seat, she pointed to the many pictures in the menu, saying things like, "Mmmm, that looks good" and "Does this have sausage or bacon?"

The waitress approached, smiling widely at Kelsey's animated behavior. The tag on her pocket front read, *LIZ*. Looking to me, she said, "She must be about five. I have a niece her age." At my nod, she continued, "They're so cute at this age." She smiled again as Kelsey started to speak.

In her most grown-up voice, she said, "I'll have the waffle with strawberries and whip cream." Looking up at the waitress, she firmly stated, "No sausage, only bacon."

"Okay. Is there anything else for you, your highness?" Liz smiled and poised her pen to write more on her pad. Kelsey grinned broadly.

"Do you have the large glasses of orange juice because I really like orange juice." She looked down at the menu briefly and then back up at Liz.

"Oh, yes, miss! That's a great choice." She giggled and then looked at me for my order.

"I'll have the short stack of buttermilk pancakes with sausage. I need a lot of coffee with cream and I'll also have orange juice." Giving her a brief nod, I handed her mine and Kelsey's menus.

17

She returned the nod as she took the menus and tucked them under her arm. "I'll be right back with those drinks."

Liz returned quickly, as promised, and set the drinks on the table, a small twinkle lit her eyes as she glanced down at Kelsey. As we waited for our meal, Kelsey pensively drew pictures on her paper kid's menu that had come with crayons. Watching her, I giggled with her when she'd magically make a discovery. The altitude was already getting to me though and I waived Liz over to the table.

"What can I do for you?" she looked at me expectantly with a gentle kindness in her eyes.

"Can I get a large glass of water please?"

"Sure thing!" Looking over Kelsey's picture, she exclaimed, "Wow! That's a pretty awesome drawing. What are those things?" she pointed at some scribbles on the paper.

Kelsey pointed to them and said, "I don't know, but they're funny animals that I dreamed about. I think they're called Santa." She shrugged her shoulders and went back to her coloring.

Liz laughed, "Kids have the best imaginations." She walked away saying, "I'll be right back with that water." She returned, stating, "Your food will be up soon."

"Thank you." Rummaging through my purse, I finally located the ibuprofen bottle and promptly swallowed three of the little pills. Our food arrived and I found it hard to finish my meal as the weight of the upcoming meeting, the pain of losing my only sister, and exhaustion, forced my appetite into hibernation.

The Tree and the Tablet

Kelsey, having finished her meal in record time, noticed that I was sitting quietly looking out the window with my meal unfinished and asked, "If you're done with those, can I have them?"

Trying to sound happy, I replied, "Absolutely," While lifting the plate to push the pancakes off onto hers. She noticed the sausage link and stopped me.

"Ewe! No sausage please." She made the funniest face. Nodding in agreement, I finished pushing the pancakes off while keeping the sausage contained to my plate. Sighing heavily, she asked, "Can you please pass me the syrup?"

"So sorry, is there not enough on there?" A slight smirk crossed my lips as she took the syrup and poured a generous amount onto the remaining pancakes. She was soon quick at work eating the pile of syrup with pancakes swimming in the middle. It was amazing that she could eat so much for such a tiny creature. It seemed that she may have a hidden pouch that went from her stomach down to her left leg to hold extra food.

Liz soon approached, "Is there anything else I can do for you?" Shaking my head slightly I could feel the grimace make my lips purse. She cocked her head to the side slightly as she watched me, "Here you go then." As she laid the bill on the table, she said, "Joe will ring you up at the counter when you're ready." She looked over at Kelsey, "Thank you for coming in today. It was a pleasure to serve you, your highness." She smiled broadly and bowed to Kelsey.

19

Kelsey giggled, "Thank you."

Gathering the check, Kelsey, and Peanut, we paid the bill on our way out.

Once again, we stood outside in the brilliant sunshine. As we walked across the parking lot, I thought about the impact it would have on Kelsey to go to her home with her parents being gone. Considering her carefully, I wondered if she'd be okay with going to the house with me or if I should spare her the emotional trauma and leave her with Andrea's best friend, Carolynn, instead. Deciding to just ask her if she would rather go there, I plucked up the courage, and asked cautiously, "Hey there, Kells?"

"Yeah?" She looked at me sideways, curiosity etched on her brow.

"Would you rather go to Carolyn's place and wait for me?" The minute the words left my mouth, I regretted it. Instantly, panic flew across her face and she looked like a doe in headlights trying to figure out whether she should stay or run. The fight or flight response was truly never more visible than in that moment, as it was embedded in every feature of her expression and her lower lip trembled as tears started to form in her brilliant blue eyes.

"No!" she emphatically exclaimed. Squaring her shoulders and turning to face me full on, Kelsey was almost hysterical when she continued. Her little hands clenched at her sides, her breathing raggedly moving through her clenched teeth and her eyes blinked rapidly as she swallowed hard to keep from crying.

The Tree and the Tablet

Suddenly she blurted out, "Don't leave me, please!" Tears were forming in her beautiful eyes and I wished I'd kept my mouth shut for once instead of speaking my mind before blurting out things.

"Kelsey, Sweetie! I'd never leave you. Not ever! Do you hear me?" Nodding her head yes with tears in her eyes, I reached over and hugged her tightly to me. Stroking her hair, I pulled away and placing my hand under her chin, I raised her face to look her in the eyes, "Kelsey, I was only asking because I want to make sure you're okay with going to the house, but if you want to, then we can go together and I won't leave you. Alright?" She began to relax a little.

Her little lips were pursed together in the most perfect pout and she nodded her head vigorously while trying to smile away her tears. "Alright then," I said, "jump in back with Peanut and buckle up." We hugged again, and I got her situated in the back seat. It was almost noon by the time we rolled up into the circular driveway on Cherry Hills Lane. The house was one of those built to look like a grand estate with pillars in the front and a large entryway. There was already a silver Mercedes in the driveway. Just as I turned off the engine, the front doors flew open and Jody, the maid and part-time nanny, came running as fast as her chubby little legs would carry her.

Andrea was a terrible housekeeper and even worse at cooking. They'd hired Jody when Kelsey was only two weeks old to help Andrea out for a couple months. She was so amazing that

21

they just kept her on full-time after the couple months were up. Jody was a sweet, older lady, with a round cherub-like face. She was very outgoing and exuberant. Never afraid to speak her mind, but mindful of what she said. Big brown eyes that were framed with red lashes surrounded by strawberry blonde hair streaked with silver lit up at the sight of Kelsey stepping out of the car. Jody's laugh sounded like a wind chime, soft and melodic, and her slightly high pitched but soft voice was so soothing to hear. She wrapped her plump arms around Kelsey and then turned to give me a hug. She was kind of short. Standing at just about the height of my shoulder, I couldn't help but have to scrunch down to give her a hug.

Trying to look happy, it was also easy to see that she had been crying and there was a shadow of sorrow in her eyes. Leaning down toward Kelsey and smiling widely, "How was your flight, sweetie?"

It was like a flood gate opened and Kelsey just poured out the information. Looking at me sideways and squinting her eyes together in mischief she started explaining, "Aunt Maggie fell asleep on this strange man on the plane."

Jody looked at me skeptically, but seeing my blush, replied, "I bet she did. She looks exhausted." Looking back at Kelsey, she asked, "Was he cute at least?"

Laughing loudly, Kelsey blurted out, "She snored on him! Isn't that funny?"

Jody smiled begrudgingly and winking in my direction, she

The Tree and the Tablet

started laughing as well. "Ah, Maggie, you do know how to impress them, don't you?"

As I slapped her on the arm, I beseeched, "Quit encouraging her. You're such a bad influence". Giggling slightly, I leaned over conspiratorially, whispering, "And, Yes, he was very nice to look at."

Jody's broad grin could be seen from space. It was so radiant and filled with silent approval as if she sensed something when I spoke of him.

Letting her down gently, I snickered, "Don't worry, we won't be seeing him again, he left rather abruptly." Jody seemed sad by this news but looked back to Kelsey with a jubilant smile on her face as Kelsey continued with her explanations.

"And he was a good pillow, huh, Aunt Maggie?" This, of course, was followed by the most raucous peels of joy, but it felt so good to laugh. We continued to chit chat about the complexities of sleeping on strange men as we made our way to the front door.

For a moment, we almost forgot. Just then, we entered the foyer of the large estate. I could smell the aroma of Jody's cooking as it wafted through the house to the doorway. Looking around expectantly, the gravity of the reality we faced suddenly struck us mute as we all suddenly became quite silent as if we were entering a tomb. The happiness from moments ago was quickly replaced with a solemn sadness that was so thick, it was almost as tangible and visible as a wall that we walked through upon entering.

Kelsey's shoulders drooped and she looked around expectantly. Then, she glanced up at the stairs with a look of longing in her eyes as if she were willing her parents to descend the long staircase to greet her.

Clearing her throat softley, Jody whispered, "I got your rooms ready." Realizing she had barely spoken, she took a shaky breath and quickly followed in a normal, but reverent tone, "Maggie, Mr. Jacobs is in the study waiting for you."

Making eye contact with Jody, "That explains the Mercedes in the driveway." Turning and leaning down, I placed a hand on Kelsey's shoulder to get her to look at me. "Kelsey, why don't you take Peanut out back and then go up to your room with Jody while I go talk to Mr. Jacobs."

It was like a light switch had been flicked. "Okay." She leaned over and unzipped the soft kennel that contained Peanut and skipped toward the back door calling Peanut out with her. Jody mouthed the words, "she'll be ok" to me as I longingly watched Kelsey go out to the backyard with my little dog in tow. I'd much rather be playing in the backyard than talking about wills and the final arrangements with Jaxon's attorney, Clinton Jacobs.

Smiling at Jody and giving her a half hug, "Thanks for everything. You truly are a gift." Jody blushed profusely which contrasted sharply with her strawberry hair. She turned and followed Kelsey out the back door.

Walking into the study, my stomach dropped as I looked

The Tree and the Tablet

above the fireplace opposite the desk to see the most recent family portrait. It showed Andrea dressed in a black turtleneck and her stomach painted to look like a pumpkin. Jaxon was sitting next to her dressed like a Chef, holding a pot below Andrea's swollen belly. On the other side of Andrea, Kelsey stood in a princess outfit holding a plate in one hand, a fork in the other, with a crazed expression. She managed to pull off a manaicle look that was accentuated by a hungry stare at the baby bump and pot. It was so them. They were always having fun and making jokes. A tear slipped out.

Turning away from the photo, Mr. Jacobs had stood up from behind the desk and reaching out my hand to shake his, he said earnestly, "Miss St. James, I'm so sorry for your loss. This won't take long." Clearing his throat, he sat down. He was a thin man. Almost anorexic looking. His aquiline nose curved downward at the tip toward his lips which gave him a hawk-like appearance. His eyes were small in his face and his hair was dark grey with large ears protruding from the side of his head.

Taking the seat across from him in the leather chair facing the window that looked out into the yard, I could see Kelsey throwing a ball for Peanut. A small smile flitted across my lips slightly at the contrast of the view of the happy child and dog playing in the yard and the somber lawyer sitting across from me.

"Jaxon and Andrea recently updated their wills. They both left everything to the children; however, since Dylon was part of the accident, everything defaults to a trust for Kelsey. The

Trustee is listed as one Daniel James BlackFeather. Have you any knowledge of Mr. BlackFeather?"

Shaking my head, "No, I've never heard of him."

"Well, I have a meeting with him later today. I'll give him your contact information. You'll also receive a copy of the contact information that I have for him." Tilting his head to the side, "Interesting, he lives in Washington." He squinted at the papers in his hand and turned the page, "the trust is fairly simple and basic. It states that all money will be held in trust until Kelsey is eighteen, at which point, she'll gain her full inheritance. A stipend amount of a thousand dollars a month will be automatically deposited into your bank account at the beginning of every month for use in the care of Kelsey and if there are any emergencies or needs for more money than that, then you'd need to contact the trustee, Mr. BlackFeather, in order to obtain the funds upon his approval." He looked up at me over his reading glasses to acknowledge I had heard him. "Of course, if something should happen to Kelsey prior to her eighteenth birthday, the remainder of the estate will be transferred to any living heir after fees are withdrawn for the Trustee. If there is no other heir, the money will be divided evenly between Mr. BlackFeather with the leftover portion to be contributed evenly to the various charities outlined in the will.

Shocked, I looked up at him sharply and exclaimed, "That's too much!" I wasn't even upset that I didn't get a share. I didn't need it. I just didn't think that I needed that much money every month to care for one child.

His surprise at my response halted him briefly. Holding up his hand to stop me from interrupting him, he calmly replied, "Never-the-less, the will states clearly that you are to do whatever it is that you see fit with the money as long as it will help Kelsey to have a happy and balanced life." He lowered his head and continued in a monotone voice, "The house will be sold and all holdings will be transferred to the trust account. A safe deposit box has been set up to hold the jewelry and sentimental items that are to be passed along to Kelsey when she turns eighteen." He turned the page, "Jaxon's made arrangements in his will to be buried in the family plot next to his parents. His final arrangements have all been handled and his service along with a memorial for your sister and Dylon will be in two days at Olmeyer Chapel."

Mr. Jacobs appeared to have suddenly taken ill or sat on a rather large and uncomfortable rock as his face became pale and he wriggled in his chair. "Miss St. James,"—clearing his throat—"Andrea had a special request for her remains. Also, there is the matter of what to do with Dylon, due to the unusual circumstance of his complete post-mortem birth."

Inhaling sharply, "What do you mean? I didn't know Dylon survived the crash."

"Oh, I'm sorry about that. That's not what I meant." He swallowed hard. "It's actually common for a baby to be partially born after a fatal incident to the mother. In this case, though, the emergency personnel pulled him from the birth canal to try and save him but it was too late. He was deceased upon impact and there was nothing they could do to bring him back." My heart plummeted into my stomach again. Seeing my crestfallen expression, he said, "Again, I apologize for my blunder." looking down, he mumbled, "I thought you knew."

Shaking my head briefly, a new wave of sorrow swept through me as I recalled in a whisper, "I asked if he survived but they said he was gone. They didn't elaborate on what the situation was and I didn't ask any other questions."

Nodding his head like a pigeon, he sighed and responded matter of factly. "Understandable." He cleared his throat yet again. "Well, um, anyway, it's customary to bury the child with the mother, but"— Hands shaking slightly, he reached for the glass of water at his left and took several large gulps. He clutched the papers in front of him now with a seemingly nervous intensity. Briefly, I wondered what got this man so worked up about the funeral arrangements for my sister. A troubled expression covered his face as he looked up at me uncertainly from his papers. Beady, golden eyes darted from me to the papers in his hand, and his pronounced Adam's apple bobbed up and down convulsively.

Firmly, I stated, "We'll bury him next to his father and mother, of course." Now he really looked nervous. Clearing his throat for the fourth time, — "I'm not sure how to say this, but your sister didn't want to be buried."

"Okay," Confused and curious, I wondered why it was such a troublesome thought for him, but undaunted, I ventured a guess, "She wanted to be cremated?"

Fidgeting with the papers again, he said, "Um, kind of." He looked like he was going to pass out.

Envisioning him falling backward in a faint because he had become so pale, I started to sit up. To his credit, he didn't lose total control of his senses, but it was maddening the way he was looking at me. What the heck had him so tongue tied? *For goodness sakes, why can't this man just speak the words?* My blood pressure felt like it was rising with every moment, and I just wanted to scream at him to spit it out. It took every muscle in my body and ounce of fortitude I had, not to lean over the desk, grab him by the front of his shirt, and shake him. Could he make this any more uncomfortable for me? Moments seemed like eternity as I waited for him to come to grips with what he needed to tell me. Finally, at the end of my rope, I took a deep breath and stated as calmly as I could, "Listen, Mr. Jacobs, this is going to take an extraordinary amount of time if you don't tell me what's going on."

Wiping the sweat from his brow, he blurted, "She wants to be cremated and buried as part of a tree!" This statement was followed with a nervous laugh. It was almost as if he vomited the words, they came out so fast. *Was I hearing things?*

"What???" As the words finally registered, an abbreviated laugh erupted from somewhere inside the room. Realizing it was me, I asked, "You're kidding, right? I mean, is that even possible?"

"No, ma'am! I mean, Yes, ma'am!" More fidgeting, "I mean, I'm sorry to say that I'm not kidding."

Placing my hand on my face and sighing heavily, I looked up at the ceiling. My inner thoughts raced, *Dammit, Andrea! When did you decide this? We had talked about this stuff a little when Mom disappeared, but I really hadn't wanted to discuss it and this tree thing was just weird, even for her.* To Mr. Jacobs, I calmly replied, "Well, this is something new then. However, even though I'm surprised by her decision, it seems like something she'd come up with. I suppose you have all of the pertinent information? Such as what I'm supposed to do with the tree or what the name of the company is that does this work?" Shaking my head, "You know this is ridiculous, right? I've never heard of such a thing."

"I understand. It's something fairly new and a company right here in Colorado has pioneered a way to turn the ashes into a biodegradable tree base that works to fertilize the tree while allowing the person to support the regrowth of the dwindling forestry in the world. It's an interesting prospect." Handing me a brochure with the picture of a tree on the front, he spoke in a reserved tone, "I've set everything up, but you could choose another option since it's something fairly new. There are no stipulations in the will about following this request."

Slightly stunned that the solicitor would suggest not

The Tree and the Tablet

following the will, I asked, "Why would I do that? If she wants to be a tree then far be it for me to stop that from happening. This *is* what she wants, right?"

He nodded begrudgingly. "It's just not something traditional. Are you sure? I mean, what will people say?"

Now a little perturbed by his judgment of my sister, my defenses rose, "Well, I'm not worried about what others will say. Besides, it's what she wanted. As for Dylon, I will have him buried with his father. I presume you took care of Andrea's cremation?"

"Yes. I'll call Olmeyer's and have them prepare the casket for Dylon and set up his headstone. Do you want Dylon in the same plot with his headstone next to Jaxon's?"

"That's fine." Flipping through the brochure, "Mr. Jacobs, did you do any research on this company to determine if they're on the up and up?" Looking out the window over his left shoulder, I could see that Kelsey, Peanut, and Jody were on their way into the house. They appeared to be chatting about something serious. The back door opened and closed followed by the sounds of footsteps mounting the stairwell to the bedrooms above. Peanut's little feet pitter-pattered across the floor. Peanut loved Kelsey. They were like little partners in crime. Where one went, the other followed, and vice versa. Turning a page in the brochure, I looked to Mr. Jacobs for a response.

"Yes, I did. It's a company that turns the ashes into a

biodegradable urn which is then buried with the sapling inside. Evidently, by making sure the tree is at least two years old, it's better able to adjust to the process of replanting. However, you can choose to get one that's up to ten years old. The two choices that your sister specified in her will for the types of trees are, the red maple, or a pink dogwood."

"Of course she did, because those are my two favorite trees." I mumbled under my breath.

"What was that, Miss St. James?" He was looking at me with a puzzled expression.

"Nothing." A soft sigh escaped my lips as I glanced up from the brochure in my hands to the unassuming lawyer, asking, "She didn't happen to mention where I'm supposed to plant this thing, did she? I mean, I'm assuming she doesn't want it planted in the forest or something, right?"

"She states clearly, in paragraph twenty-one, section three, that she wants the tree planted firmly in a highly visible area of the garden of your back yard where you and any of her surviving offspring may be able to, and I quote, '*look upon it and talk to it as if I am there with you*'."

"Alright then." Rolling my eyes and again looking to the sky, "*Andrea, I'm not sure what you're thinking, but using my love for trees is very clever.* Certain it was some kind of afterlife joke from her to me— one last prank if you will, I threatened her silently, *Andrea, when you and I meet up again, I'm gonna kick your butt!* A short burst of laughter erupted at the thought of getting

The Tree and the Tablet

her back, but then I sobered, recalling my setting and simply stated to the puzzled Jacobs, "Sure, Why not? Sounds like something Andrea would do."

"Here's the rest of the information pertaining to the trust, the will, and all of the bank and storage information." He laid the paperwork on the desk and pushed it toward me. "The ashes have already been placed in a temporary urn for the memorial service. They can be delivered to the company in Estes Park after the funeral. I've taken the liberty of contacting all friends and extended family members per the list attached to the wills." Looking down at his side where there was a beautifully ornately embroidered deep blue velvet bag about the size of a fist, he cringed. Ashen faced and suddenly looking extremely uncomfortable again, he glanced at me while laughing shakily. It was almost like an afterthought, "Oh, I almost forgot."

Reaching down, picking up the bag by it's golden draw string using his pen as if it were diseased or contaminated, he placed it on the desk in front of me and handed me a sealed envelope. My name was scrawled on the surface in what looked to be Andrea's handwriting. Speaking rather rapidly, "Here's something from your sister." He stood up as if to leave, stating rather succinctly, "If there are no further questions, I've concluded this reading of the will." I got the impression of a mouse trying to escape becoming dinner as he hurriedly put his things away.

Shrugging my shoulders at his odd behavior and picking up the satchel to look inside, his eyes went as wide as saucers.

33

Stopping in the midst of his actions, he held his hand out toward me in the fashion of a traffic cop stopping traffic, exclaiming in a squeaky voice, "Please, Miss, wait until I leave!" There was a pleading in his voice unlike anything I'd ever heard. It almost sounded as if he were frightened.

He hurriedly explained, "Ever since Andrea and Jaxon came to my office to rewrite the will and asked me to place that thing in my safe, I've had relentless nightmares of my long-deceased mother-in-law." His eyes scrunched up and he visibly shook as if he had the worst chill of his life. The way he said "*thing*" was as if he were talking about some odd creature. "I don't care to see it again."

Somewhat startled but wanting to alleviate his fears, I gently set the satchel back on the desk, "I must profess that you've got my full attention and my curiosity, but out of respect for your feelings, I'll look at it later."

"Thank you, Miss St. James."

He took his kerchief from his front pocket and wiped his now wet brow. Looking remarkably relieved he asked, "Now, I'm sorry, but do you have any questions regarding the will?"

Staring at the satchel, wondering what could possibly have caused such a drastic reaction, I replied somewhat distractedly, "Everything seems to be covered and in order. I have no further questions, thank you." Looking up from the desk, "I trust you'll take care of the final arrangements for the sale of the house and sending Kelsey's things to my home in Allyn?"

"Yes, yes." He replied rather hastily. "Everything's been arranged. The real estate agent will be contacting you for the final list of things that you'd be willing to let go with the house, but I'll be in touch with Mr. BlackFeather to finalize the trust for Kelsey. You're allowed to go through the house and collect all of the photos and memorabilia to keep for Kelsey as well as choosing items for yourself. However, everything that's left behind, will be sold at an auction or donated to charity." As he made his final declarations, he finished placing his items into his briefcase and stood up. He seemed a little shaky at first but then took a deep breath and started to round the desk toward the door, all the while with his eyes on the satchel.

Standing up, "Thank you, Mr. Jacobs." Extending my hand toward him to conclude our business.

Eyeing my hand, he stopped and shook it vigorously, "Yes, yes. You're welcome." His eyes darted back to the satchel, "Again, sorry for your loss." Turning back toward the door, he kind of scurried as if he wanted out of that room as fast as he could but didn't want to seem offensive. Joining him in his escape from the room, which now seemed to be closing in on me, we made our way to the front door. As we walked—at a brisk pace—he said quietly, "You know, I can still contact Olmeyer's and we can just bury Andrea's ashes in the family plot." Looking at me out of the corner of his eye, he said, "No one will know."

Mid-stride, I gasped slightly at his suggestion as it really took me aback. Stopping and looking at him squarely, trying to hold back my frustration, I spoke in metered tones. "No. These are Andrea's last wishes. I'll honor her wishes." Taking the last couple of steps toward the door, I turned to him, "Thank you, again." Opening the front door, I ushered him out. "Drive safely."

"Good-bye, Miss St. James." Handing me a business card, he added, "Feel free to contact me should you need anything." He half smiled and his small eyes squinted against the bright Colorado sunshine. As he walked toward his car, he spoke to no one in particular, "Blasted confounding weather." Shaking his head, he stepped into his silver Mercedes. I watched him fumble with his briefcase, start his car, put on his seatbelt and drive away.

Glancing up at the sun briefly, then shielding my eyes, I stepped back and closed the door. My mind was racing. *Good grief. A tree? What was she thinking? And what was in that satchel?* As I stepped away from the door, the letter was heavy on my mind and while I couldn't wait to read it, I was also a little afraid of what it might say. Curiosity and uncertainty did an odd waltz in my mind. Well, this ought to be interesting.

CHAPTER 3

As I closed the door, I turned to walk into the house. Contemplating going back to the study to read the letter and look into the satchel, I headed in that direction when I overheard Kelsey and Jody in the kitchen. The smell of something delicious wafted through the air. Inhaling the tantalizing aromas, I figured it must be getting close to dinner time. My hand was on the knob to the office, but I stopped, deciding to look at it later. My mind needed a break from the emotional battering it had been taking. Time for a little distraction. Releasing the door knob, I turned toward the two people who could sooth my soul and walked into the kitchen. They were placing the plates of food on the table and taking a seat next to Kelsey, and unsettling silence drifted over us as we quietly ate dinner.

However, the entire time, all I could think about was that darned letter and satchel. Jody took Kelsey up to get a bath and put on her pajamas for bed. Standing next to the study door, I watched them walk up the stairs talking about which pajamas Kelsey wanted to wear. Peanut, having followed them up, stood at the top of the stairs and turned to look down at me. She whimpered as if she knew what I was about to do and I waved at her, "Go on, girl. I'll be right there." She stood there a moment longer, cocking her head from side to side, as if she were trying to decide whether to follow me or Kelsey. The loud giggle from the bathroom turned the tides in Kelsey's direction, and Peanut turned to run down the hall toward the bathroom.

Turning on my heel, I opened the door to the study and slipped inside. For a moment, in the dark, it looked like there was a figure standing by the desk and I jumped, inhaling sharply with fear. "Hello?" No answer. Shakily, I reached behind me and turned on the light. All I saw was my own reflection in the window. Laughing at myself for my overreaction, I walked over to the desk and snatched the satchel and letter up, deciding to just take them to my room to explore. The satchel was heavy. Curious now, I decided that I'd grab a cup of tea on my way up and headed to the kitchen.

After preparing a cup of Darjeeling, I settled myself in the middle of the queen bed of the guest room to read the letter and open the satchel. Excitement and curiosity warred within me. Opening the satchel slowly, I poured the contents out onto my left hand and was surprised at the ornately carved amulet that landed securely in my palm. It was beautiful.

Looking to be from some sort of ancient time, there was an oval, milky-white stone about two inches long by one inch wide. It shimmered in the light. The mounting looked to be twenty-four karat gold and had carvings all around it that looked like birds and other types of designs that I'd never seen before. At the top of the amulet, where the chain ran through, was an all-seeing eye. It reminded me of something I'd seen on one of those shows about ancient Egyptians or the back of a dollar bill. Turning it over in my hand, there were a bunch of symbols arranged in a circular pattern starting in the center and working toward the outer ring of the amulet. In the very center, there was an opening about three centimeters in diameter that you could see the stone from behind. Hmmm. My chest tightened when I caressed the words on the back andthe sensation was slightly frightening which propelled me to set the amulet on top of the satchel on the bed.

Looking away, I picked up the letter. Written on the front of the envelope in Andrea's handwriting were the words, "To my beloved sister, Maggie." Reverently, I ran my fingers over the letters. Closing my eyes, I felt the raised edges and the indentation made by the pen strokes as I visualized Andrea writing those words. My imagination saw her scrawling those words meticulously over the paper with the marble encased pen I'd purchased for her when I went to Greece two years ago. Sighing and holding the envelope to my chest as if I were hugging Andrea, I finally pulled it away and turned it over, opening it gently to find a letter folded neatly inside.

Dearest Maggie,

I wish you weren't reading this right now, because that means I'm not with you anymore. Firstly, I love you. I'm so sorry about the burden I've left you, but I'm absolutely positive that you'll take great care in protecting and raising Kelsey. —

Stunned by her words, "Did she know that Dylon would die?" The sound of my words spoken aloud reverberated through the room, slightly startling me. A shiver crept along my spine with a sense of something unknown. Glancing over my shoulder toward the cracked door, there was nothing there, but I stared a little longer toward the opening waiting breathlessly for what...I didn't know. Seeing that the situation hadn't changed and there was still a void in the gap left by the barely closed door, a sigh escaped my lips. *"Well, what did you expect?"* Shaking my head, I returned to the letter.

—I'm sure you have questions about the amulet, so I'll try to fill you in. The most important thing I can tell you, is that the amulet is very powerful. Take every precaution to keep it hidden and safe.

As you know, Jaxon and I have been trying to find our parents even though they were legally declared dead five years

The Tree and the Tablet

ago. About a month ago, one of our clients, who deals in ancient antiquities, came to us with an offer we couldn't refuse. Carolynn turned us on to his work. He'd heard from her that we were looking for a way to find someone we'd lost, and since he owed us a substantial balance on his accounts, we made a deal to accept an ancient Mayan amulet called a Soul-Seer. It's very old and it's said that the souls of those who are lost can be channeled through the moonstone. It's supposed to possibly have other powers, but we weren't concerned with those. The Mayan's had many beliefs and traditions that we're still learning about, but taking a chance, we decided to believe this one. Some of the ancient writings link the Mayan beliefs to those of the ancient Egyptians, but I'm not sure how. This stone will allow the wearer to see and speak to their lost loved ones. It's like a channeling device of sorts. Almost like what you and I used to do as kids. I know it sounds crazy, but you have to believe. Please. Your life depends on it.

We were warned that if the amulet wasn't used properly, it could cause great harm. The consequences of using this amulet are what made us fear for our lives and Kelsey's safety. I sent Kelsey to stay with you under the guise of getting ready for Dylon's arrival, but it was because Jaxon started having horrific nightmares. Shortly after that, we contacted Mr. Jacobs and asked him to change the will and keep the stone safe. We spoke to Jaxon's buddy from college, Daniel BlackFeather. He consulted the elders in his tribe, and he said that we opened a portal of some kind, because Jaxon used the amulet in a way it wasn't meant to be used. I was so afraid because he changed, Maggie. Jaxon became obsessed with the amulet and was rambling about how we were all going to die. I had to protect Kelsey from all the things that she'd already witnessed. That's the real reason I sent her to you. This is the real reason she was having nightmares. Not a silly movie she watched. I'm sorry I lied to you.

We tried to contact Mr. Caulker, the man who gave us the amulet, but shortly after Jaxon started having nightmares and visions of his parents, Mr. Caulker was found dead in his Larimer street loft. I was so frightened. I saw the pictures, Maggie. His eyes were missing. I didn't know what else to do.

Daniel spent some time with us right after we sent Kelsey to you and he bound the amulet with a ritual, but he says that might not hold its power for long. We're still looking for a way to remove the curse. A man named James Maxwell has been working in the Mayan ruins at Chichen Itza and Tulum for the last twenty years. He said he'd heard of the amulet and was very upset when he learned we'd used it without researching it first. After we contacted him, he was researching the amulet's powers and how to control it when he went missing. He said there are some ancient alien researchers that believe that it's a doorway to the god's or another world and that if it is used properly, it will possibly allow communication with aliens. I thought he was crazy at first, but now... I don't know what to think anymore. I just wish we'd never gotten it.

I know that this all sounds absurd. But, Maggie, you should see the texts and research. It's incredible. We had some documents that showed the links to the ancient Egyptians and possibly to aliens, but our house was broken into and the documents were taken after we gave the amulet to Mr. Jacobs. Daniel went searching for Mr. Maxwell who'd disappeared. The last we heard from Maxwell was that he'd gone to the Olympic National Forest to try and find a cave there that's supposed to have a tablet that can control or channel the power of the amulet.

I know you don't believe in this sort of stuff, but please promise me you'll be careful with it. Keep it safe. If you have any questions, contact Daniel. He'll know what to do.

Lastly, I suppose you're wondering when I decided on the tree thing. It was a last minute change to the will. I had a dream I was back in that fantasy land we used to go to in our minds as kids. In the dream, a beautiful woman, like an angel, told me that I needed to have my ashes turned into a tree. It was weird, but I felt like it really needed to happen so I changed the will when we went to take the amulet. The company that does this type of work had come up as an advertisement when I was scrolling through my social media account. I didn't tell you because there was no time. I really hoped it was all a bad dream, but I'm just glad that you and Kelsey are safe.

I love you, Maggie. Please take care of Kelsey for us. I'm so very sorry we did this to you.

Love, Andrea

Shocked, I set the letter on the bed, shaking my head. What the heck happened? Did they just go crazy? Maybe they were poisoned? I knew Andrea and Jaxon were trying to make contact, but this is ridiculous. Looking at the letter and then to the amulet, tears slipped down my cheeks. My mind whirled. To have gone through all of this and not share it with me was unfathomable to me. We'd always been so close and never kept secrets like this. The only thing my mind kept sticking on was that she knew she was going to die. Why would she have gone to great lengths to send Kelsey to me, write a new will, and write this letter? Reeling from the pain of this realization, the anguish coursed through me in pulsating waves. Picking up the amulet and speaking to it as if it were alive, I commanded, "If you are truly able to bring back those we lost, show me my sister." Nothing happened and I cried harder, "Dammit, you stupid rock, show me Andrea!"

Just then I heard an agonized cry from the doorway and Kelsey ran into the room like the hounds of hell were on her heels, "Nooooooooo!" She cried. Grabbing the amulet out of my hand, screaming at me on her way to the window, "Don't say that! You don't know. This necklace took my mommy and daddy away! I know it!" She flung the amulet out the window with all of her strength and dropped to the floor crying hysterically. She hugged her little arms around her curled up legs and balled herself up so tight that I couldn't see her face. Kelsey just rocked back and forth hugging her legs and crying, repeating over and over, "You don't know. You don't know." Shaking her head back

The Tree and the Tablet

and forth.

While initially surprised by her outburst, I knew that she was very smart for her age and had moments of extreme comprehension. However, my heart plummeted at the sight of her small form wracked with pain.

Slowly, I crouched down in front of her, placing my hand on her arm, "Please, Kelsey, it's just a necklace. Is this why you were having nightmares?"

She stopped rocking. Big, beautiful, blue eyes, wide with fear, looked up at me, filled with anguish and flooded with tears, she nodded her head.

"Oh, honey. That's silly. The necklace didn't take your parents away. Your mommy and daddy were in a horrible car accident. That's all." Gingerly, my hand strayed toward her to stroke her hair.

Searching my face, she frowned. "You don't believe it!" Shaking her head, she looked at me pleading, "You have to believe. I know!"— she whispered. — "They didn't know, but, I saw it."

Trying to comfort her, "Kelsey, I know that what happened to your mom and dad was a terrible accident and I'm just as sad that they aren't with us, but it simply wasn't a necklace that caused it. It was just bad luck."

She looked at me and just cried. "You don't know." She started repeating again. Calmly, encircling her in my arms, I picked her up and went to the chair near the window. Rocking her slowly and singing her the lullaby that my mother used to sing to us, *All the Best Things,* from our favorite movie, I was finally able to get her to sleep. She'd been crying so hard that every couple of breaths, she'd hiccup like she was gasping for air. Her hair was matted to her face where the tears had gathered and I gently pushed it away from her face. There was still a look of fear etched on her brow and she mumbled in her sleep, "You don't know." My heart hurt for her. "*Oh, Andrea,* — I cried inwardly as I clutched my beautiful niece close to me — "*What the hell happened?*"

Sitting there, holding her close, it seemed like an eternity passed. Seeing that she had calmed and was breathing regularly with less hiccupping, I decided to take her to her room. As I placed her in her bed and pulled up the blanket, she rolled over sighing heavily, snuggling into her blankets. Looking down at Kelsey, I couldn't help but wonder what exactly it was that she saw and how I was going to help her.

Stepping out into the hallway, it was like a magnet was drawing me toward the stairs. A wave of fog fell over my thoughts and almost as if I had no control over my own feet, I found myself wandering toward the back yard where Kelsey had thrown the amulet. Aimlessly winding my way through the hedge maze in the backyard, I stopped at the center.

There, in the center of the fountain was a statue of the Greek goddess, Venus. Sitting as if it had been perfectly placed within the hands of the goddess, was the amulet. The haze I'd been in, was starting to lift. Looking back at the immense distance between the window and the fountain, I wondered whether Kelsey was practicing being a baseball pitcher. There was at least a hundred feet between the center of the maze and that window.

Pulling up my pant legs, I waded into the fountain to retrieve the amulet. The moment I touched it, an electric current pierced my soul. Almost instantly, my mother's voice encircled me, singing about my favorite things as if she were standing right there.

Still holding the amulet in my hand, I turned around and there was Andrea. Startled, I jumped and just about swallowed my tongue. Tentatively, my hand stretched out toward her, but she was transparent and my hand went right through her. Mouth hanging open, I closed my eyes and shook my head violently, whispering to myself, "It's not real. I'm dreaming."

"Maggie, you're NOT dreaming." The apparition admonished me in a soothing, Andrea-like voice.

Opening my eyes slowly and exhaling through my teeth, I garnered my courage to ask, "What are you," as my voice wavered with fear and I blinked my disbelieving eyes trying to clear my obviously stilted vision.

The apparition that resembled my sister looked at me sternly, "Magpie, it's me!"

Only Andrea called me that. Shaking my head in disbelief and waving my hand as if to erase the vision, I swallowed hard, starting to close my eyes against the view, "No. Nope! Not real."

"Magpie, Please. You need to listen carefully, I only have a minute." The appeal in her voice caused me to stop my frantic movements and my eyes roamed over her as I briefly wondered why I was still standing there. Her voice caressed me gently, "Take care of Kelsey. Protect her at all costs. Put the amulet away. Trust no one. When you receive the tree pod, bury the amulet under it. I don't know how I know this or why you have to do this, but it will keep you safe. Promise me, Maggie!" She pleaded with me. Blatantly staring at her, my response was a stunned silence. "Please!"—she looked like Andrea, but it just wasn't possible, my mind reeled—"Maggie, I'm begging you."

Her figure started to shimmer and waver in front of me. "Remember to trust no one, especially those you think you can trust"

Feeling a bit rebellious, I snarked back at my dream, "What will you do if I don't?"

The figure became dark and brooding and Andrea screamed. It felt like a large hand had reached in and grabbed hold of my heart. My breath caught in my throat and everything went dark. I'm not sure how much time went by but it was still dark when I woke up on the ground next to the fountain soaking wet from head to toe with the sprinklers spraying me in the face.

Looking around, the amulet was lying on the ground next to me. Placing it in my pocket, I got up feeling utterly exhausted and went toward the house. The entire time, all I could think about was whether I dreamed about Andrea or if it was real. Once in my room, I placed the amulet carefully in the satchel, put it in the bedside table drawer and dried myself off.

After dressing rapidly, I climbed into bed, wrapping myself in the warmth of the fluffy comforter in an attempt to get warm. My whole body felt like it had been completely sapped of strength. Reaching to turn the bedside lamp off, the weight of my own arm suspended in mid-air was almost more than I could bear. As I flicked the switch, it was all I could do to pull my arm to my side. Cringing against the strain, the sound of the lullaby swelled over the night sounds drifting in through the cracked window from the maze. Realizing I must have forgotten to close the window, the struggle to decide whether to close it was lost as I realized my exhaustion was winning the battle. Too tired to go close it, my eyes turned toward the clock, which reflected back at me with a blinding blue light illuminating the numbers, 3:33 a.m. Weird. With a deep sigh, I turned my head toward the lilting sounds coming from the garden and soon drifted off to sleep.

CHAPTER 4

*J*ody and I spent the next week while waiting for the funeral date, going through everything in the house. There were a couple of items that Jody asked for, and I gave them to her. I figured if they were going to go to charity, why not give them to Jody. Andrea and Jaxon would have wanted it that way.

Andrea's best friend, Carolyn, called, "Hey, I was wondering if I could come and help you go through Andrea's belongings?"

A chill crept up my spine, "That's not necessary, Carolyn. Jody and I have this."

"Well, there might be something of mine within her things." she sounded a little out of breath.

"Can you describe it to me? That way, Jody and I can look for it." I offered.

"Umm. Well, I can't remember what it exactly looks like, it's been so long since I've seen it is all." She laughed nervously. "I mean, I think I lent it to her a while ago."

"So, you're not certain what it looks like or what it is?"

There was a silence on the other line. I thought I heard whispering in the background.

"Hello? Carolyn? Are you still there?"

"Yup, here. I have to go, I'll call you later."

"Okay." my goodbye was answered with a dead silence followed by the sound of my phone beeping to let me know the call was lost. Immediately, I thought of the conversation with the Andrea spirit dream. Carolyn called a couple of other times but I let them go to voicemail. She never left a message, which I also thought was odd.

One day, while we were going through some of Andrea's clothes, I asked Jody about Daniel. She laughed hesitantly, "Well, I don't know him that well. I only met him once about a week before Andrea and Jaxon..." she stopped mid-sentence and looked off with a sad expression. Collecting herself, she said smiling gently, "Sorry."

Touching her arm, I replied, "No, you don't have to be sorry." We hugged.

She looked at me sideways, "Anyway, the story I got, is that they went to school together. I think he majored in microbiology or something like that, but he decided to go into forestry work later." She picked up a blouse to fold it. "They were pretty close in college, I guess." She laughed, "Jaxon said they were *joined at the* hip." At my quizzical expression, she elaborated, "Evidently, they were so close that whenever they would go anywhere, all their friends called them Jack Daniels. It was a huge party joke." Looking a little uncomfortable, she chuckled. "That's about all I know, but I'll tell you, if I was younger, I'd go after him like a chocolate cake!"

Laughing hysterically at her, "Oh, I see. So, he's a good looking guy?"

Winking at me, she smiled broadly, "Well, I wouldn't kick him out of my bed for eating crackers, if you know what I mean."

Laughing, I slapped her playfully on the arm. "Jody, you're a hoot." She shrugged and smiling smugly, she took the box of clothes out to the hallway.

After the amulet incident, I found Kelsey in her parent's bedroom almost every night crying. We'd sit there in their room and cry together. We laughed and talked many times over about how much we missed them and reminisced about the many different complexities of Andrea and Jaxon. It was a healing process. As we worked through the sadness and the loss, we also rejoiced in the many things we loved and would cherish about them. Kelsey didn't speak of the amulet again.

She and I were always close, but these times spent together reminiscing were bonding for us, except if I asked her what happened before she came to stay with me. She'd just get sad and shut me out. After the third attempt to bring it up with no response or large teary eyes, I decided to let it go. She'd tell me when she was ready.

As part of our nightly routine in Andrea and Jaxon's room, I would sing her the lullaby, carry her to bed and then go back to my bed. However, I woke up every night at 3:33 a.m. in a cold sweat and heard the lullaby as if it were coming from the bedside table. The night before the funeral, I opened the dresser to find that the amulet was glowing within the satchel. After taking the satchel containing the amulet and putting it in my backpack surrounded by every stitch of clothing that I brought with me, the music stopped.

Finally, the day arrived for the services. Jody had made all the arrangements for the memorial reception afterwards at the house and arranged for caterers to deliver food. Arrangements had been made for parking and a valet service was ordered to assist in the job. Jody was an amazing cook, but I'd insisted that she have time to grieve and not spend all her time in the kitchen preparing for the reception.

Kelsey and I got up that morning to two feet of snow. My phone rang as I stared out the window at the blanket of white which startled me slightly. The caller ID showed it was the Limousine service.

"Hello?"

"Miss, this is Mark, your driver for today."

The Tree and the Tablet

"Oh, Yes. Is there a problem?"

"I'm just calling to let you know that the lot where the cars are kept hasn't been plowed yet and I'm waiting for him so I can get the car out and head to your pickup location. Has anything changed with the plans for today?"

"No, I'm not aware of any changes."

"Alright, I should be there a little late. I'll call if there are any other issues, but the service is pretty reliable."

"Okay, thank you." He hung up the phone and I looked up the number for Whiteman's mortuary service. Hearing Jody in the hallway talking to Kelsey, I went to the door and opened it, "Jody, can you call the reverend and let them know to delay services?" At her confused look, I expounded, "The limo driver said they're clearing the lot, but he'll be late."

"Sure, honey. You want me to give them a specific time frame?"

"No, just let them know we'll be late." She gave me a thumbs up and ushered Kelsey down to stairs to have breakfast.

After showering and putting myself together, I made my way downstairs. Jody had popped her head into the bathroom while I was showering to let me know the reverend was running late as well. Since she and Kelsey had gone up to change after breakfast, they came down to meet me in the foyer at the foot of the stairs. They were both in black, and Jody had arranged Kelsey's hair into a loose braid with a black ribbon woven into it. Little curly wisps of hair framed her beautiful little face and tears were brimming in her eyes. She looked pretty, but so sad. Clasping her hand in mine, we left the house to make our way out to the car. Jody had spent the night and had had the foresight to have her oldest son, John, come over with her so he could clear the steps and driveway the next morning if it snowed. She was always spot on with the weather, even when the weatherman was wrong.

John was about twenty four years old, he'd been doing the landscaping and cleanup services at the house for the past two years along with two other young men. John did an excellent job. Standing next to the steps to help us down to the car, making sure we didn't slip, he'd laid out a healthy amount of ice-melt which appeared to be doing its job.

As we entered the limousine, I overheard Jody talking softly to John, "I love you, squirt." I wanted to laugh as he was definitely not little. He stood a foot taller than her at least. "We'll be back soon."

He wrapped his arm around her and squeezed her tight, "Okay, Mom, I love you, too." As he helped her into the car, he smiled gently toward me, "Everything will be ready when you get back."

Nodding at him, "Thank you, John." and with that he closed the door.

What a good kid he was. Just as the Limo pulled out of the driveway and onto the road, the sun came out, nearly blinding us all with it's brilliance. The driver was prepared, putting on his metallic reflective sunglasses as we pulled out on the road toward what seemed to be another grim reminder of my aching heart.

We arrived at the mortuary about five minutes after 9:00 am. There was a large group of people already there, and Carolyn came through the group as soon as she saw me and Kelsey arrive. People were lined up, signing the guest book. A large board was posted near the registration book that had many different photos of Andrea and Jaxon dressed in their finest clothes at various charitable events throughout town and in family photos.

On the sanctuary near the podium, there was a large wreath of flowers placed in front of the presentation area of Jaxon and Dylon's caskets. Andrea's urn was sitting on a pedestal in front of the flowers. A large easel was placed near the caskets showing Jaxon and Andrea with her large belly in a loving embrace. Carolyn hugged Kelsey and was crying, or trying to seem like she was crying but she was carrying on so much, it seemed a bit fake and I sighed softly as I looked around. She always seemed so dramatic with her reactions. Andrea had always told me that Carolyn had had a rough life in some southern city —I could never remember where exactly— and that she was a little extra, but that her heart was in the right place so I tried hard not to say anything about her behavior. She made a fuss at trying to wipe her tears with her handkerchief, but there wasn't much for her to wipe away.

Noticing that I was watching her, she spoke with her ridiculous southern accent, "Andrea used to tease me so,' she waved her flimsy piece of cloth in my face, "We could never go out after those chick flicks we went to because my makeup would be so messed up from crying." She dabbed at her eyes and hiccupped. Gritting my teeth, I tried to smile reassuringly at her, but I just wanted to slap her. She was still talking except I had no idea what she was rambling on about. She reminded me of a cat with her dark eyes and bright red hair that was almost orange. Looking down to keep from analyzing her anymore, it was difficult not to see the pained expression on Kelsey's face.

She looked like she was ready to leave. My stomach was feeling queasy. Jody, sensing that things weren't going well, piped up, "Um, Carolyn, we should go to the restroom and clean up your face, dear. You wouldn't want Andrea to look down and see you with your makeup all streaked would you?" Stopping mid-sentence, Carolyn's eyes widened, "Oh? Oh, yes, I mean. Thank you so much," she said to Jody. Turning to me as Jody pushed her toward the ladies' room, she said, "I'm so sorry, I'll be back soon." As they entered the restroom, Jody looked back at me and winked. Sighing, I was never more happy to have a reprieve from someone as I was that moment. As I stared up toward the ceiling I sent a silent *Thank you* to Andrea for hiring Jody.

Leaning down to Kelsey, I asked, "You doing okay, Kells?"

She nodded her head, but responded with, "I don't know."

Lifting her in my arms and hugging her close to me, we went into the room to sit down and wait for the services to start. Sitting in the front row, I stared at the flowers. The birds of paradise

The Tree and the Tablet

were a nice touch. It was her favorite flower. Not really the sort of flower you'd see at a funeral though. It all felt so surreal.

The pastor approached me and handed me the memorial program, "Is there anything that you feel needs addressed that isn't in the program?" His kind smile searched my face for an answer.

Tears welled in my eyes as my fingers caressed the cool paper that was slightly embossed, "No, everything looks fine to me."

"Alright, then, since we're already behind schedule, I'll announce that the service will start in five minutes and we'll get this part done. Is that alright with you?"

Nodding in the affirmative, I felt my mouth form the word, "Yes." But there was no actual sound that left my lips. He walked away quietly into the antechamber where he announced in a clear and concise manner, "If everyone could please be seated, the memorial service will start soon." People started filtering into the finding seats. They just kept coming. The room looked like it would hold about one hundred fifty people and it was already packed. Since I didn't know many of these people, I assumed they were probably clients of Jaxon's and Andrea's, or knew them from their charity work since they were successful lawyers at two of the top firms in Denver.

I'd met a couple of them a time or two at some events but never really took the time to get to know any of them except for Carolyn, and I didn't really want to get to know Carolyn because something about her always made me feel on edge.

Many different people got up and talked about how amazing Andrea and Jaxon were, and how the world was missing out on such great people. It was all a blur. As I sat there with Kelsey next to me, crying and numb, my heart hurt so much. It was like it just happened all over again. Everyone got up as we all started walking toward the doors. It was time to take the caskets to their plots. The pall bearers lifted the two caskets and started walking toward the doors.

Walking outside, it was so cold but so bright. The sun was shining through the clouds giving the appearance of a path made up of sun rays shining their light onto the burial plot like a beacon. A beautiful large stone was set up that read, *Boyer Family*. It was ornately carved with the names of the family members that were buried there. Jaxon's parents' names were there even though there were no bodies. The memory of that day was so vivid it was like it was just yesterday. It seemed so odd to bury two caskets that had nothing in them. Again, there was a speech and afterward, Kelsey and I placed roses on the caskets. The ashes would be sent directly to the company for the tree and then the tree would be delivered to my home within the next two weeks.

After the burial, we returned to the house with a mile of cars behind us. We arrived at the house where the valets had arrived and were preparing to take cars, parking them down the street by the golf course. Jody, myself and Kelsey walked into the house which had been transformed to accommodate the wake. There were two chairs sitting next to the front door now for myself and Kelsey to sit in. Kelsey looked up at me with huge teardrops in her eyes. "Auntie, I want to go to my room now."

Dropping to my knees, I hugged her fiercely, "I love you, Kells. You go ahead up to your room. It's okay, baby." She nodded and I looked up at Jody who was patiently standing next to me. Jody nodded as if an unspoken question was answered between us.

Taking Kelsey by the hand, Jody led the way up the stairs toward the back of the house and the quiet retreat of her bedroom. Looking longingly in their direction, I couldn't help but wish I was there with them, instead of waiting for the hordes of people to enter that front door or to hear a thousand condolences and well wishes.

Plucking up my courage, I removed my jacket and walked calmly back to the kitchen/dining room area. The house was so beautiful and large. The great room opened into a large area that had several different rooms off it. Everything had been set up on the side of the great room facing the kitchen and dining room. Additional seating had magically appeared throughout the space to accommodate the extra people. Taking a glass, I filled it with wine and sat down in a chair facing the garden. The garden was always so beautiful. Even with the fresh snow, it was like a magical wonderland just outside the doors.

Staring into the surreal scene, it was difficult not to notice the beautiful robin that perched itself on the ledge of the deck. It seemed to be looking at me. As it tilted its head from side to side, it appeared as if it was trying to become accustomed to having eyes so far apart, but still trying to see me through the window. What a funny little bird. Briefly, I wondered if it was hungry and cold. I couldn't recall seeing robins in the garden during this time of year before. How odd. Stepping up to the French doors, I reached for the handle wanting to see if the bird was injured, but was halted by the sound of the front door opening ushering in Carolyn who was flamboyant explaining, "I just know it's alright, Harold."

A male voice behind her said, "Well, I still think we should ring the bell, Carolyn."

Spotting me from across the room, she was still talking loudly to a couple of older people while walking straight toward me. The male, who I recognized as a partner in the firm Jaxon worked at from a prior dinner party, seemed slightly perturbed but also mildly embarrassed. I turned from the door, and smiled softly to him while slightly waving my hand to let him know it was okay and then made my way toward a strategic spot at the entrance in order to greet the people heading my direction. . . And so it went for the next hour. People saying how sorry they were, me thanking them and directing them toward the food. After the continuous flow dwindled to a couple of stragglers, I was finally able to find Jody, taking a moment to look around for the little smile I needed to see, "How's Kelsey doing?" Slightly

The Tree and the Tablet

disappointed that she wasn't nearby, I looked to Jody for reassurance.

"Oh, honey, she's gonna be okay. It's a lot for a little one to take. She's sleeping right now."

As I started in the direction of the stairs, Jody placed her hand on my arm. Glancing down at her round face, her eyes reflected an inner peace I didn't feel, but knew that meant everything was alright.

"She ate some food and we read a book. She's sleeping peacefully with Peanut curled up next to her. Probably best to leave her be right now."

Knowing she was right, I sighed and gifted her with a small smile. I didn't quite feel like it was an accurate reflection of my feelings just then, but it was the effort that counted, right? "Thank you, again, Jody. Are you sure you don't want to move to Washington with us?"

"I wish I could, honey. You know how much you and Kelsey mean to me. I'll visit you as often as I can. I just can't leave my family." She looked so sad in that moment, like I just strangled her favorite stuffed animal.

"I know." Attempting another smile to try and dispel her sad look, I cleared my throat, "I saw John earlier. He was looking for you. Better go ahead and see what he needs, I think he's in the kitchen." Her knowing eyes skimmed my face lightly before she turned and mumbled, "I'll be right back," as she scurried off toward the kitchen.

Again, I found myself drawn to the French doors leading out to the garden. Funny that I never really left the area except for a few moments when I was pulled into a conversation. Almost like a magnet kept me there. Or maybe it was the wine. Topping off my empty glass, I turned back to the view.

Again, I was amazed to see the beautiful robin. The coloring was not quite what I was used to. Brighter and more brilliant coloring, I'd never seen on a robin before. The orange appeared almost as a shiny copper with a prism effect that caused every nuance of light to glint off of its chest. The feathers were a deep, rich brownish gray and the white was as brilliant at the snow. The eyes seemed almost to be a deep shade of cobalt blue rather than the usual black of a bird. It turned and looked right at me again from the side, blinking its eye and then looked away. Lost in thought, I found myself wondering again if I was seeing things. Then, I saw him.

Standing on the deck, looking at the robin with the same curiosity as my own. He was just as handsome as I remembered. His dark hair was combed back, but longer than I remembered. He wore a sleek black suit with a crisp white shirt that contrasted sharply with the bronze skin showing through the opening at the neck. The suit fit him superbly as if it had been tailored just for him. The outline of his physique could clearly be seen through the material without revealing too much other than his muscular build.

Oh, dear lord. Who is he? Why was he on the deck?

Pressed up against the window panes so tightly that my breath was fogging the window, my pulse was racing. Afraid that a mere hint of air on the window would cause the apparition to disaapear, the breath hung stagnant in my lungs. Like a cool glass of water on a hot day, all I could do was drink in the vision of him standing there. Ouch! There was this ache deep in my belly that curled itself throughout my body in this delicious but painful way. As I stared at him, I licked my lips, suddenly thirsty. Remembering the fresh glass of wine in my hand, I gulped it down while my eyes remained fixed on the vision outside. Empty now, I set the glass on the credenza in front of the window without looking.

My hands were now pressed against the glass as if somehow, I could magically feel him through the invisible force that was separating me from my heart's desire. Looking him over from head to toe, my eye caught on the shiny black feather wrapped in leather with silver and turquoise hanging around his neck. Just then, the robin flew from its precarious perch on the snow-covered railing and as it flew between us, he looked up from his musings to watch it fly away. The bird became a blur and our eyes locked. Deep, hypnotic pools of green enveloped me. A gasp escaped me followed by shallow breathing as my world seemed to freeze, this one moment in time enveloping me with its cloying sweetness. Suddenly, I was drowning in a haze, the air being sucked right out of me in one big whoosh. Arms like jelly burned and tingled with a numbing sensation. Quicksand was pulling me down, sucking me into a deep abyss and then nothing. Sweet,

Kathryn O'Brien

peaceful, nothing.

CHAPTER 5

The sun was shining right into my eyes through the open curtains. Rolling over to shield myself from the intensity of the sun shining through the window into my face, my thoughts began to solidify. Wow! What an amazing dream. Swollen lips, parched and aching throbbed from the memory of the most intense kiss I'd ever had with my dark godlike mystery man. My heart pounded and my belly ached with the memory of those kisses. A sigh escaped me. I could still feel his arms around me and his firm body pressed against mine. It was such a vivid dream that I could still smell him. As I laid there for a minute, rubbing my temples, I tried to remember the events that lead to my trip into the bedroom. Everything was sort of fuzzy, and no matter how much I struggled with my brain, I couldn't remember going to bed. After attempting to figure out what was real and what was a dream, my head was starting to hurt.

Oh, well. I must've had more wine than I thought I did. Pulling back the comforter and sliding my feet to the floor, now things were really getting strange. It seemed I had veered from my normal nightly rituals as I wasn't wearing anything other than a t-shirt and a pair of panties, rather than a tank top and comfy shorts. Hmmm. People do odd things when they've been drinking. Pulling on my old hoodie and a pair of loose fitting jeans that were lying on the chair next to the end of the bed, I grabbed a scrunchie from the bedside and put my hair into a loose ponytail. Slowly meandering down the hall, I poked my head in to check on Kelsey. She wasn't in her room. Panic started to creep through me until I heard her laughter in the backyard.

Walking to the end of the hall facing out toward the high pitched squeals, I glanced through the window to see her chasing Peanut through the garden. Every couple of feet, Peanut would run under a bush and then stealthily crawl out behind Kelsey, letting loose a quick bark. Kelsey would jump and turn around giggling ferociously and then start off after Peanut again. A smile crept across my face at the sight. They were so adorable together. Knowing that Kelsey was safe, I made my way downstairs to the kitchen.

"Good Morning, Love." Jody handed me a cup of hot coffee and smiled gently at me. "Are you feeling better?" She felt my brow like a mother checking her child for fever. A look of consternation etched on her brow.

Nodding assuringly, "Mmm, Hmmm. I guess I just needed some rest." Taking a moment to let the smell of the hot brew in my cup drift into my nostrils and feel the warmth seeping through the ceramic mug, I closed my eyes and took a sip of coffee. From the moment it passed my lips, I savored the smooth flavor and the heat as it briefly sat in my mouth and then found its way across my palate to gradually slide down my throat, warming me from the inside-out. For that simple moment in time, life is good. There's nothing like a cup of coffee in the morning to melt away the cobwebs and rejuvenate the soul.

"Mmm. Your coffee's amazing, Jody. I buy the same brand, but it never tastes as good when I make it." Jody smiled knowingly. "I must've had a little too much to drink yesterday. I don't remember going to bed." Looking at Jody quizzically, I couldn't help but notice a gleam in her eye and the hint of a whimsical expression that played on her lips. Somehow, I felt like Jody wasn't telling me everything.

"Yes, well, with everything going on, it's no wonder you fell so hard. You really did need the rest though." She touched my shoulder. "Everything's been arranged. I packed Kelsey's bag and the movers will come tomorrow to pick up everything else." She sighed.

"It's too soon." I said, dejectedly. "I'm not ready to leave." Looking around at the house and thinking of all the memories that were made there, a thousand thoughts were flying through my head. Turning back to Jody, "I feel close to her here." Glancing down at my almost empty cup, a tear slipped out and rolled down my cheek.

Wrapping her arms around my upper torso, Jody replied, "You know that Andrea wouldn't want to see you so sad. Besides, it will be easier for Kelsey to heal and move forward once you are back in Washington." Giving me a firm squeeze, she relinquished her hold on me, touched my cheek tenderly and went back to her dishes in the sink. "Your flight leaves at 6 pm tonight. I was thinking I could make you some snacks for your flight so I started some s'mores brownies for Kelsey and some cheesecake bits for you."

"Awe, Jody, you didn't have to do that. You've already done so much."

"Nonsense. I don't know when I'm going to get to spoil you girls again, besides, it makes me happy to do this. I also made some peanut butter doggie treats for Peanut." Placing a pot on a draining rack, she turned to me and looking concerned she said in her most maternal voice, "You need to take better care of yourself. You aren't going to be any good for Kelsey if you don't take care of yourself."

As I started to speak, she raised her hand, "Hear me out." My mouth snapped shut. "As I was saying, open your heart and stop hiding behind your work. I see you. I know what you are doing. You think that if you guard your heart, then you won't get

The Tree and the Tablet

hurt, but that's not true. Let yourself love. It'll all work out. I promise." She smiled and tilted her head to one side. Reaching out toward me, she tucked a stray lock of my hair behind my left ear. It felt like my mom was standing in front of me. I'd heard this all before. Mom was always telling me to let love in.

Sighing heavily, "You're right, Jody. I know you're right. It's just so hard." Jody raised her eyebrows at me. "Okay, I'll try harder."

"I'll take that for now." Turning and lifting the coffee pot from the plate, she filled my cup. "You best get packed, it's already almost noon, sleepyhead."

Gasping, "Noon?"

Nodding and chuckling, she turned back to her chores, "Yes. Truth is I was starting to get worried. If you hadn't shown up when you did, I would've gone up to wake you. But you needed that sleep because you're right back to your beautiful self. Go ahead now. There's lots to be done before you have to go. I had the rental car agency pick up the car and John will drive you to the airport in the Lexus."

She was always a step ahead of me. It was almost like she could read minds. She turned and looked at me pointedly. My eyebrows rose sharply in response. She laughed and turned back to the cooking.

"By the way" I said, smiling mischievously, "I made arrangements for the ownership of the Lexus to go to you and the F-150 Lariat to go to John."

In the process of rolling out pie dough for miniature pies, she was surprised enough to drop the rolling pin and gasp. Spinning around toward me and squealing at the same time, she literally bounced the three steps toward me and hugged me ferociously while crying. "You sweet, amazing, girl! Thank you so much. I can't find the words."

Well, I guess she's not psychic. She always loved the Lexus and said that when she could afford it that she might buy one for herself. "It's the least I could do. You are family. Besides, John's going to need a nice truck to start his landscaping business. Consider it an investment."

Pulling away and wiping her eyes on her apron, she said, "Go ahead now, before you get me to crying again." She shooed me out of the kitchen and I laughed as I walked over to the French doors. As I watched Kelsey and Peanut playing, a glint of copper caught my eye. It was the little robin there again. Strangely, it appeared to be watching them as well. Turning its head, it looked at me. *Funny bird.* The snow had magically almost melted completely away except for in some areas where there was more shade. Rays of sunshine streaked through the cluster of cottonwood trees and lit on the different areas of the garden like a highlighter bringing attention to a cluster of columbines that somehow survived the snow, melting my aching heart a bit.

Not sure why, but I looked to the right side of the deck. Nothing to see there. My heart dropped into my stomach. The robin took flight and the disappointment was tangible, but in an effort to find a second of happiness, I turned away.

Sighing, *"Margaret St. James, stop daydreaming!"* I admonished internally. It wasn't real... Or was it? Shaking my head vigorously and releasing a soft chuckle, I decided that Jody was right. I should get myself packed. With that thought, off to the shower I went.

A couple hours later, feeling clean and refreshed, I took one last look around the house, mentally preparing myself for the leaving. Mine and Kelsey's bags were sitting by the front door. Peanut's kennel was sitting there, waiting for her to be placed inside. Kelsey's giggle traveled across the space and I glanced up to see her sitting at the island in the kitchen. Jody had just handed her some brownies and a glass of milk. Peanut was lying on the floor in the sun next to the open French doors. She lifted her head slightly from the floor, perked up her ears and looked at me. Laying back down, she sighed and closed her eyes to resume soaking up the miraculous sunshine. Kelsey must've worn her out this morning.

As I walked across the great room toward the kitchen, Kelsey saw me. Jumping down from her chair, she crossed the span of the room at a dead run. "Auntie!" She screeched as she ran and dove into my arms. Picking her up and spinning her around, I snuggled her close. Funny how kids always greet you like they haven't seen you in a year even if it's only been a few minutes. I love that.

Twirling her in circles in the middle of the room, I giggled with her. "What have you been up to today? I saw you and Peanut playing in the backyard earlier."

"You did?" A doubtful expression was on her face. "I didn't see you." Her face lit up and she almost shouted, so filled with excitement, "Auntie, I saw a beautiful robin earlier. It landed on my shoulder and it kinda scared me at first. I love robins. Me and Daddy used to always sit on the deck and talk to them together." It truly was dizzying to listen to her sometimes. She had a knack for speaking rapidly with such excitement that it always took me a couple seconds to catch up to what she was saying. As the information was absorbed by me, I noticed a look of consternation cross her face for a moment. "I never saw this one before, though." She smiled and shrugged as if it was only a momentary fleeting thought that entered and left her head just as quickly. It was like watching a door open and close. Setting her down on the floor, I looked up at the open door to the deck briefly and then back to her. A new thought must've entered her head as suddenly her face lit up and tugging my arm insistently she jubilantly proclaimed, "Jody made brownies! Come on!" Relinquishing my arm, she sped away from me.

Smiling and shaking my head, I looked after the skipping child who relinquished my arm to resume her brownie consumption, wondering where she got all of the energy. Shrugging my shoulders, I followed her into the kitchen.

Jody handed me a plate while watching Kelsey dig into her brownies, "I already fed Kelsey, here's a plate of spaghetti to tide

The Tree and the Tablet

you over since you haven't eaten today." Smiling, she admonished me, "You know you can't survive on coffee alone. Even though you think it's one of the main food groups, it's not!"

"Oh, thank the lord, you read my mind. I'm starving!" Setting the plate on the island, I quickly slid into my seat and started shoveling the food into my mouth. It was so delicious. As my stomach mumbled its approval of the nourishment hastily making its way through my esophagus, I found myself wishing I could put Jody in my pocket and take her with me. Cooking was not my forte'. She was truly a master chef. Wow! Just Wow! So good. It didn't take long to clear my plate of every last morsel. Looking up from my now empty plate, our eyes locked.

Jody stood by with a knowing smile on her face and giggled at me. "Goodness, you weren't hungry, were you? Did you even breathe?"

Feeling a little sheepish, my shoulders lifted involuntarily, "I guess so. Is there any more?" Chuckling to herself, she scooped up another helping and placed it in front of me. Eating more slowly now, I asked, "What time are we leaving?"

"John returned the rental car yesterday as you asked. I told him to be ready to leave by three so you have time to get to the airport in this traffic." Peering sideways at the clock over the stove, a sad expression crossed her face. Glancing at the clock myself, I realized it was already a quarter past two. Panic struck, it was almost time.

"Jody, come with us to the airport. I'll buy you a ticket and

75

you can fly back in a week." Hope crept into my voice.

"Yes, Jody! Come with us! Please, please, please!" Kelsey jumped down, and straddled Jody's legs. Looking up at Jody with the sweetest smile, she wriggled her eyebrows and repeated herself with a lengthy, "Pleeease?"

Reaching down and cupping Kelsey's sweet face in her hand, she removed her from her legs and dropped to her knees to hug Kelsey. Pulling back to look her in the eyes and pushing a lock of wayward hair around her ear, Jody sighed, "We already discussed this, right?"

Kelsey nodded. Smiling timidly at Jody, "I thought you might change your mind?" It was partly a pleading question and partly a statement.

Jody raised one strawberry colored eyebrow at Kelsey's antics, "I'll come soon for a visit. I promise. You and Aunt Maggie need time to adjust to your new life. Everything will be okay, Sweetie."

Kelsey looked sad, but soldiered through and replied with an ethereal smile, looking like a little angel, "Okay. I understand. I love you, Jody. I'll just have to miss you until I see you again." She hugged Jody tight. They pulled back, looked into each other's eyes and placing their foreheads together, they started to laugh.

Struggling to her feet again, "Oof! I'm getting too old for this!" Wobbling and attempting to stand up, I moved around the counter to help her to her feet.

The Tree and the Tablet

Giggling like children, we both sort of lost our balance in the effort. As we steadied ourselves, I hugged her to me. "I love you! You're like a second mother to me. Please keep in touch and let me know if you need anything."

Hugging me back, she whispered in my ear, "I love you too, sweet girl. You and Andrea have always been like the daughters I always wanted." Tears in our eyes, we separated.

Without warning, a flash of coppery feathers surrounded us and the little robin was circling our heads. Chaos ensued and Jody grabbed for the broom in a flurry of screeches and hoots. Sensing it was in imminent danger of being harmed, the bird seemingly halted in mid-air, then flew right out the open French doors. Huffing, puffing, and trying to slow our pulses, we looked at each other perplexed by what had just transpired. Jody looked at the door and glancing back at me, she exclaimed slightly out of breath, wide eyed and flustered, "Goodness, that's never happened before!"

Without a chance to process any further what had just happened, John opened the front door causing us all to jump and turn toward it, "Are you ladies ready? We'd better go if we want to beat the traffic."

CHAPTER 6

After many hugs, kisses, and fond farewells, we boarded our flight for an uneventful trip home. The driver picked us up at the terminal. We arrived at the house in Allyn around midnight, after having him stop at Burgers by The Bay to pick up some food that we could eat at home. Opening the front door, I was greeted with an immediate sense of relief. As if being away was slowly sucking the life from me.

Upon entering the front door, you could see straight through the back-French doors right in front of the dining room area. As the driver placed the bags inside the door, I handed Kelsey the food. She made her way to the dining room to eat while I tipped the driver and thanked him.

Peanut was ecstatic to be back home as well. Initially, when I unzipped her kennel, she ran through the house jumping on all of the furniture, causing Kelsey to giggle and dance excitedly at her antics. After opening the doggie door, I went to put the bags in the rooms.

When I returned to the dining room, I noticed that Kelsey was half asleep while still trying to eat her cheeseburger. "Hey, Kiddo, looks like you're ready for bed."

Wiping her face with a napkin, I turned her toward me. As I picked Kelsey up to take her to her room, Peanut returned from her third trip out the doggie door to relieve herself and followed me into the guest room, which would now become Kelsey's room. It was the room directly across from mine and just made sense to put her there permanently. Normally, I'd insist on Kelsey brushing her teeth before bed, but she was entirely tuckered out. Once tucked into bed with her favorite teddy bear, Mr. Snuggles, I started to sing the lullaby but noticed she was fast asleep.

Peanut followed me through the single-story rambler to the kitchen. She sat looking at me sideways while I poured a nice large glass of wine. As I glanced around my little slice of heaven, a sigh perforated the peaceful silence. It was so good to be home.

The living room was situated in the front of the house to the left of the front door with large bay windows facing out to the driveway. The ceilings were vaulted to the peak of the roof and gave the impression of a grand opening. Beyond the entryway was the open kitchen with a large center island covered in a light granite in a marble design. There was a beautiful subway tile backsplash with stainless steel appliances. The cabinets were a rich mahogany. Hand-scraped hickory hardwood floors flowed through the house. The garage was situated off the side of the house and entered through the kitchen with my study just off the side for privacy and quiet, which also contained a three-quarter bath and Murphy bed for additional guests. To the right of the living room was a wall with a coat rack and coat closet next to the door.

It was a quaint rambler with three bedrooms and two bathrooms. Growing up in this house, I had worked alongside mom trying to make the house as beautiful inside as it was outside. Large windows faced out toward the water and allowed the cool summer breezes to flow through the house. The sanctuary of my bedroom opened out to the garden and waterfront as well. Under each of the picture windows, were built in window seats where I could snuggle up with a good book on the colder days and view the bay. Beautiful, heavy damask, thermal, olive green curtains hung from the ceiling to the floor with hazy sheers to diffuse the light. Living on the bay had its perks. My little piece of heaven was mine alone.

Walking to the French doors leading onto the deck from the dining room, I stepped out into the night and settled into my favorite swinging chair under the stars to contemplate my solitude. Looking out at the expansive backyard, I saw the years of work I spent helping Mom develop her little oasis that was now bathed in the light of the full moon and twinkling little lights strategically placed throughout. The moon was reflecting on the bay. The night was very still. Normally, there were the sounds of crickets and other insects this time of night as well as the sounds of the owls. It was so quiet though. Like the calm before the storm. It was kind of eerie at first.

There were sections of the yard that covered different desired spaces. On either side of the yard were giant draping weeping cherry trees. Along the back of the house was a large deck that had a pergola with the swinging chairs on one side and a small dining area on the other, complete with outdoor cooking area. In the furthest left corner of the yard under an expanse of seventy-five feet tall pines there stood a seating area surrounded by perennial shade-loving plants and flowers. In the center back of the yard, there was a fire pit with driftwood seating around it and beyond that was the bay.

On the right side of the yard, there were various toy structures that I had accumulated through the past five years for Kelsey to use when she came for visits. Everywhere there were roses, a favorite of both me and mom, and other perennial flowers. Along the back of the house were many different and assorted baskets that were used to plant annuals such as my petunias and violas. There were walking paths that were lined with little statues and even a retreat by the water set up in the form

The Tree and the Tablet

of a Japanese Zen garden, with several species of Japanese maples and assorted flowers as well as a sand and rock garden. There were lights everywhere. Not large lights, but small twinkly barely visible lights that made me think of little fairies visiting and hiding amongst the bushes.

Finally, there was a path leading away from the Zen garden and fire pit area to the dock and boat house beyond the pines, down the hillside. It was only about ten feet above the beach and waterfront. The whole boathouse and dock was a floating entity that raised and lowered with the water of the bay. Currently, the tide was in and I could see the small structure as the water was almost as high as the hill. When the tide was out, there was a sixty foot ramp that had to be climbed to reach the dock and boathouse. Or, you could walk down the hillside into the beach area from the side where there was a built-in rock and concrete reinforced stairway. It was lovely.

My favorite place to be was on my deck. I was soaking in the loveliness of the retreat, when I heard Peanut barking. Looking toward the patio doors, I thought I saw the shadow of a person run out of the door, and then I heard Kelsey running through the house at a dead sprint. "Auntie, Auntie!" Panic was evident in her voice.

Setting down my glass, I jumped up and turned to run toward the opened door-way. We collided just inside the door and I held her tightly to me for a brief moment before dropping to my knees and allowing my eyes to roam over her face, "What is it? What's

83

wrong?"

She just cried softly and held onto me so tightly. "I thought I was alone." She was becoming hysterical and very distraught.

Stoking her beautiful hair and looking into her eyes, I assured her that I was real. "Look, see?" I said as I pinched myself, "Ouch! That hurt." Rubbing my arm, I looked at her trying not to laugh. "I'm real as ever and you aren't alone, Kells. Pointing to her heart, I told her, "Even when our loved ones aren't right next to us, they're still right here, where our love lives."

She placed her hand on her heart and asked, "But how do they get there?" I saw her eyes sparkle.

"I just mean that the love you have will never go away and they will always be close to you if you remember the love." Watching her closely, she nodded.

Looking at me skeptically, "Do you promise?"

Making the motion of etching an "X" across my chest, "Cross my heart." She was settling down now. Holding her close to me, I remembered all the nightmares and the need for comfort when I was a child that caused me to seek out the comfort of my mother's bed, "How would you like to sleep in my room tonight?"

Already getting sleepy again, she nodded and then said, "Don't forget Mr. Snuggles."

"Sure thing, sweetness." Lifting her in my arms, we made our way to get Snuggles and then went to the bedroom. Setting her down in my bed, I spoke softly, "I have to go lock up. I'll be right back." No response and the sound of soft, even breathing was the reply.

Smiling, I went back out on the deck, grabbed my wine glass, called to Peanut, and locked up. As I changed my clothes, cleaned my face and brushed my teeth, I couldn't help but wonder how long it would take for her to be okay with being alone. Pulling back the covers and curling up next to her, I couldn't resist reaching out and pushing a stray lock of hair away from her face. As I extinguished the lamp, my voice seemed barely above a whisper, "I love you, Kelsey." Silently, I prayed I could be what she needed to overcome the pain of loss when my heart was so torn. Sleep came swiftly that night.

The sound of loud knocking at the front door woke me. As I sat up, I realized that I wasn't awakened at 3:33 a.m. Relief flooded my brain. Looking around I noticed the French doors to my room were open and a small light entered through the opening as the shears fluttered in the light breeze. It was remarkably warm for this time of year. Kelsey was playing with Peanut in the backyard. Giggling and barking pierced the quiet morning. It startled me that she had snuck out of bed so stealthily. This would be something we definitely needed to talk about. She'd never broken the rules before, so I wasn't quite sure why she decided to go outside while I was sleeping. Hoping this wouldn't become a habit, I rolled over with a groan.

Pulling the covers back, I got up and grabbed my sweater

85

from the end of the bed, closed the French doors in my room, and headed to the front door. Opening the door, I was bum rushed by a very disheveled looking Sherri. Her hug was ferocious. Laughing hysterically, I hugged her back just as tightly. Sherri was about my height with a very firm body. I admired the beautiful grandmother of three and wished that I could be as hot when I got to be her age. Her twinkling blue eyes were the color of a cloudy sky, her hair was silky white and her smile was a mile wide as she exclaimed, "I missed you so much! How are you? How was everything? Are you ok? How's Kelsey?" My head was whirling.

Placing my hands on her shoulders, I said, "Good morning! I missed you too, but I was only gone for a week." Gently, I steered her toward the dining table and asked, "Would you like a cup of coffee?"

Finally taking a gripping breath, she sighed, "Yes, please!" She sat down at the table looking out into the back yard.

Turning toward the French doors, I said, "Hold on, sweetie, I have to talk to Kelsey." Opening the door, I called out, "Kelsey, can you come in please?"

Looking at me she replied, "Coming, Auntie." She and Peanut headed toward the doors. Something caught my eye and looking to the right I saw what looked like the shadow of a man walking into the lilac bush at the base of the weeping cherry tree. Rubbing my eyes, I looked again and saw nothing. Shaking my head, I turned around to wait for Kelsey.

The Tree and the Tablet

Upon entering the large dining room, there was evidence that Kelsey had been up for a bit as I looked over to see that there was food in, and around, Peanut's food dish. Also, it was difficult to miss that there was a small, but disarrayed menagerie of various food types and dishes which suggested that Kelsey had eaten breakfast. Turning toward her as she entered, I said, "Who was that man in the yard?"

She looked at me, confused. "What man, Auntie? It was just me and Peanut."

With a worried expression now, I asked, "Have you forgotten the rule about going in the backyard alone?"

Hanging her head and having the sense to look contrite, she said, "I'm sorry, I know you were really tired and Peanut needed to go outside, so I let you sleep." Looking excited and proud of herself, "Look, Auntie, I made myself breakfast and fed Peanut for you."

Sherri giggled. Kelsey turned toward her, but I stopped her, taking her by the shoulders and kneeling to get on her level, looking her in the eyes, I said, "You need to let me know when you want to go into the back yard. Even when I'm asleep, you should tell me where you're going, so I don't worry about you. Okay?"

Blazing blue eyes lit up in comprehension. "You mean like when I get upset when I can't find you?"

"Yes! Exactly. I know that you were scared I left you last night, but I promise I'll always be close by and while you may feel

87

the same, it's now my job to make sure and keep you safe. Because there is water outside and we have coyotes and cougars in the area which will not usually attack an adult, you may be in danger from an animal like that. Please promise me you won't go out without telling me again."

A dawning understanding crossed her face and she whispered, "Yes, Auntie. I understand. I'm sorry you were scared."

Hugging her closely, I whispered, "I love you, Kells." The conversation must have gotten too serious as she suddenly pulled away and giggling, she turned toward Sherri.

Bouncing across the room, she landed with a thud into Sherri's lap and said, "Where are my friends?"

Sherri looked at me over the top of Kelsey's head as if to get approval from me. I nodded and smiled, which let her know I was finished and she relaxed. Looking at Kelsey, Sherri explained, "Well, the boys went out on the boat with Grandpa Dave and they should be back in this afternoon."

Going into the kitchen, I started a pot of coffee. Standing at the sink waiting for the coffee to brew, I listened to Kelsey beguile Sherri with the harrowing stories of our adventures with Mr. Robin.

"Wow!" Sherri exclaimed. "Did you know that in some legends, it's said that a spirit can return in the form of a bird?"

Kelsey and I both looked at Sherri simultaneously and at the same exact moment said "Really?"

She laughed, "Of course, but it depends on the story, there are some legends that say it's an eagle, some people believe it's a sparrow, and others say it's a raven. However, I've never heard of a robin except in some old stories about spirit guides. There are other stories that just generalize it to a bird of some kind." Kelsey and I looked at each other.

Kelsey's smile could be seen from outer space as she exclaimed, "It's my Daddy. I just know it! Auntie, we have to call Jody and tell her to catch the robin for us." She hopped down from Sherri's lap and ran to me. Clasping my hand to her and hugging it, she said, "Please, auntie."

Scowling at Sherri, I made eye contact with Kelsey as I softly replied, "Honey, it's just a story. We can't catch a wild robin and put it in a cage. That would be sad for the robin. Could you imagine being put in your room and never being allowed to leave it?"

Kelsey put her head down and became very sad. "I just thought that I could have Daddy close to me."

Pulling her close, I hugged her and said, "I know, Sweetheart. I understand."

Pushing me away from her, she shouted, "NO. YOU. DON'T!!!!" It pierced my heart as she ran out into the backyard. Frantically, I followed after her and stopped dead in my tracks at the back door. Kelsey was standing like a stone statue, her gaze transfixed on the most beautiful robin sitting on the back of the chair looking at her. It looked exactly like the one in Colorado.

How odd. It couldn't be. Maybe there was a new species of robin with the same brilliant coloring. Kelsey walked toward the bird and held out her hand. "Here, Daddy." She said to the bird. It flew to her outstretched hand and at that moment, I exhaled. The bird cocked its head to peer at me from one blue eye and then flew over to the ledge. Kelsey looked over her shoulder at me and sneered, "I told you it was Daddy." The jelly that my legs became wouldn't support my weight causing me to promptly sink to my butt right there and begin to cry.

Sherri, having witnessed the entire episode, said, "Are you okay, hun?"

The robin stared at Sherri, then back to Kelsey and took flight into the trees. Catching Sherri's eye, I asked, "What the heck is going on? That can't be the same bird? Can it?" We both glanced up to the trees that harbored the new resident robin. Shifting my gaze upward toward the sky, and speaking under my breath to no one in particular, "This is not funny." The skies decided at that moment to streak lightning across the clouds and shout with thunder as if it were angry in response to my comment. This sent us all scurrying into the house as the rain came down like a sheet falling from the above and obscuring our views of anything and everything within five feet of us.

Once inside, Kelsey started dancing in circles and shouting, "Hooray, Hooray. Whoop, Whoop!" Shaking her little butt and repeating over and over, "I knew it, I knew it."

My head was spinning. Was I losing my mind? That's not

possible. Peering over to Sherri, her face was white. Suddenly alarmed, I asked, "What's wrong?"

Shaking visibly, she replied in a panic, "Dave and the boys are out there!" Her slender finger extended toward the meley erupting over the bay.

Turning to look out the door, I exclaimed, "Oh. My. God!!!"

Kelsey stopped dancing and turned toward Sherri now with fear in her eyes. I ran for the phone.

CHAPTER 7

"Yes sir, David and his three grandsons. They are three, five, and six. She's with me. I understand. Yes, sir. We will. Thank you." As I hung up my phone, my eyes skimmed across the room to see how Sherri was doing. Her face was stark white, as if all the blood had drained out of her. Her eyes were fixed toward the window, watching the intense wall of water, unblinking, as tears silently slipped down her face. Looking past her through the window of the French doors, the rain was coming down so hard, it almost looked like a waterfall, causing the water to bounce and foam as it hit the deck. She'd tried to call Dave's cell phone but kept getting the voicemail. Desperation clung to her like a cloak.

It almost looked like hail, but upon peering through the window, this was clearly just the most intense rainstorm I'd seen in the area in years. The sky had gone from a light blue with scattered puffy white clouds to this immensely thick and dark gray which almost made it look like night was coming. It was only ten in the morning. Taking in a deep, calming breath, I poured Sherri a hot cup of coffee and stirred in two small teaspoons of sugar just the way she liked it. Picking up the cup, I turned toward her.

Walking over to her, I placed the cup of hot coffee in her hands and sat in the seat next to her. Drawing her attention to me, I spoke softly, "Honey, the coast guard's out looking for them." She raised her beautiful eyes to me, shimmering and glistening with tears. I continued, "They have my number. Dave might've seen that the weather was turning. You know he wouldn't do anything that would endanger those boys. He's pretty good out on the water and he always keeps the weather radio with him as well as an emergency beacon, life vests, and all of the necessities." She kept slowly nodding her head at me and sniffling.

My hand skimmed across the linen tablecloth to grasp a napkin and pass it to her as I continued to speak in dulcet tones meant to calm her, "In the meantime, the sheriff's sending a man to the waterfront park and ramp where they put in, to see if they have come back in." Attempting a reassuring smile while placing my hand on her upper arm, "They'll be fine. I just know it." Looking down at her hands, which were slightly shaking and barely holding the hot cup of coffee, she took a slow, staggering breath to calm herself. Taking a sip of her coffee, she shivered. Slowly, I rose from the table and made my way over to the couch to grab a fleece blanket I kept there for those chilly winter nights. Returning, I wrapped it around her shoulders.

Helplessness seeped through my bones, causing a chill. It made me suddenly envy the blanket I'd just placed around my best friend. Sherri resumed her watch on the unforgiving skies and distant waters of the bay that couldn't be seen no matter how hard she strained her eyes.

Kelsey was parked in front of the French doors, her forehead pressed against the cold glass, trying to peer through the intense wall of water toward the bay as well. Her breath fogged the window in small bursts of condensation that would slightly fade, but not quite disappear, and then cloud again in a small circle with each breath. Speaking softly as if she were afraid to make too much noise, she asked, "Auntie, do you think Daddy is okay?"

Exasperated, I gasped. Trying to reign in my frustration with her, I realized she was just a child and trying not to sound mean, I said evenly, "Kelsey, I think the robin's fine. We really need to focus on positive thoughts of Mr. David and the boys getting home safe, Okay?"

She turned her head slightly toward me, glancing at me from the corner of her eyes, she sighed but responded in a petulant voice, "Alright."

Just then, something small flew straight at the window of the French door. A flinch jolted my body as I thought it was going to hit and shatter the window. Then it just stopped. Perched on the deck, in front of the window, was the robin. It looked sideways at the window of the French door and reaching up with its little beak, it pecked on the glass.

Stunned, I just stared at it. Kelsey jumped up from the floor, her face appeared happy yet super intense and serious all at the same time, "Look, Auntie. It's Daddy. He's okay."

Frustrated now, I stomped over to the door and opened it roughly to shoo it away. As the door slid open, it flew straight toward the bay. In the distance, I could make out the figures of a man holding a small child and two smaller figures walking toward the house. The rain had begun to let up, but they were silhouettes against the rain and fog. My mouth fell straight to the floor. Standing there, mouth agape and absolutely flabbergasted, I exclaimed, "I'll be damned!" Turning to Sherri, I said excitedly, "Come quick, you need to see this."

Sherri was looking down at her coffee. Setting it on the table, she lifted her eyes to the vision outside. Jumping out of her chair, she literally appeared to fly off the deck in the direction of the approaching figures. Tears and excitement ensued. Peanut, having followed Sherri out the door, was running around everyone barking rambunctiously and barely bouncing out of the way of the feet of the people at the other end of the yard. Following closely behind her, I jumped off the end of the low deck and ran out to help bring the family in from the rain.

Dave was still holding three-year-old Raiden, who he passed into the arms of Sherri. He lifted six-year-old Wren, as I hoisted five-year-old Ryder up. We ran the rest of the way to the house to get out of the rain. Setting Ryder on the floor just inside the door, I was barely able to get out of the way as Kelsey ran over to hug her friend, "I'm so happy you're here. Did you see my daddy? He's a bird." She laughed. "Was it scary in the storm," she continued exuberantly, not waiting for a reply, "Daddy helped you get here, didn't he?" Ryder just looked at her and smiled. He was always a shy and quiet child. Kelsey made up for that by talking enough for the both of them.

As I was closing the door to shut out the weather, I saw the little robin fly over and land in the weeping cherry tree on the right side of the yard. Shaking my head violently, my mind screamed out, *NOPE! Nope, nope, nope.* Closing my eyes against the thoughts raging inside me, I told myself not to think about it. Taking a deep breath and plastering a smile on my face, I turned to the family and called out to Kelsey as she and Ryder had moved further into the house, "Kelsey, let's get some blankets and towels from the linen closet in the bathroom."

The family was quickly removing items of soaking wet clothing. Kelsey and I made our way down the hallway toward the closet and on the way there, Kelsey asked, "Are you sure it isn't Daddy?"

Pulling linens out and piling them in Kelsey's arms, I replied stiffly, "I don't know what to think, but I don't want to talk about it right now, okay?" Solemnly nodding at me, I continued, "Let's go take care of Sherri and her family and we can talk later. Agreed?"

Sighing, she said, "Okay, Auntie." As we turned to go back into the dining room area I swear I could feel her smiling smugly behind my back.

As we entered the dining room and started handing out blankets, there was a lot of laughing and chattering going on at the same time from all of them. Wrapping towels and blankets around them, I wasn't really focused on what was being said. After gathering the wet shirts, coats, and socks, I went to put them in the dryer.

Returning to the dining room again, I watched my best friend. Her eyes were now lit up with such love and adoration as she listened to the children and Dave relate their harrowing experiences. It sounded as if they were simply telling a story of a grand adventure. She was smiling so brightly, it looked like sunshine. Making my way through the group, I walked into the living room and turned on the gas fireplace, "You all can move your chairs over here to get warm. The clothes are drying." They all said thank you in their own ways and started moving the dining room chairs over to the fireplace. Walking toward the kitchen, I called over my shoulder toward Sherri, "I'm going to call the sheriff and coast guard to let them know everyone's safe." She glanced over to me and said, "Okay" as she nodded. Turning

The Tree and the Tablet

toward the kitchen island, I grabbed my phone and dialed the non-emergency number to the Sheriff. The other line rang twice and a pleasant young man's voice answered, "Sheriff's office, how can I help you?"

"Hello, my name is Maggie, I called earlier about a grandfather and his three grandson's out in the storm on the bay."

"Oh, yes, ma'am. The Sheriff and a couple of men are out doing a search and rescue in the bay with a coast guard boat. What can I do for you?"

"I'm calling to let you know that the people they are searching for have made landfall at my home."

"Oh? That's great news. Can you hold the line while I relay the information to the group?"

"Yes, I'll hold." After a fairly brief time, the young man came back on the line.

"Alright, ma'am. The coast guard requires a follow-up so the Sheriff and an EMS team will be coming to your residence on Sherman road to check on the individuals and take a statement. Please advise the individuals to stay put so we can complete the protocols."

"I'll do that. I think they're all fine, though."

"I understand but it's a procedure that we have to do with any waterway emergency. It really shouldn't take long."

"Okay. I'll let them know. Thank you."

"You're welcome, ma'am. The sheriff will be there soon."

"Alright, Goodbye."

"Goodbye."

Disconnecting the line, I signaled to Sherri as I walked over to her, "The Sheriff has to do a report, so they'll be coming by to check on you all and then take a statement."

Looking to Dave, they both nodded and said, "Okay."

"Are you guys hungry?"

Five voices chimed in with affirmative responses which made me giggle. "Okay, then, I'll get started on that."

"Can I help?" Sherri asked.

"No! You just stay here with your family. I got this." She tried to stand up, but I placed a firm hand on her shoulder to keep her in place. "No, really."

While I was in the kitchen, I made some little sandwiches and started another pot of coffee. As we were waiting, the boys were busy eating and laughing about random comments they made to each other. Kelsey was perched next to the French doors again, eating some grapes. Sherri and Dave were huddled close, whispering to each other while warming up by the fire. Peanut was curled up in her little bed next to the fire as well.

Everyone looked cozy enough for the moment. Sherri briefly left Dave to get him a cup of coffee. On her way to him with his hot coffee, she winked and smiled at me warmly mouthing the words, "Thank you." As she sat back down next to him.

"You're welcome," left my lips just as silently as her

gratification, but she didn't see as she had turned her adoring eyes back to the love of her life.

Settled in a chair at the island, nursing a cup of coffee, I stared blankly out the front window. Soon, the sheriff pulled into the driveway along with the paramedics. Looking toward the group, I said, "They're here." Walking to the front door, I ushered Sheriff Cooper into the room along with the volunteer fire department's Emergency Medical technicians on duty. As everyone was being checked out, I stood to the side with the Sheriff.

"Hello, George." I said to Sheriff Cooper. "How's Shirley doing?"

He looked at me, smiled, "Better than yesterday, but every day is different." He looked down and cleared his throat trying to get control of his emotions. Looking up, he smiled and said, "Thanks for asking."

Returning his smile, "Let me know if you need anything."

He nodded. "By the way, Shirley said to tell you how sorry we are about your loss. She wanted to bake you some cookies but she just couldn't get up." Sorrow drifted across his face again like a wave and just as quickly as it came, it was gone as he turned his attention toward the group excitedly chattering at the same time.

Resting my hand on his forearm, I replied in a soft voice, "It's okay. You tell your beautiful wife that me and Peanut will be coming around for a visit soon."

A gentle smile lit his features briefly, "She'd love that. She really gets a hoot out of your little dog." Looking around, he spotted Peanut laying on her bed near the fire and his face glowed with adoration for her. "She keeps asking me if there's some obscure law that would allow me to steal your dog." He laughed a singular bark. Peanut looked up at him and growled. Caused him to laugh harder. Holding out his hand, he exclaimed, "Okay, no worries, Peanut, I'll let her know your feelings on the matter." As I glanced at Peanut, she calmed down as if she understood what he said. We looked at one another and chuckled. "Well, enough said."

George and Shirley Cooper were longtime residents of Allyn. Shirley used to be a teacher at the grade school in Grapeview which was a short distance down the road. George had been a sheriff in Mason county for over thirty years, but chose not to retire yet as they needed his health insurance for his wife. Shirley was forced to retire after twenty years with the school due to a diagnosis of lung cancer two years ago. She'd never smoked a day in her life, but when she was younger, she worked as a waitress in the local bar for seven years before she decided to try her hand at school, and eventually at teaching. She and I met through Mom as they were best friends and spent a lot of time together.

The EMT's finished up and gave everyone a clean bill of health. The female, Janice, asked, "Who wants a sticker?" All the children held up their hands, "Me", "I do", "Yes, please" were the responses. As the EMT handed out the fire Marshall stickers,

The Tree and the Tablet

the other EMT reached in his bag and pulled out a bunch of plastic junior firefighter hats which turned out to be another big hit causing a chorus of "Thank you" and excited child chatter. Turning to Dave and Sherri, the male EMT stated, "Everyone looks to be in good health, but if you have any of the symptoms we talked about earlier such as trouble breathing, a fever, or lethargy, please don't hesitate to call us or go to the hospital."

"Thank you. We will. Thank you for your time," Dave replied. Janice turned and nodded at Sheriff Cooper, "They're all yours," and they headed out.

Smiling at the boy's antics, George looked to Dave saying, "Tell me what happened today."

Dave glanced at Sherri, turned his eyes to me, smiled and then, making eye contact with the sheriff, he said, "You won't believe me, but, we were out on the water. The skies were clear when we left and the forecast for today was supposed to stay that way, otherwise I never would've gone." The sheriff was rapidly writing in his notepad. Dave took another breath and then while exhaling, he said in a rush, "It was the darnedest thing I've ever seen." He stopped and looked at Sherri again.

She nodded and he continued, as if there was an unspoken conversation that just took place. "Well, the clouds started forming out of the blue and then lightning and thunder. We just brought up the anchor to start in. I was telling the boys that it looked like the weather service was wrong and we were going to head in. Suddenly, there was a wall of water that just fell on us. It was raining so hard, we couldn't see the shore or even make out which way the shore was with my compass. It just kept spinning." He pulled the compass out of his pants pocket and looked at it. "Hmm. Funny, it appears to be working now." He shrugged and placed the compass on the side table. "I cinched down the boys more tightly into their life jackets and we spread our raincoats out over our heads as I tried to radio in to get help. There was only static. Then, there was a flipping bird flying around us in a panic. I'm surprised it could fly in that amount of rain." He stopped and ran his fingers through his thin grey hair.

Sheriff Cooper looked up from his frantic scribbling and said, "Did you say a bird?"

"Yeah." Dave replied. "Not a seabird either, but like an orange and grey thing. I swear it looked like a robin." He chuckled while shaking his head, "I know it sounds crazy."

Standing in the kitchen, cleaning up the dishes from the sandwiches while they were talking, a gasp escaped my lips and I dropped the plate I was holding which caused it to hit the floor, shattering into several pieces. "Are you sure?" I asked, looking at Dave in amazement.

Cocking his head to the side to look at me, he squinted his blue eyes and said. "Yes. It was different though, almost like it was shiny."

The sheriff cleared his throat drawing attention back to him. "That's odd for sure." He went back to scribbling in his book.

Sherri touched his shoulder and said, "I'll be right back."

The Tree and the Tablet

She got up and rushed to the pantry to get the broom while I knelt down to pick up the larger pieces of the broken plate.

Dave looked at Sheriff Cooper and continued, "Anyway, it kept flying and whistling at me and it would fly away in the same direction and then fly back. After the third time, I figured it wanted me to follow, so I started the outboard and tried to keep up. The bird disappeared and there was Maggie's boathouse straight in front of me. We tied off, took off our life vests and climbed the hill."

He rubbed his hands on his pant legs as if they were all of a sudden quite sweaty and he didn't have any other place to wipe them. "It was the oddest thing I ever saw." He looked at the Sheriff, shrugging again, "But we're here and we're safe. Maybe I was seeing things and maybe I wasn't. I don't care how it happened." He stated the last part matter-of-factly and looked at his wife pointedly. Sherri and he exchanged smiles. "I'm blessed to have had a way to find the shore and get myself and the boys back to my sweet Sherri." His words made Sherri glow. She positively radiated with love.

Sheriff Cooper finished his writing and said, "Well, Dave, I've seen some odd things in these many years that I've been doing the job and I've never heard of a bird leading someone to shore in a storm before, but I agree with you." Wrapping the pen and book together with a rubber band, he placed them in his front pocket and reached for his hat, "you're a lucky man, indeed." He handed a card to Dave. "This is the case number. If

105

you think of anything else, give me a call."

Turning toward the front door, "Well, it looks like everyone is in good health and very lucky to have made it back home today. I have all I need. I'll submit my information to the coast guard for review if they request it, but my end is completed." As he reached for the door, he stopped, then turned and smiled at no one in particular, "You know, there're legends that say birds are spirits of our lost loved ones sent to watch over us." With that, he tipped his hat and turned toward the door, he stared out the glass side windows saying, "Looks like the rain's letting up." As he reached for the door, "You all take care." He closed the door behind him and I sank into the nearest chair watching him get into his car, radio dispatch, and then drive away. The only thing better than a drink right then would be a nap! That's exactly what I needed right then.

CHAPTER 8

*L*ooking at the clock, I noticed it was almost four. It was getting late. Having returned the dry clothing to the family, they'd gotten dressed. The sky was clearing and after what was a very minimal discussion, it was decided that Sherri would stay at the house with all of the children. Since Dave had dropped off Sherri before they went to put the boat in the water, I'd give Dave a ride to the boat dock to retrieve their vehicle which had all of the car seats in it. Besides, I'd been waiting quite a while to pick his brain about the bird incident since he had ties to the local Quileute tribe and was familiar with some of their legends and lore.

Once we were in the car, Dave was buckling his seatbelt

when he looked up and said, "Sherri thought we should talk." He was fidgeting with his hands in his lap now as I pulled up in the driveway toward the highway.

Looking at him, slightly surprised, but not completely shocked, I chuckled. He smiled, "What's on your mind? As if I can't guess."

Raising my eyebrows at him, the blinker clicked on and clacked softly in the background while I formed my thoughts. Seeing the way was clear, I pulled out and headed toward the waterfront park and public boat dock. Quickly glancing sideways at him and then back to the road, "Is there anything specific in your tribal lore about robins?"

He laughed and then looked a little serious for a moment. "You know, now that I think on it, there isn't anything specific that I can recall; however, there are some websites that have information about different tribes and their beliefs." My sigh of frustration was difficult to hold in. Looking at me with understanding and compassion, he said, "I vaguely recall my grandmother sharing a story with me when I was little about a little boy named Opichee but that's from a southern tribe." He shook his head as if trying to clear the cobwebs.

Excitedly, I asked, "Can you remember anything about the story?" He shook his head and eyed me apologetically, "I'm so sorry, Maggie. I just don't remember it that well." When my face clearly showed a look of exasperation and sadness, he added, "I'll ask my Grandma if she can remember, but don't get your hopes

The Tree and the Tablet

up. She's getting up there, and it's difficult for her to remember things these days." He fell silent for a bit. The sound of my blinker broke his concentration. Raising his eyes to the surroundings, "Oh, we're here."

"Yeah," I nodded as I pulled into the park. Seeing his Ford Explorer parked at the end of the driveway with his boat trailer attached, I turned in that direction. Parking next to his vehicle, I smiled as I said, "Thank you."

Having reached for the door, he paused with his hand on the door handle and looked over his shoulder at me. "Maggie, I know what you're thinking about the little robin." At my little gasp, he said, "Don't be surprised by the way Mother Earth sends messages to you. There are things that happen beyond our understanding." Smiling, he continued, "I can't say for certain, but I believe it's entirely possible that the robin may be a spirit guide. He may be who Kelsey thinks he is, but there's no way of knowing for sure."

Sighing heavily and looking down at my hands as if there were suddenly something very interesting about the shape of my fingers, I said, "I know it sounds ridiculous, but I just can't get over all of the coincidences." Looking up at him, I shook my head slightly and then stared out my window at nothing in particular.

"It's okay." He said, "We all need hope sometimes. There's always a bigger purpose to the great spirit and her ways. Let Kelsey have this. It may help her get over the loss." I turned to look at him, and he smiled gently before reaching for the handle again. "I'm just glad that little bird showed up when it did." Opening the door, he turned back one last time and said happily with a broad grin on his face, "I'll see you back at the house." Jumping out of my pickup, he closed the door and got into his own vehicle, leaving me to ponder our discussion.

On the way home, I had much to think about. As I entered the driveway, I decided to accept everything for what it was and not put too much thought into it. If this is what Kelsey needed to help her accept the loss of her parents, then I'd do what I needed to for her to be ok. Still, it was going to be difficult to overcome my own fears and skepticism. Placing the truck in park, I stepped out of the vehicle, clicked the key fob to set the alarm, and locked the doors when I noticed that I was being greeted by a smiling group of children at the front window. They were so cute.

Ryder and Kelsey were hugging and grinning like they were up to something. Wren and Raiden were dancing around and giggling while Sherri was trying not to give in to them and lose her composure as well. They all stopped and waived out the window and screamed, "Maggie!" Running toward the front door. It was comical to watch as they all plowed into each other from the living room into the foyer. If it weren't for the large windows that exposed them to my view, I would've missed that they all slipped on the rug and went tumbling to the ground right in front of the door. There was a tangle of arms and legs and uproarious laughter. Slowly opening the door, I was greeted by a sea of flailing arms and legs that echoed a roar of jubilation from its depths. We all pitched in trying to disentangle the children from each other while they continued to laugh and frolic. Peanut was boisterously bouncing around the menagerie of children and yapping incessantly at the giggling bundle of children. Finally, we were able to successfully separate the mass of arms and legs. As everyone was finally starting to settle down, Wren went over and closed the door which prompted Kelsey to nudge Ryder.

Making eye contact with me, Ryder shuffled his feet and blushed as he stammered a little, tucking his hands behind his back and swinging his body from side to side as he asked, "Maggie, can Kelsey spend the night at our house tonight?"

Kelsey jumped up and down and clasping her hands together in a prayer type pose, she begged prettily, "Please, Auntie?"

Sherri piped up, shrugging her shoulders, "I told them they'd have to ask you because you might have plans for tomorrow."

"Hmmmm." Thinking to myself, *Well, if I let her go, then I won't have to talk to her about the bird tonight. Then again, I kinda want to talk to her about it.* But, looking at her glowing face filled with hope, and the excitement on the boys' faces was what decided the matter for me. Even though we just got back from one of the most trying times in my life and reluctant to let her go because she was so precious to me, I knew that I needed to trust my gut and let her have this or she'd resent me for it. Getting on her level and cupping her little face in my hands, I asked, "Are you sure, sweetie?" At her insistent nodding, I smiled, "You know I'm right here if you need me, okay?" She continued to bob her head up and down eagerly, "Alright, go pack your bag." She and Ryder ran for the bedroom giggling and talking excitedly all the way. Getting to my feet again, I turned to Sherri, "Haven't you had enough fun for the day?"

A glimmer twinkled in her eye and a look of comprehension flitted across her face as she spoke softly, "Not as much as you have. Besides, it's a lot to deal with for you." At my look of consternation, she laughed. "It's totally up to you. If it's too soon or if you need more time before you let her go, I'll explain to them."

Wringing my hands, I tried to come to grips with the war raging through me and finally released my pent-up breath in a slow sigh, "No, it's fine. She needs to have some happiness away from my gloomy butt."

Wrapping her arm around me, she gently reassured me, "It'll be okay, Maggie. I promise, if she asks to call or wants to come home, even in the middle of the night, I'll bring her to you."

Shrugging my shoulders, I smiled and glanced at her sideways, "Well, just so you know, I was planning on going to see Shirley tomorrow. I'm not sure Kelsey could handle that after everything else."

Sherri released her firm hold on my shoulders to glance over at Dave. They exchanged the warmest sentiment toward each

The Tree and the Tablet

other. Turning back to me, she said, "That's fine. Why don't you make a day of it and do whatever you need? We're going to have dinner around six so I'll see you then. The kids will have the day to play and you'll be able to have some you-time. Self-care is an important part of taking on children and keeping a level head." There was the psychology major chiming in as I expected.

Dave piped in sounding somewhat like a child bragging about a new toy as he dove between us and whispered conspiratorially, "Yeah, Mags, I'm gonna make some super delicious ribs on my new smoker."

Reaching around him, she grabbed me, hugging me fiercely and whispered in my ear, "I love you, ya'know?"

Hugging her in return, I whispered, "Yes, and I love you, too." Wren and Raiden had joined Kelsey and Ryder at some point back in the bedroom. They were now all giggling their way back down the hallway toward us, excitedly talking about the latest kids' movie that was out on digital format for them to watch tonight. With a final intense squeeze, Sherri and I separated with a wide grin.

Dave turned to the children, "Well, kids, let's get going." He opened the door to a stream of children funneling through in a straight line headed toward the SUV.

"Dave, Kelsey's car seat's in the back of the pickup." Snatching the electronic key fob of my coat pocket, I pressed the button and unlocked the doors to the truck.

Turning toward the truck, Dave called over his shoulder,

113

"Thanks, Maggie, you're awesome." The rain had completely stopped, and the clouds were clearing.

As Kelsey was getting ready to follow her friends out the door, she stopped and looked up at me. Dropping to my knees in front of her so that I was on eye level with her, I brushed a stray lock of hair from her face and curled it gently around her ear as I smiled at her, "Have fun, kiddo. Just remember, I'm only a phone call away if you need me."

Seeing Sherri staring at her, she pursed her lips and mumbled, "I know."

Hugging her close and sensing she was struggling with embarrassment, I whispered in her ear, "I love you, Kells."

She pulled back, wearily staring at me and then looking around to see if anyone was watching she rolled her eyes and pursed her lips as she pushed away from me and said, "Okay, see you later." Turning on her heel, she followed the others out the door. That was odd. I wondered briefly what was going on.

A frown spread across my lips, but I tried to cover it up. Getting up from the floor, I took a deep breath and shrugged while slightly shaking my head. Looking after her, I uttered, "What was that all about?"

Sherri, having watched the exchange, placed her hand on my arm, "She's trying to adjust. It'll take time. She loves you and you know it."

Standing there, looking after her, "I know."

Sherri walked out to the car and helped wrangle the children

The Tree and the Tablet

into their car seats. Once everyone was settled, they all yelled loud and long from the inside of the vehicle, "Bye, Maggie!!" Waving exuberantly from their seats.

Laughing and waving back, I yelled in the same exaggerated way, "Bye!" They pulled out of the driveway. As I turned to close the door, the robin flew up to the railing on the front porch and sat there with one eye on me. Slightly startled, I remembered my vow to try to go with the flow so I laughed out loud to see what the bird's reaction would be. Since he didn't budge, I spoke to it, "Hello, my little friend. What a busy day you had." The bird cocked its head sideways at me and then hopped up and down while spinning in circles on the railing. Hmmm. What odd behavior. Looking closely at it again, I asked it, as if it could answer, "Jaxon? Is that you?" The bird moved its head in an up and down motion and all prior attempts to accept what was meant to be flew right out of my head. As I screamed, I tripped over the door jamb and spun around, slamming the door, and pushing my back against it as if it would be knocked open again.

Slowly sliding down the door, my butt hit the floor while my back was still pressed firmly against it. An incoherent stream of words flowed from my lips as if hearing the sound of my own voice would make me less freaked out, "No, that's not possible. I'm seeing things. Get a grip, Maggie. Did that little bird just nod its head? No, it did not. Listen to yourself. That's crazy talk! But, What if? Nope. Just stop." Noting that I was beginning to hyperventilate, I tried to calm myself by taking several deep breaths. Turning my head slightly so I could look out the long windows next to the door, I peeked to see if the bird was still there. It was gone. A shuddering breath escaped me. Taking in another great gulp of air, I let it out slowly. What is going on? Am I losing my mind? I must have sat there for quite a while because suddenly I noticed it was dark and my butt was asleep, and my stomach was rumbling with hunger.

Gathering my wits, I got up and locked the front door. Since it was night, I decided to close the curtains and turn on the lights. Looking around, I noticed that Sherri must have cleaned up while Dave and I were down at the boat launch because everything was neatly put away. My stomach grumbled loudly, and I decided I would just have one of the leftover sandwiches that was in the fridge from earlier. Pulling out a turkey and cheddar on rye, I eagerly began munching while I puttered about the kitchen preparing to pour myself a large glass of wine.

Peanut whimpered at me. Turning toward her, "Awe, sorry, sweetie." Pulling out a cup of food for her, I walked over and poured it in her bowl. She dove into her bowl like she hadn't eaten in ages, and I reached down to scratch behind her ears. Walking over to the sink, I rinsed my plate off, and placed it in the dishwasher. Grabbing my glass of wine, I headed out to the deck. Reaching over to get my wool shawl on the way out, I huddled myself down into its thick warmth.

The clouds were completely gone now and the moon was high in the sky. It glistened on the water. Still no crickets tonight.

Sitting in my wicker swinging chair, staring out into the darkness, I couldn't help but wonder about the events of the day. My mind was running through every moment as if it were a video, pausing periodically to analyze different events. Was I imagining things? Was it truly Kelsey that was manifesting this, or was it me?

Finishing off my glass of wine, I decided it was time for bed. "Peanut, come on." She half-ran, half-hopped, which made her look like a bunny, up the stairs and scampered into the house. Moping, I made my way around the house and locked up and slowly ambled my way down the hallway toward my bedroom. Briefly, I paused outside Kelsey's door and stared at the empty bed. Only a couple hours in and I already missed the little minx. As I was brushing my teeth, my eyes kept wandering to the large soaker tub in the corner. Settling on the decision, a nice bath with some bath salts would do wonders to help me relax. Every muscle in my body quivered as the hot water enveloped me in its gentle cocoon of luxury and tranquility. The gentle scent of lavender filled my nostrils and I closed my eyes, laying my head back on the fluffy towel at the head of the tub, a sigh escaped my lips.

Suddenly, the most beautiful green eyes filled my vision, which caused me to catch my breath. It felt like drowning. The need to inhale was overcome by my inability to take a breath as my heart thudded wildly in my chest. The sensation of the water touching my skin became gentle hands running across every pore as my heart raced even faster. It felt so good. He opened his mouth to say something and out came barking. Puzzled, he disappeared in a haze and was replaced with the vision of bubbles. The burning sensation in my lungs triggered the need to inhale. Starting to take a breath, my mind caught on the realization of water in my mouth as it passed over my lips and onto my tongue. *Air doesn't taste like soap.* My mind struggled to grasp what was happening.

Becoming more alert, I discovered it wasn't a dream but a reality in which I was choking on my bath water. Quickly, I sat up out of the water. Struggling to catch my breath and clear the water from my airway, I continued to cough and sputter. Finally, able to get air into my lungs without choking and clearing the tears from my eyes, I looked around to see my green-eyed stranger was gone. Peanut was next to the tub barking as loud as her little self could. Climbing out of the bath and wrapping a towel around me, my breathing began to steadily improve. Peanut was licking my toes. "I'm okay, girl." She looked relieved and finally left my side to go to her little bed satisfied that she'd done her job.

Looking over at the cursed tub that lured me in as if it were an evil entity, I said, "Maybe next time I'll just take a shower." Laughing at myself, I dried my hair and pulled on my tank top and shorts. Slipping between the cool cotton sheets, I felt a renewed sense of loss. My heart ached. Shivering as if all the warmth had just seeped out of my bones, I hunkered down deeper into my bed. So tired. Closing my eyes, a single tear slipped down my cheek as I fell into a mind-numbing sleep.

CHAPTER 9

*S*tanding on my back deck looking out toward the water, but there was no water, only a thick dense fog. It almost felt heavy like a wool blanket laying on me. Suddenly, Andrea appeared out of thin air floating on the thickest layer of fog. Surprisingly, I wasn't scared, just confused. Even in my dream, it seemed strange to me that she was there so I asked her, "Why are you here?"

Her response was a whisper on the wind. "Don't fear what will come. I'm here to help you. Look to Kelsey and all will be right. She knows more than you think." She floated toward me, and leaning forward, she wrapped me in her ghostly arms. Electricity flowed through my veins but then was replaced with a *deep sense of calm and comfort. My eyes closed in an effort to concentrate on the soothing effects of the hug and just as quick as she had appeared, she was gone. The wind whipped around me, blurring my vision due to my hair flying in my face. Still trying to clear my hair from my face so I could see where she went, I was startled by the intense sound of a large conspiracy of black birds which rose out of the dense fog.*

The wind calmed and immediately in front of me appeared a robin which shuddered and blurred until it transformed into Jaxon. My heart was racing, but I felt calm. He spoke softly, sounding almost melodic like the sound of a bird singing, "Maggie, look after Kelsey. Tell her every day that we love her." He vanished and the robin appeared again. Singing it's beautiful song, it rose into the fog toward the trees. Finally, my mysterious stranger appeared before me. He held out his hand smiling gently at me. Those beautiful green eyes beckoned to me, drawing me in. When I reached out my hand to take his, he turned into a stunning six foot raven and flew away singing a raucous song that remarkably sounded like the words, "Trust me, trust me, trust me." As I reached out my hand toward the sky, a blinding light pierced the fog. Shielding my eyes from its brilliance, I turned away. Darkness surrounded me...

That was when I woke up. The sun was shining through the windows which is rare in December. The dream felt so real. It was so similar to the one that I had in Colorado. I'd put the amulet in my safe when we got home. A little part of me wondered if it was still there. Picking up my cell phone, I found that it was only 7:00 am. Well, might as well get going. Peanut was anxiously awaiting my feet to hit the floor. As soon as I turned toward her, she started jumping and yapping excitedly at me. A grin crossed my lips, "Yes, I know. You want to go out?" She danced around in a circle and stood on her hind legs. Chuckling softly, "Okay, let's go." Rather than let her out from the bedroom, I decided to just open the dog door in the dining room. Walking over to the kitchen to start a pot of coffee, I looked out and saw that there was a very thick fog. Odd, when I left the bedroom, it seemed like the sun was shining because it was so bright in my room. The mist was so dense that I couldn't see where Peanut went when she dove off the deck barking.

The thick low-lying cloud was moving around almost making it look like things were hiding in it. The wind was moving it around but it wasn't dissipating. It seemed like there was a man walking around in it. Then, I thought I saw Carolyn's face swirl in the mist. Jumping back in surprise, my heart raced. My dream flared in my memory and cautiously, I leaned over, quietly opening the window so I could listen to the sounds outside. Nothing, it was eerily quiet and there were no signs of any people moving around. Peanut was quiet as well. Shakily, I called for her, "Peanut. Come." She soon stood at the end of the deck wagging her little nub of a tail at me. Relieved, I smiled at her. *My imagination is just running wild again.* There it was again, the image of a person, or at least the outline of a person, but Peanut would've let me know if there was someone in the yard. A female voice drifted toward me from the gloomy silence. The faint sound of a woman singing. *Raindrops on Roses and whiskers on kittens.* Alarmed, I recoiled from the window again, yet I continued to stare out the window from a safer distance. No. It couldn't be.

Startled but unable to peel my eyes away from the swirling shadows, something small and dark approached and landed on the deck near Peanut. She looked over at it, and leaning closer to see what was there, I realized it was the robin. Peanut licked it on the head and then ran off into the dense curtain. The robin looked thoroughly pleased with itself and just sat there quietly. A bubble of laughter erupted from me of its own accord. My hand flew to my mouth to stifle further outbursts. Even my dog was hallucinating or losing its mind. Normally she would've tried to eat that bird. The laughter released me from my fear and with a deep calming breath, I shrugged my shoulders, deciding to spend my energy on getting myself a cup of coffee and taking a shower. The bird could wait.

After showering and dressing, I returned to the vanity in the bathroom, As I was drying my hair something by the tub caught my eye. It was such a stark contrast to the bright white of the tub, that I couldn't help but notice it. At the base of the tub, near the headrest was a solitary large black feather. Crinkling my brow, I thought, *"That wasn't there last night."* It wasn't there this morning either, as I definitely thought I would recall seeing it.

The Tree and the Tablet

Startled but curious about its sudden appearance, I walked over and reached out to it tentatively as if it were a wild animal that may flee upon contact. Grasping it by the quill, I began turning it in my hand and running my finger along its spine. It was so soft. Absolutely magnificent. Upon further examination, it was the most beautiful specimen of a raven's feather that I'd ever seen. It almost seemed luminescent as it glittered and shined in varied shades of blue and black. It was so shiny it almost reflected the light like a mirror and it flashed brilliantly with every movement blue to green to black. Fascinating. Glancing around, I wondered, "But how did it get here?"

Carrying the feather with me into my room, I placed it on the dresser in front of the oval mirror. As I put the feather on the dresser, I saw the amulet sitting there. Gasping, I grabbed it. *That's not where you go.* As a knee-jerk reaction, I went into my closet and kneeling to open the hidden door on the floor under my shoe rack, I found it open. Sitting back on my haunches, I shook my head. Talking to the amulet, I demanded in my most stern paternal voice, "Do not remove yourself from this spot again," and placed the amulet in the safe, turning the lock forcefully. Checking again that it was locked, I stood up and placed my hands on my hips, I scoffed at the offending item, "There! Let's see you get out now."

Walking back into the bedroom I saw Peanut come in and turned to quiz her, "Did you bring this feather in when I was in the shower?" She just stared at me blankly and cocked her head to the side as if she were considering what I was asking her. My burst of laughter must've startled her as she jumped back and then ducked her head wagging her nub. Leaning down to scratch behind her silky ears I said, "Well, even if you did, I'm not mad. It's beautiful."

She wriggled her small blonde and silver body along my hand and panting a couple of times she made a small growling sound to indicate she wanted to eat. Smiling, "Oh, I forgot your breakfast." She yipped at me and ran to the kitchen. "By the way", I called after her, "if you're opening the safe, you're not allowed to do that." Giggling at my own keen wit, I proceeded to follow Peanut into the kitchen where I placed a scoop of food in her bowl. She dove in.

Looking out the window, I could see the fog had lifted and the sun was shining. Shrugging, I gathered Peanut's leash and called Sherri. The phone rang a couple times followed by a soft, "Good morning, you. I wondered how long you'd wait to call. Dave and I were taking bets."

"Oh, really?"

"Yeah. He won darnit."

"What? I didn't call early enough?" Glancing across the room to the clock, I saw it was only 8:00 am.

She laughed, "Well, I guess that's early for you. But still."

"Is everyone up?"

"Yes. The kids had breakfast and they're all in the backyard playing."

The Tree and the Tablet

"How'd she sleep?"

"She was mumbling in her sleep around 3:00 am, but I couldn't make out what she was saying and she didn't seem upset so I let her continue her dream. It was over pretty quick though and she woke up in good spirits this morning."

"That's good. Is it normal for kids her age to have a lot of talking in their sleep?"

"It can be. Especially when they're trying to work through things. Try no to worry too much. It'll pass."

Choosing to take her advice, "Alright. I just wanted to check on her and let you know I'm heading out."

"Okay, you wanna talk to her?"

"If it's not a problem."

"Hold on." There was a rustling sound followed by the opening of a sliding screen and giggles. "Kelsey, your auntie is on the phone."

In the background, I heard, "Can you tell her I'm busy?"

"No, ma'am, you need to come talk to your Auntie." This was followed by an exaggerated, "Ugh, fine!"

Rustling again, a small and disgruntled voice rang through, "Hi, Aunt Maggie."

"Hey, kiddo. What's going on?"

"Nothing." Another flat response.

"Did you sleep okay?"

"Yes."

"What'cha doing?"

"Playing." Her continued flat tone was beginning to bother me. A lot.

"Are you mad?"

"No. Can I go play now?"

"Sure. I..."

"Okay, Bye!"

"...Love you... Bye?" Too late, she passed off the phone.

Sherri came on the line. "That was short and sweet." She chuckled.

"Yeah. Must be some fun game." I tried to laugh but it must have come off stilted.

"You know, she's only five. It's just a phase. Give her time to adjust."

Sighing, "I know. Thanks."

"Don't worry, I'll try to pick her brain a bit if you want."

"No, that's alright. Let her enjoy her time with the boys. It's been a lot to deal with for quite some time. I'll talk to you later."

"Sure, sweetie. Have fun. Dinner's at 6:00 pm."

"See you then. Thanks for everything, Sherri."

"My pleasure. See you later." The phone went dead.

Standing at the island, I stared at my phone for a moment. Kelsey had never been so short with me. Maybe her dream bothered her more than she was letting on. Mentally shrugging, I resolved to talk with her later about it and try to find out if it was a one-time thing or if this was going to become a pattern.

Glancing at the clock again, I realized it was late and called

The Tree and the Tablet

to Peanut so we could leave. We drove over to Sheriff Cooper's house to visit with his ailing wife, Shirley. She looked weak and frail, but always had a smile for me and Peanut. Working my way around her kitchen, I prepared some herbal tea for us to enjoy in the sunroom situated off the back of the house where she was seated. Their house was modest but perfect for her and George and it was situated on a small sloping lot on the hillside that presented a beautiful view of the bay.

Peanut jumped into her lap and closed her eyes, blissful and content to be stroked by one of her favorite people. Watching her out of the corner of my eye as I slowly took a small sip of my tea, it was easy to see she was trying to find the words she wanted to say. Choosing to relieve her of her burden, I ventured, "So, how are you feeling these days?"

A whimsical smile played across her lips as she spoke, "I had the most wonderful dream last night."

"Really? What did you dream about?"

She raised her cup to her lips to sip at the hot liquid as she thought about her response, "Well, it really wasn't very detailed, it just made me feel good." Setting her cup down, she stared thoughtfully out the window. Appearing to mentally shake herself, she returned her pensive gaze to me and promptly changed the subject and in a much more somber voice, "I'm very sorry about your family. How was the service and how's Kelsey doing?"

"It was beautiful, but a little odd." I quickly cleared my

throat, swallowing to keep the lump of emotion down, "Kelsey's doing alright, I suppose. She's been a little bit of an emotional rollercoaster, but nothing I can't handle. I'm sure it's normal." Sighing softly, I took to studying my cup of tea and tracing my finger along the intricately woven design along the rim of the hand hewn mug. One of the things I loved about spending time with Shirley was viewing all of her beautiful hand made pottery and dishes. "Either way, as soon as I can, I'll get her enrolled in school here and I'm hoping that making connections with other kids will help her adjust better."

"The elementary school has an awesome school counselor. Just make sure to let them know the situation. It might be a good idea to talk to them before winter break so they're prepared for her when they go back to school after new years."

"Yeah, I figured I'd wait to have her start after the first of the year." Glancing up from my cup of tea, I saw her studying me. "What?"

"You said the service for your family was odd. Want to talk about it?"

"No, it's really nothing to trouble yourself over. There was just a passage in the will that 'Drea added that she wanted to be cremated and turned into a tree." A nervous giggle escaped me.

Her eyes squinted as she hesitantly queried, "A tree?" At my nod, she inquired, "What type of tree?"

"It was a choice that was left to me, but it was either a maple or a dogwood. I chose the dogwood, of course."

The Tree and the Tablet

"Naturally. I wonder if I should tell you about my dream after all?" It seemed as if it were more a private musing rather than an actual question meant for me.

At her silence, my curiosity was like a balloon inflating in my chest, and trying not to sound too impatient, in my calmest and most nonchalant voice, I prodded, "Well? What happened in your dream?"

Her eyes twinkled and she replied, "You were never very good at hiding your feelings from me, and I can tell you aren't quite telling me everything."

Slightly startled by her astuteness, I stammered, "It's just all the weird stuff that's happened since I left here. I mean, the whole thing is odd. I really don't know what to tell you and what not to tell you."

"Ahhh, I see. Well, I'll tell you mine, and you tell me yours. Deal?" As I nodded rapidly, she continued, "Good!" Setting her cup down on the little table next to her, she absently stroked Peanut and took a slow breath in, "Your mom came to me and told me the time was near." A small gasp escaped my lips, but she kept talking, "There was a beautiful robin sitting in a magical glowing tree. Suddenly, I was in a large throne-room with her and she told me to watch the skies, that there would be a sign. Everything went dark and a vision of you standing near a giant pool of purple flashed before me. That's it. George woke me up. He said I was mumbling or something." Her laughter tinkled across the space like a windchime stirred by a gentle breeze. She picked up her cup again and looked at me expectantly, "Well? Your turn."

She was always pretty direct. "Wait, what were you mumbling? I mean, did George say?"

Waving her hand dismissively, she said, "Oh, yeah, something about, *Don't lose hope* or something like that." She laughed, "It was just a dream, but you need to tell me what happened while you were in Denver."

Something about her fragile appearance or her sudden sadness made me stop from telling her everything, especially about the robin. Maybe it was my need to protect her somehow, but I just decided to keep that part to myself. "It really wasn't bad. Just weird." Picking up the cup from the table next to me, I took a sip of the now tepid tea. As the cup softly clanked against the table, my eyes danced across the floor and sought the view out the open window. Steadying my nerves and enveloping myself in a calm I didn't feel, I expounded, "The whole tree thing kinda threw me for a loop. That's all." Seeking her understanding and hoping she wouldn't prod further, I looked to her gently.

Seeming to understand my unspoken plea, she smiled, "What a beautiful day." She gestured toward the sun laying upon the water in the bay, sparkling like a shiny penny. It wasn't difficult to notice her spirit and strength waning as the time ticked by and we both quietly gazed at the tranquility that lay before us.

As she sat there, stroking Peanut and basking in the warmth of the sun, she almost looked like she was glowing. Her skin was

The Tree and the Tablet

a pale white from months of illness and seclusion. She seemed content though and was smiling softly as she started to doze off in the reclining chair. It seemed like a good time to leave. George came into the sunroom just as I was preparing to go. He gathered her up in his strong arms, carrying her toward her room with her head nestled against his shoulder. She looked like a child in his arms. He turned to me and said, "Thank you for coming by, Maggie."

Shirley roused herself and piped up, "Yes! Thank you!" She reached out her frail hand to me, the skin almost looked transparent.

Gently, I grasped her slender fingers in mine and replied, "Well, I couldn't miss seeing such a beautiful person on such a splendid day!"

Shirley laughed, "Beautiful? Hear that, George? She said I'm beautiful." She started to laugh again which turned into a fit of coughing. George, recognizing the need for a breathing treatment, turned to take her into her room. He mumbled to her softly, "You are very beautiful. Stop that laughing or you'll cough yourself right out of my arms." She wheezed something in return, but I couldn't quite make it out.

Grabbing Peanut, I commented loudly to be heard over her attack, "I'll let myself out, George!"

He half turned on his way through the bedroom door. Looking at me solemnly, he mouthed the words, "Thank you" and went into the room at the end of the hall.

Peanut and I got in the car. Determined to make the best of my day and not dwell on the continued perplexities, I patted my little companion on her head and rubbed her ears, speaking to her jovially, "Well, how about some Christmas shopping and a trip to the groomer for you?" She looked at me sideways and then just laid her head between her front paws on the seat. "I agree, but it's almost Christmas and I think we should at least buy Kelsey a few presents." Peanut looked at me, not even bothering to lift her head. If dogs could achieve a look of impatience, I'd swear she rolled her eyes at me. What a big attitude for such a little creature, of course, it was probably my imagination attributing human traits to an animal, but she was sure cute with her made-up attitude. Giggling at her antics, real or implied, she slightly perked her ears up. Putting the car in drive, I commented, "Try not to look so excited."

After dropping Peanut at the groomer's, I made my way to the waterfront shops in the small port town about thirty minutes northwest of the house. It was a quaint town that boasted an indoor flea market, antique shops, and a multitude of dining experiences in a sprawling waterfront shopping experience. Parking my car some distance away due to the vast number of seasonal shoppers, I made my way along the waterfront toward the shops. I could've gone to the mall, because it was the same distance, but preferred to go to the local vendors and support the local economy rather than big businesses such as the many department stores in the mall.

The Tree and the Tablet

Stopping in a Christmas decoration store, I asked the older lady at the counter, "Do you have someone who can deliver a tree to my home?"

"Why, yes, we do. Sara hasn't been too busy this year." She pulled out a beautiful red leather appointment book from below the counter. "It looks like she has an availability to deliver and decorate your tree three days from now. Will that work for you?"

"Oh, that would be wonderful. Please stick with the birds of winter theme like the one in the front window."

"Yes, ma'am. That particular tree and decorations runs six hundred ninety-nine dollars with taxes."

A slight gasp escaped my lips, but I honestly wasn't sure what to expect since I'd never had a tree in my home. At least it was fake. "That'll be fine." I handed her my credit card and waited for her to ring up the transaction. She handed me the book to fill in my name and address. Placing the card back into my wallet, I turned to leave. "Merry Christmas!"

Her cheery voice followed me out of the shop, "Happy Holidays to you."

It was planned that Kelsey and I would go to pick out a tree on Black Friday because Dylon wasn't due until the following week. I thought it would be nice for us to pick out a tree and go shopping together for Christmas but then...Well, best to focus on today. We would have decorated it together and I felt bad not decorating it with her, but I'd never put up a tree at the house because I always spent Christmas in Colorado. Honestly, I just

133

wasn't in the mood. Once the decorating was done by the delivery person, I got to keep everything and could reuse it every year. The decorations were chosen carefully, thinking about what Kelsey was used to and what would be important to her. Feeling satisfied with my decision, I was walking along, window shopping, when a small glass bird caught my eye. Thinking how beautiful it was and that Kelsey would love it, I went in. As I stared at the bird in the window, a reflection of a woman caught my eye. She looked remarkably like Carolyn, but that was ridiculous, why would she be there? Spinning around to confront her, there was no one there. Gasping, I glanced back at the window to find I was all alone, looking at my own reflection. *Weird.* Shrugging, I made my way into the shop to check out the bird.

Speaking with the shopkeeper, she pointed out a hanging mobile type lamp that had several different types of birds floating around, made of various shades of glass, and it lit up with little lights that made the birds look like they were glowing from within. It was so beautiful, and it reminded me of the little robin with its coloring being so similar. Paying for my purchase, I waited while the girl at the counter gently wrapped the light fixture in soft paper and then placed it in a box to be gift wrapped.

The paper that she chose was a metallic gold with little red cardinals all over it. I took the bag with the wrapped gift and headed out the door. For just a moment when I exited the doorway, I thought I saw my mysterious man across the street. He was staring straight at me. He stood there in tight blue jeans

The Tree and the Tablet

and a button-down white shirt that was open at the neck. There on his chest was the most beautiful black feather hanging from a setting of turquoise and silver on a leather necklace dangling between his lapels. Our eyes locked. My heart began to race, and I exhaled a slow breath that sounded like a whistle.

The sun took that opportunity to move itself from behind a cloud which blinded me from the amazing view I was gazing upon. My hand instinctively flew up to shield my eyes from the blinding sun. When I gained the ability to see again, he was gone. *No, nooooooo!* Why? Glancing both ways for traffic, my feet took over with a mind of their own and propelled me across the street to where I'd seen him. Running into the shops and looking around, it was as if he'd vanished. My heart dropped. It was probably just my imagination again.

As my eyes dropped to the curb, I ran my fingers through my hair in disappointment. Something caught in my vision and I noticed right at my feet was the very same black feather wrapped in a leather thong and adorned with a turquoise and silver setting. Reaching down, I gathered the beautiful necklace to me. It wasn't a dream. He had to be real. Looking around again, hoping to catch a glimpse of him, he was still not visible.

I decided that I'd leave my name and number with the lady in the shop directly in front of me just in case he decided to come back and look for it. It just had to be his. As I exited the store, I looked at my phone to see the time, it was getting late. Just as I looked up from my phone, a raven swooped down and grabbed it right out of my hand. As I ran after it, I yelled loudly, "Stop, you thief!" It flew straight up, swiftly disappearing from sight. Standing there with my hand shielding my eyes, I just shook. Anger coursed through me. Damn birds. If they aren't haunting my dreams and my house, they're stealing my phone. Shrugging my shoulders, I decided I'd just go get another phone tomorrow.

I stopped to pick up Peanut on the way home. She looked adorable with her little red bow in her hair. When we got to the house, I let Peanut outside and walked back to my bedroom to freshen up before dinner. Deciding to put the feather necklace on my dresser next to the raven feather from the morning, I reached to set the necklace down and noticed the other feather was gone. Wondering where it had gotten off to, I looked around for it, but it was nowhere to be seen. *How odd? Did I dream it? I think I'm going crazy.* No. I promised myself that I wasn't going to over analyze this stuff. Shaking my head, I walked toward the bed. As I turned to sit on the bed and remove my shoes, I saw the feather on my pillow.

Startled, I looked around half expecting to see some apparition. Picking it up and looking at it as if I suspected it would jump out of my hand and start running around the room I said softly, "Alright, this isn't funny." Slowly turning back toward the dresser, I set the feather next to the necklace. It seemed as if the two feathers were magnetic. When I placed the feather next to the necklace, the two were drawn together by some invisible force. So strange!

The Tree and the Tablet

Oh, well, I don't have time for this, I need to get ready to go to Sherri's for dinner. The doorbell rang and I just about jumped out of my skin. Laughing at myself and my ridiculous musings, I went to the front door to see who was there. Upon opening the door, there was a short, stocky, but burly looking gentleman standing there with a clipboard. His jacket said, Lifetree, Inc. Founded in Estes Park, Colorado. Just behind him stood the most beautiful fifteen-foot-tall dogwood tree in full bloom of beautiful pink flowers. That was odd. Dogwoods don't usually bloom in winter and two-year-old Dogwoods aren't fifteen feet. tall.

He cleared his throat. "Are you Margaret St. James?" My head involuntarily nodded as I continued to gaze curiously at the tree. "I have your sister's ash-pod tree here." Looking back toward it and then back at me he asked, "Where d'you want it?"

CHAPTER 10

*A*fter giving it some thought, I decided to place the tree about fifteen feet from the back of the left side of the deck toward the center-left of the yard. The gentleman made a large production of marking the spot and testing the wind with a wetted finger. After this, he stood back and looked over the spot and tried to visualize the placement. He said this was to determine if the tree would be happy in its placement. It was everything I could do not to start giggling at him.

Not wanting to have to do the work myself, I just sat by and watched him with a twinkle in my eye and laughter barely bursting beneath my interested and calm facade. After listening to him carry on mumbling under his breath for a bit about proper placement of the tree, I calmly interrupted, "Just so you know, I'm an arborist." He stopped his mumbling as I continued, 'I think this is firstly, my yard and secondly, that I, being a tree specialist, would know where a dogwood tree, cornus-florida, would prefer to be placed." Having stated the last part and thrown in the scientific name of the tree for good measure, I quietly waited for the information to sink in.

Raising his eyebrows skeptically at me and looking at the tree again, he said, "Well, excuse me but I think this tree is very special. Not every tree I deliver is this large or in full bloom in winter."

"Oh, I totally agree with you on that. I'm not sure what happened but this is definitely not a two-year-old tree."

"Yup, I think you got the one the boss was saving for himself by accident."

Slightly startled by this news, I wondered, "Maybe we should send it back?"

"No, ma'am." He exclaimed, looking over his shoulder at me. "That's not allowed. Once a tree's been placed with its pod in the receptacle, there's no return unless the tree dies." He laughed raucously at that and mumbled something under his breath.

What a strange little man. Peanut kept barking at the poor guy, so I had to lock her up in her kennel, which she hated. While the gentleman, whose name I discovered through our witty discourse as being Bobby Roberts of Broomfield, Colorado, was

The Tree and the Tablet

digging the hole for the tree, I remembered the dream I'd had in Denver of Andrea. Slipping into my room, I went to my safe to retrieve the amulet so I could place it in the hole before the tree was planted. It almost seemed as if it were pulsing in my hand.

On my way out to the back yard, having glanced at the clock on the wall, I noticed it was almost 6:30 pm and decided to take a minute to call Sherri so she wouldn't worry. David picked up the phone. An exaggerated "Hello," met my ears.

"Hey, Dave. I..."

"Hold on a minute." In the background I heard, "Sweetie, it's Maggie. Here, I gotta check the ribs."

Laughter was followed by, "Hi, hun. Sorry I didn't answer the phone. I must not have your home number programmed. Thought you were one of those weirdos that's been calling lately."

"Yeah, I called you from the home phone because a stupid raven flipping swooped down and stole my phone today." I chuckled.

"What?!? You're joking."

"No, I'm not. Little jerk flew down while I was on Bay street and took my phone right out of my hand. I've never seen anything like it." My laughing started again as I remembered my antics in the street. "Oh. My. God. I think I actually chased after him and called him a thief. I must've looked like a crazy woman."

Her echoing enjoyment met my ears, "Oh, Maggie. What are you going to do?"

"I guess I'll call the cell phone provider and see if this is covered under my insurance. But right now, I have other issues to deal with."

"Really, what's up?" Her voice sounded suddenly less joyful and more concerned.

"Everything's alright, I just wasn't expecting Andrea's tree to arrive today."

"Is it there now?"

"Yeah, I was getting ready to head over to your place when the tree guy showed up. It's kinda weird though, the tree is huge, and the guy is kinda off, if you know what I mean. But I think he's overall harmless." Just then, Bobby traipsed across the yard and flung his hands up in the air animatedly as he appeared to be talking to himself. Shaking my head, I watched him pace back and forth a couple times while he was clearly talking but I couldn't make out anything he was saying. Leaning sideways, I couldn't see anyone else out there. Maybe he was talking to the tree? Sherri was chatting away on the other end of the line, but I wasn't paying attention, so I missed it, "I'm sorry, sweetie. I think I should go see if this guy needs help."

"Oh, okay. Are you gonna make it over?"

"Well, I'm thinking probably not."

"Do you want me to send Dave over to keep an eye on things?" Concern was laced between her words as the pitch of her voice sounded a little deeper.

"No, I'm sure it'll be fine. Besides, I have bear spray. It

The Tree and the Tablet

works great! You know...for those long walks in the woods and funny little men planting trees." I chuckled.

A short burst of laughter met my joke followed by a more intense, "Seriously, though. Please be careful. If you want, why don't you just let Kelsey stay again tonight since they're having so much fun."

"Are you sure? I mean, I'd really love to have her home with me. I miss her so much." Sighing, I asked, "How's she doing?"

"She's fine. She already asked if she could stay over again anyway."

"Really? I wish I knew why she wanted to stay away. What do you think is going on with her?"

"I'm not certain. She seems like she's confused or upset but won't open up with me or Dave. I was going to wait until you came over for dinner and see if we could get her to talk a bit about her feelings."

"I just wish I could get inside her little brain and help her. Has she had any episodes with the bird over there?"

"No, not at all." She took a deep breath and let it out slowly. "You know, Maggie, this is big for her, I'm sure she'll talk about it when she's ready. If you want to come get her, I'll get her ready for you."

"I don't know what to do. I don't want to push her. I know she loves me, but I don't understand why she doesn't want to be here." Even in my own ears, I sounded whiney.

"I'm sorry, honey. You know, the boys really struggled a lot when they came to live with me and Dave. They kept wanting to go to their friend's homes rather than stay here with us. Looking back on it, I remember when we asked why, they said that they didn't want to hurt their mom by loving us too much. Kids do things for the darndest reasons."

"Oh, I remember that." Glancing out the window, I could see Bobby talking to the hole and laughing up to the sky. What an odd character. "Do you think that's what's going on with her? She's just not sure how to handle it? I mean, you don't think it's this whole business with the bird, do you?"

"It could be. Listen, give me a call after everything's done and let me know what you want to do. If you want her to stay tonight, it's really no trouble since Dave wants to go pick up the boat tomorrow anyway. The forecast calls for clear weather too."

Thinking about it for a moment, I asked hopefully, "Can I talk to Kelsey?"

"Let me see where she is." Sherri set her phone down and I could hear her in the background calling to Kelsey. "Kelsey, your Aunt is on the phone. Can you come and talk to her?"

"No, that's okay. I'm gonna play."

"But she's gotta go and won't be able to come to dinner."

"Okay. Tell her I'll see her later. I'm gonna go play now." A squeak of hope in her voice, she asked, "Did you ask her if I could stay for a sleepover again?"

"She said yes, but you really need to talk to her. She loves you bunches and would really like to hear your voice."

The Tree and the Tablet

The "yes" was followed by a squeal of happiness but her voice quickly became impatient again. "I have to go potty. Tell her I'll call later."

Sherri picked up the phone. "I'm sorry hun, not sure how much of that you heard, but she had to go to the bathroom and said she'll call you later."

Glancing down at the small satchel in my hand, I recalled that I was supposed to bury the darn thing. My heart felt heavy, but I needed to go deal with Bobby and the amulet. A sense of urgency took me over and I responded, "Yeah, alright. I'll just let her stay the night again, I'll get her tomorrow when you bring her home. I have to go though. Love you."

"Okay. Love you, too. Don't worry, honey. It'll be fine." She tried to sound chipper for me.

"I'm sure you're right." The sadness creeped into my thoughts, but I tried to sound positive so she wouldn't worry too much, "If she wants to call, that's fine, otherwise, I'll try to call later. I'm feeling kinda wiped. If I don't get ahold of you, I'll see you tomorrow. Tell her I love her and have fun."

"Alright. Call if you need me."

"I will, Bye."

"Bye," she said. As I hung up the phone, I glanced through the kitchen window to the view of Bobby returning to attempt to move the tree next to the hole for burial, I moved toward the door. Odd that I thought of it as a burial rather than a planting. He limped away again.

Setting the portable phone on the dining room table, I went out to the back yard. Hearing his voice still in the front yard, I made my way to the opening in the earth wondering briefly if he would be able to plant the massive tree without help. Glancing skyward, I thought toward the heavens, "I hope you're right," briefly wondering if I was doing the right thing. Making up my mind to follow my gut, and the apparition, I dropped the amulet in the hole still encased in its satchel. Getting down on all fours, I covered it quickly with some loose dirt. It worked out well because the satchel blended with the dark, rich soil. Getting to my feet, I inspected the base of the tree which was wrapped in some sort of biodegradable purplish skin that seemed to glow, appearing iridescent. The day seemed suddenly gloomy in comparison to the bright hues reflected in the material. Briefly, I wondered where the ashes were. Weirdly, as I put my hand gently against the base material, I could feel a pulsing sensation through the covering. Gasping, I quickly pulled my hand away and jumped back from the odd feeling. *Don't lose it now. It's just a tree. There's no way it has a heartbeat.*

Bobby came around the corner from the side yard at that moment and startled me. Squinting his eyes at me suspiciously, he asked, "Everything okay here?"

At a loss for words, I mutely nodded in his direction. "I've never seen such a wrapping before," pointing to the roots.

His eyes widened slightly for a split second, but he responded with a soft chuckle, "Oh, that?" He leaned over and

The Tree and the Tablet

wrapped his arms around the trunk of the tree just above the soil and hefted with all his might, steadily moving the tree closer to the opening. "That's a new product meant to protect the roots." Standing up from his labor, he huffed a couple times and said, "I forgot the organic planting mix. Be right back," and with an awkward turn, he started back toward the gate muttering to himself animatedly, "Gotta go get the "special" dirt for the tree," his fingers made invisible quotations in the sky as he spoke and swiftly made his way to his truck.

He returned shortly. As he spread handfuls of a green-hued substance, I queried, "What's in that, I've never seen anything like it used before."

His response was a bout of crazy sounding laughter. He stopped suddenly and shrugged his shoulders, "It's just a compost mix with vitamins and nutrients to help the tree take root." At my skeptical look, he said, "It's new, specially formulated for tree pods." Figuring that would shut me up, he gently maneuvered the tree into its resting place.

Casually remarking on the great effort it took for him to put the tree in the ground, "You'd think that for a tree that size, they would've sent two guys or a skip loader to take care of planting."

An abrupt, "Yup," was the only response as he completed the job, filling in the sides, watering, then completing the fill-in, complete with a final tamping and moisturizing with the hose. It was getting darker by the minute. Turning to me, he said, "There you go ma'am." He turned back to the tree and looking like a puffed-up rooster proud of his conquest, he put out his chest and whistled through his teeth. "Yes, ma'am, that's a beaut." He turned, and grabbing his paperwork off the deck, said, "Well, my work is done. I'd best be on my way. Merry Christmas to you and that little girl!"

Shocked, I started to think back about our prior conversation, trying to remember if I'd told him that Kelsey lived with me or that I had any children. How did he know that? He smiled, winked at me, then turned on his heel and made a funny salute, where he placed his hand on his heart and then moved it in a figure eight movement, then straight out to a third Reich type salute toward the tree. Turning on his heel, he hobbled his way through the side gate.

Calling out after him, "Thank you."

A wave behind his head in my direction was his reply. Funny little man. As soon as I was sure he was out of ear shot, I laughed. I couldn't help it. It was the funniest thing I had seen all day.

Taking a moment to admire the tree, I realized that I didn't receive any paperwork from Bobby confirming the delivery of the tree or what to do if there was a problem. Hoping to catch him before he made it out of the driveway, I walked briskly for the front door by cutting straight through the house. Peanut took that opportunity to protest her placement in the kennel for the billionth time. Turning my head toward the hallway, talking to her on my way through, I responded with, "I know, I know! Just a minute!" Reaching out, grasping the knob, and opening the

The Tree and the Tablet

front door, my mouth fell open as I saw that the truck and strange little man were both long gone. Well, that was quick! Staring toward the street, I remembered I'd gotten a brochure from Mr. Jacobs so I'd just have to contact the company on Monday since it was Friday and already too late to call.

Shrugging, I turned and closed the door, locking the dead bolt. Peanut was soon released from her prison. Wine...Yes, that was a good idea. Purposefully, I went to the kitchen to obtain a glass and choose a bottle of my favorite blackberry merlot. What a crazy day. Normally, I would have dinner first, but I just wasn't hungry.

Peanut had already made her way into the back yard through the open French doors. She stood at the base of the tree cocking her head from side to side as if she were listening to something. I could just make out her silhouette in the flickering lights on the deck. That was an odd behavior. Wandering over to the French doors, flicking the switch, the flood lights enhanced the ever-darkening view. The sun was setting which provided a very small amount of natural light. The tree seemed to glow in the soft hues of pink provided by the sunset. It was a little creepy looking.

Gingerly stepping out onto the deck, my eyes darted around expecting something to jump out at me. Moving slowly across the deck, I made my way to the tree. It seemed as if it were glowing brighter upon my approach. As I was standing there, I could have sworn I heard my name being called. Peering around through the depth of sunset, seeing no one near, I gradually inched my way around the tree, noticing a large spot on the tree that looked like a human face. It was facing out toward the bay. I didn't recall seeing that when it was planted, but then again, I was a little distracted by the strange little man who was planting it. A soft voice echoed around me. It was pulling me in as I leaned closer and closer to see if I was imagining things. There it was again. So faint but clearer.

"Come closer, come closer. I can't see you. Where are you?" With a will of its own, my hand steadily crept closer to the whispers. My hand was so close to touching it when, suddenly, the knot twisted and fluttered and Andrea's face peered back at me, the indentations in the tree bark looked like tendrils of hair moving in the breeze around her face. It spoke, "There you are."

Heart racing, I jumped back away from the tree and screamed, dropping my glass of wine. As I turned to run, out of nowhere a tree branch became tangled around my arm. A terrified scream was ripped from me as I pulled frantically to escape the grip, "Let me go!"

All I could hear was Andrea's voice saying, "Calm down! Maggie, calm down!"

Gripped with a terrifying and overwhelming fear like I've never known, I felt like I was choking on the very air as my lungs suddenly started burning from the exertion to be released. Succumbing to the fear, my legs crumpled, and consciousness left me.

Waking up next to the tree, the wine glass was in my hand

The Tree and the Tablet

and Peanut was curled up by my side. I jumped up realizing I wasn't in the clutches of the tree and braced myself as I studied my arm. There were only a few small scratches where I'd seen the branches clutching at me, but when I looked at the tree, there was no face. Just a tree. One small branch was hanging from the tree. Getting to my feet and clutching the branch, I ripped it away from the tree. My imagination made me believe someone said, "Ouch!" But I just shook my head and laughed. This is ridiculous. Giving the tree a stern look, I said, "You deserved that," and huffed my way back to the house. Peanut stood there next to the tree with her head cocked to one side watching me. Angrily I shouted, "Peanut, Come!" She ran across the yard and leapt onto the deck scurrying into the house through the open door. I could've sworn I heard a faint whisper, "Good night."

In response, I stared ruefully at the tree. Shaking my head in disbelief I turned to enter the house, assuring the doggie door cover was in place and the French doors were locked firmly closed.

Looking around to make sure everything was secure, I placed my wine glass in the kitchen sink before going to get ready for bed. As I changed my clothes, I couldn't help but notice the black feather wrapped in silver and turquoise. Picking it up, I stroked it tenderly as I thought of my wonderful mystery man. Loneliness and pain swallowed me whole as I longed for some relief from my emptiness. Not really certain what the connection was, but I just couldn't rid myself of the overwhelming urge to be around the man I met on the plane. He was always a thought in the back of my mind. For the first time in a long time I prayed in earnest, "God, if you can hear me, please bring this man into my life for good." Sighing, I set the feather down, then crossed the room to climb into bed. Slipping between the cool cotton sheets, I thought about Kelsey. Missing her cherubic little face that reminded me every moment of my sister, I couldn't wait to see her. With hope in my heart I closed my eyes and drifted off to sleep.

It felt like I tossed and turned all night. My mystery man was in my head. Oh, the sweet agonizing torture. Every time I'd get close to him, he would turn into a raven and fly away. I just couldn't catch him. Finally, there was peace and I slept the sleep of the dead. The doorbell rang. Peanut ran down the hall barking. Rolling over to look at the clock while shielding my eyes from the sun coming through the shears in the windows, I blinked at the offending numbers in my view. 7:30 am? Why would someone think it's appropriate to ring my doorbell so early? It rang again. Oh, good lord. Rolling to my side, I sat up. Grabbing the scrunchy from the bedside table, I made my way to the door. Whoever it was, they were standing with their back to the door looking out at the parking area where a bright red pickup was sitting. Irritated, I angrily opened the door and asked as calmly as I could, "Can I help you?"

Turning around to make eye contact with me, was the man of my dreams. "Yes! You can." Was his husky reply. I tried sucking in great gulps of air to keep myself from losing it, but it didn't work, and my body lost total control of its senses. My mind had decided to stop working properly and uttering something totally incoherent, I lost my bearings with reality and crumpled to the floor in a pile of oblivion.

CHAPTER 11

Coming to, my first thought was that something was seriously wrong with me because I didn't consider myself to be so weak that I would faint at the drop of a hat. I seemed to be passing out and waking up in strange places a lot lately. Second thought was much more disarming. My eyes were still closed but as the haze lifted, I could feel what was most assuredly some amazingly strong arms surrounding me. There was also the strong but distinct sound of a human heartbeat against my ear. Thump-thump, thump-thump. It was such a soothing sound. It was very nice, but in my muddled thoughts, I pondered whether my bed had come to life or if I was being held by someone.

Hazarding a guess that my prior experience wasn't a dream, I slowly opened my eyes. At first, all I saw was a blinding light. Then, to my utter horror and explicit pleasure, I was being held in the arms of none other than my raven-haired god. An audible groan erupted as I faced the combination of embarrassment and pleasure. How could one person cause so many conflicting emotions in me? Suddenly, the gravity of what was really happening took hold of my clearing brain. Anxiety caused me to panic and out of a pure need to be alone with my embarrassment, I struggled to be free of his arms.

"Whoa. Hold on, there." He implored softly as he attempted to help me extricate myself from his grasp. It almost felt like he didn't want to release me. "Maggie, please calm down!" He asked calmly. Shaking his head, he muttered, "Andrea said you'd react this way."

As he spoke my name, I ceased my squirming. Eyes wide with shock and realization, I barely heard the comment about Andrea before stiffening in his arms again. The flush in my cheeks was hot and uncomfortable as I turned my face toward his. Narrowing my eyes in suspicion, I asked, "What did you just say?"

Frozen in place, waiting for his response, he must've decided it was a good time to remove me from his lap. He swiftly scooped me up and set me down on the sofa next to him as if I were no more than a sack of potatoes. Jumping up from the sofa, I turned on him. Swaying on my feet, the room blurred briefly and then

The Tree and the Tablet

righted itself. Seeing my disorientation, he appeared to consider whether he should hold onto me as his hand extended toward me and then as quickly retracted. He sat there calmly, a smug smile crossed his lips as he gave a devil may care response, "What? I didn't say anything." Was he mocking me from the plane incident?

When I analyzed the situation and mentally ran through all of our past encounters, I was suddenly struck dumb by the sudden and overwhelming comprehension that there was something I was missing. My head was still foggy, which caused me to struggle with figuring out the exact particulars. It was like standing in a huge surf as the waves of information battered my foggy brain. Dawning awareness and understanding hit me in the face like a brick. Covering my mouth with my hand, I gasped at the fact that I just realized I knew who he was and he had known all along who I was. "Oh my god!"

He looked so comfortable on my sofa, casually laid back with an air of confidence surrounding him. All the pieces were falling into place within the puzzle of my mind, "You knew?" Disbelief rocked me, "All along, you knew who I was?" He had the nerve to look contrite as he flashed a grimace at me. However, this was quickly followed by a smooth grin showing his perfect white teeth that I now wanted to punch. My eyes widened with the affirmation I read in his response and more sternly, with accusation dripping from my voice, I almost growled in exasperation, "You knew!" The outraged scream that followed was purely involuntary.

Clenching my fists, I stormed to the back door, and flinging it open, I stepped out into the cool air to calm myself. Pacing back and forth, I was livid. How could he do that to me? I noticed that he stepped out onto the deck but chose to ignore his presence as I thought of all the times we'd made eye contact. All the times he could've relieved me from my torment. Running through a gambit of questions in my mind, I muttered to myself, "Why? What was the purpose? Was he following me? He knew who I was and what was going on but still chose not to let me in on his dirty little secret." Stomping my foot on the deck in frustration, I exclaimed loudly. "Darn it!" Betrayal, pain, outrage, frustration, fear, confusion, and joy...Yes, joy, at having him be close. All these feelings directed at him, and also, at my sister, who knew somehow what would be happening but hid it from me. Why?

Ultimately, the real reason I was angry, was because all the signs had been there and I missed them. He took advantage of my state of mind! Reflecting on the moment we first met on the plane. Absolutely beside myself with grief and then taken in by his handsome face, I failed to notice that the woman in the picture was me. It was me when I was in college. That was a rough year for me and seeking to start over after two breakups in a row, I'd dyed my hair black. He knew on the plane who I was. He never said a word. Standing there in the middle of my deck, I became fully aware of the sudden realization that I was face to face with none other than Daniel BlackFeather. His resemblance to the little boy in the photo on Jaxon's library wall was unmistakable.

Feeling a myriad of emotions flowing through me, I turned and stared at the tree. Ha! The robin was now perched on a limb of that tree and was singing away happily hopping from limb to limb as if it were dancing. Not a care in the world. Silly little bird. Staring at it angrily, I sought to silence the joyful little bird with my own voice, "Oh, Shut up!" As I turned around to pace again, I noticed Daniel standing to the side of the doorway. He was smiling as if he were holding in laughter. That's it! "And you!" My index finger pointed at him and ground out through clenched teeth, "Go away!" Storming past him again and into the house, I marched my way straight into my bedroom. Approaching the dresser, I grabbed the blasted raven feather necklace and turned to stomp my way back out to the deck and confront him. Shockwaves coursed through my body as the brick wall of his chest stopped me in my tracks and knocked the wind out of me. "Oof!" Stumbling backward, I was caught by the waist and lifted into very strong arms.

There was something about the smoldering look he gave me that flooded me with longing. My heart was racing frantically, but I was still so angry. Trying to push away from him, my body lied and my efforts were feeble at best, but before I realized the peril of my body's betrayal, I noticed his soft gaze was centered on my lips and he started moving slowly toward them with his. I couldn't stop him and mesmerized, I felt like the two raven feathers and found myself unable to pull away, as if he were a magnet and I was steel. He bridged the gap between us and the kiss was electrifying, sending jolts through every fiber of my being. As our lips touched and my world went spinning out of control, I found that I could barely breathe. Odd, but even though this was our first kiss, it was as if I had felt this before, but couldn't remember when; however, the sensation was so intense and overwhelming, I just couldn't get enough. I felt myself melting into him and that was when I realized that he knew that too. He knew I wanted him. His right hand had moved to palm my cheek and when his hand slipped to cup my neck, his thumb gently stroked my jaw as he sought to deepen the kiss. If I didn't stop him now, I'd be lost if he kept going. *God help me! It feels so good!*

How dare he use his charm and my own desire against me. As if finally finding a will to overcome my passion, a renewed anger pried its way through the veil of pleasure I was experiencing. Pushing myself away from him forcefully, I slapped him across the face so hard it left a mark that looked exactly like my handprint. Seeing the red mark getting darker by the second, I almost felt bad about that. He looked surprised. *Good!* He shouldn't underestimate me. He was standing there a little dumbfounded with his arms spread wide and his palms face-up. When he started to say something, I interrupted him and slammed the feather necklace into his open palm, screeching vehemently, "Get out!"

He took the feather necklace and put it around his neck. It dangled on his chest between the opening of his unbuttoned shirt. Speaking calmly, he said in his beautiful voice, "I know you're angry, but I can explain."

Pushing past him, I made my way back down the hall toward the deck to get away from him, my voice a practice in patience but bridling with a deep anger, "I don't want to hear it."

Stepping out onto the deck, Peanut was standing there watching me closely and I put my hands in the air, pleading, "Why?" Our connection was strong and his presence was so electric that I could physically feel him when he stepped out onto the deck behind me. Spinning to face him, I went off into a crazy place in my head. Pointing my finger at him, I sought to placate my raging brain with a fallacy, "You're a dream. You aren't real." Turning toward the yard and motioning outward, "This tree, the amulet, the stupid bird, they're all some big hoax, right?" Looking at him pleadingly, I laughed when he didn't respond, "Next thing I know, Peanut will be talking to me!" Arms flailing wildly, I paced back and forth, breathing heavily and trying not to explode as heat built and flooded throughout my body in waves.

Abruptly, I stopped to look down at Peanut. She jumped up from her seated position where she was calmly watching me lose my mind to wiggle her little nub and bark at me excitedly. Turning to Daniel, "Oh-Ho, See, I told you!" Throwing my hands in the air, exasperated and borderline psychotic, "She just said I'm right." Hysterical and maniacal laughter perforated the silence around us. I sounded like a mad woman. He looked at me concerned with a questioning expression on his face. Guessing his thoughts, I said, "There's only one way to prove I'm not crazy." Looking out toward the yard, and then back to him, the gap between us had gotten smaller and I could see his intentions on his face. He was gently and quietly walking toward me, he put out his hands to try and calm me as if I were a wild animal getting ready to flee. I saw him coming this time as I dodged to the right. He tried to follow but I was too quick and dove to the left at the last minute. Leaping off the deck, I made a mad dash toward the tree.

He followed after me, "Maggie, stop! Please! I can explain. Will you just listen?" He begged in a calm but beseeching voice.

As I dove around the tree I planted my feet firmly and stood facing the knot in the tree, stating matter-of-factly, "Andrea Michelle, you better materialize yourself right now or I'm not talking to you ever again!"

The tree fluctuated and fluttered, the bark shifting and swirling. With a deep sound like that of an awakening giant yawning, the face appeared and the branches moved causing the robin to lose his perch. Whistling and flapping his wings crazily, he flew away and then back again landing in the exact same spot on the same branch. The face that appeared just then looked like it had just woken up from a nice deep sleep. "Geez, Magpie. What is it?"

Daniel stopped right behind me. Letting out a massive

The Tree and the Tablet

exodus of breath that sounded a lot like a balloon losing all of its air at once, "Holy hell! Is that Andrea?"

Smiling triumphantly, I turned to face him, "See, I'm not crazy." Gleeful laughter erupted from me and I did a little jig in the yard. Clasping my hands in front of me and continuing to giggle insanely like a child who was up to no good, I danced a circle around Daniel. He didn't look happy at all.

Looking at me as if I was off my rocker, he exclaimed in awe and shock, his deep voice reverberating into my soul, "What have you done?"

Stopping, mid-skip, I looked at him in surprise. He couldn't mean me. Confused by his accusation, I dared to ask, "Me?" At his wide-eyed silence, I laughed incredulously and asked sarcastically, "What have I done?"

"Where is the amulet, Maggie?" A stilted expression crossed his face as he questioned me.

Without uttering a word, I pointed at the ground near the base of the tree.

"Please tell me you didn't bury it!?!" It was more of a statement than a question. What did he know that I didn't?

Slowly nodding my head as I pointed at the tree and responded irritably as if I were a child getting in trouble for another of Andrea's pranks, "She told me to!" Without waiting for a response from him, I turned to the tree and said, "Dammit, Andrea! Even in death, you're still getting me into trouble!" Stomping my foot like a petulant child, I turned away and stared

163

out at the water. Raggedly, my breath moved in and out as I tried to control my emotions, but I was so lost in my own thoughts and feeling sorry for myself that I didn't hear Daniel approach.

He silently slipped his arms around me and feeling overwhelmed and shaken to the core, I chose to accept the comfort he offered. His presence came with a multitude of mixed feelings. Yet the connection was too strong to deny and I found myself turning into the shelter of his arms as I cried my heart out. To his credit, he stood there calmly and gently stroked my hair, whispering that it would be okay. Finally, I pulled away and wiped my moist face on the sleeve of his shirt. Slightly surprised by my brazenness, he laughed.

Trying to appear as if nothing had happened, as if I hadn't just wiped tears and snot on his shirt but knowing that my face was now bright red and splotchy from crying, I smiled anyway. Giggling, I shyly let my gaze roam over his face settling on his eyes, "Ummm, Sorry about all that"— I waved toward...well, everything — "How about some coffee?"

The tree shook and then I heard Andrea's voice saying in a most exasperated tone, "Dammit, Jaxon, I know you can't really control it but please stop pooping on me!"

Daniel and I turned to see the little robin dancing around trying to avoid moving branches while chirping loudly. There was a long stream of robin poop dribbled down across the top of the face in the tree. Daniel and I looked back at each other, our eyebrows both raised and realizing the hilarity of what had just happened, we both started laughing so hard we were holding our sides from it. Every time we thought we were done we'd turn to look at the tree and start laughing again. All the while, Andrea was saying, "Oh, ha, ha! Very funny!" And "If you two are done laughing it up, can one of you please get something to clean this off?"

We were finally able to gain our composure long enough to breathe regularly. Daniel, having noticed the hose laying on the ground near the tree with a nozzle attached, lifted it up asking, "Is this thing on?" At my nod to the affirmative—I was still having trouble talking without wanting to laugh—he sprayed Andrea square in the face.

She sputtered and coughed. The visual display of the bird poop now running from the top of her face into the area of her mouth made us start chuckle again. Convulsions coursed through my body and I grabbed my side where a stitch had started to ache from the extended hilarity.

We both heard Peanut barking in the living room which alerted us that someone was in the driveway. The humor left my face and I looked at the tree. "Not a word! Do you hear me?" The face quickly vanished to be replaced with the appearance of a simple knot in the tree.

Daniel glanced over at me, one eyebrow raised in a silent question. Jumping up on the deck, walking toward the door, I checked my reflection in the glass of the door. Noticing he wasn't following, I turned to him and waved to him to come along, slightly breathless, "It's Kelsey," and I ran into the house just as the front door opened.

"Hello? Aunt Maggie?"

CHAPTER 12

Stepping into the dining room, "I'm here." She ran toward me and I dropped to my knees to hug her close to me.

She hugged me tightly in return. "I missed you."

Leaning back to see her face better, I smiled, pushing a stray lock of hair from her face and curling it around her ear, "I missed you, too." Such a difference in her tone. I searched her face to try and figure out what caused the sudden change in attitude.

Not even noticing that we were joined by a strange man or that anyone else was in the room, Kelsey continued in a hushed voice, "I dreamed about mommy and daddy last night. I couldn't wait to get home to talk to you because I wanted to tell you that I love you, just like mommy said I should." She jumped into my arms again and giggled, then pulled back to touch my face.

Watching her little chipmunk face, so beautiful and full of life. Her deep dimples seemed to shine with her exuberant grin. "I love you, too, precious girl." Still holding her close in my arms, I booped her nose with my finger and we both giggled.

She suddenly pulled back from me and said, looking over my shoulder, "Hi. Are you Daniel?" As I turned slightly to be able to see him, he nodded and smiled at her. She calmly replied in the most mature voice, "Mommy told me about you in my dream. You're here to help."

He cocked his head to one side and knelt down to her level. With the warmest look on his face, his deep voice replied, "Yes, Kelsey. I'm here to help."

Stepping to my side, she reached out her hand in an offer of a handshake. He took her hand, shaking it gently. "Nice to meet you, Daniel. Didn't I see you on the airplane?"

He chuckled and his eyebrows lifted, "Well, Miss Kelsey, it is my pleasure to meet you as well."

Noting how observant children are, I also realized that Daniel opted not to answer Kelsey's question about the airplane. She didn't press the issue though, but I would definitely be asking about that later. Briefly, I was curious about the fact that she only recognized him from the flight to Denver and asked slightly confused, "Haven't you two met before?"

Kelsey turned her attention back to me, "Nope. Well, we

The Tree and the Tablet

met on the plane but I didn't know his name. I saw a picture of him one time, but he looked a lot different, he was really little, and he and daddy were playing soccer in the picture so I didn't see his face. Daddy talked about him before, but Daniel never came to our house before." She shrugged her shoulders, cocking her head to one side thoughtfully.

A broad grin spread across her lips as she looked back to the front door where David stood. "I'm going to go put my stuff away." With that, she turned and walked down the hallway toward her room grabbing her backpack from the floor on her way.

David stepped into the doorway with a concerned expression, "Sherri's waiting in the car with the kids for the signal to go down to the ramp."

Standing, I introduced the two men, "Dave, this is Daniel. He's an old friend of Jaxon's."

Daniel stepped forward and shook Dave's hand, Nice to meet you, Daniel." He turned to me, "I'll just go down and get the boat. Can you let Sherri know I'm on my way?"

Nodding, my head, "Sure thing." David stepped out onto the deck, "Hey, nice tree."

Replying softly, "Thanks." He shut the door and walked toward the boathouse. Daniel still stood close by and I could feel his eyes on me. Heading toward the front door, I motioned toward the kitchen and said, "I'm just going to go talk to Sherri for a minute. Have a seat, I'll be right back," and walked out the door.

Stepping out onto the front porch, I walked steadily toward Sherri's inquisitive gaze. Reaching the open window of the SUV, her voice dripped with curiosity as she tried to see through my front window, "Who's that? He looks cute." Looking past my shoulder to the red pickup, her eyes twinkled, "Nice truck. You know what they say about guys with big trucks." It was a statement, not a question.

"Stop." Chuckling softly at her teasing, I reminded her, "You know I don't know what that means. My experience with men is limited. Remember?" Knowing her for as long as I did, I was only mildly embarrassed by her innuendos. "That's Daniel BlackFeather, a friend of Jaxon's."

Her brows drew together, "What's he doing here?"

For some reason, I lied, "He's the trustee for Kelsey's inheritance." Well, that part was true. "He came to talk about things and see if there was anything we needed." That was a lie. I took a deep breath to calm myself so I wouldn't blush. Since I was a child, I'd struggled with my inability to lie without it showing on my face.

She nodded. "He's cute."

"Yeah, I guess so." Another lie. Either I'm getting good at lying or Sherri is being purposefully obtuse. Choosing to take that moment to change the subject, I stated, "Dave is down at the boathouse and said he'll see you in a few."

The boys were starting to get louder and more rambunctious

The Tree and the Tablet

in the back seat. Sherri made eye contact with them in the rear-view mirror, "You boys settle down. I'm trying to talk to Maggie." They immediately complied. Leaning out the window, she threw her arm around me and hugged me close. "Well, I'd better go. I don't want to keep you from your company. I love you, girl."

Reaching into the open window, I returned the squeeze and replied, "Thanks for everything. I love you, too." Leaning back, I waited for her to drive away.

The boys waved and laughed, shouting in a long drawn out way, "Bye, Maggie!" in unison.

Chuckling, softly, I waved at the boys, "Bye, Boys!"

Sherri shrugged her shoulders in a devil may care attitude and laughed with the silly boys as she put the car in gear and headed toward the pull-out. As I closed the front door, I couldn't help but grin at their antics while shaking my head ruefully.

Stopping in the hallway, I called out, "Kelsey? Honey, are you hungry?"

She yelled from her bedroom, "No. I ate at Sherri's. I'm sleepy though, is it alright if I lay down with a book?"

Not knowing what to say, I thought, why not? "Okay, let me know if you need anything."

A faint, "Okay," drifted down the hallway and I knew she was probably pretty close to falling asleep. She was always sleepy after spending time with the boys. She ran like crazy trying to keep up with all of them.

Turning toward the kitchen, Daniel was standing next to the

coffee maker with a cup in his hand. Smiling roguishly at me, "I took the liberty of making coffee. I hope you don't mind." He pulled out a second cup and asked, "How do you take it?"

Watching him pour the hot liquid into the mugs, I wondered briefly what I was doing but then decided that a cup of coffee might put things into perspective. "Just some creamer from the fridge will be fine." He pulled the creamer out and started to pour it into the coffee, glancing over at me, I moved my hand in the air in the way you would to show him to keep going. Finally, I said, "That's good."

He laughed this deep booming laugh that was so rich, I couldn't help but be reminded of the bird poop. He placed the creamer back in the fridge and coming to sit next to me at the kitchen island, placed my cup in front of me. We sat silently enjoying our drinks. Unable to hold my tongue any longer, I turned toward him and said, "Why didn't you say anything to me on the plane?"

He set his cup down and looked up at me sheepishly, "Andrea didn't want me to get involved unless it looked like you were in trouble."

Taking a deep breath, I asked, slightly concerned, "When did she talk to you and why are you here now?"

Placing his hand on top of mine which was resting next to my cup, he said, "Honestly, Maggie, we thought it was safest for you and Kelsey if I didn't alarm you in any way. I didn't know they were going to die."

The Tree and the Tablet

"But then, I still don't understand why you didn't say anything on the plane." My anger was starting to rise again.

"Jaxon asked me to come to him. We spent a couple days together trying to undo the curse he was under. With the information I had, I came back here to look for more clues on how to help them." He rifled his hand through his hair. "I knew you were here with Kelsey, but she told me that you didn't believe in the things she did and we knew that if things weren't handled in the right way, you might not cooperate. That was before the accident." His eyes sought my understanding. I stared at him, waiting for more, "I received your photo in an email along with a brief note to watch out for you and Kelsey but not alert you to our past conversations no matter what."

"But I don't understand why?" A tear slipped down my cheek. "I don't get it. We were so close. She never kept secrets from me."

"I can't answer that. I only know she didn't want to put you in more danger. Besides, I never thought they would die." He looked down into his mug and I could see the sadness flit across his face. He looked back up at me with a sober but pained expression.

However, as I stared at him, I could also see sincerity in his eyes, I couldn't help but feel he still wasn't telling me everything though. "I just don't understand the need for so much secrecy." Frustrated, I pulled my hand out from under his and made a point to examine my fingers. Looking back up at him, tears started to form in my eyes, "Why didn't she just trust me? Maybe I could have helped before it was too late?"

His beautiful green eyes widened in shock and then a deep sympathy reflected back at me. Shaking his head, "Maggie, there was nothing...".

Interrupting him, "No! Don't! You and my sister had no right to keep me in the dark." Trying hard not to cry, the tears just kept flowing like a dam had burst and a flood was coursing its way down my face, "You don't know what it's like to lose everyone you love." Turning away, I tried to get a handle on my raging emotions.

"You're wrong, Maggie." Peering back at him over my shoulder, a flicker of some faint emotion crossed his face and was just as quickly covered up. As I turned back to look out the window, he continued, "And you still have Kelsey." Grasping the back of my chair, turning me back toward him, gently, he placed his hand under my chin and raised my head to look in my eyes. "That's why I'm here."

Something in his gaze was reassuring but still mystifying. Steadying myself, I asked, "Why? What's going on?"

He took a deep breath and ran his fingers through his hair which pulled his hair away from his face to then have it fall forward like a dark, mesmerizing waterfall. It was clear to see he was struggling with how much to tell me. "Why can't you just tell me what's going on?" Motioning toward the tree in the backyard, I said, "I think at this point, someone needs to start being honest about what's really happening here. Don't you?" Frustration made me grab the pull-cord for the blinds and slam them down to cover the view of the offending reminder of my sister's conversion into a leafy creature from beyond.

He sighed, "Maggie, there are forces here at work that are very ancient and powerful. If things aren't done properly, and the tablet isn't found soon, you and Kelsey won't be the only ones impacted by this."

Even more confused now, I scoffed at him, "Tablet? What tablet?" *Of course, the tablet that guy was looking for, but did Daniel know about the letter 'Drea left for me?* He was just looking at me as if I'd lost my mind again, which prompted me to ask, "Are you kidding me? This is a joke, right?"

He shook his head solemnly. "No, Maggie! This isn't a joke." Clearly his frustration was taking control now as it tainted his voice, which made him sound harsh, "Why can't you let go of your guarded view of what you think the world is and see what's going on?"

Irritated by his judgment of my beliefs, I jumped up from my stool and turned on him. Now I was pacing like a caged tiger and feeling the blood pulsing through my veins, I exclaimed, "Listen to yourself. You sound like some stupid made-for-TV science fiction movie. Reality has definitely taken a trip to another universe." A short burst of maniacal laughter exploded from my lips. Pain struck right between my eyes as if someone had just thrown a large stone at me causing me to look up at the window that was facing the tree. *Can this be true? All of this is just too much.* As I stood there staring at the shrouded window, a deep sigh was drawn out of me. Leaning forward to brace myself on the countertop, I whispered, "I don't know how much more I can take of this."

A deep growl caused me to look at him again. His eyes flashed like a lightning bolt illuminated them briefly, "This is NOT a joke, Maggie. You need to listen to me. Andrea and Jaxon are gone, and the man who was supposed to be looking for the Tablet has gone missing."

As I watched him closely to see if his eyes would do that thing again, "So? What has that got to do with me? Or Kelsey for that matter?"

Looking at me dumbfounded, "You can't seriously be that clueless to what's happening. Andrea told me a little about your childhood and your struggles." My eyes flew open and I gasped, but he continued, "She told me that even with your experiences, you had a hard time with the possibilities of things beyond our world. I didn't think you could be faced with facts and still deny what's right in front of you." He got up and walked over to the curtain, pulling on the cord to the blind which flew open to reveal the tree outside. "I just didn't think it would be this difficult for you to let go of your bias with this staring you in the face." He motioned toward the tree. Returning to sit in the chair next to where I continued to pace, his gaze was level with mine for a moment. In exasperation, he sighed, "Didn't you read the letter

The Tree and the Tablet

she left you?"

I'd stopped pacing to give him my full attention, "Okay," I ground out. "What's really happening?" Rolling my eyes, sarcasm dripped from my voice as I broke down my view of the situation, "I mean other than some weird amulet thingy has possessed the people I love, brought my sister's spirit alive in a damn tree and put a robin in my yard in winter." Glaring at him, "What else could possibly be happening here that I need to be aware of?"

Suddenly, out of the corner of my eye, I saw Kelsey. She was standing in the hallway with her mouth hanging open. Glaring at Daniel, he looked over my shoulder, and looked toward Kelsey as she stared out the window.... "That's my Mommy?"

"Kelsey, honey, it's not what you think." Immediately, I tried to move toward her.

Daniel read the scene and started to get up to walk toward Kelsey. She darted for the door. Glancing over at him and throwing my hands in the air, "Great!" I said as I flew out the door behind Kelsey.

Daniel was step for step with me. As we reached the tree, the robin flew over and landed on Kelsey's finger. She walked around the tree. "Mommy?"

Suddenly the tree shifted, and Andrea said, "Hello, little dove."

Kelsey ran over and hugged the tree. "I knew you'd find a way, Mommy." She cried and hugged the tree.

177

My barely contained tears of earlier flowed freely now at the sight of mother and daughter united. The most agonizing sounds were coming from the most precious child I knew, and there was nothing I could do but stand there and watch it happen. It was almost like she was happy and sad at the same time. Absolutely torn in two by what was happening, I just stood there and watched it unfold. Daniel had the good sense to stand by wordlessly as well.

After a while, Andrea said, "Kelsey, honey, I need you to be brave and to keep this our little secret."

Kelsey stood back and asked, "Why?"

Andrea's face flickered and shuttered in the tree bark. "Honey, if you tell anyone, then they may think you're sick and take you away or think that I'm bad and dig me up and take me away. Do you understand?"

She nodded in comprehension and said, "Mommy, will you stay forever?"

Andrea smiled, "I'm not sure how long I have, Pumpkin. I'll stay as long as I can."

Kelsey started to cry, "Don't leave, Mommy. Please?"

This was killing me.

Andrea soothed, "Hey, this is not the strong girl I raised. You're my little angel and I love you no matter where I am. Do you understand?"

Kelsey nodded and sniffled loudly. "Okay, Mommy."

Jaxon had been perched on Kelsey's shoulder and he flew

The Tree and the Tablet

up into the tree. Andrea seemed to be listening as Jaxon started making odd sounds for a bird to make. It was kind of like clicking and grunting noises combined with tweets and other bird sounds. Andrea glanced up and said, "Okay, honey." Looking back at Kelsey, "Sweetie, Daddy said that he'll be here as long as he can, too."

Kelsey's face lit up, "Really?"

"Yes, my love." One of the branches moved slowly through the air until it was a short space from Kelsey's face, a petal moved toward her and gently caressed her face. "Butterfly kisses, love. I need to rest now, okay? It takes a lot of energy to show myself to you." She yawned.

"I love you, Mommy. Get some sleep." The face vanished, and the tree shuddered to a standstill. Kelsey turned to me, "Can I put up a tent outside?"

Tenderly, I watched this child whom I loved beyond words, "We can talk about that later, alright?"

Seeing that I wasn't about to discuss it right now, she nodded and said, "I'm gonna go draw a picture of Mommy and Daddy.

Deciding to let it go, I put my hand on her shoulder and said, "Okay, sweetie." She was smiling and humming the entire way into the house

Turning to Daniel as Kelsey closed the door to the house, I said, "What's happening that I need to know about?"

Just then the tree shuddered again, and Andrea said, "Maggie, is Kelsey in the house?"

Glancing at the closed door, I said over my shoulder, "Yes."

Sounding relieved, "Good!"

Since she sounded worried, I asked, "What's happening, Andrea?"

"Maggie, our time is short. You have to find the tablet. Put Kelsey somewhere safe. Take Daniel with you. He knows the area." She sounded frantic.

Moving closer to the tree, I asked, "Whoa. What's going on?"

Daniel stepped up, "Andrea, talk to me. What's happening?"

"Daniel, the amulet gives me limited energy, but it also shows me things. I know that my time is limited, but I also knew that by burying it under the tree, I'd be able to communicate. I don't know how I knew. Maggie, if you look on the ground, you'll see that my flowers are shedding. When the last petal falls, I won't be able to communicate with you in this way. I'm not sure how they are linked but this tree is special."

Remembering what Bobby had said about the tree being special, I asked, "Wait, what are you saying?" Glancing over to Daniel and then back to Andrea, "You want me to go off into the woods with this man that I don't really know, and look for something that I don't know how to find?"

Daniel spoke up, "Maggie, that's why I'm here. I came because my team that was scouting and searching for Mr. Maxwell, found his backpack and his journal as they were tracking someone or something through the woods, but he's missing."

Turning toward him, I asked, "And you think I'll be able to find him?"

"No, I think you're the key to the prophecy he wrote about in the journal."

Now who's crazy? Giving him a sideways glance, "How do you know it was about me?"

He cocked his head to the side, mimicking me, and gave me that infuriating look. Like he expected me to just believe him. Choosing to ignore him, I waved my hand in the air, "Never mind."

Looking back at the tree, Andrea said, "He's right, Maggie! I don't know why, or how I know this, but you're an important key to solving the riddle. You need to go with him."

Flabbergasted, I threw my arms in the air, "Well, alrighty then. If you say so, then I'd be crazy not to listen to a talking tree proclaiming to be my sister and a strange man who says he's here to help me." A little more flippantly, I remarked to the air in general, "What have I got to lose, besides my mind of course." A fake laugh was followed by an exaggerated sigh. My stomach rumbled and deciding I was done with the conversation, I stated firmly, "I'm hungry," abruptly walking toward the house.

As I stepped up to open the door, I could hear Andrea saying, "See, Daniel, she can be reasonable, but I think she's still struggling with it all."

Sensing his eyes on me, I spat out, "I can hear you," as I opened the door.

Daniel chuckled and responded, "I think she'll be fine."

Choosing not to storm back over to give them both a piece of my mind, I closed the door and went in search of food. As I rummaged through the kitchen and located the fixings of a great omelet, I couldn't help but think that it could be a little exciting to enter into an adventure with Daniel, who I now liked to think of as Captain Mysterious. Giggling, I reveled in the new nickname I made up for him. But then again, what am I thinking? There isn't an adventurous bone in my body. I could die out there and then who'd take care of Kelsey? It would be so nice to be able to wrap my head around this thing.

Kelsey entered the kitchen and brought me out of my thoughts, "I want to go with you."

"Go with me where, sweetie?" The question left my lips, but I already knew the answer and eyebrows raised, I asked, "So, you were listening?"

Scrunching up her face and giving me a sideways glance, uncertainty crept into her voice as she asked in a worried whisper, "Well, a little. Are you mad?"

Turning and lifting her into the chair at the end of the island, I looked her in the eyes and said, "If, and I mean *If*, I decide to go help Daniel, you have to stay with Sherri." She started to interrupt me, but I placed a finger across her lips, "Shhhh. I said, If." She nodded. "Besides, we won't be leaving for a bit, and you're supposed to start school soon. You can't go off into the woods with me if you need to go to school." Her eyes started to tear up. Changing tactics, I decided to play on her heartstrings a little. Feeling guilty over using such a tactic, I knew it was the right way to approach it. In a very soft and soothing voice, I asked calmly, "Who'll look after the tree and the robin for me, if you go with me?"

Kelsey's eyes lit up and she excitedly responded, "Okay, I'll stay."

A brief smile lit my face before I asked, "You want some food?"

She jumped down and said, "No, I'm still full from breakfast. I'm gonna go play with my dolls." She skipped off to her room. A movement caught my eye and shifting my view, I saw that Daniel had silently entered the room. A soft look shone through his eyes as he watched our little exchange, or maybe that was my perception.

"You're very good with her," his voice rumbled low in a soothing tone as he spoke.

"Mmm-hmm." As I turned back to fixing my amazing omelet, I couldn't help but wonder when I was going to get used to him just appearing like that. Sneaky, sneaky.

Finishing up the omelets, I placed one in front of Daniel, he looked away from his view out the window and smiled his appreciation. No words were necessary as I set the plate down and slid into my seat. Just as I was going to place the first bite of food in my mouth, a blood curdling scream pierced the silence and my heart fell to my knees.

Turning toward the sound, one word escaped both of our lips at the same time, "Kelsey!" Daniel and I jumped up to run down the hall the instant the word was uttered. As we reached the doorway, the window was hanging open where we could see the little man, Bobby Roberts, was driving away with Kelsey's tear-streaked face looking out the window.

My world crashed down around me, and I crumpled to the ground. What I didn't see at that moment was that Daniel had leapt over my sobbing form to dive out the window trying to get to Kelsey. A thick fog had rolled in and by the time Daniel got to his truck to follow, they were gone. As I glanced out the window to where he'd gone, he seemed to be swallowed by the fog.

Crawling across the floor and fighting to see through the veil of tears falling from my eyes, I peered out the window, waiting. I didn't hear the truck engine start. Where was he? The only sound that met my ears was like the flapping of large wings, but it was probably my imagination. Then, he was there. As if he just appeared out of thin air. Startled, I jumped, but then realizing it was him, I watched him as he walked up to the window without her. Shaking his head and looking lost, his eyes met mine and my world slipped away as I was drawn into an abyss like none I've ever known. A river of tears flowed across my face as I abruptly sat on Kelsey's bed and allowed the new pain to wash over me.

CHAPTER 13

"Why, Daniel? Why did Bobby take her?" Unable to pull myself from the edge of Kelsey's bed, I floated in a haze of anguish as I tried to grasp the reason why the tree-man would return to take Kelsey.

Daniel sat next to me. "Maggie, do you know who that was?"

Glancing up at him through the waterfall of tears that blurred my vision. "Yes, that was Bobby Roberts. He delivered and planted Andrea's tree."

Daniel now looked perplexed. "No, that was Mr. Maxwell."

My mouth dropped open. Stammering in confusion, "But...How? And why?" In a panic, I jumped to my feet and turned toward the door, "I'm calling the police!"

Daniel took hold of my arm firmly and stopped me in my tracks, "That's not a good idea."

Looking down at his hand holding firmly to my upper arm, I spat out, "Let me go! They can help! Why wouldn't we call them?" Wiggling and pulling, I tried to break free. My eyes met his, pleading, "Daniel, we're wasting time. Let me go!"

He faced me full-on and grasped my other arm with his free hand to keep me more firmly in place. "Maggie, No!"

My eyes drifted back to his hands. "Daniel?" My mind reeled as I tried to figure out why he wouldn't let me call the police or try to find my niece. Everything in me cried to move quickly as each second was a nail in her coffin. On the verge of full-blown hysteria, I cried, "Please?"

Calmly, with a deep sympathy in his voice, he looked into my soul as he held me firmly in his grasp, "I need you to stop and listen for a minute."

Daggers shot from my eyes as I willed him to release me. "You really need to let me go." Teeth clenched together in a show of mind over matter, I gritted out in a low growl, "Now!" He finally caught the hint and as soon as he released me, I started toward the doorway.

Sighing heavily, "Maggie, stop." His voice was calm and rich as he held me with his eyes, "Please, think carefully about what you'd tell them." His breathing was slightly ragged with emotion. "I understand your pain. I lost a sister when I was young. But you need to take a deep breath and think about everything that's happened. What will you say to the police?" He waited a moment and searched my face for what? Understanding?

Stopping in my tracks, a moment from walking through the threshold of Kelsey's bedroom door, I stared at him and let

the words he spoke sink into my subconscious. Thinking about all the events of the past couple days, my eyes widened in comprehension. I choked out, "Oh, Dear, Lord, Even George will have a hard time with all of this."

"George?" Another look of confusion crossed his face.

Waving my hand dismissively, "Never mind, not important." Remaining frozen in place, I tried to think of some way I could explain to the local police what was happening and why Kelsey had been kidnapped. Frustration coursed through me and I grunted in acquiescence, "But what are we going to do? I need to find her." Fear for her safety made the tears start again, "She must be so scared."

He simply nodded. His words were filled with compassion, "I understand. The police will think you're crazy or that you did something to her. Our chances of finding her are better on our own. I can promise that I'll do everything in my power to find her." His voice trailed off as he focused his attention on something beyond my vision.

Watching Daniel, he looked over to the bed and leaning over, picked up a piece of paper that was sitting on the edge of the bed. His eyes narrowed as he read it aloud. *"Bring me the tablet or she dies. You have three days. I'll be in touch."* Daniel crumpled the paper up and held it tightly in his clenched fist. "I have to make a phone call." A determined expression on his face, he turned and left the room.

It was as if I were suddenly released from quicksand, but my feet felt like they carried the caked on remnants of heavy soil as I walked over to close the window. Thoughts were spinning in my head. As if my limbs had a force of their own, I followed him into the living room.

He was on the phone staring out the window. "Yes. He just left here. Get here by morning. Alright. No, I'm staying put for the night. Okay. Bye." He placed his phone in his pocket and turned to me. "I'm staying here tonight. I don't think it's safe to leave you here alone."

Nodding absently, I asked, "There's others?"

"Yes. It's just a couple of people that I trust, but we've been actively searching for Maxwell since I was contacted by Andrea and Jaxon."

"Oh." Trying to keep myself busy, I started cleaning up.

"Hey, don't put that away." He motioned toward the food I was reaching for. He walked toward me, "I'm still hungry."

Looking at him as if he were crazy, I asked, "How can you eat at a time like this?"

A serious expression on his face, he leaned forward and reached for his plate, "Maggie, I can't imagine what you're feeling right now, but, no matter what, I need to keep my strength up and so do you." Sitting down in front of his plate, he patted the

The Tree and the Tablet

seat next to him, "This next couple of days are going to be very trying for both of us. I suggest you fill your reserves. You'll be no use to Kelsey if you starve yourself."

Picking up his fork to dig into the food that had grown cold, I couldn't help but feel a little out of sorts. Looking around, I suddenly noticed that I didn't hear Peanut alert me when Kelsey was taken. Where was she? Alarmed, I called out for her, "Peanut! Peanut?!? Peanut, come!"

Setting down his fork, he recognized my anxious calls. Looking down the hallway, Daniel asked, "Would she hide?"

Shaking my head slowly, I started walking from room to room calling her. Daniel suggested we look outside in case she'd tried to follow Kelsey. A curt nod in his direction and we headed outside. The fog had lifted slightly, but a chill was in the air as I stood in my driveway, my arms clasped around me. Looking around and calling for her again, I shivered but it wasn't from the cold.

It was one of those deep in the bones, foreboding type of shivers. Silence floated on the breeze and I focused all my energy on listening, but I didn't hear anything. No barking or whimpering or any other type of response met my ears. The lack of sound was deafening. Daniel was over by the window, kneeling down. Reverently, he touched the ground and then looked as if he were following a line in the earth.

He stood up and turned to me. Holding my breath, I waited in anticipation. "She went with Kelsey." It was a statement made in confidence.

Exhaling, I asked, "How do you know?"

Pointing to the ground, he stated matter-of-factly, "There are her paw prints in the gravel. If you follow the trail, you can see that her prints stop right near where the vehicle was stopped. If I'm right, she jumped into the vehicle when he opened the door to put Kelsey in the truck."

Spinning on my heel to face the road and peering off into the distance my voice was low as I pleaded with the heavens, "Dear God! Please protect them and keep them safe."

Daniel wrapped his arms around me from behind and said softly in my ear. "He wants the tablet, Maggie. With all that I've learned about Maxwell, I'm sure they'll be okay."

Every fiber of my being ached with defeat. The agony of not knowing where they were or how we'd find them. The uncertainty of all the "what if's" circled in my head filling me with an emptiness and dread like I'd never known. Feeling crushed from the inside-out, I turned into his embrace and cried.

Being held in his arms felt so good. The smell of him filled my senses. It was calming. Taking a deep breath, I decided that this is the last time I was going to cry, if I could help it. Standing to my full height, wiping the tears from my eyes in embarrassment, I whispered, "Thank you."

Turning from Daniel, I walked into the house and went straight to the back door. He followed me.

Guessing my intent, "Maggie, are you sure you want to tell

them?"

Half turning toward him as I walked through the doorway, "No." I continued to the tree. Bracing myself, I called out, "Andrea. Something's happened. Kelsey's gone. She's been taken."

The tree shimmered and fluctuated as it came to life with a horrendous cry. "Nooooooo! Not my baby." Jaxon was perched in the tree and at the same moment of her agonized cry, he took flight, spinning and twirling in the air as if he were a broken kite being battered by gale force winds. He finally settled down and landed on the tree again. He made awkward sounds and Andrea replied, "Yes, my love, find her." He flew away like lightning was on his tail feathers.

Andrea spoke calmly and hesitantly, as if she were trying to reign in her emotions. "Jaxon will be searching for her. If he finds them, he'll return here if it's safe or send his thoughts to me if he's not too far away."

Daniel spoke up at this point, "I already tried to find them."

Andrea responded, "I sensed Maxwell nearby. It was him, wasn't it?" The tree quaked slightly, "I don't know what happened to him, but I sensed something strange about him and it was like a whisper in my mind."

Stunned, I asked, "How did you know?"

The branches of the tree vibrated gently. "I felt him yesterday, too. I don't know how I knew it was him. I never met him in person before, it was like a whisper in my mind. He seems a little crazy, though."

Turning to Daniel, I asked, "But why would he want the tablet and not ask about the amulet?"

Daniel looked at me with a sheepish expression, "Because there's two amulets?"

Andrea and I spoke accusingly at the same time, "How do you know that?"

Daniel took a step back defensively, "When my team found Maxwell's belongings, it was because he dropped them running from Joseph in the woods. He jumped off a cliff into a lake and we assumed he was dead because we couldn't see him come back up. I searched but couldn't find any signs that he had exited the water below." Stopping his discussion of the facts to think for a moment, he remarked, "That would explain the limp though."

Thinking out loud, I said under my breath, "Interesting, but I assumed the limp was due to a deformity rather than an injury when he delivered the tree. But how did you know he had a limp?"

Daniel was still talking, "Tatyana and Joseph are researching exactly how he came to possess and deliver the tree, but we suspect he knew something was up and that's why he went to Denver. We believe he's also responsible for the murder of Mr. Caulker, the antiquities dealer that gave Andrea and Jaxon the amulet." At my questioning look, he responded, "I noticed the limp when I was studying the tracks outside the window." Returning to his discussion, "As I was saying, Maxwell wrote everything in his journal." Looking back to the tree, he continued, "He's slightly crazy, but I don't believe he'll hurt Kelsey. He just wants the tablet. He only sees her as a tool to get what he wants." Kicking at the dirt near his boot, he angrily exclaimed, "I should've known and come to you sooner." A low growl rumbled across his lips.

Turning to face him with a white, hot rage enveloping me, "How could you keep that a secret?" He flinched, "You knew all of this prior to today and did nothing to protect her?" He had the nerve to look ashamed, but wisely chose not to respond. Looking at Andrea, I asked, "Did you see anything that would help us find him?"

Andrea's face was anguished, "No. I'll try again. Jaxon and I have a mind-link of sorts and he'll let me know if he sees anything."

Daniel chose that moment to speak up, "Maggie, I had no way of knowing he would do this. I'm so sorry I missed the signs."

Facing him, I asked, "Really? You were aware that he was a dangerous man who *KILLED* someone, and you had no idea?"

He looked like a wounded puppy, "I really didn't think that she'd be in danger, but I promise you this, we'll get her back." More succinctly he stated firmly, "I. Will. Get. Her. Back."

Giving him a stern look, "For your sake, I hope you're right." As I watched the petals on the ground lift and float in the breeze, then drift back to the ground, I spoke softly. "Andrea, we'll be leaving tomorrow after Daniel's team gets here. I'll come out to speak with you again after I get something to eat and take a shower. Rest for now and focus on Jaxon." Walking past Daniel, I stopped as I stepped up onto the deck. Stiffening my resolve, I looked over my shoulder, saying in the sweetest voice I could muster, "Come on Daniel, as you said, we need to keep our strength up so we can be on our game tomorrow." Sarcastically, tears in my eyes, I added, "We can't have you wasting away while a poor child is in the clutches of a deranged maniac."

He nodded and reassured Andrea again, "We'll find her." Meeting me at the door, we stepped into the dining room together.

Making my way to the kitchen, for a moment, I let my eyes roam the empty space as I tried to reign in my emotions. Turning away from him, frustrated that I had to wait to go after Kelsey, I asked softly, "Would you like your food reheated?" I prepared to warm up my omelet and made myself a pot of coffee while waiting for it to reheat. When he nodded, I placed his plate in the oven as well. He sat down to watch me, almost like a bird of prey wondering when to best pounce. *Or maybe he was more like a rat, hiding in a corner, waiting for the moment to slink across the room.*

Grinning to myself at my private thoughts, I continued with my preparations. Setting the food in front of him, I also got us each a new cup of coffee. We sat down and ate in silence. After cleaning the dishes, I decided to go take a shower. Daniel said he was going to make some phone calls and get some things arranged.

Stepping into the shower, my body tingled with the sensation of the hot water hitting my skin. Taking a couple of deep breaths, I melted into the heat. As the tension gradually seeped out of my body, my mind started to wander through all the things that had happened since the day Andrea called me to take Kelsey. It seemed like such a long time ago, but it was only a month since everything in my world went sideways. Eventually my thoughts landed on the day I met Daniel. Even though we'd had barely any time together, I kept feeling like our paths were meant to be intertwined somehow. Now that he was here and I was dependent on him to help me find Kelsey, what did this all mean? The main question that kept recurring in my mind was, "Why?" Why did this happen? What was it about Daniel that I couldn't stop thinking about him? Was he really interested in helping me? Did he feel the link between us? What role did he really play in all of this? Who was he and why did I have such a strong connection to him? I just couldn't shake the feeling that it was all important and had something to do with my future, but how?

There had to be more to what was going on and I really needed him to let his guard down and start sharing everything with me. But, was I willing to do the same? What if we can't find the tablet? Shaking my head, I quickly resolved to stop that line of questioning in my mind. Gathering my wits, I finished my bathing ritual. Standing in the water with my mind cleared, my belly full, and my heart open to the possibilities, I focused my thoughts outward toward Kelsey. *"Kelsey, if you can hear me honey, we're coming to get you. Hold on baby. Auntie loves you."*

For a split second, I thought I heard her respond in my mind, *"Aunt Maggie? Please hurry."*

It startled me so much that I slightly slipped in the shower and as I attempted to catch myself, I dislodged the caddy that was hanging over the faucet-head which caused several bottles of soaps to fall clattering to the floor.

Shortly, there was a knocking at the bathroom door followed by Daniel's voice, filled with concern, "Maggie? Everything okay there?"

Feeling a little embarrassed, I quickly responded, "Yes, I'm fine, just dropped the soap." Ugh, I can't believe I said that. Hysterical laughter flew from my lips and I admonished myself for being such a dunderhead. Daniel reminded me to be careful and I swear I could hear him chuckling as he walked away from the door.

Once I was dry and dressed again, I decided to let my hair air dry. Brushing it out, I allowed it hang loose down my back. Heading into the living room, Daniel stopped his perusal of what looked to be a map, to look up at me upon my entrance into the room. My face felt very hot and my heart beat a little faster as I turned toward the kitchen. Asking over my shoulder, "Is there any coffee left?" Stealthily, he had crossed the room and stepped up behind me, he slid his hand around my waste to turn me toward him. Catching my breath, I looked up at him and noticed that his eyes had changed colors. The color was somehow deeper and richer than I remembered them to be.

"Maggie." He breathed my name as if it were a sigh on his lips and he leaned forward to place the gentlest but most stirring kiss upon my lips. Drowning! I was definitely drowning. My heart felt like it would pound itself right out of my chest. Just when I thought I'd totally lose all control of my senses, reality crashed around me and the deep pleasure that was curling itself through my belly came to an abrupt halt as he released my lips from their very pleasant perch upon his own. When he pulled back, he looked at me longingly for a moment and abruptly released me as if he could sense my anguished guilt-ridden thoughts. He mumbled "I'm sorry." as he slinked away.

Standing there trying to catch my balance and return my breathing to normal, my heart was pounding in my ears and all I heard was the thrumming of blood rushing through my veins. Instantly, the warmth left me and was replaced with an emptiness and severe longing to run up to him and put him back into my arms. It was a small consolation from the pain of my worried thoughts of Kelsey, but the void was a reminder of how truly alone I was feeling. It was all compounded with the aching caused by the loss of his warmth and I wondered what had caused him to stop.

Looking up from my gaze on the floor, he was sitting on the

sofa again with his map in his hands, as if he hadn't moved from his precarious perch to uproot my world. Raising my hand to my lips, I could still feel his warmth like a silky layer of softness lingered there. If it wasn't for the slight swelling of my lips and the nerve memory of the sensation it invoked, I would have thought it was a dream. How did he do that? Just sit there like nothing happened? Was this some sort of game?

Then, I remembered that I was supposed to be angry with him for his secret keeping. Confound it all. My foot itched to stomp the ground in frustration. Admonishing myself to let it go, I turned toward the coffee maker, seeing that there was indeed coffee. I quickly prepared a cup and went to sit at the table. Broodingly, I found myself staring out the glass doors toward the water and the fog that was rolling around in the harbor.

Picking up my portable phone, I called Sherri.

When she answered I tried to sound upbeat, hiding my raging pain as I said, "Hi."

"Hey, girl, what are you doing?"

"Not much."

"Is everything okay?" Concern tinged her voice.

"Yeah, I'm fine." The lie stuck in my throat. Swallowing a sip of coffee to mask it, I explained, "Just sitting here, drinking a cup of coffee." Thinking back on the conversation about why we wouldn't be involving the police in the search for Kelsey, I continued to lie to my best friend. It killed me to do that, but even I knew it was all ridiculous as I barely believed what was

The Tree and the Tablet

happening. How would she take it? "Hey, I just wanted to see if you could come by on Wednesday and unlock the house for the Christmas tree delivery person? She's supposed to show up around 10:00 am and set up the tree and decorations."

"Sure, honey. What's going on?" More concern.

"Kelsey and I are gonna take a trip to the coast. She suggested it so we could hang out together."

"You want me to come over and help you pack up for the trip?"

Sensing she was trying to figure out my lie, I laughed, "No, that's alright. I got this. Besides, you have your own family to deal with. Thanks for coming by. The key is still hidden under the rock."

"Alright. You're sure everything's okay?"

A little exacerbated, I chuckled, "Yes. Everything's fine." Not knowing how long we'd be gone, I swallowed the lump and said as calmly as I could, "Thank you for being my friend. I love you."

"I love you too, honey. Have fun."

"Okay, Bye."

"Maggie?"

"Yes?"

"Call me if you need me, okay?"

"Sure thing. Talk to you later?"

"Okay, Bye."

Hanging up the phone. It felt like I just kept ripping a band

199

aid off of the open wound that was my heart and it hurt like hell. Would the pain just stop coming? Taking a deep breath, I returned to broodingly staring out the windows at the relatively calm day that seemed to mock my mood.

The day was slipping away. It would be dark soon and I felt so tired, like all my strength had been sucked right out of me.

Daniel approached and gently placed his hand on my shoulder so as not to startle me. "Maggie, can I sit with you?" I nodded. He took a seat next to me, placing his map on the table in front of him. He pointed to a mountain range and a heavily forested area, but I wasn't focused on his words. All I could think about was his luscious lips. Kelsey was God knows where, probably frightened out of her mind and here I was thinking about kisses. What was wrong with me?

"Maggie? Are you okay?" He sounded concerned.

Shaking my head as if I were awakening from a dream, I said, "Yes, I'm so sorry. I'm just suddenly feeling exhausted."

He smiled at me—A gentle, no frills, kind-hearted type of smile. It melted my soul. "Why don't you go take a nap? We can go over the plans for tomorrow when you wake up."

Looking up from the map, I replied, "Yes, I think I will." As I stood up and turned toward the hallway, my world spun out of control and I crumpled. His strong arms wrapped around me. A feeling of intense peace and security filled me, and I gave in to the mind-numbing abyss that had been threatening to engulf my world.

The room melted away and there was only the feeling of him against me. He carried me so gently, but so securely, that I felt as if I were floating on the wings of a hundred butterflies. Gently, I landed upon the soft down comforter of my bed and snuggled into the cool, but comforting cloud. My thoughts were soon drifting through a vortex of whirling and shifting colors that twisted around me until my mind landed firmly in a dark room filled with dirt. The musty smell of the wet earth clung to my nostrils and there was the pungent aroma of ferns and wildflowers. My ears cued in on the sound of water rushing all around me, but I couldn't see it. In the distance, I heard the cackling laugh of some deranged soul.

There was soft sobbing coming from behind me, but the room was so dark, I couldn't make out what was causing it. In my mind, I imagined a light beaming from my hand and used it like a flashlight to see what was surrounding me. Turning from side to side and trying to see into the intense darkness of the dirt-filled room, I stopped abruptly and said, "Kelsey? Is that you?"

Kelsey looked up from her little corner where she was holding Peanut and whispered, "Aunt Maggie? I can hear you, but I can't see you. Where are you?"

My heart screamed with pain, "Oh, honey, I'm not sure what's happening, but we'll find you. Are you safe?"

"Yes, the man that took me gave me food and blankets. Peanut's keeping me company."

"Sweetie, I'm not sure how I'm able to see you and talk to

you but stay safe. We'll be there soon. I love you."

Sounding confused but optimistic, she replied, "I love you, too, Auntie. Please hurry. I'm scared."

A crazy sounding scream filled my ears and I sat up in my bed. Sweat was pouring down my face, or maybe it was tears. My body felt like it was wading through mud. As I began to come to, I could feel that Daniel was holding me, rocking back and forth. His voice sounded strained, "Maggie, please wake up."

Tensing up, I pulled away to look at him confused, "Daniel?"

He brushed the hair from my face and asked, "What the hell, Maggie? You scared me half to death."

CHAPTER 14

Placing my hand on Daniel's chest, I asked, "What happened? I blacked out." Suddenly feeling protective of my experiences and not wanting him to think I was crazy, I decided not to share everything that had just happened. The duplicity of what I wanted from him and why I didn't share with him right now, hit me like a ton of bricks. But until I could get him to share with me, I felt it was a good idea to guard myself as well. Besides, I wasn't quite sure it was even real.

"Maggie, you collapsed, and I carried you here to put you in bed, but you started moaning and thrashing." He looked at me intently to make sure I was okay. "You started crying out and I couldn't wake you." His face was really pale.

Looking down and away from his prying eyes, I couldn't help but to smile at the thought that he was concerned for me, but then I was instantly ashamed for wanting him to care when all I should be focused on right now was finding Kelsey.

Drawing my attention away from my own deprived thoughts, Daniel squeezed me tightly, asking, "Maggie, what happened? You were in a type of trance. You opened your eyes but looked right through me." He leaned away trying to regain eye contact with me but let his hand slide slowly down my arms and rested one hand on my left arm. Shivering at the delicious and exciting sensation that movement caused, I took a steadying breath. *Dammit, how did he do that to me? How was he able to make me focus on him and nothing else?*

Looking up to his beautiful gaze, I could see his expression had turned hard and demanding. Inhaling sharply at my surprise. What did I do wrong now? He almost seemed angry. I continued to lie, "I'm fine. I don't know what happened. I must have just had a dream." The lies seemed to come easier. *Don't get used to this, Maggie. It's dangerous to spin a web of lies, you'll get trapped.* My mother's words came back to haunt me and I admonished myself as I continued my storytelling, "I used to have weird dreams when I was a kid, too." As I laughed to take the edge off, "My mom always told me that I'd have strange dreams where I could look right through her and still be asleep. She called them night terrors. She also said I had a penchant for turning up in strange places or just disappearing, but I don't really remember any of that."

His face softened slightly as he looked at me skeptically, asking, "Are you sure you're alright?"
Nodding, I tried to reassure him. "Yes, I just have these spells when I get stressed out." *Was it just a dream? It seemed so real.*

It was easy to see he was still frustrated with me, but I couldn't figure out why. Thinking I did a pretty good job with my explanation, I couldn't be certain, and I always felt on edge or like I was second guessing myself when I was around him. What an enigma he was. He appeared like he wanted to say something more but not certain if he should, he exhaled sharply. Seeming resigned with my misinformation he sighed. Running his fingers through his hair, he shook his head. "Well, best to get some sleep then. I wouldn't want you to be too stressed and suffer from a spell when we're out in the wilderness." A knowing look crossed his face, but was just as quickly replaced with a stern expression. Standing up and turning toward the door he looked back at me over his shoulder at the doorway and said, "Get some rest. I'll be here if you need me." Stepping out into the hallway, he left the room closing the door behind him. It might have been my imagination but I thought I saw a fleeting look of consternation cross his face through the crack as he glanced back toward the closing door. When the door latch clicked, signaling that I was alone, I sighed audibly.

Relieved that he let it go, I wondered briefly if he knew I was lying. I just couldn't read him. Laying back on my pillows, I stared wide-eyed at the wispy, sheer material that was draped across the top of the four-poster bed as a canopy. It was a shimmering fabric that looked like the inside of an abalone shell with the light flickering across it. It was a large expanse of pearlescent material shimmering with pink, purple, and turquoise ribbons of color worked through it.

On breezy summer nights I liked to light candles and open the windows to allow the material to shift and shimmer in the flickering light. The effect was quite extraordinary and entranced me with its undulating and swirling colors. Using meditation breathing techniques and focusing on the movement of the fabric proved to be hypnotic. That was the reason I chose that material. It calmed me and it also reminded me of the many dreams I had as a child. It also helped me think clearer about the things that were troubling me.

Thinking back on what I recently experienced, I couldn't help but to recall the many times when I was younger that I would have visions or go into a trance. It had been years since I felt this way and I thought I'd outgrown it. I used to cry myself to sleep at night because of the frightening visions. Mom always said that gifts came in different types of wrapping, and that I should be thankful for what I'd been given. My visions had stopped when I was a teen or maybe I'd just learned to control them. It was scary when they started up again right before 'Drea announced her pregnancy with Kelsey. Even though mom thought I should be thankful, I'd looked at the visions more as a curse than a gift and

The Tree and the Tablet

I was happy when they went away completely after Mom disappeared. As a matter of fact, it had been approximately five years since I'd had a vision at all. When I was a child, there had been one particularly frightening vision I'd had that put me in a funk for two weeks. I couldn't even remember it now. After that, I tried to block them out and only had visions every once in a while, between my teen years up until Mom went missing. It was a mixed blessing though. My last vision was of Mom screaming for help in a body of water. That was three days before the incident and the phone call from the Barbados port authority. Shuddering, I shook myself mentally and tried to let it go but I couldn't help thinking that it might not be the worst thing to happen right now.

If the visions help me find Kelsey, then I'm going to use them to my advantage. With that thought, I yawned and rolled over. I'd lost track of time thinking about my past, but I was more determined to find a way to get Kelsey home safe and sound. Even though I still hadn't slept, I felt rested. Time to go talk to Andrea.

As I entered the dining room, I noticed the door to the backyard was opened and the curtains fluttered in the cool breeze that wafted through it. Stepping out onto the deck, I saw that Daniel was sitting on the ground near the base of Andrea's tree. A gentle chanting came from him like the rumble of a seismic eruption underground. It was mesmerizing. A deep feeling of calm enveloped me as I felt a stirring in my soul at the beautiful rhythm of the melody he was singing. Never had I heard such a sweet and soulful song before. An earthquake seemed to be occurring within my body as I allowed the sounds to surround me and penetrate my being. There was a bowl perched on Daniel's lap with what smelled like sage burning inside.

Slowly, I approached. His eyes were closed. He was wafting the smoke toward the tree using the raven feather that was on the thong around his neck. The embers glowed fiercely in the alabaster bowl. A gentle glow was emanating from the turquoise stone encircled in silver at the end of his feather. Curiosity, as well as some undefined sensation of an invisible rope surrounding and pulling on me, seemed to propel me toward him. Looking to the tree to see if Andrea was alert, I could see that the bark was fluctuating and moving in rhythm to his song. Her face appeared to be at peace, and she was mouthing the words to his chant.

Before I noticed he was looking at me, it felt as if his gaze caressed my skin causing goosebumps to rise on my arms. They appeared to have changed from their normal seafoam green to a brilliant emerald color. Entranced, I continued to move forward. Suddenly, my heart felt like it was on fire and I struggled to breath. Stopping abruptly, I clutched my throat. He was still intently staring at me. He'd stopped moving and the bowl was gone. Dropping to my knees, I looked to him for help, but he didn't move. Reaching my hand out toward him, the air seemed to shudder and shimmer in a bright glowing light that twisted and turned in on itself.

Now on all fours, I swore there was a large black bird rising behind Daniel. It was the most remarkable looking bird I ever saw. Taking the form of a Raven, it spread its wings and all the while, the song became louder and louder. Inky black eyes filled my vision. My breathing was shallow and I struggled to suck air into my lungs as I screamed inside my head for it to stop. His face turned toward me, but his eyes looked through me and with an immense clap of thunder which caused me to go deaf, a bolt of lightning struck Daniel. It appeared to engulf him and the giant raven opened its beak to let out a shrill cry. The scream was ripped from me for real this time, using what seemed to be the last of the air that was available in my lungs.

Darkness engulfed us like black ink spilling over a white piece of paper. It was so thick, I thought I could feel it surrounding me. A sense of doom cast itself over me like a heavy velvet cloak. *Is this what it feels like to die?* All the oxygen within me felt like it was being sucked from every pore and orifice in my body, which caused me to convulse uncontrollably. My hands grasped the earth as I tried to pull myself forward toward him. Still, I couldn't look away. Were my eyes playing tricks on me? What was happening? I couldn't move and in my mind, I was crying out to Daniel to help me, but no words left my lips. Feeling like I couldn't hold on any longer, the pain in my lungs was excruciating and my heart felt like it would surely stop beating any moment.

Suddenly, it was as if a curtain had been pulled back. The world righted itself and I could breathe again. Blinking rapidly and sucking in great gasping breaths, I noticed that Daniel was no longer sitting on the ground in front of me. As I turned my head to search for him, I saw him standing next to me. The ringing in my ears subsided, and I finally heard the words he was saying. He was kneeling next to me trying to help me to my feet.

"Maggie? Are you alright? Talk to me. What's happening?" Shaking my head as I tried to continue to clear the confusion, I looked at him like he was out of his mind.

Staring at him accusingly, I asked, "What the hell *was* that," while trying to right my world and gain my equilibrium.

He looked confused by my question. Cocking his head to the side and peering at me expectantly he asked, "Why don't you tell me?"

Tilting my head to match his, I asked, "You didn't see any of that?" He shook his head with a look of concern on his face.

Covering my face with my hands, I thought that I was losing my mind. How was it possible to have seen all of that and not have him see it? Looking at him more intently for any clue that he might be hiding the truth behind those beautiful green eyes, there was nothing but concern reflected back at me. Exasperated, I remembered all the times as a child where I was teased and abused by the other kids for my trances and visions. The school counselor told me that I had an active imagination and said that the only way to make friends would be for me to keep those

The Tree and the Tablet

things to myself. Again, I chose not to share with him out of fear. Getting to my feet, I looked over at the tree. Andrea's face wasn't visible and I shrugged the event off, "it was nothing." All those years of conditioning myself not to tell anyone about my visions kept my mouth sealed tightly and I sensed he wasn't buying it.

At his questioning look, I forced a fake laugh and gave him the most cavalier smile I could muster, "I'll be fine. I just tripped." He still looked like he didn't believe me. "Honestly, I thought you were standing right in front of me and when I fell, the wind got knocked out of me. That's all."

"Maggie, you know you can tell me anything." His voice was calm and even but his look was one of disbelief and concern.

Waving him off and trying to sound sure of myself, I laughed and said, "I'm fine! Really!" Internally warring with my insecurities, I turned toward the tree and Andrea, promptly putting an end to the discussion and ignoring the entire episode.

"Andrea? Have you heard from Jaxon?"

The tree fluctuated and shimmered and Andrea spoke hesitantly. "Maggie, what's going on with you?" She sounded uncertain and afraid. Her voice quivered with the sound of unshed tears. "You know I couldn't bear it if anything happened to you too?" It felt like a question rather than a statement which caused me to feel defensive.

Dammit, I thought to myself, even when I was younger, couldn't hide anything from her. Irritated, I snapped, "Nothing. I'm just tired."

211

Andrea rolled her eyes, "You know better than that. You don't need to be like that. I'm just trying to look out for you. Kelsey needs us all to be on the same page."

Frustrated and scared like a cat in a corner, I snarled, "Andrea, lay off already! I get it. There's nothing you need to worry about right now." At her look of concern, I reigned my emotions in and asked calmly, "I'm sorry I snapped at you. I'm just worried. Did Jaxon find anything yet?"

Daniel grunted under his breath, "Sure," and I shot him a scathing look that caused him to put his hands up in front of him in a posture of defense.

Andrea looked down in concentration and then glancing back up at me, she said, "No, nothing concrete yet, but he thinks he found a clue. He's following it now and will report back as soon as he knows something. He's showing me a picture of a small town to the west of here but he's trying to find a sign or something that will help us find it."

Turning to look out at the water, my mind raced. Where could she be? Running through my visions and thinking out loud, I said, "He should look for a place where there is running water and caves."

Daniel had stepped up behind me sensing my troubled thoughts. Speaking softly so as not to interrupt my thoughts, he asked, "Why would he do that?"

Startled that he was so close to me, I suddenly realized that I'd spoken my thoughts, rather than keeping them in my mind

The Tree and the Tablet

and I abruptly turned, shaking my head as if to clear cobwebs. "I don't know. It's just a feeling." At his questioning expression, I said a little gruffly, "Call it a hunch." Trying to hide my angst, I turned back to Andrea. "Remember that wierd thing I lost?"

A knowing grin split across the formation of her mouth in the tree bark and she said, "Really? Have you found it again?" She sounded more excited than I was.

Nodding absently while chewing my lip, "I think so, but I'm not certain."

She started to talk excitedly but also concerned and skeptical, "Magpie, How?"

Staring at the ground, I gently shook my head. My eyes darted apprehensively toward Daniel and then back toward her in a pleading manner, "Please, Andrea?" Rocking my head sideways and raising my eyebrows in an effort to indicate that I didn't want him to know, I attempted to sound calm when my insides were churning with apprehension, "I'm not sure." She started to speak again, and I stepped closer, giving her my most pleadingly dramatic expression, "Please?!?"

She seemed to understand my barely spoken plea not to share any further information with Daniel there to hear and making eye contact said, "I understand. Let me know what I can do." With a curt and hopefully imperceptible nod, I mouthed the words, "*Thank you,*" followed by a loud proclamation, "I'm going inside. It's getting late. I'm sure it'll be too dark for Jaxon to continue his search for the night and suddenly I'm famished again. I'll come see you in the morning."

A branch sneaked through the air and gently plucked a stray lock from my face. "I love you, Maggie."

Smiling gently at her and playfully swatting at the branch, "Geez! Do you know how weird that is?"

She laughed, "Sorry."

Grinning at her, "I love you, too." Turning on my heel, I walked into the house. Not stopping to see if Daniel followed, I sensed his closeness as if he were a dragon on my back.

It was getting dark quick and the absence of a moon made it sort of creepy. No wonder I was hungry. As I reached for the door handle to go inside, I turned to ask Daniel if he was hungry and my eyes met the beady ink black eyes of the raven. Gasping, I stumbled backwards. Tripping over the threshold of the door frame, my eyes and hands simultaneously sought out something that I could grab hold of to steady myself. Daniel's hand stealthily slipped through the air and grasped my wrist to catch me. When I looked up at him again, he had magically returned to normal. The raven's eyes were gone, and I took a couple steadying breaths to cover my confusion.

Snidely, Daniel quipped, "If you keep falling over like this, I'm going to have to buy you a set of padded body armor. I can't always be here to catch you, y'know?"

A small squeak escaped, and I laughed as I blushed, "Yeah, right."

He shook his head as he chuckled at me and as we stepped

into the dining room, I couldn't help but wonder what it all meant.

CHAPTER 15

As I stood in my pantry, digging around, looking for food items, Daniel laughed, "Do you think you have enough ranch dressing?"

Following his eyes, I saw that his view landed squarely on the partial case of extra-large bottles of ranch dressing I had purchased by accident when I ordered from my online food vendor. Chuckling at the site of twelve jugs stacked in a row on the middle shelf. A cursory glance over my shoulder and I replied, "Well, you know, I felt it was necessary to be prepared for any occasion including the next zombie apocalypse."

"Well, I'm sure that no matter what you eat, it will be well seasoned."

"Yes, well, better to be safe than sorry is my motto."

His view must have shifted as he soon noticed the wine fridge on the other side of the pantry and sighing in appreciation, he crouched down and withdrew a bottle of a locally made blackberry merlot. Noting his choice, I remarked, "My favorite, I know you're supposed to drink red wine at room temperature, but I prefer this one chilled."

A broad grin spread across his face, "I know the winery well. A very good choice. And I agree, it's best chilled."

"By all means, please open it." Heading out of the pantry, I pulled a bottle opener out of a drawer and handed it to him. He graciously accepted and I followed up by pulling two wine glasses from the cupboard for him to fill.

Soon, I had determined we would be eating a basic salad of greens and tomatoes with a couple leftover sandwiches from the other day. It was quick and easy, and he sat silently watching me prepare the food. Occasionally, I'd look up to find him watching me with a soft smile on his face. He handed me the glass of wine and I nodded with a brief, "Thanks," as I continued the preparations. Suddenly shy and aloof, I couldn't think of anything to say and it seemed he was alright with my choice not to make idle chatter during the food prep. Choosing to sit at the island to eat, I put the food down and motioned for him to take a seat.

Grabbing the bottle, he set it on the counter in front of us and sat next to me. "Thank you, Maggie. I know this must be a lot for you." Studying the meal placed before him, he mockingly observed, "Well, all doesn't seem to be lost. I was worried when I saw your almost empty pantry that we might have ranch soup, but again, you surprise me with your resourcefulness." Lifting a turkey on rye, he waggled his eyebrows at me, and said, "But this looks very promising."

Not to be outdone, I retrieved the bottle of ranch next to me and laid it across my arm like a sommelier, asking politely in a snooty sounding voice, "Would you care for a sampling of our most desired salad pairing, sir?"

Trying to stop himself from chuckling at me, in a serious voice, he asked, "What year is this bottle?"

"It's of the finest quality, Sir, I assure you." Flipping open the cap, I asked hastily, "Would you care to smell the cork?"

"Don't mind if I do." As he leaned over to take a whiff of the salad dressing, I squeezed the bottle slightly which caused a small splattering of ranch to shoot out and cover his forehead. Not expecting it to do that, I started cackling like a deranged lunatic and promptly set the bottle on the counter as I reached for a napkin to wipe his face. He grabbed my hand and held it in his, staring at my fingers briefly before he let his eyes wander to my face. Our eyes locked on one another and I held my breath in anticipation. Releasing my hand abruptly, he spouted in a stoic voice, "Madam, I have decided not to endorse your establishment on the basis of poor customer service and lack of culinary options."

Blinking at him in confusion, he began to raucously laugh at my bewildered expression. Realizing he was joking, I sputtered and soon found myself engulfed in a joy that caused a tingle throughout my entire body. Raising my glass in silent toast of his ability to bring me out of my funk, "Touché, sir." He clanked his against mine, and smiling broadly, gulped down his entire glass of wine. Not to be undone, I mimicked him, and he immediately filled both our vessels with another round of blackberry heaven. With another drink in hand, I remarked, "I'll be certain to convey your complaints to the owner." His response was a gentle smile and a nod followed by another rapid emptying of the sweet nectar. The rest of the dinner was amiable with very few words and very many glasses of wine. As I finished my last bite of sandwich, my eyes drifted across the countertop taking in the scene. Not quite sure how or when it happened, but I was surprised to see two empty bottles sat on the counter. Glancing up at the clock and nursing what might have been my fourth glass of wine, I spoke softly, "I know I've been tense. It's all been a bit much for me, but I wanted to say that I know you were trying to do the right thing, and, well, thank you."

His eyes widened in surprise. His reply was steady and soft, "Earlier, when I said I understood about your pain. It was the truth. When I lost my sister, my relationship with my mother changed drastically so I also lost her. It has been very difficult for me. Since the day Jaxon contacted me, I've been trying to help. I hope you believe that." He sighed softly and his eyes pleaded with me for compassion. Just being in a room with this man and sharing a meal in silence made me feel better. I didn't think it was possible, but his hold on me seemed to be stronger than I thought it could be after only having spent a limited amount of time with him.

Nodding, "I'm not sure why—I mean, I barely know you, but somehow—I believe you." Getting to my feet to start clearing the dishes was when I realized that I was most assuredly tipsy. He must've recognized my slight stumble or my inefficient movements and was soon at my side helping to clean up after dinner. Putting my now empty wine glass in the dishwasher, I turned and walked away. His eyes were on me and I felt it like a caress between my shoulder blades.

Slipping down the hallway, I quickly retrieved some blankets and a pillow for him to sleep on the sofa since the third bedroom was currently being used as storage. We went through the house silently together and made sure all the doors and windows were locked.

For a short time, I'd allowed myself to be distracted from the things that had seemed so overwhelming and focused my attention on the only other thing in my life that brought me some small pleasure. . .

Daniel. . .

I couldn't help but to study the events that brought him into my life. He was a blessing and a curse all together wrapped in a tight package of enigma and wonder. Allowing my thoughts to drift away from the most perplexing human I'd ever met, I was soon overwhelmed with the thought that tomorrow couldn't be here soon enough as a stab of sadness pierced my heart thinking of Kelsey all alone. My heart nearly broke from the feelings of loss and helplessness that engulfed me.

Pushing my pain aside, I said a quick prayer. *Dear God, please be with her and keep her safe,* I thought as I stared toward the back door. As I attempted to project my prayer outward into the world, I stood at the end of the hallway, just inside the dining room. Slowly and lost in hopeful thoughts, I turned toward my bedroom for the night, looking down at a spot on the floor that held no particular significance, a shuddering sigh escaped my lips as I said, "Good night, Daniel." When I looked up, he was standing in front of me.

Startled, I gasped and slightly jumped backward. *Damned sneak* flitted through my mind just as he caught me by the waist. His left arm slid around me and reaching up with his right hand, he cupped my cheek. My gaze focused on his masculine chest. Gently, he slowly ran his thumb along my jawline causing a tingling sensation to erupt where he had touched me. As if sensing my thoughts, he calmly reassured me, "Don't worry, Maggie. We'll find her." Sighing, I nuzzled my face into his palm.

The simplest touch from this man soothed me and lit a fire in my belly at the same time. Slowly, my eyes raised up to meet his and my soul was pierced with a longing like nothing I've ever felt before. Every thought in my head disappeared when he was

The Tree and the Tablet

near. It seemed like every time this man touched me, I was in a new and exciting form of being. Every time was like the first time. The connection between us was always electric. He made me feel like a lightbulb with a pull string. The slightest touch was enough to make me vibrate and come to life instantly. Was it possible to feel this way every time someone had physical contact with another person?

Pulling me closer, his eyes seemed to be looking everywhere, at every part of my face, as he meticulously and methodically drew me toward him. The air caught in my throat, my mouth seemed parched, and all I wanted was a cool drink of Daniel. My brain screamed at me to pull away, to stop this madness. However, my aching soul and treacherous body rebelled violently at that thought.

Again, I was drowning in the loveliest sea of green. *Oh, Dear Lord! He's going to be the death of me,* I raged inwardly. My heart was beating so hard, I knew he could surely hear it or feel it. As my breast pressed against his torso, I was forced to lift my eyes even further to meet his. The strength of his arms encircled me like a shrine of protection, and the electricity of his breath upon my lips was so thrilling, I thought I'd die from the anticipation of what was yet to come. Lightning struck as our lips touched, and every fiber of my being became a beacon of longing erupting within me. My head was spinning with excitement.

What started out as a gentle, insistent touching of his lips upon mine, and a gentle aching in the pit of my stomach, soon raged into a terrible fire that threatened to consume me. His mouth devoured mine. My breathing became ragged, and every fiber of my being was taken in by him. The power and strength that radiated from him made me shiver, but it wasn't fear, it was the most intense desire I'd ever felt. Intoxicated by his command over my senses, I wanted.... Well, I wasn't exactly sure what I wanted other than to drag him so close to me that we would become one person.

Heat pulsated outwards from him and seared my skin beneath my shirt. My body responded with its own powerful heat pushing back toward him. We were like two magnets, irreversibly drawn together. Random thoughts flew through my head and just as quickly were eradicated by the powerful intensity between us.

It was such a deep and all-consuming desire. Grasping him desperately to me, it felt like I couldn't get him close enough. No matter how I tried, he wasn't close enough, yet that didn't stop me from trying. A guttural moan escaped him, or maybe it was me. My head was so filled with fog, I couldn't decipher who was doing what. I was most assuredly dying. Drowning in the most blissful way possible. *If this is death, then kill me again and again,* my mind raged. He moved his kisses from my lips down along my jaw and blazed a path from my ear to the crook of my neck. *Oh, dear god. What is he doing to me?*

Delicious waves of pleasure coursed through me. Panting heavily and trying desperately to get air into my lungs but also wanting to be totally consumed by him, I struggled against him as if I were wrestling with myself but losing my war on sanity at the same time. I moaned softly. He took that opportunity to capture my mouth with his again and delve even deeper into the core of my existence with his powerful aphrodisiac. *I'm going to faint.*

He broke away from the intense kiss, and breathing raggedly, he said quietly, "I'm sorry, Maggie." The whispered words were barely audible above the sound of my racing heart. *What did he just say?* The fog was slowly dissipating, and it was difficult to mistake the sound of agonizing pain in his voice as he rested his head against my forehead, "You should get some sleep." Taking a deep breath and stepping away from me, he sighed.

Oh, God! Crushing, agonizing pain and emptiness filled me. Arms that were once filled with a strong presence were suddenly left aching for what was gone. My heart felt like it was going to burst into a million pieces. Why did he keep pushing me away? Frustration, anger, and confusion coursed through me. Determined not to let him see, I gathered my wits and with a steadying breath, I pulled myself up to my full height. Squaring my shoulders and trying to look unfazed by what had just taken place, I plastered a fake smile on my face.

Looking up at him, I replied sweetly, "Yes, you're right. Good night." Turning on my heel, placing one foot steadily in front of the other, I attempted to focus my energy on absorbing the sensation of the cool flooring against my bare feet as I headed down to the doorway leading to my room. His piercing gaze was like a cool blanket on my back this time. As I closed the door behind me, I heard him mumbling something about dreams, but my heart wouldn't hear the words. Throwing myself across my bed, I quickly forgot my promise to avoid crying and gave in to the tears that were burning in the backs of my eyes. They flowed silently. Exhaustion took hold, and I cried myself to sleep.

A bright light pierced the veil of my mind as I struggled to see what was in front of me. A booming sound pounded in my brain like the sound of a large drum causing me to turn my head to my right. There, in a white gown surrounded by an ethereal glow and only an arms-length away from me, was the most extraordinary creature I'd ever seen. The light was so bright and intense, but I couldn't look away. Neither did I have a desire to shield my eyes. In awe, I couldn't help but think that she was almost the exact image of what I thought an angel might look like. She was speaking, but I couldn't hear what she was saying. A dawning comprehension spread across her lovely face and made her beautiful violet eyes shimmer.

Reaching out one fine and delicate hand toward me, a soft finger touched my forehead. A sudden jolt like a low-current electric shock pierced my frontal lobe and entered my body at the point between my eyes where Hindu's believe the third eye is. There was a popping sound that reminded me of rice cereal after milk had been added. This was soon followed by a muffled sound, deep and muddled.

Then I heard it, the most beautiful and soothing voice I'd ever heard. Instantly, a feeling of euphoria filled me, and a deep

The Tree and the Tablet

abiding calmness surrounded my entire being. It struck me that the sensation was sort of like that feeling a baby would feel upon hearing the comforting sound of their mother's voice for the first time. The encompassing shine around the woman diminished gradually until standing before me was a being of amazing beauty and grace. Flowing white hair that easily reached her calves, delicate features, tall and slender, dressed in a gossamer, iridescent white dress that shimmered with every movement, moved closer to me.

Smiling softly at me, her mouth opened, and a sweet musical sound flowed from between her lips. While she was speaking English, her mouth movements didn't match. "Little one. Can you hear me?" Blinking rapidly, I nodded slowly. Another soft smile, "Time is short. You must right the wrong. Go back to your beginnings and seek the knowledge you have lost. It is the only way."

Puzzled, I asked, "What's happening? What must I do? I don't understand...".

She interrupted me, "Seek to use your gift and you will find the proper path. There is so much more within you. You must remember. I cannot help you with this. I must leave you now, but please don't give up. Our time is short and we need your help." She started to fade away.

"Wait! What does that mean?" My hand stretched out toward her to grasp empty space and in that moment, she was gone. A shuddering quake started and there was a deep rumble

227

that seemed to be coming from below me. The ground began to shake more violently and then fell out from under me causing me to plummet head-first into nothing. I was falling through space and time.

Particles of the ground that used to be below me now floated up to me as I fell past them. As I raised my arms to shield myself from the flying debris, a large piece of earth gouged my arm, sending blood spewing out like little bubbles. Clasping my hand over the wound in my left arm, I screamed and closed my eyes, not wanting to see my demise rise up to crush me from below. Just when I thought there'd be no end to the maddening fall, I landed with a thud. It felt like my soul slammed into the presence of my human form. Sensing that I was still alive somehow, I opened my eyes and the darkness of my room met my gaze. Looking at the clock on my bedside table it read 3:33 a.m.

Rolling to my side, I stood up and walked to the French doors that led out to the deck. Opening the door, I stepped outside into the cool dark air. There was no moon tonight. It was so dark that the only light was that of the twinkle lights in the bushes. Smiling to myself, I thought of the time Mom and I had decided to put them in when I was five years old and had just had a particularly bad dream that caused me to wander through mom's room and outside.

Mom had followed me, but it had been extremely dark, remarkably similar to tonight. She'd tripped off the back deck while she was trying to find me, which caused her to scream out

The Tree and the Tablet

with pain. Somehow the sound of mom in pain woke me, and I was suddenly frightened because I didn't know where I was or how to find her in the dark. Moments later, I tripped over her and landed roughly on her head. After she soothed my fears and we had both calmed down, we laughed for a bit about my falling on her head. She ended up with a small scar on her forehead, but it was barely visible and she called it a love mark. She'd always wink at me when she'd explain to someone what it was.

Reaching the end of the deck, I sat down on the edge. Ruminating on the dream, or were they really visions and not dreams at all? The angel-lady had said I needed to find what I had lost. *Was she talking about my visions or my ability to communicate telepathically? Or was it more? Blast it all, why couldn't someone just say what they meant?*

Five years I'd spent blocking everything out. Before that, I'd spent many more years trying to shut it out with some success. It had taken one devastating loss for me to close my mind. After the vision of mom, and the ensuing pain and realization that I could've prevented what happened if I'd only told mom that I saw her in danger. If I'd listened to the warnings and embraced the vision of her surrounded by water, just maybe... That was when I decided that I was done with visions and shut the doors of possibility. Having been hurt by my telepathic abilities with 'Drea as a teen, I hadn't used that form of communication with her either.

After mom and Russel disappeared with Jaxon's parents, I

kept having a recurring dream that Mom was alive. But after eighty days of continuous fruitless searches for her at my insistence, combined with a dwindling search team, I decided that I was wrong about them being alive. That's when I worked diligently to shut the dreams up and stopped holding out hope for something that wouldn't happen. By ignoring them and blocking them out, eventually, they stopped completely. Maybe, if I'd kept them, I could've prevented 'Drea's death. Looking up at the stars, I chastised myself for that pattern of thinking. Honestly, my visions had never served a purpose before, they'd just been scary images that didn't make sense.

Now, looking back on my past, and all the visions that I'd had, I could see that there was some truth to them. Andrea and I used to be able to communicate through space and time using our minds only. Well, it was only me. We tested it once, but Andrea couldn't get through to me unless I initiated it. That's why I thought it was odd that Tree-Andrea could communicate with Bird-Jaxon telepathically.

We never told mom about our ability to talk in our minds. Andrea never had the visions, either, unless she was with me. We knew that I had a special gift, but I saw the effect it had on mom, so I hid it as much as I could to save her from her own fears. However, I was never able to really control how I reacted to my dreams or visions. They were so strong, and she always caught me. If she knew I was hiding my visions from her, she never let on. My sleep visions were so much more intense than the ones I had during the day.

A cold breeze wafted over me, reminding me that I was sitting outside in December with only a pair of shorts and a T-shirt on. Talking to myself about the absurdity of sitting in the cold in the dead of winter, I stood up and went back inside. As I turned to close the door behind me, I thought I saw a shadow moving toward the dining room doorway. Stepping back out into the yard, I looked over and there was nothing. Shrugging, I figured my mind was playing tricks on me and went back inside. Snuggling down into my nice warm bed, I started practicing my meditation breathing. Soon, I was fast asleep and wandering through the corners of my mind searching for something I'd lost.

CHAPTER 16

The sun woke me as it shined through my open curtains onto my face. Peace and serenity filled my soul. There was nothing like the feeling of sunshine in the morning. Something about it invigorated me and made me feel alive. Most people would probably say the same thing, but it felt somehow different in my mind. It felt like I was a rechargeable battery and the sun's rays were the energy source I needed to regain my power.

Sitting up and stretching my arms widely to absorb as much as I could of the glorious rays, I became aware that I felt different somehow. Closing my eyes, I focused on the feelings of energy coursing through my body. Pushing my thoughts outward, I concentrated on Andrea.

A whirling and spinning sensation coursed through my mind, causing me to feel slightly off balance. Soon my world righted itself and I was standing face to face with Andrea; however, I wasn't looking at a tree, it was Andrea in human form. Almost as if I were on some sort of astral plain. The sky was the loveliest shade of iridescent purple filled with shimmering clouds of gossamer looking material. The floor beneath me was the most luscious and verdant green and felt like the softest moss under my bare feet. Blinking my eyes as if I were trying to focus, I looked up again and Andrea was smiling at me.

"I knew you could do it, Magpie." She exclaimed exuberantly. Dancing in a circle around me, she laughed and grasping me tightly, we were both giggling and dancing as we lost our balance and tumbled to the ground. It was as if she hadn't died. My heart raced as I realized I could feel her, see her, touch her and I felt wonderfully alive. My mind took over and sighing, I rolled to my stomach. Propping myself up on my elbows, I looked long and hard at my sister laying on the soft ground next to me.

"Andrea,"— afraid of the answer but posing the question anyway — "how is it that you're here when in the real world, you're...." Looking down at the soft earth and toying with the lush sponge-like material, I couldn't finish my question.

Running her hands over her body with a quizzical expression and looking at me, "I'm not sure." A brief frown crossed her brow, "I thought you did this."

"No, it wasn't me."

She looked as puzzled as I felt. Taking a moment to think and looking back at the sky, "I feel like I'm sharing space though"—Looking back at me, she asked, "Isn't that odd?"

"Yes, I suppose it is." *Was Andrea really here or was it just my mind playing tricks on me?* 'Well, it doesn't really matter, I'm just happy to have you here with me now." My grin split my face in two as I rolled onto my back. Grasping her upturned hand in mine, I sat up. Releasing her hand as I turned to look around and take in all the sights, I'd forgotten how beautiful this could be. It was almost like another world.

There were strange animals grazing in the distance that looked like a combination of a hippopotamus and a flamingo with a large round body covered in pink feathers and sporting a large bill that was curled downward. The head was broad and had large eyes. Large tusks protruded from beneath the bill, and the entire weight of this odd creature was balanced on two spindly looking legs. A chuckle caught in my throat at the odd site. What an amazing imagination she had. In the past, I'd always assumed it was Andrea's imagination fueling the strange visual representations when we would have our mind-links since she'd spent hours drawing odd pictures of things that we would see in these episodes.

Sighing and sitting up next to me, Andrea placed her hand on mine, which was still resting on the soft earth. "Isn't it

235

beautiful, Maggie?" She asked in awe.

Nodding my head, I turned to her, "'Drea, was it always like this?" My arm swept through the air indicating the expanse of the amazing visions stretched out as far as the eye could see.

"Oh, yes! Don't you remember?" Our eyes met for a moment and suddenly, it was like a key clicked in a lock. A flood of memories, sights, and sounds, as well as physical sensations and remembered smells, swirled through my mind.

Taking in a deep breath, refocusing my eyes, and exhaling, I exclaimed, "Oh....My.... God!" Tears filled my eyes.

Reaching over and wiping the tears away, she smiled gently, "Oh, Maggie, don't cry! It'll be okay."

Laughing, I replied knowingly, "Yes, it will!" Jumping up and grabbing Andrea's hands to pull her up next to me. Looking her in the eye, I asked, "Are you ready for this?" She nodded hesitantly but smiled reassuringly. Excitement coursed through me, "Okay, 'Drea, here we go." Instinctively, I raised my hands up, palms outstretched toward her.

Raising our arms in front of us, fully extended, and placing our hands approximately one inch from each other palm to palm, I closed my eyes and focused my energy outward. It felt like pushing out with one hand and pulling with the other, even though we weren't actually touching. Drawing on Andrea's energy, it felt like a force was circling between us and through us at the same time. A blue light flared between our hands, quickly becoming a line of light that held our hands from separating. Mist

The Tree and the Tablet

began to rise between us and with a sound like that of rushing water, Kelsey began to materialize between us. Her form was thin, like a wraith; however, her voice was strong like she was standing right in front of us. She didn't seem phased by what was happening at all. She smiled and asked, "Aunt Maggie? Mommy?" She looked at Andrea again, her eyes wide, "Mommy, you're alive?"

Smiling down at her, "No, love. We're in your mind."

She frowned for a moment. The sadness was quickly replaced with a giggle. "It feels funny in my tummy. Like I'm being tickled by the feathers on my scarf."

Grinning down at her cute little face, I said, "Yes, it does feel funny! It's a sort of magic trick." She giggled again. "Kelsey, I need you to focus for me. Listen carefully and tell me, what do you see and hear? Think about all the things that have happened. What have you seen? Did you see anything on the road when you were going to where you are? Any signs or posts or any stores or buildings?"

Kelsey put her head down to concentrate and looking up at me, she shook her head. "I'm sorry, Auntie, I fell asleep." She clenched her little fists in frustration. A sad look crossed her face, "I was so tired right after I was put in the big truck, I barely saw Peanut jump in and snuggle under the seat." She started to cry. Her voice trembled as she asked, "Are you going to come and get me today?" Her voice came now as a whisper, "I don't like it here." She looked over her shoulder, frightened eyes made

237

contact with mine.

Andrea tried to reassure her. "There's my brave girl, I love you so much."

Kelsey looked up at her, her lower lip quivering. "Mommy. Please don't leave me."

Andrea looked down on Kelsey lovingly, "Oh, sweet, angel. I'm always right in your heart, baby. I'll always be with you. Even when you can't see or hear me." Looking at mother and daughter, so sad and separated by tragedy, I couldn't help but feel a deep sorrow. However, that wasn't going to help Kelsey right now.

"Shh. It's okay, sweetie," my voice was calm and steady as I tried to sooth her. My heart hurt so bad. A desire to reach down and pluck her from wherever the hiding place was engulfed me, but I knew it wasn't possible and it wasn't helpful right then as I needed her to focus on her surroundings so I could find her. "Kelsey, I'm trying to get to you. Is there anything you can tell me? Are you eating? Are you warm?"

"Yes, he is giving us food and blankets. He talks to himself mostly. I just sit here quietly and pet Peanut." She smiled at that last confession.

"That's good, sweetie. What kinds of things does he say?"

Scrunching up her little face in consternation, she tilted her head sideways, "He mostly just mumbles a lot, but he talks about a... omelet?"

A small giggle at her word usage escaped me as I said, "You mean an amulet?"

The Tree and the Tablet

Nodding, she continued, "Yes, and dragons, and stones or birds made of rock and ledges? No, legends," she enunciated the word slowly, "but I don't really know for sure." She stopped and thought for a second, "Oh, and he said something about seven sisters and fingers." She looked at me, seeking approval.

Not really understanding what that meant but trying to comfort her and help her feel like she was being helpful, I lied smoothly, "Oh, Kelsey, that's really good." She smiled and I felt my power weakening, "Kelsey, I'll try to reach out to you like this again, but make sure you are a very good girl and listen carefully. Eat your food and try to stay still. I'll do everything I can to get to you. Do you understand?"

She nodded her head vigorously, "Do I have magic, too?"

"I'm not sure, sweetie." Inwardly, I wondered if this was magic, or if it was something else. Feeling like my energy was fading, I quickly reassured Kelsey, "Stay strong, love. We're doing everything we can to find you. I'll try to contact you again tonight if I can. Daddy's out looking for you too." Kelsey clapped her hands happily. "We love you, sweet girl."

She started to fade, "I'll be strong. I love you." Her voice faded as she spoke. With a popping sound, the light went out and the mist vanished. She was gone.

Tears streamed down Andrea's face. "Oh, Maggie!" Fiercely, I hugged her close.

"Andrea, we'll find her. I just know it." A voice that I recognized as Daniel was echoing around us calling my name.

239

Pushing myself away from Andrea, "I have to go back. I'll check in when I get a chance. Stay positive."

Andrea smiled and nodded. "Stay safe, Magpie."

The gossamer clouds fell around me pooling on the ground. A pulling sensation could be felt in my chest like someone had tied a string to my back and then strung it through my chest. It was as if someone then pulled the cord forcefully jerking me forward into an unknown and unseen destination. In my mind, I was falling with my eyes shut. Telling myself to open my eyes, I was suddenly transformed to a sitting position in the center of my bed seeming like I never left. Sunshine poured through the windows and Daniel opened my bedroom door. "Maggie?"

"Don't you ever knock?" I asked tersely.

Clearing his throat, he replied shamefaced, "Oh, I called out, but you didn't answer. I'm sorry." He was backing out of the doorway pulling the door closed. Popping his head back in the open door, briefly, he chirped, "The team will be here in an hour." He hesitated briefly to add, "Coffee's ready." He was already pulling the door closed again.

"Wait!" The door opened again, slowly, "Sorry, I'm not a morning person." He smiled as I hesitantly added, "Thanks for making coffee."

Another huge grin, "No problem. You might want to hurry, or I may drink it all," he teased.

His smile was infectious, and I returned it, "Okay. Thanks, again."

The Tree and the Tablet

As he closed the door, I jumped out of my bed, pulled on some jeans and a baby blue t-shirt, and quickly threw my hair into a messy bun. Quickly, I made my way into the kitchen to get a cup of coffee. Upon entering the kitchen, I saw that he'd packed a backpack full of stuff and there was a spread of scrambled eggs, toast, bacon, and juice on the island. Raising my eyebrows, I looked at him, "You did this?"

Shrugging his shoulders, he smiled and said, "Eat. You need to be ready. We'll have a lot of hours of hiking ahead of us."

At a loss for words, I sat down and filled a plate, "Wow! Thanks!" He nodded at me and handed me a cup of coffee. As reveled in my first sip of the warm brew, I could tell, he had been observant as there was the perfect amount of creamer. Smiling broadly, I nodded at him in affirmation of a well-made cup of joe and we both ate hardily.

He offered to clean up and asked me to go pack a backpack that he handed me. "No makeup or silly stuff. Just necessities."

"That won't be a problem, I rarely wear makeup." A devil-may-care grin was plastered on my face as I walked back down to my room to pack a couple pairs of pants, socks, shirts, and underwear. After washing my face and hands, I pulled out my hiking boots and some wool socks and headed back down the hallway. It must have taken longer than I thought it would because no sooner had I put on my boots then the doorbell rang. Startled, I jumped, and I swear it took a full thirty seconds to get my heart back out of my throat and into its natural position within my chest.

Daniel walked across the living room toward the front door holding his hand out to stop me from rising to answer the door. Upon opening the door, a boisterous and beautiful woman of a little over five foot came barging in the door followed by a younger male who appeared to be Native American. The woman stopped in front of me and looking over her shoulder at Daniel, she said, "You are introducing us, yes?" Her accent was not too thick, and I could tell she was probably from some other country. If I had to guess, I'd say the accent was Russian. She placed her hands on her hips, still waiting. Tapping her foot impatiently, she expounded, "Well? You are waiting for me to maybe sniff her butt like dog?" Squinting her eyes, she continued to stare at him.

Daniel laughed hysterically. "Tatyana, this is Maggie St. James." He waved in my direction.

The vivacious woman now turned toward me and said quite matter-of-factly reaching her hand toward me, "It is nice to meeting you. I am very exciting to start this trip." Having reached out to shake her hand, she pumped my hand vigorously with hers and asked, "You are ready to go?" *Was that a question or a statement?*

Daniel then turned and said, "Maggie, this is Joseph." He turned and allowed Joseph to step forward from his hiding place behind him. He was smiling slightly at Tatyana and reaching up with two fingers, made a slight salute and nodded his head, "Ma'am."

The Tree and the Tablet

Raising my hand partially, I sort of gave him a little wave and said, "Hi."

Tatyana then turned to Daniel and said, "Well, the moon is not waiting on you. Let us go." With that, she grabbed Daniel's pack and headed back out the front door. Joseph followed behind and Daniel stepped over to where I sat stunned and silent.

Well, this ought to be interesting.

Daniel smiled and said, "Yes, it should."

Turning to him surprised, I wondered for a moment if he could read my mind, realizing that I probably said that out loud. He just turned to me and said, "You should probably watch what you say around Tatyana." At my questioning look, he shrugged and said, "Or don't, it's not my butt." Laughing, he handed me my pack and said, "I let Andrea know we were going to be leaving when you were getting packed. Do you want to say goodbye?"

Geez! When would I learn to keep my mouth shut? Feeling a little peeved for speaking my thoughts out loud, I was still excited and anxious to talk to 'Drea, so I replied over my shoulder, "Yes, I'll be right back," and headed out the back door.

"Andrea." The tree came to life.

"Maggie." The bark shifted forming the shape of a smile on her lips. "It was real, wasn't it?" She exclaimed. As I nodded, her excited squeal perforated the silent morning air and while I was a little surprised by the affirmation, inside I'd already known the

243

answer to my unspoken question. Sensing my next questions, her branches fluttered even though there was no breeze and she spoke in a rush, "Jaxon's searching based on the information I gave him."

"Has he found anything else that would be helpful?"

"He said that there is a sign that read Sold U C?" She said it more like a question than a statement. My mind worked through what she said and inhaling sharply with comprehension, I smiled.

"Sol Duc!" Excitement made me jump up and down as I exclaimed. "It's an area west of here that has a hiking trail, a valley, waterfalls, and the River is fed by a grouping of inlets called the seven sisters." Clapping my hands together quickly, I exclaimed, "Yes! That must be it!"

"Oh, Maggie." Andrea sounded so hopeful. Seeing that I was firmly set on my idea, she commanded me "Well, what are you waiting for? Go get my baby!"

Laughing and filled with eagerness, I said, "Yes, Ma'am." Smiling and turning on my heel, I left my home and my sister without looking backward. Stepping out the front door into the sunshine, I looked up at Daniel and said, "Well, the moon's not waiting on you." Laughing raucously over my shoulder at him, I stepped lightly to the truck waiting outside and noticed that Tatyana was scowling at me, I flashed a funny little smile in her direction and jumped into the passenger seat.

CHAPTER 17

*L*ooking the window, I could see that Daniel was still standing on the front step contemplating my words. There was a small frown on his face, but he must have decided that time was pressing as he made his way to the truck and jumped into the driver's seat. Looking at me sideways, he asked, "Any ideas on where we should go?"

"Oh, Yes!" My voice squeaked slightly —too excited— clearing my throat, "Let me see your map and I'll show you."

"Here you go." Opening the map wide, I swiftly pointed at a spot that he'd already marked on the map with a red "x" surrounded by a large circle. Looking up at him with a question in my eyes, he responded, "Based on the writings in the journal, we had figured the tablet to be somewhere in the area that's marked." Attentively, I watched him move his slender finger across the map as he outlined the riddles and drawings in the journal which seemed familiar to him.

Glancing over the map to make eye contact, I asked, "But, where's the journal?"

Daniel reached into his backpack and handed me a leather-bound notebook covered in dirt and smudged with bloody fingerprints. Tentatively reaching for the journal, I dreaded what I'd find within it. Looking up at him questioningly, he shrugged, "I presume it's from his many months in the forest. I've tried to clean it, but it won't come off."

Sighing, I said, "Well, we have a ways to go to get there, so we should probably be going. I'll see if I can make any sense of the writings in the journal while we travel."

Smiling gently at me, "We have tried to figure out his writings, but if you have some other information from Andrea and Jaxon that will help, I welcome a new set of eyes." He put the truck in drive and reached out the open window, signaling for Tatyana and Joseph to follow us.

Pulling the vehicle out into the highway, I looked back at my home briefly and wondered if I'd ever be back. Chiding myself for being silly, I sent a little prayer outward to the universe to watch over Andrea, Jaxon, Kelsey, and Peanut. Soon, I refocused my energy on the task at hand... Deciphering this ridiculous journal.

The Tree and the Tablet

Flipping through the pages on the old leather-bound book, I could see how the passion for the ancient Mayan legends was woven into each and every page. There were drawings and hieroglyphs and various phrases written throughout. The edges of each page were slightly frayed and worn with staining from being continuously touched. There were smudges and fingerprints throughout. One page, in particular, caught my interest. It contained a drawing of a clawed foot and below it a phrase and poem of sorts was scrawled across the page.

Beware the Golem. Hmm. This sounds interesting, I thought.

Beware the Winged Warrior who perches precariously upon the precipice of peace.

On the side of the page there was a rough drawing of a creature that looked remarkably like a jade dragon but had a more squared looking head. My fingers gently traced the outline of the drawing and I felt a little tingling sensation as excitement and uncertainty coursed through my veins. As I read the words written below the drawing, I became intrigued to see what it all meant. The words of the poem danced in my vision...

He who travels the lands of woe
Will surely find a friend or foe.
A heart so pure will find the scrolls
That the winding paths will unfold.
His sight obscured will shift and wane

Kathryn O'Brien

And soon the world will feel the pain
Of the wanderer's weary flights
Throughout the long and troubled nights.
You must look deeply through the mist
To find the seer's catalyst
Viewing creation's cloaked desires
Feeding the flames of hidden fires.
In the tree of ancient power
Lies the seed of the God's flower.
The flame of a lover's pain beget
The moon-stone seer's amulet
The lover's pain will right the wrong
Bringing forth the sister's song
Truth of light and virtue strong
She who sings the golem's song
Can hold the key of divine light
To wield the words of strength and might.
Beware the beast that lies within,
Whose raven's claws will surely win.
Only purpose of truth and light
Will save you from the dragon's plight.

Looking up and glancing out the window to watch the scenery passing by, I considered the riddle and its words. *What did it mean? What was the dragon's plight?* Shrugging, I decided to come back to it later and promptly placed a small piece of scrap paper in the folds so that I could find it easily. I happened to see Daniel eyeing me curiously but he didn't speak so I refocused my energy on trying to find more information in the book.

As I thumbed through the pages, I couldn't help but notice that there were a multitude of drawings throughout with scrawling handwritten notes next to each. Some of the information was difficult to decipher and understand as I didn't know what the different symbols meant. As I turned the page, I found myself staring at a drawing of a creature that looked remarkably similar to the one that I saw when I was in my dream state with Andrea. My breath caught in my throat and I choked on my own saliva because I'd inhaled so sharply. The force of my coughing sent me forward, leaning against the dash. Daniel reached over and whacked me on the back. *Not helpful.*

Putting my hand up, I waved him off. In a strangled voice still trying to control the urge to cough, I sputtered, "I'm okay. Just inhaled wrong." He looked at me skeptically and handed me a flask, "It's water."

Still lightly coughing and swallowing convulsively to try and stop the process, I nodded and opened the flask, taking a long swig. Slowly, I could feel myself starting to gain control. As I was handing back the flask, I could see a grin on his face that belied his concern and laughing with him, I said, "Thanks."

He smiled again and said, "My pleasure." Glancing sideways at me for a brief second, he quickly looked back to the road and asked, "Is there anything you want to discuss?"

Playing with my lower lip, I decided to forgo a conversation about the mysterious creature until a later time. Asking instead, "How much further? I kind of need to use the restroom."

He smiled knowingly and replied, "There's a rest stop at the base of the mountain before we head up to Sol Duc, which is about another 10 minutes out. Do you think you can hold it that long?"

My eyebrows rose in surprise. That was fast. It seemed like we had only left a couple minutes ago, and we were already almost there? Tilting my head sideways, "Do you have some sort of special fuel in this truck?" Looking out the back window, "I mean, I haven't been absorbed in the journal for the entire three-hour ride, have I?" A quick glance at my watch proved the fallacy of my words, but still, it seemed like time was standing still.

Briefly, he scrunched up his eyebrows in a concerned look, asking, "Can you wait ten more minutes?"

Nodding, "Sure." With a sideways glance, "Daniel?"

"Yes?"

"Do you know anything about the area?" My lower lip started to ache from chewing on it so much.

"Well, there are some legends, but the language has been forgotten and there are only vague interpretations left because the actual meaning of the words is sort of...lost." He glanced at me, "Why do you ask?"

Looking out the window, I wondered aloud, "Well, I read

something in the journal about seven sisters and a great warrior chief named Duc who became lost in the forest." The clouds had parted, and the sun shone through at that moment right into my eyes. Closing my eyes against the glare but rejoicing in the heat that radiated on my face, I continued, "There was a reference to a well of souls and in the corner of the drawing on that page, I saw the word Sol spelled the same as the area." Glancing at him, "Do you think they're related?"

Squinting his eyes against the sudden brightness, "I thought so, too." His smile beamed at me so brightly, I almost melted right there on the spot. The light glinting in his green eyes made them appear a brilliant soft green like the color of Colombian emeralds. It was fascinating the way his eyes changed color with his moods or maybe it was just different lighting that caused it. Either way, it was one of my favorite features on him.

A slow blush rose across my face and smothering my need to reach out and touch him, I sat on my hands and asked, "Have you heard of the falls of the seven sisters?"

Raising his eyebrows at me, he turned back to driving and very quietly, he asked, "How did you know we needed to go to Sol Duc?"

Still not ready to share everything with him yet, I lied. Well, it wasn't a full lie, it was a partial lie. I'd convinced myself that it wouldn't hurt to keep a little to myself and besides, I couldn't have him thinking I was totally bonkers, could I? A curt smile crossed my lips, "Andrea said that Jaxon had found a sign but when she told me what it said, it took me a bit to figure out what it meant." Trying to hide my face, I turned away toward the sunshine. "I used to go camping at Sol Duc a lot when I was younger. It was my favorite place to be. That's when I decided what I would study in college."

Smiling to myself, I remembered when Andrea and I got lost in that very same forest. It took us hours to figure out how to get back to the camp, but I'd paid attention to the many books I read about moss growth and how certain trees and plants will grow toward the sun even when they don't have an actual line of sight to the sun based on the way the trees reacted to the sunlight and the photosynthesis.

Interrupting my memories, he asked, "What did you study?"

"Well, initially, I was going to be a lawyer." Out of the corner of my eye I saw his surprised expression which was accompanied by a short bark of laughter which caused me to chuckle. Turning toward him, I sputtered, "I know. Could you imagine me standing in front of a room full of people, talking?" He didn't speak but waited for me to continue, "Anyway, I always had a passion for trees, so I changed my major to arboriculture."

He nodded as he spoke in a deep and appreciative tone, "I decided to drop law classes to study forestry because of my love of the woods."

Facing him, I couldn't hide the beaming smile and total adoration directed his way. I'm pretty sure I audibly sighed, because he sort of looked at me and tried to hide that he knew

The Tree and the Tablet

why. He was applying pressure to the brakes and turning off the road into a clearing. We pulled up to an area for hiking that had a parks and recreation restroom at the end of the parking lot. A large sign read, *Sol Duc National Park*. As he put the truck in park, I smoothly jumped out, closing the door behind me. Seeing the restroom sign on a building at the end of the lot, I felt the tingle of urgent need pressing on my bladder as I trekked in that direction. Wondering if he was watching me walk to relieve myself, a flush of mortification crept up my cheeks. Swallowing hard, I put my head down and headed into the structure.

That was when I heard Tatyana's voice ring out in her broken English, "Hey, why you are stopping here?"

Daniel's deep voice rang out strong and certain, "Because this is where we need to be."

She didn't argue as I heard a door close, she hollered, "Yoseph, get out!" This was followed by the sound of another car door slamming shut, but I didn't hear much else as I was entering the restroom and the heavy door closed behind me. Once inside, I entered a stall and took care of business. Oh, good Lord. It felt like I'd drunk two pots of coffee.

As my bladder began to relax, my eyes closed in relief, I started to feel like I was swimming in a murky pool. My world shifted and as I took some deep breaths, I realized that my inner senses were tuned into something. Calmly, I focused my energy outward and was surprised when I suddenly was looking down on the restroom exterior through an interesting set of eyes. It was like looking through one eye and seeing one thing and looking through the other, there was a different view. Almost like looking through a prism and it made me dizzy. Suddenly, I heard, "Maggie?" I just about fell off the toilet as I realized that I'd somehow made a mind-link with Jaxon while I was using the restroom.

Almost instantly, I became fully aware of my surroundings and broke the connection. Taking a few deep breaths, I righted my world and exited the stall. After washing my hands, I quickly dashed some cold water on my face and got my angst under control. That was entirely too uncomfortable; however, I now knew that Jaxon was nearby.

As I was stepping out of the restroom to start back toward the truck, Tatyana was coming in and we ran full into each other. She spun as I hit her and turning on her heel managed to balance herself and me while settling us in the correct positions on the opposite of where we once were. Inhaling sharply, I uttered, "Sorry."

She looked me over and nodded curtly with a disapproving expression and said, "I guess I am having to watch out for you if you can't be watching yourself." With that, she promptly headed into the restroom without another word. Exasperated, I chuckled and shook my head as I continued toward the truck and Daniel.

Awestruck, I found myself totally dumbfounded by the brilliant view of Daniel that was before me. For some reason, he'd removed his shirt and was standing in the sunshine like some half

The Tree and the Tablet

naked god. The muscles rippled on his chest and arms as he reached into the back of the pickup and pulled out a backpack. It must have been heavy, as his muscles bulged under the strain and I was totally mesmerized. Joseph had said something to him from the other side of the pickup and he turned smiling at his words. He laughed and his brilliant white teeth sparkled against his beautiful bronze skin. The light glinted off his shiny black hair and made it look like there was a band of turquoise on his head. I was standing there like a lovestruck teenager when Jaxon decided to make himself known to the others.

Like a bombardier dropping a payload, he swiftly flew across the clearing from a branch in the trees and smoothly dropped a load of poop right in the middle of Daniel's head. The look of horror and utter astonishment that crossed his face sent me into fits of giggles. He turned toward me and crossing his arms, gave me the sternest look he could muster. Promptly, I fell to the ground and began laughing so hard I could barely breathe. Hysteria soon took hold.

Tatyana had exited the restroom just in time to witness the entire thing and standing next to me, she let her guard down just enough to join me in my explosion of humor with her own great gulping guffaws that made me laugh even harder. As I was attempting to bring air into my lungs, she suddenly snorted and that sent us both into another fit. Daniel cursed and grabbed a rag, pouring some water on his head while Joseph tried to remove the offending offal from the crown of Daniel's head.

Kathryn O'Brien

Jaxon landed on the back of the pickup and began tweeting and chirping excitedly. Not sure if my brother-in-law did it on purpose or if it were an accident but I just couldn't get the sheer look of outrage that crossed Daniel's face out of my mind. Trying to catch my breath, I laid on the ground watching the shifting sky above me.

The clouds moved in rapidly, darkening the sky and a flood gate opened, which promptly drenched all of us before we had a chance to collect ourselves. That was a sobering experience and soon we were all standing near the truck attempting to gather our belongings so that we could make our way inland toward the lake. After a cursory look at the map and a determined direction, we started our journey into the land of unknown possibilities. Jaxon hopped onto Daniel's pack and we were soon on our way.

Looking down at my wet feet, I couldn't help but feel a little slighted at the sudden gloom that cast its shadow on our journey. Refocusing my gaze ahead of me and deciding that determination would win the day, I said a little prayer as we started our miserable hike. The entire time, I wondered what we would find. Only time would tell, but we were running out of that too.

CHAPTER 18

Trudging along the trail, I pulled the journal out and turned my focus to the intricate writings while trying to keep my eyes on the group so that I wouldn't get lost, which is extremely easy to do in the dense forest. There were a multitude of smaller, less conspicuous trails that led off the sides of the main trail we were following. The plan was to make our way to the edge of the lake where the seven sisters creek fed into it. From there, we would make camp and determine where to go next.

Daniel handed me the journal, "You should keep this. So far, your view on things has been a bit different and I think you might bring a new perspective to some of the other areas as well."

Beaming under his positive appraisal, I responded, "I'll do my best."

Once again, Tatyana gasped loudly, "Daniel?" When he turned to face her, she spat out, "This is the only clue we are having. You are sure is good idea?" Even though her voice was strong and steady, she sounded very apprehensive, "She is not part of team." She glanced over to me and then back to Daniel to wait for his response.

Quickly I offered, "I don't want to cause trouble, if she wants to carry the journal, I can..."

Daniel interrupted me, "No, Maggie. You will keep the journal and continue to look through it for clues." Turning back to Tatyana, he addressed her in a calm voice like he would speak to a child, "Maggie is with us because of her niece. She is more a part of this team than any of us. She **will** keep the journal for now. Everything else we need to know is right here," he said tightly as he pointed to his head. "Any other questions?"

She grudgingly gave in and was quick to shake her head as she turned to stomp off.

Joseph winked at me when Tatyana had stormed off toward the trail and briefly stopped to deal with her pack saying, "Don't mind her. Her bark is worse than her bite." At my doubting look, he laughed and said, "Underneath her rough talk is the heart of a playful kitten. Trust me."

Staring at Tatyana who was busy preparing her pack with exaggerated, stiff movements, I shook my head doubtfully, and

The Tree and the Tablet

said, "Yeah, right."

He just grinned and shrugged, "You'll see." He made his way over to help her lift her ridiculously large pack onto her back. Seeing that she was so petite, the thing looked immense on her. However, she stood to her full height under the weight and I admired her spunk and tenacity. They put their heads together for a moment. It appeared they were talking quietly to each other as if they were the closest of lovers. It was then that I noticed the light in his eyes when he looked at her and the returning expression of tenderness when she looked at him. *Ah, ha! They're in love!* They had both turned and looked at me and I immediately busied myself with my own preparations.

As I walked along, I thought about that revelation as I watched Joseph calmly keep pace behind Tatyana. He would casually reach out a strong hand to steady her every time the weight of her giant pack caused her to begin to sway off the path. It all made sense though. They made quite the cute couple. Two opposites but totally complementary to one another. Kind of like molten lava meeting the ocean. He was the ocean, all calm, cool, and collected. She was the lava, fire, brimstone, and passion. Together, they made an island.

I want an island, I thought as I glanced up ahead to where Daniel was trekking determinedly toward our destination. My heart skipped a beat and instinctively my tongue darted out to moisten my suddenly dry lips. He turned to look back at me as if he sensed I was watching him. Instantly, I looked back down to my work of studying the journal.

Following a sound to my right, I never looked up and continued to look through the book in my hands. Lost in my reading of the journal, I skimmed several pages studying every nuance. Something caught my eye on the page in front of me I hadn't noticed when I was looking at it just a few moments ago. Suddenly, it made sense. Following another sound to my right, I kept trekking along and read the map in front of me. It showed a clawed hand. Between the fingers were what looked like small rivers. Trees were drawn all around them. Below the drawing was a verse that said, between the fingers of the seven sisters lies the key. Next was a drawing of a rocky outcropping at the base of the fingers. My mind ran through the many different possibilities of things that it could mean. Stopping for a moment and looking up, I was startled to see that I'd wandered off on one of the side trails and that I had lost sight of the team. Surely someone would have noticed if I were too far back and said something? Peering around, there was no sign of the group. How the heck did I manage to get lost? Scolding myself for keeping my face in the book when I should have been focusing on the group ahead, I realized that it wasn't their fault. They were trying to keep to the trail and probably hadn't even noticed. The forest was so dense, I should've paid better attention.

Shouldering the blame for becoming lost, fear gripped my heart, and I started panicking. Closing my eyes, I focused my energy on drawing in several deep breaths. Reminding myself that

The Tree and the Tablet

I'd be able to focus better if I was calm, I worked on my breathing for a moment. Once I gained my wits, I turned around and started back toward the main trail.

After several hundred yards, I came to another small trail that led off to the right of the one I was on. Looking up, I checked for any kind of sign that it was the direction I should go. Not being able to remember what the other trail looked like and seeing that every tree was covered in a thick coating of moss, I suddenly felt overwhelmed. *Well, they say, if you're lost, stay in one place and someone will find you.*

With that thought in mind, I quickly looked around and assessed my situation. There was a large stump of a fallen tree next to where I stood and I decided to make a shelter and settle in under the cover of it. Pulling a rain cover out of my pack, I rigged it up to provide me a roof of sorts, laid my waterproof pack on the ground and promptly sat down to nibble on some granola that I'd found in my pack.

Either the storm was getting more intense or I'd been walking for a lot longer than I thought I had. Darkness was setting in. Pulling my pack out from under my rear end, I rummaged through it and found a glow stick and some items to allow me the ability to start a fire. Smiling to myself, I started gathering items to build my fire.

It wasn't difficult to build a fire, there'd recently been a windstorm in the area which caused some of the loose, dry, wood to fall from the trees. This made it much easier for me to gather the things I'd need to keep a fire going for an extended time frame. There was a heavy weight sleeping bag rolled up, attached to the bottom of my pack. After clearing the debris from under my covered area, I laid it out and got comfortable.

After taking a couple gulps off my water bottle, I thought to myself how suddenly calm and comfortable I felt. Briefly, I wondered why the group hadn't noticed I was missing yet, but then again, I was the one who got lost. I laughed raucously and found myself snorting. Another nervous chuckle escaped my mouth again and I settled into my space to review the journal some more, reflecting on the writings within it. The fire was blazing nicely which lulled me into a warm state of fuzzy sleepiness. Soon, I was drifting off into a befuddled state of euphoria. My eyelids drooped and I was sound asleep.

A haze of purple clouded my vision. Suddenly, there was what looked like gnarled and clawed fingers in front of me. Feeling as though I were looking at myself, I was confused because it wasn't me. Seeing haggard clothing, I ran my hands over it and was shaken by the unfamiliar cloth in my grasp. There was a small puddle of water where some minuscule light reflected within it. Slowly leaning forward and bracing myself for what I may see within the puddle's reflection, I took a deep breath in preparation and closed my eyes as I reached the edge.

Grappling with my need to see, but fearful of what would present itself to me as my reflection, I stuck my neck out to hover over the shiny surface and opened my eyes. As they began to

The Tree and the Tablet

focus on the image, I gasped. Placing my clawed hand up to my face, I was looking at a dragon. *But Dragons aren't real, are they?* With everything I'd been through lately, I decided to go with it.

In reality, it couldn't be anything else as the huge eyes looked like those of a cat with large yellow orbs staring at the reflection in the water, which blinked repeatedly. Poking my nostrils and running my claws along the jagged fangs protruding from the front of my snout, I was amazed by what I saw. The tattered cloth had been replaced with what looked to be layers of rocks. Or maybe it was scales. It was too dark to tell. Inside my head, I heard a deep rumbling voice. "Hello, Earth Child, daughter of Valor. I have waited long to feel your presence again."

My mind whirled. In my own feminine voice, I heard my words, "Are you talking to me?"

A deep rumbling laugh followed. "Yes, little one. I have been waiting for you to arrive. I feel your presence is near."

This has got to be a joke.

"What is a joke?" Came the rumbling question.

"What?" Realizing the dragon could hear my thoughts, I replied, "Oh, sorry, a joke is when you tell someone something that's unbelievable or funny." The reflection of the dragon cocked its head to the side and scrunched up its face as if it were trying to determine the meaning of what I had just said. I expounded, "You know? To make someone laugh?"

"Ahhh. I remember this." His face seemed to relax with comprehension. "It has been a very long time since I have laughed." He sighed. Looking over his shoulder, he proclaimed in a hushed voice, "There are others nearby. I smell them. Mostly I feel the presence of the tiny one and the small animal."

Gasping, I asked, "You are near to Kelsey and Peanut?"

"What is a Kelsey and a Peanut?" He chimed quizzically. He then said, "There is one who smells badly though. That one is not quite right and there is a smell of fear and unbalance about it."

Calming my racing heart, I asked, "The little one is named Kelsey and the other is a small dog named Peanut." I smiled mentally at his look of understanding followed by a mirrored smile in the pool of water. "Can you tell if they are okay?"

"Yes, they are fine. No need to worry. The little Kelsey has a strong warrior's heart and her little Peanut is very good at keeping her calm."

Sighing with relief, I queried, "What's your name?"

Steady and strong came the response, "I am Duck, the guardian of the tablet of power, a guide to those who are of the house of Valor, possessing the eye of Shalandria and seeking to right the wrong." I giggled. I really couldn't help it. Pulling himself up to his full height and glaring into the pool of water he retorted, "What is funny that I have said?"

"I'm sorry, Duck, but your name doesn't fit your stature or your appearance. Who named you?"

"It was many years ago, but my creator, Shalandria, of Valor, gave me this endearment when I was brought into being."

"You mean when you hatched?"

Duck shook his head slowly. "No, she created me from the stone within these caves for her daughter as a wedding present." His voice became deep and monotonous as he calmly recited, "I am of this earth, brought into being by the Goddess. I was transported to this land as a guide to the tablet and protector of the house of Valor until the day that she who is of earth and fire will come into her power. She will unleash the sacred song of the seven sisters and bear the strength of the amulet's fire to vanquish the evil one's heir into obscurity with love and light." His voice trailed off as he completed this prophetic phrase.

Reminded of the words within the journal I wondered aloud, "But, who is that and what does it mean, Duck?"

At that moment, Duck turned rapidly away from the pool. His next words met my ears as if they were a whisper that was quickly fading on a breeze, "Someone approaches. I must leave you now. Rest now, daughter of Valor, for soon you will need to focus much of your energy toward the greater good." A deep silence met my ears.

"Duck?" Calling out again, "Duck?" A deep nothingness responded to my pleas. Darkness was closing in on me and reaching out my hand which now looked like my own, I whispered once more into the void, "Duck...." the silence surrounded me and my soul was calmly lifted into a state of bliss as I drifted into a calm and soothing slumber.

CHAPTER 19

The first sound I heard was the calm and soothing birdsong of a robin somewhere nearby. Shortly after that came the raucous cry of a really loud and annoying raven. Opening my eyes and squinting in the direction of the offensive screeching, I found the largest black bird standing on a branch of the fallen tree, hopping up and down, back and forth and staring at me with an accusatory look. I laughed, "Well, good morning, Mr. Happy Pants!" Giggling again at myself for talking with a crow, it cawed flamboyantly at me one more time before it flew away. The little robin made its way down to rest on the ground near me. Looking at me sideways, I guessed that I'd been found.

"Good Morning, Jaxon." Shivering slightly, I wrapped my arms around myself and looked for some wood to throw on the dying embers. Glancing up through the trees, I guessed that it was somewhere around dawn, but without being able to see the exact placement of the sun, it was difficult to determine the time. Fiddling with the fire for a bit, I came to the realization that I was going to be leaving soon and decided to throw dirt on the fire rather than wood. As I shivered again, I sat pensively and watched my remaining hopes of warmth dwindle under the moist earth I'd kicked over the embers as I listened to my surroundings. Looking at Jaxon, I tilted my head sideways and asked a bit tersely, "So, I assume this means that you'll be able to lead me to the team now?" I was slightly miffed that Daniel hadn't come to my rescue. After all, if Jaxon could find me, then so could Daniel.

My frown was aimed at the dying coals of the fire, while I contemplated my next move when the beautiful bird hopped up and down and twittered the most awkward sounds. Again, I was awed by the interesting and odd noises he made having never heard anything like it from a robin before. Surfacing from my contemplation, it made me grin. Glancing around for a spot to relieve myself, I quipped, "Well, then, I'll need some privacy for a moment and then you can lead me to them." He responded by turning his back to me. My laughter was so loud, a group of startled bushtits soared into the air from its hiding spot a few feet away. It was quite comical that I was standing in the woods, talking

The Tree and the Tablet

to a robin.

After I was finished, I packed up my belongings and prepared for our trek out of my hidden fort. Piercing Jaxon with an expectant expression, I bowed low, sweeping my hand outward and sarcastically spouted, "After you, my liege." Laughing at myself, I waited for his response.

He flitted from branch to branch, waiting patiently for me to catch up to him while keeping me within sight. As I hiked along, I thought about the writings in the journal and my odd conversation with a stone dragon named Duck. It was funny but a couple of months ago, I never would've given credit to having a conversation with a dragon. In addition, I definitely would've chided myself for having girlish fantasies of dragons and pixies or talking trees and birds; however, I had yet to talk to or see a pixie. So, there was that to look forward to. Looking back, my life had never really been extraordinary except for the little telepathy stuff that I did with Andrea when we were kids.

Thinking about Andrea now, I realized that I needed to communicate with her, but I had to focus on Jaxon. She must be so worried. I'd take a moment when we got to camp and communicate with her about what was happening.

In no time, we were entering a clearing and I could see the wide expanse of the lake sprawled out before me. My first thought as I looked at the cool stream-fed waters was that it reminded me of Daniel's eyes.

No sooner had the thought crossed my mind then coming

out of the water was the god-like man himself. The sun shone brightly down onto his bare skin which was covered in tiny droplets of water. Throwing his head back, the dark mass of his glistening hair threw water in an array that caused a rainbow to shoot out behind him.

Looking up from the water, his eyes locked with mine and he unabashedly strolled right out of the lake in front of me. All six feet of muscle-formed man came straight toward me. A pair of tightly fitted black shorts covered his midsection but the rest of him was all man. Clenching my jaw, lips parted slightly, to keep my mouth from dropping open in awe, my breath whistled through my teeth. He looked like an Olympic swimmer all muscled and shiny with not a speck of hair to be seen. My eyes were burning for lack of blinking as I drank in the vision before me.

Licking my lips, I sucked in the small amount of saliva that was forming in my mouth at the sight that made me want to become a cannibal. He looked yummy, all I could think about was licking that water off his torso. All thoughts of my recent hurt flew away as my eyes met his. While his long strides closed the distance between us, I caught a knowing look and a slight grin on his face before it was quickly covered under a more serious demeanor.

Grasping me by my shoulders and looking me over from head to toe, he pinned me down with his eyes as he proclaimed in a gruff voice, "It's a good thing we have Jaxon here. You really

The Tree and the Tablet

need to be more careful!" With that, he let his hands drop and stepped around me to walk away. My mouth fell open so fast, it might've hit the ground if I hadn't caught it. What just happened? This was not the welcome I'd envisioned. Feeling shattered, I turned on my heel and marched after him all fire and brimstone. My blood was boiling. He just treated me like a senseless child. There was no — *Oh, Maggie, thank god you're okay!* — followed by kisses and cuddles.

Coming up behind him, I tapped him on the shoulder. When he spun around, I slapped him square across the face, grinding out angrily, "Jerk!" To his credit, he stood there dumbfounded for a split second, and then grasped me by the shoulders to pull me into him. Instantly, I knew exactly what he was planning, but that moment had passed. Ducking low, I spun around breaking his grip. On my way out of the embrace, I stomped on his foot.

Hopping up and down on his other foot, "Ouch," he exclaimed as he turned toward me. "Maggie, what the hell?" He honestly sounded surprised at my reaction.

"How dare you think you can treat me like that?" Fuming as I turned to face him and sent him a scathing look, "I was lost, alone in the woods and you sent Jaxon to find me. Then, when I return, you treat me like a child who wandered off?"

Stomping my foot on the ground, I spoke in a barely audible whisper that was filled with innocent pride and pain, "My niece is out there alone and frightened and you have the audacity to

271

send a bird to find me? Stop playing your childish games with me. You won't touch me again!" A bewildered expression crossed his face, but I was done with conversation. If he couldn't understand what he did was wrong, then I wasn't going to explain it further. "Which tent is mine?" He had the good sense not to speak and simply pointed across the way to a small green tent.

Turning toward the tent, I walked away with my back held straight. As soon as I entered, I dropped to my knees and tears formed in my eyes. Wiping at my eyes angrily, I chided myself, "No more tears, Maggie!" Determined to change my attitude and stop hiding behind my emotions, I set my pack down and looked through it for a change of clothes since mine were moist from sleeping on the ground.

After changing and hanging up the others to dry, I grabbed an apple to eat and settled down with a cup of coffee. Tatyana had quietly set the cup inside my tent when I was rummaging through my bag. She hadn't said anything, just opened the bottom of the tent flap and slipped the hot mug of coffee under the flap. The kind gesture brought a smile to my lips. Sipping my coffee, I crossed my legs and practiced my meditation breathing. Now was as good a time as any to let Andrea know how things were going.

Focusing my energy outward, I was soon standing face to face with Andrea. "Drea!" Relieved to be close to a friendly face and having successfully connected with her, I exhaled and hugged her tightly to me. The uncertainty of whether I would be able to communicate with her from such a large distance, had silently weighed on me. The vision of her and the feel of her in my arms, made me feel suddenly overwhelmed and I held onto her a little longer and tighter than usual.

Pulling back and searching my face, "Maggie, what's happened?"

Not wanting to worry her, I stepped back with a weak smile and replied, "Nothing." At her doubting expression, I waved her off and explained, "We're at the campsite. I had a communication last night with a creature that lives in the cave where Kelsey and Peanut are being held." Andrea clapped her hands in front of her and her expression became hopeful. Interrupting her, I continued, "We aren't there yet." At her crestfallen expression, I reassured her, "Don't worry. She's safe and I think we'll find the cave today."

Andrea smiled, but her voice revealed her fear as she quietly pleaded, "Oh, Maggie. Please hurry. I can't stand the thought of my baby all alone in a cave." She turned away from me. Her shoulders shook with her silent tears. Stepping over and placing my arms around her, I just held her.

"Andrea, Jaxon's with me and everything will be okay." She turned around and looking me in the eyes, she took a deep breath to steady herself.

"Maggie, I trust you. I know you can do it." She hugged me again. Her image started to waver and become transparent.

"Drea?" Reaching out to her fading image.

She looked at me fearfully. Her hand moved toward me as if to hold onto me, her voice became weak, "Maggie, please hurry! The tree...." the whisper trailed off and with a pop, she was gone.

Deep down inside, I felt desperation grasp hold of my heart like the talons of my new dragon friend. Without warning, I found myself falling through a spiraling vortex and taking a deep breath, I landed with what felt like a thud back into my body. Opening my eyes, I was still sitting cross-legged in my tent, but Daniel was sitting in front of me, staring at me with a questioning expression on his face.

Surprised, I stammered, "Daniel, wh-wh-what are you doing here?"

Still off balance, I was mildly shocked when he clasped my hand gently in his. He raised it up to his lips. "I'm sorry, Maggie." Trying to respond, he placed his finger on my lips. "Please, let me finish." Blinking in confusion, I nodded while continuing to consider his eyes. "Maggie, I can't give you what you want, but I can't deny what I feel for you either." My heart leapt out of my chest at the admission. "I didn't handle losing you in the forest very well."

I arched a brow. "You think?"

Looking up at my sarcastic tone, he grinned cheekily. "Please accept my apology for the way I responded. But also, I need you to understand why I didn't go looking for you when I discovered you missing."

"I'm all ears." Sarcasm oozed from my pores.

Taking a deep breath, he explained, "I felt responsible, but I was also angry. I was mostly angry at myself. Somehow, I also knew that I needed you to find your way without my help." He sighed and looked down. "As soon as I spoke my concern for you, Jaxon flew off into the forest." Running his other hand through his hair, he met my gaze, "I'm not sure what it was, but a feeling came over me and I knew you were safe. You are so strong, but I knew you could find a way to overcome the odds on your own." Taking a deep breath in, he absentmindedly stroked my fingers with his, "I'm not the person you think I am..."

Nodding again, I continued to peruse his face to determine the merit of his words as it seemed like there was something he wanted to say but not sure how.

Knowing I expected more, he let out a ragged breath. He continued to hold eye contact with me and shifted his focus, "Maggie, I think it's time you came clean with me about what's really happening with you."

As I started to shrug my shoulders and deny anything, he interrupted me, "Please. I'm not blind."

Looking away, I made a point of grasping my coffee cup which was significantly cooler now and seemed as if it had moved about six inches further away. Bringing the cup to my lips, I couldn't help but glance over the rim at his beautiful face. He was patiently waiting for a response. Setting my cup down, in that moment, I chose to continue to hide my ability. Not sure why, but an alarm bell rang in the back of my head. I wanted to tell him about my gift, but I just couldn't. The effort it took to not confide in him made my heart race. Swallowing a huge lump in my throat, I looked him in the eye steadily as I calmly replied, "There are things I have learned in my past. I use meditation to clear my head and help me focus on details to find solutions." The words kind of spilled out of my mouth. It was easy to see he was disappointed, and he wasn't buying it.

He reached out and gently pushed a stray lock of hair behind my ear which caused a delicious shiver to run up my spine. All my resolve was crumbling. As he pulled his hand back, he slowly drew his fingers across my jaw and cupped my face in his large hand. "Maggie," there was a pleading sound to his voice, "please share with me." He was caressing my other arm with his strong fingers while he rubbed his thumb along my lower lip as if he were trying to coax the information he sought from my lips.

A deep sigh escaped as I breathed, "Daniel." Leaning toward him, I couldn't stop. My eyes fluttered closed as he pressed his lips against mine. Lost. That's it. Completely lost. Time stopped and my heart beat a crazy rhythm within my chest. At that moment, I was willing to give him anything his heart desired even at the expense of my previous words. I was drowning in his smell, his taste, his...

Wait, what was I doing? Firmly placing my hand against his chest, I pushed him away. He was still staring at my lips. His breathing matched mine. Hoarse and intense with raw emotion,

The Tree and the Tablet

I said, "You're the most despicable human being." His eyes flew open and the jig was up. Instantly, I knew. Or did I? Was he just using my attraction toward him to get the information he wanted? Pain, anger, and distrust contorted my face. "Ohhhh. You!" As I stood up, I shouted, "Get out!! Now!"

To his credit, he rose calmly to his feet, bowing under the low ceiling of the tent and said, "Maggie, why can't you trust me?" There was no remorse in his expression. Only disappointment. Did he feel bad about using my passion to manipulate me? I glared at him accusingly.

Stomping my foot, I pointed to the door. "OUT!"

A brief flicker of what looked like sadness crossed his face. Bowing toward me like a gallant knight, he replied, "As you wish, milady." He mockingly saluted me with a pounding hand on his chest followed by a raised fist while clicking his heels together and abruptly left the tent.

Really? Shaking my head, I was totally befuddled by his response. As I stood there watching the tent door flap in the breeze, I wondered, *Why can't I trust him?* Was it me, or him? Well, that doesn't matter. What matters is finding Kelsey and the tablet. Time is wasting away while I stand here trying to figure out the enigma that is Daniel. No sense thinking about it any further, I admonished myself. My energy needed to be focused on more important things than one very puzzling man and his ability to flip me on my head every time he crooked his finger or smiled at me sideways. With that thought in mind, I grabbed the journal and

Kathryn O'Brien

stepped out into the light.

CHAPTER 20

As the sunshine hit me in the face, I couldn't help but wonder about the weather. It was December and felt like it was April. There were clouds but it was almost like we were in a protective bubble of sorts. Shrugging my shoulders, I decided to not look a gift horse in the mouth and just roll with it.

Putting on my best devil-may-care expression, I marched over to where Daniel stood and extending my hand toward him, asking, "Can I see the map please?" Glancing at me skeptically, but deciding not to question why, he handed me the map.

Tatyana and Joseph came out of the woods with broad smiles on their faces. They were laughing and talking as they approached. Joseph walked up next to Daniel and asked him, "What's up?" With a shrug from Daniel and a nod in my direction, Joseph decided to take a seat next to me on the ground and peruse my face for a clue of my intentions. Promptly, I ignored him and went about my task. Joseph, determined to give me some space, stood and walked over to where Daniel was now talking with Tatyana.

Unfolding the map, I searched for the waterfalls I knew would be close by. Finding the red circle on the map, there were several areas with little wavy crosses and one area stood out to me more than the others. There were no crosses next to it, but my mind knew there was something missing. As I shook my head in confusion, I wondered aloud, "It couldn't be that easy, could it?"

Daniel, Tatyana, and Joseph all stopped what they were discussing to look at me quizzically. Glancing up from the spot on the map where my finger rested, I said, "It's not marked on the map as a waterfall." Daniel smiled. At that moment, I knew he understood exactly what I was thinking.

"No, because the water fall only exists during winter rains and runoff in the spring. Otherwise, it's just a small creek." He turned and grabbed his pack off the ground. Excited, he remarked softly, "I can't believe I missed that."

Speaking quickly to Tatyana and Joseph in a brief huddle, he turned and started to walk away. Glancing in my direction he called over his shoulder to them, "You two can stay here. We should be back soon. If not, you know where to look." They both nodded.

Reaching out a hand to help me up, I ignored it and helped

myself up. Nonchalantly, I dusted myself off and walked over to my tent to retrieve my pack. As I turned around, he was standing behind me. Handing him the map, I said, "Shall we?" He nodded and we headed off along the creek that fed the lake. Jaxon followed along flitting from tree to tree. Every once in a while, he would let out a little chirping noise.

We walked along quietly for quite some time. The combination of the sun beating down and the weight of my pack caused me to start sweating. Having stopped near a spot where the water was a little shallower, I reached into my pack to retrieve a bandana. While I was soaking it in the water, I noticed that Daniel silently had removed his pack and was rinsing his face off in a spot where the water was cascading off the rocks above. Again, he'd removed his shirt. *Geez, couldn't this man keep his clothes on?* I wondered to myself as I drank in the sight of his chiseled body. He glanced over at me and I realized I was staring again. Busying myself with the bandana and wringing it out, I wiped it across my chest and neck. Making a big deal out of soaking and wringing out the bandana again, I couldn't help but to glance sideways to see if he was watching me. Surprised, I looked around and he was gone.

Instantly, I stood up to get a better view of my surroundings. Losing my balance on one of the slick rocks I was standing on, I did this odd sort of dance, waving my hands this way and that, trying to catch my balance, but it was too late. Splash! Instantly, freezing cold water penetrated all of the little nooks and crannies in my nether regions and the sensation of the cold water trickling across my mid-section had the effect of making me gasp, and sputter profusely. The water was coursing across my stomach and rushed just under the line of my breasts as it was about a little over a foot high. It was agonizingly painful due to the extremely low temperature.

Screaming like a banshee, I jumped up and ran to the bank of the creek. Looking like a crab freshly plucked from the ocean with my arms spread askew and my head leaning forward to assess the damage, water was dripping from all over me. Hearing Daniel's laughter nearby, brought my attention to the fact that he was standing under a tree about four feet from where I stood. Unfortunately, it was easy to surmise that he'd seen the entire episode. Mortified, I could feel the heat rising in my cheeks as I tried to overcome my embarrassment. Replaying the event in my head, I started laughing hysterically at myself.

"You look like a drowned cat." Daniel continued to laugh.

He was right, but I didn't need him to point it out. Not quite knowing what to do with myself, now that I was soaked, I walked casually over to my pack, picked up the discarded bandana and tied it around my now wet hair. Placing my jacket around my waste, I turned to Daniel with a nod, "Ready?"

He was still smiling as if he were trying to keep from laughing. Nodding his head at me, he motioned outward with his right hand and said, "After you."

Turning on my heel, I continued our hike up the creek side

toward our destination. My senses were heightened, and I could swear that I felt eyes watching me, but looking around in the trees, there was nothing in sight. The further up we went, the thicker the woods grew. The forest seemed to be closing in on us. It was difficult to keep right next to the water while we wound our way along the creek that was soon becoming a river due to the amount of brush and lush grasses growing right up to the edge of the water. Reaching a Y in the river, it was easy to see how the other water flowed away from the current course at a forty-five-degree angle. There were several boulders that allowed us to get across the river to the other side without getting too wet. After crossing over, we turned to follow the other waterway back down river in the opposite direction from where we were.

Hours passed but we finally reached a bend in the river. Rounding the bend, it appeared that the river just disappeared and there was a sudden drop in elevation. We slowly climbed down along the edge of the water to where we could gain a solid footing again. About fifty feet down the river there was a clearing right next to a fallen log that spanned the river like a natural bridge of sorts. It appeared that, again, we were on the wrong side. Looking down at the chasm below and seeing the rushing water was quite the hindrance to my wanting to cross the log.

Beside the fifteen foot drop we'd just come down, there was an additional twenty-foot drop to where the swirling white water was cascading through the earth's opening. The opening was only ten feet across, but it looked very treacherous. The log was large though, and it appeared that it would be quite easy to cross it while standing. However, that would mean that I needed to get over my fear. Palms sweating, blood rushed through my head in a pulsing pattern which sounded like an internal drum machine between my ears. Gathering all of my courage, I decided to allow Daniel to cross in front of me so I could take a couple extra minutes to get my bearings and convince myself that I just needed to not look down. As I stepped up onto the log, my legs froze.

Daniel recognized my fear, "Maggie, keep your eyes on me and walk in a straight line." He smiled encouragingly, "You can do this. I'll be right here."

Staring into his beautiful green eyes and seeing his reassuring smile, I took a deep breath. One foot moved in front of the other as my eyes attempted to steadily watch him. Crossing over on the fallen log was faster and easier than I'd anticipated.

"Okay?" he asked as I stepped down.

Releasing my pent-up breath as I reached the other side and pride welled within me as I applauded my own bravery. Nodding, I stepped down and goofily grinned up at him, "Thanks." Andrea would never believe I did that. I was always a chicken when it came to heights.

He simply smiled and nodded. Turning and looking back toward the drop, it was much easier to see the shape of the river from where we now stood. Awestruck, I couldn't help but marvel at the view before me. It looked exactly like a hand with water running between the fingers in the form of small waterfalls.

The Tree and the Tablet

Pulling out the journal, I flipped to the page that had the drawing of the hand. Pointing to it, I motioned toward the waterfall. Daniel nodded to me which indicated that he understood exactly what we needed to do.

As we inched our way around to the side of the waterfall, we could see there was a very thin ledge that led behind the water in between the rocks. Pointing to the ledge, I shouted to be heard over the sound of several waterfalls flowing at once, "Do you think that will support our weight?"

He was looking at it skeptically as well. Suddenly, he reached over my head and grasped a large vine that was hanging over the edge of the outcropping. Tugging on it to check its ability to hold weight, he yelled over the sound of the raging water, "Stay here. I'll check it out."

Briefly, I nodded my agreement and watched tensely as he swung out and placed his foot on the ledge. Jaxon had flown over, landing on a tree branch that jutted out from the rocks just above my head. He appeared to be watching intently as Daniel stepped out onto the ledge.

Slowly, he edged his way across the tiny ledge and disappeared behind a wall of water. Anxiously, I waited, and it seemed like hours passed as I looked at the spot where he entered, hoping that everything was okay. His head popped out from the spot where he'd entered, and I let my breath out, slightly dizzy from having held it for so long. His boyish grin reminded me of a child having caught his first fish. The joy and excitement of what he must have found caused me to rush forward toward the ledge. Looking back toward Jaxon over my shoulder, "You'd better stay here. Your robin's eyes may not be well suited to a cave."

    Daniel yelled something at me, but it was drowned out by the rushing water. Looking toward the sound of his voice, I realized too late that I'd stepped out a bit too far. Suddenly the world seemed to be falling or maybe it was me who was falling. Screaming, my hand flailed out desperately to catch myself from falling into the vortex of water that was churning thirty-five feet below. Just as my life started to flash before my eyes, a strong vice closed around my wrist. A jolt of lighting shot through my body as my weight was suddenly held in place by a force I didn't expect. My eyes went up instantly toward my hand being held by a much stronger, darker hand. Looking beyond that I could see a forest of green reflected back at me in the shape of two eyes staring into mine. "Hold on, Maggie! I've got you!" he shouted.

    Reaching up with my left hand, I grasped the hand that was holding onto mine. As I struggled to get a good grip with the cold water that was rushing around me, he pulled me up and into his arms behind the waterfall. Standing there, pulses racing, breathing out of control, I knew in that moment that I never wanted to be separated from him again. The electricity that I felt every time we touched, no matter what the situation, told me that there was something between us. Cringing, I briefly wondered if I'd ever be able to let my guard down and fully trust him.

Stepping backward into the cavern, he leaned over and gently set me on a rock outcropping to catch my breath. Turning and dropping to his knee, he rummaged through his backpack and pulled out a flashlight. He motioned to me to stay put and nodding my agreement, I reached for my pack to get a drink of water. Looking around, the light barely penetrated behind the waterfall, but there appeared to be a very large opening behind where I sat.

The light from the flashlight briefly disappeared at the back of the hollow and then reappeared, steadily moving toward me. The sound of the rushing water bounced off the walls of the cavern, but an odd effect kept it from drowning out the sound like it had outside. As a matter of fact, I could hear everything as if it were amplified. My ears picked up the sounds of small rocks falling, and the scurrying sound of small animals as well as the sound of Daniel's feet softly walking toward me. No sneaking up on me this time.

Placing my water bottle back into my pack, I looked up at him as he stood in front of me. "Well?" Tilting my head to the side waiting to hear a response.

Reaching out a hand to help me to my feet, he replied calmly, "Come with me."

Standing to my feet and swinging my pack onto my back, I eagerly followed like a puppy trying to please its master. Inwardly mocking myself, I chided, *I swear, if I had a tail, I'd probably be wagging it joyfully.* Following him blindly, we reached the back of the grotto.

There were a few different caves that led off in different directions. Daniel pointed to a larger one that appeared to have been used recently. As my affirmative response we entered. It was so dark in the cave that it seemed to swallow the light from the flashlight as if it was dimming it somehow. Even with the flashlight we could only see about a foot in front of us. Reaching the end, there was a lever that protruded from the right side of the cavern wall. It looked almost like a door handle.

Something about it seemed off to me. Just as I was about to speak, Daniel reached out and pulled it. Too late. Looking back at me apologetically, we both screamed as the floor opened and we slid into a deep abyss. The world suddenly came abruptly to a halt as I fell headfirst into something extremely hard. The blackness engulfed everything, and the scream stopped just as abruptly as it started. Darkness was quickly replaced by nothingness and the last thing I felt was the warm trickle of something flowing into my eyes before I succumbed to oblivion.

CHAPTER 21

A voice echoed in my mind. It sounded like the woman from my dream. "WAKE UP!" Awareness filled my core and radiated outward. Taking in a deep breath, I found my chest was constricted. A splintering sensation shot through my head. Confusion clouded my brain as I tried to recall where I was, and what had happened. Trying to clear the fog, but unable to overcome the intense pain that was radiating through my skull, I gingerly felt my head above my eyebrow where the pain was centered. There was a large knot with a gash at the center that felt like it had scabbed over. The sound of my labored breath echoed through the chamber and briefly I wondered how long I'd been lying there. Trying to open my eyes was difficult as what I assumed to be blood from the wound had clotted over my right eye preventing it from being opened easily.

Fortunately, I hadn't lost my pack in the fall. Trying to sit up to reach it, I discovered that the reason I was having such a hard time breathing was because there was a large object laying across my abdomen and chest. Feeling it gingerly to try and figure out what it was, a moaning rumble sounded from the lump and I realized it was Daniel. He was coming to and must have realized he was laying on me as he suddenly sat up and away from me which caused me to gasp with the relief of pressure. His voice came a little raggedly at first, "Maggie?"

"Yeah, I'm here." I touched him gently on the arm. He shivered. Opening my good eye to try and see, it was just as dark in this chamber as it had been in the tunnel that was now, what I assumed to be, somewhere above us. In a bit of a daze, I asked, "What happened?"

He coughed, "I'm thinking it's some kind of trap, but not sure where we landed." My eardrums ran with the sounds of him unzipping and re-zipping various pockets on his backpack. "Are you okay?" he asked. His voice sounded strange, almost like he was talking through a straw. There was a strange wheezing sound that punctuated each word.

Grimacing in pain at the various sounds coming my way from his non-stop movements, which had the effect of feeling like little hammers hitting me in the head, I replied as calmly as I could and tried to sound as unfazed by our current dilemma as possible, "I hit my head on something and can't open my right eye." A clicking sound was followed by a small and insignificant light bouncing off my one good eye which caused me to flinch.

"Oh, Sorry. I found a smaller flashlight in my pack." Came the reassuring and strong voice - followed by a wheeze. "Hold on." Sensing the distance close between us, he soon had a wet compress pressed to my eye. Such a gentle touch from such a strong man. As he finished his ablutions to my eye, he asked, "Can you try to open your eye for me?" The wheezing sound continued.

"What's wrong with your voice?" I asked, a little crossly as the sound of my own voice was just as irritating to me.

"Nothing, I think I broke a rib." At my gasp, he added, "No big deal, I'll be fine." He tried to reassure me, but I couldn't shake the feeling that he wasn't being entirely honest with me.

Fine, two can play that game. Gingerly testing the eye, I could open it with minimal tension and finally was able to see to the extent of the limited range afforded by the tiny light in his hand. Somewhat relaxing now, I reported, "Thank you. I think it'll be okay."

He sighed with relief and stated matter-of-factly, "The gash on your forehead is very small, no-stitches-kinda small, but it bled a lot and I was able to clear most of the excess." As he turned away from me to put away the rag he used, I looked around. Not really seeing anything, I returned my attention to Daniel.

"Where do you think we are?" Trying to hide my fear, I silently hoped my inquiry didn't come out as shaky and frightened as I really was.

Shining the light around, he turned toward me and handed me the water flask, "Not sure, but we should probably look around to see if we can find a way out." Getting to his feet, he reached down his hand to help me up.

As I got to my feet, I swayed slightly prompting him to steady me. "Are you feeling dizzy?"

I couldn't explain what I'd felt, but it sure wasn't dizzy. It was like someone put a needle and thread right through my stomach and yanked it, pulling me in a sideways direction. Taking a breath, I replied as calmly as I could, "No, just thrown off by the darkness." He held me close for a moment. Wondering if he sensed it, I acknowledged I really needed that just then. If he knew, he didn't let on.

"Shall we?" He asked as he removed himself from my arms and grasped my hand.

The light was insignificant in the bleak darkness of the cave. We soon came to a wall. Standing there, I could feel a soft and gentle breeze coming from my right and on instinct, we headed in the direction of the air flow. There was the distinct impression we were slightly working our way at an upward angle. My heart was racing as I felt a sense of familiarity. Suddenly, my eyes clouded over which caused me to gasp loudly. Daniel stopped and asked, "What's wrong?"

Not being able to explain it, I stammered, "I don't know..." How was I supposed to tell him I couldn't see. After all, we were

The Tree and the Tablet

in a dark cave. As suddenly as my vision had clouded over, it was replaced with a sort of greenish-gray vision that illuminated every nook and cranny of the room in a soft glow. Softly, I whispered, "It's okay, Daniel." Looking at him, his eyes looked white and his breath was like little puffs of clouds extending out in front of his face. It was sort of like putting night vision glasses on and I sighed. It was amazing. Sensing the presence of an unseen force, I reached out with my mind.

"*Duck? Is that you?*" A deep rumble sounded directly in front of us.

"Hello, Child." He said aloud. His voice sounded deep and excited. "It is very nice to see you here." As his breath wrapped its warmth around us, I couldn't help but feel at ease. It turns out the air flow we were following was Duck's breath.

Daniel tensed up next to me at the sound of Duck's rumbling voice. Placing my hand on his arm and again, I tried to reassure him. "It's alright, Daniel. This is Duck. He's a friend."

Daniel turned to me and asked, "What is that noise? And what is a duck doing in here?" He was moving the flashlight around rapidly but from what I could see and sense, he couldn't quite figure out what was happening.

Grasping his hand in mine, I laughed and said, "Calm down." As he stopped his frantic search through the deep blackness of the cave, I enlightened him as best I could, "Duck's a dragon."

Daniel snorted, "Now who's losing it?" Looking around

again, he said skeptically, "I hear air, I feel warmth, but I see nothing."

Duck decided to help illuminate the situation and, taking in a deep breath, his belly turned into a bright red spot that resembled embers in a fire. He released his breath very slowly and deliberately, which caused the glowing red color to move from his belly up his long neck toward his mouth. He opened up his mouth and flames shot out above our heads. Right before the release of the fire, the radiance was so intense that I could make out his facial features in the soft light and the large cat-like eyes that watched Daniel warily.

Daniel jumped back grabbing me and throwing me behind him. "Whoa!" He yelled as he tried to defend me with his miniature flashlight. Duck shook his large head and I laughed hysterically at the sight of this big man trying to stave off a flame breathing dragon with a flashlight the size of a pencil. The dragon looked confused by what he was seeing and hoping to stop a huge misunderstanding which would surely end in harm befalling either of these two proud creatures, I forced myself to sober up and speak rather quickly, "Daniel, stop! He won't hurt us. He's a friend!"

Being able to see better in the dark, I swiftly maneuvered my way around Daniel and placed myself in front of Duck as a shield. Something about me standing guard in front of a large dragon who was easily two feet taller than me at the shoulders must have penetrated his panic as Daniel was finally able to hear my words. Taking a breath while looking down at me, he asked, "But...how do you know this creature?"

"It's a long story," I replied with a sigh. *Well, there's no escaping it now. The cat, or dragon, is out of the proverbial bag.* The jig was up, and I knew I now needed to tell him everything. *Well, maybe not everything.* Daniel started to talk, but placing a finger across his lips, I looked up into his eyes and reassured him, "I'll tell you what you want to know, but you have to promise to listen patiently and not interrupt. Okay?" He looked past me into the darkness and then back down to me. He nodded his acquiescence to my demands. "But first...," my thoughts shifted direction as I turned to the dragon.

"Duck, can you help us get out of this cave?"

"Oh, no." He replied shakily. "I'm so sorry, daughter of Valor, but the only way out is to find the tablet of power, speak the words of making, and sing the sister's song."

Totally defeated, I stopped to think for a minute. "Duck? Can you tell me how to get to Kelsey and Peanut?"

"Yes." He replied firmly. My heart soared. However, he paused.

Suddenly concerned, and slightly alarmed, I asked in a gentle voice, "Duck, what aren't you saying?" He bobbed his head back and forth, then dropped it low. His actions reminded me of a child dancing from one foot to the other in an effort to decide what he should do. "Duck, out with it!" The words came out as more of a command than a request.

"You have to get us out of this cavern to get to your Kelsey." Sensing he had more to say, I waited patiently and tapped my foot on the hard stone floor. To Daniel's credit, he sat patiently off to the side, wheezing steadily. Shaking my head, "And?" The question was meant to prompt him to share more.

The words spilled out of him like water from a pitcher, "You have to get the tablet so that you can release us from this cave." My eyes flew open in comprehension.

"You mean we're trapped here until I figure out how to retrieve the tablet from some unknown hiding place?"

He nodded in confirmation. As my breathing increased with anxiety and my mind whirled, *How am I going to get to Kelsey? I can't find the tablet. What am I going to do?* The questions kept repeating in my mind and I became more and more agitated with every thought. In no time, I was beginning to hyperventilate. Daniel must've been concerned because he started to rise from his resting spot on the floor of the cave. Absently, I put out my hand, but realizing he couldn't see it, I firmly placed it on his shoulder to keep him put. Staring at Duck in a very not pleased sort of way, I took a few calming breaths and asked, "Duck? Do you know where the tablet is?" He watched me pensively waiting for me to finish speaking.

Nodding his head vigorously, he replied excitedly, "Yes, mistress!" Now he was impatiently jumping from one front foot to the other and doing a sort of jig. If there was room, he probably would've spun in circles. His nostrils flared, and a puff of fire shot out from his mouth as he belched loudly.

Waving my hand in the air at the foul odor of brimstone, which smelled a lot like burnt rubber, "Calm down, Duck."

"Oh, mistress, I'm so sorry. I just got too excited." He looked down dejectedly.

"It's quite alright, Duck." He perked up. "But where's the tablet?"

"But you must know, daughter of Valor." At my questioning look, he added, "It is behind the veil of the weeping maiden's tears."

"Well, then," I said, totally flabbergasted, "lead the way." Extending my arm outward, Duck looked at me with a total lack of comprehension as to what he should do next.

"But you must know, it is for you to find your way to the land of Valor and the hidden Glenn of the Sacred Tree of Life. Then, you must sing the sister's song to find the tablet." He sat his rump on the floor and looking over at Daniel asked, "Mistress?" Concern tinged his voice as he asked, "Is he alright?"

My mind was still reeling with the comprehension that the only way out of this confounded cave was to sing a song I didn't know and find a veil of some sort in the dark. Realizing that Duck had asked me a question, I turned to him, slightly flustered and asked impatiently, "What are you talking about?"

He was frantically motioning toward Daniel with his front foot; one clawed toe pointing straight at him. "Your friend seems to be having a problem."

Turning toward Daniel, I could see that he had slumped forward and there was no more wheezing. My heart leapt into my throat. Kneeling to get closer to him, I could hear that there was a very small sound coming from him and the breath was very minimal. "Daniel. Daniel?" Grasping his shoulders, I gently shook him. There was no response other than the silence caused by the air flow completely stopping. *Oh. My. God.* "Nooooooooo!" The agonized scream tore from my lips.

As he fell to his side on the floor, his jacket fell open to reveal that he had a knife embedded in him. Instantly, my mind recalled all of the steps to performing **CPR**, and laying him on his back, I listened to him, felt that there was no air and his heartbeat was so faint I couldn't tell if it was still beating. I began compressions. Frantically, I listened and then puffed two breaths. Listening again and feeling for a pulse, nothing. Compressions, breath, breath, listen. Still nothing. Unshed tears stung my eyes, but I refused to give up. As I was about to begin compressions again, Duck stepped forward and placed his giant foot upon Daniel's chest, a glowing ember began to burn under Duck's foot. The glowing grew to a fire and afraid that Duck was sealing the deal, I cried out and tried to pull Duck's foot from Daniel's chest. "Duck. You're killing him."

It was useless. Duck's foot was huge and heavy as he was made from stone. "No...wait." It was as if the fire was pushing the blade out of Daniel and I could see it slowly moving outward until it dropped to the floor beside him. Duck then leaned over and

The Tree and the Tablet

breathed a puff of smoke into Daniel. The fire within him grew and glowed and then raced out through his throat and the open wound then out into the room. Duck moved his large foot from Daniel's chest. I started crying. He was so still. My heart hurt so bad. How much more could I lose? Placing my face in my hands, I started to cry in earnest.

"Are those tears for me?" The sweet sound of Daniel's voice broke through my agony and turning toward him, I could see that he was smiling at me.

Throwing myself on him, "Jerk! Don't ever do that to me again!" I admonished as I laid on him and listened to the sound of his heart beating stronger by the second.

His arm wrapped around me. "Easy love." He said quietly as he placed his hand where the blade had been. "I don't know what just happened, but my chest is on fire." Leaning away from him and wiping at my tears, I turned to Duck.

"Duck saved you." Turning back to Daniel, I admonished, "You should've told me what was going on instead of allowing yourself to suffer."

"There was nothing else to be done." He said calmly.

"Still." I said, at a loss for words. Turning to the stone dragon, I said, "I'm sorry for doubting you, Duck. Thank you for what you did," and I reached out to gently caress his big snout.

He shivered which sounded like rocks falling and said, "It is my pleasure to bring such joy to a daughter of Valor."

Gracing him with a broad grin and turning to Daniel, I could see he was still struggling. After rummaging through the pack and giving Daniel some water, he laid back again.

Duck spoke up and said, "I will warm you and he will rest." Agreeing with him, I set up a pack as a pillow and pulling out an extra jacket, I laid it on Daniel as a blanket. When he tried to get up, it didn't take much effort to push him back down. Brushing my lips across his, I pleaded with him, "Please rest for a bit." He started to protest but I insisted, "I'm not going anywhere and I feel like Kelsey is safe enough." At his doubtful look, I begged, "Please?"

His response was a solemn, "Alright, but not too long," as he closed his eyes and soon was breathing evenly. Funny how I noticed that the wheezing sound was gone.

Turning toward Duck who was gently breathing warmth into the cave, he glanced in my direction and queried, "Now, Mistress, shall we have a look into your mind to see if we can discover what you have lost?" Funny that he used the same words as the beautiful angel in my dream. Nodding, I sat in front of Duck and closing my eyes, I began to breath.

CHAPTER 22

Now that Daniel was resting peacefully, I sat on the cold floor of the cave, focusing on my breathing. Within the swirling vortex of my mind's eye, I searched through the mists to find what I wasn't sure of. There was no way for me to know what I sought, but I kept thinking back to the night before, when I'd had the conversation with the beautiful creature in my dream and focused on her.

Soon, I was standing in a field of purple flowers of every shade, surrounded by what looked like pink dogwood trees. Looking to the sky, there were deep purple clouds and two suns on the horizon. From my right, I saw movement. A blurred vision of two figures was moving toward me. Forcing myself to focus more, I could make out that the outlines were the beautiful woman from my dream, only her hair was a deep black and pinned up on top of her head as opposed to the long flowing white it had been, and walking beside her was Andrea. They were walking hand in hand. It seemed that they had just finished laughing at some secret joke.

Not sure why, but I was angry. How could they just be laughing and joking around, when I was trying to find Kelsey and rescue her from a crazy person? As they approached, I was growing more and more agitated and I was slightly alarmed by the intensity of feelings I'd never felt before.

Suddenly, Duck appeared at my side and speaking in a harsh tone, he hissed through clenched teeth, "Stop! You, evil being."

Gasping, I looked at him as if he'd lost his mind. His posture was that of a large dog trying to protect its master. His back was arched, and his eyes were focused on the woman standing next to my sister.

The beautiful goddess halted in her tracks and turning rapidly toward the dragon, she grasped Andrea, using her as a shield against Duck. She hissed between her teeth at me while still glancing back and forth between Duck and me. "You vile thing. You shouldn't have brought the dragon." Her form started to shimmer and shake, and a terrible thundering sound surrounded us.

Duck yelled out while attempting to encircle me with his great body. "Get back!"

Andrea seemed confused by what was happening. It was almost as if she were waking up from a dream to be faced with a

The Tree and the Tablet

nightmare. Seeing the fear in her eyes, I tried to go to her, my arm stretched in her direction. Duck blocked my effort and warned me, "No! She'll be safe."

Peering under his great form, I could see that the enchanting creature was transforming into a great black winged monster that looked like a raven. It screeched at us with its obnoxious voice, "I see my son has his hands full with you, but I'll deal with him later."

Duck released a stream of fire aimed at the head of the great bird. As it dodged to the side, it lost its grip on Andrea. Seeing my opportunity, I rushed forward. Grasping Andrea by the arm, I yanked her sideways away from the raven. It screeched and took flight. Duck had converted from a dragon of stone to the most beautifully colored creature. His scales glowed iridescent, fluctuating between teal, purple and pink just like the gossamer cloth above my bed. Like a rocket, he shot into the air and took flight after the large raven who appeared to be similar in size to him.

The battle between them raged on for what seemed like an eternity, but was in reality, only minutes. They swerved and rocketed through the clouds. The raven would stop in mid flight and shoot what looked to be lightning bolts from its eyes at Duck, and he would counter with a rain of fire upon the beast. Appearing as if it was losing the battle, the raven suddenly, in a snap of my fingers, vanished into thin air with a loud whoosh and a plopping sound. Duck made his way back to where I stood in the circle of trees with Andrea.

Breathing a heavy sigh on his landing, he mumbled, "Nasty witch."

My eyes still focused on the spot in the sky where the raven had vanished. Turning toward Duck as he landed, I asked, "Are you alright?"

Bobbing his head toward me, "Yes." He snorted releasing two small puffs of smoke from his nostrils. "I am glad I decided to follow your thought trail. I sensed the danger."

"But I don't understand. What happened?" Turning to face him, I asked, "If she wasn't a goddess sent to guide me, then who was she?"

Andrea just stared at Duck, a look of awe on her face.

"That was, Ellandra, the Trickster, The Sorceress of Doane. She is one very nasty and cunning being." He turned to look off into the distance. Turning back to me he stated, "We must hurry, there is no time to waste. We are exposed here." As he started to walk toward an opening in the trees, I lost my patience.

"Wait right there!" My voice reverberated through the clearing and what animals weren't scared off by the battle, were soon scurrying for hiding places. He turned toward me expectantly and I started to walk toward him but found that Andrea had her feet planted to the spot where she was standing. Her eyes were like saucers and her mouth hung open. Turning gently toward her, I said softly, "Andrea, this is Duck. He's my friend. I need you to come with me so that we can save Kelsey."

She blinked rapidly as if she were coming out of a trance, she looked at me sideways and sighing in resignation, started to walk with me.

Stepping up to where Duck waited for us, I asked, "What's really happening here?" At his hesitancy to speak, I repeated myself, "Duck, please. I need to know what I'm up against here."

He sighed in resignation and glancing back toward the opening, he said, "Mistress, it is not safe here, but once we get to the protection of the Glen of the Great Spirit Tree where the Veil of the Maiden's Tears is located, I will tell you what I know."

Seeing in his eyes that there was no budging him, I nodded my agreement, "Well, why didn't you tell me we were close to the Veil of the Maiden's Tears?" He blinked his large eyes at me. "Very well, Duck. Let's go."

We headed toward the opening in the trees again. This land was so beautiful. I couldn't help but wonder at all the various creatures and flowers the likes of which I'd never seen before. Beautiful and bright shades in every primary color were mixed with a pallet of softer pastel shades and vibrant greens. It was amazing. The ground was soft like a sponge beneath my feet, but it bounced back like memory foam.

As we walked, I asked Andrea, "I wonder how you're still able to be here with me." She looked at me questioningly. "The last time we spoke, you faded away because of the tree."

She looked as if she were concentrating, "I'm not sure what's happened." She looked down at the ground and then suddenly, looked up at me with an expression of revelation, "It released me." She smiled at my look of confusion. "The tree told me that I had to go, or I wouldn't be able to be with you again. Then, I was here, and that lady was talking to me." She looked ahead again. "I don't remember anything between then and you grabbing my hand."

Putting my arm around her, "Well, you didn't miss much. At least you're here now and we're able to be together. But I still don't understand how I'm able to touch you and see you solidly when this is all in my mind." My question was a voiced thought, but my mind still tried to figure it out.

Andrea shook her head and shrugged, "Either way, it's wonderful to be able to be with you again."

We walked under an arched opening that had two statues of gorgeous women standing on either side of it, their hands were raised and outstretched toward each other as if they were getting ready to play a game of patty cake. Stepping through the opening, a hush fell on us like a curtain.

Directly in front of where we were, about twenty feet away, there stood a shrine of sorts. It was like a fountain with a stunning white stone maiden standing in the middle on top of an earthen hill. She had her hand raised up and a beautifully carved robin was perched on her finger. However, it looked as if something was missing.

There was a large mound of earth in front of her that appeared to be disturbed. It looked like there used to be a tree

The Tree and the Tablet

planted there, but it had been dug up or ripped out violently. The ground oozed a deep, shimmering dark purple of rivulets that poured down into the pool at the base. As we came closer to the place where the maiden stood, visible tears, the color of the pool, were gently gliding down her cheeks, across her arms and like a waterfall over the rocks at the base into the pool. It sort of looked like a veil because of the way it flowed. Suddenly, I remembered Shirley's dream and froze. My mind reeled.

Staring at the scene before me, I was overcome with sorrow at the vision of the maiden's tears and a shiver danced along my spine. Something about the sight in front of me seemed like a dream from a far-off place that I'd once had. No, it was a dream that Shirley once had. The silence gave way to a sound like air moving in and out. The earth seemed to be breathing deeply in the center of the fountain. Andrea, still clutching uncertainly to my arm, flinched and stepped back at the sound.

Releasing Andrea's hand from my arm, I stepped toward the fountain. Upon reaching the edge, I was suddenly filled with the most intense sorrow. My heart was racing and I couldn't stop myself from crying out. It was agony. Almost like every painful thing that had broken my heart as a child came rushing back all at once. Even though I wanted to curl up into a ball, I found myself reaching forward to put my hand into the swirling purple-black ooze in the pool. Just as my finger was about to touch the inky mass, Duck hissed. "Stop!"

My hand jerked back. Turning to look up at him, he said,

"Do not be drawn into the maiden's tears. You will be filled with a longing like nothing you have ever known before. It will consume your heart and soul." He whispered the last bit in the most heart wrenching tone of voice as if saying the words broke his heart. His eyes spoke of a deep abiding love and sorrow.

Placing my hand on his snout which was right next to me, I asked gently, "Duck, tell me who she is. Please?"

Blinking his large cat like eyes at me, he sighed. "She is Valoria, the warrior daughter of the great chieftain Sol and his wife, Shalandria." Taking another deep and ragged breath, he looked up at the still figure in the middle of the mound of damaged earth. "She was once my mistress and my creator's daughter. I was created as a wedding gift for Valoria's wedding." His sorrow was prevalent as he remarked, "But now, as a daughter of Valor, you are my new mistress."

Andrea sat on a wooden bench that was placed near the fountain. She turned and looked at the statue. Taking in a deep, ragged breath and exhaling loudly while trying to clear the intense sadness from my heart, I asked calmly, "You don't have to call me Mistress."

Shrugging, "It's alright. It's meant to be."

"Will you tell me what happened here?"

Nodding his great head, Duck continued, "I was away when it happened. In this Glenn, there was a large tree with the most beautiful pink flowers on it. The Great Spirit Tree, which is also known as the tree of life, the life source of all who dwell in the

The Tree and the Tablet

land of Nohad." He spread his great wings as if to emphasize his words. He seemed a little restless but continued on. "The small bird on the Maiden's finger was her best friend and lover, Alkard, the Strong. He was a mighty warrior who served as the Captain of the guard for Valoria's father. Alkard is a member of a clan that have a special ability to transform their shape into that of a bird. His father, Opi-Chee, descended from great chief's as well."

My eyes lit up hearing that name. It sounded so familiar. Almost like a story I'd once heard as a child. Making a mental note, I turned my attention back to Duck and his story.

"On the day of the great sorrow, Mistress Valoria and Sir Alkard were going to be married." He shuddered. "I was off gathering twigs and sprigs for the Mistress to make a wreath for the wedding ceremony."

Glancing from Duck to the beautiful Valoria held captive in time, I was awed by the clear display of love expressed in the eyes of the maiden.

"It is believed that a set of guards, who were hired by Ellandra's grandmother Serena, entered the Glenn as Valoria was praying to the Great Spirit Tree for blessings. They told my mistress that Serena that Alkard was in danger and being held in Serena's dungeons. Serena was promised to Alkard, but after meeting Valoria, Opi-chee had pity on the two lovebirds and broke the betrothal. Serena was filled with anger at the loss of her birth-right and continuously schemed to get Alkard back so she could gain the power to take over Nohad by overthrowing Sol. But she knew she could never accomplish this while Valoria lived." He grunted. "Valoria should have known better." His scales rippled with a reflective wave of pink that flowed from his tail to his head and was quickly replaced with his original bright coloring. "When my mistress tried to leave to go save Alkard, the deceitful warriors stopped her and told her the only way to save Alkard from a horrible fate at the hands of Serena, was to bring her a blossom from The Great Spirit Tree."

It was plain to see the evidence of sorrow playing across Duck's face as he described the events of that fateful day. He was panting softly and his eyes widened showing a small amount of white toward the outer edges, almost like a dog in distress.

"Alkard had been out in the forest and heard of the trickery Serena had hatched. He had spies watching her every move after it was suspected that she had poisoned Opi-chee to try and stop Alkard from marrying Valoria. Alkard was racing to stop Valoria before it was too late." Turning toward his mistress and then back to me, he clenched his jaw, "She knew what would happen. To touch the sacred tree is forbidden. It comes with a price!" He sat down again and facing Valoria, "Only a dragon of earth and fire can touch the blossoms." He whispered it so quietly, I thought I had misheard him.

He shivered again. "If I had insisted that she keep her mind link with me, I would have known her thoughts. I told her to release me from her mind link filled with swooning and love. If only I had kept the mind link, I would have sensed the danger, but I was preoccupied with filling my belly after spending all day collecting decorations." Giant tears fell silently from his eyes and down his scales to land on the ground in small puddles.

Reaching out my hand and placing it on his chest, I replied softly, "It's not your fault, Duck. You must know that."

He jerked away from my touch, "You were not there, you do not know. I have sworn an oath to the house of Valor to never allow them to feel pain, or know the sorrow that my Mistress endured on that day." Taking a steadying breath, he continued. "Serena, that vile witch, convinced my mistress to climb the path of the virtuous to stand at the base of the Great Tree and pluck a blossom from the tree's outstretched arms. Serena told her that if she did this, then her true love would be released and no harm would befall her if she sought the blossom for something as noble as true love." A ragged sigh escaped his mouth. "Valoria believed her. She grasped the blossom. A great wind whipped around her, and Alkard was too late to show her Serena's trickery was false. He had not been taken as Valoria had feared." The tears were flowing freely down his great scales. "Just as Alkard reached her in his bird form, she recognized too late what had taken place. They were frozen in time in this form." He motioned toward the statue with the bird perched upon the outstretched finger.

"But what happened to the Great Spirit Tree?" I asked. "It looks like it was ripped from the ground."

"The tree was transformed from its ethereal form to that of

a real tree upon the taking of the blossom." Looking me in the eyes, "I don't know when it was taken or how it was removed without someone touching the maiden's tears, but the little man who resides in the hidden space with your Kelsey has the stench of it upon him."

"But how did he make the journey here?" I wondered out loud.

Scratching at the ground with his front paws, he began to pace restlessly. "I know not how this has come to be, only that Ellandra has a hand in all of this."

My mind whirled trying to figure it all out. Andrea had been sitting quietly and listening to our exchange. Suddenly, she jumped up from her perch on the bench and said, "But that's it."

Turning toward her, eyebrows raised, I asked, "What's it?"

"My tree." She exclaimed exuberantly.

Turning to me, a deep raging anger crossed his face. "That evil sorceress, Serena, took my mistress from me and cursed this land. Now her granddaughter, Ellandra, has taken another thing that does not belong to her family. I will rip her apart." He flexed his great clawed feet like a cat releasing the full length of his talons.

Realizing Duck was getting more and more worked up, I sought to sooth him. "It'll be okay, Duck."

A shuddering breath hissed through his teeth, and a small tear floated down across his beautiful scales as he glanced back to the beautiful woman who stood next to a great gaping hole in

The Tree and the Tablet

the ground. "Ellandra, Serena, I don't know which, but one of the houses of Doane stole the great tree and hid it away. My mistress will not be able to return to the land of Nohad until the wrong is righted by one who is a descendant of the house of Valor."

He turned away from the statue of the beautiful woman whose tears flowed freely into a swirling pool of sorrow and looked at me intently.

A smile lit my face as I realized Andrea was right. The answer was so close, but so far away.

CHAPTER 23

ooking around, I wondered, how in the heck I was supposed to get Andrea's tree from my house in Allyn. How would I get it all the way to this strange land when all I do is close my eyes to get here in my mind? And, I still need to get out of the confounded cave where Daniel is resting. A shiver of anxiety climbed up my spine as I recalled how close I'd come to losing him. With that thought came a sense of urgency.

Kicking my foot outward in frustration, the lush, fluffy flowers that were spread throughout the Glenn sent a cloud of light purple spores floating into the air. Silently, I hoped Daniel was okay. Ugh, I wish I knew how Mr. Maxwell got the damn tree out of here and planted it in my yard? My mind was swirling with questions and I didn't seem to be any closer to finding the answers or rescuing Kelsey. Turning and pacing back and forth in front of the fountain, I suddenly stopped.

Looking up at the spot where Valoria appeared to be rooted to the ground, I said, "Well, Great Spirit, if you have any keen ideas on how I'm supposed to solve this riddle and restore your glory, I'm waiting for your direction." The last part was particularly sarcastic on my part.

Staring at the statues, I waited patiently for a response I knew wouldn't come. Then, stomping my foot, sending a fresh cloud of spores floating into the air, I threw myself down, sitting on the edge of the pool to ponder what my next move should be. Laughing out loud, I said to no one in particular, "Yea, I thought not."

"Mistress?" Duck called out in a curious tone.

As I looked up at him, I could see in his expression that he was alarmed. His head was tilted to one side and he stared off toward the entrance to the Glenn. Following his gaze, I could see a familiar form wending its way through the forest outside the entrance. No! it couldn't be. But how?

As my mind tried to grasp what I was seeing, I stood and turned from my musings to face the approaching individual and the onslaught of emotions ripping their way through my heart. Mesmerized by the vision in front of me, my feet took control and propelled me hesitantly toward the opening. Soon, I was standing in the archway that led into the Glenn. Blinking and gasping in shock, I was suddenly confronted with such anguish

The Tree and the Tablet

and fear. Was this real? But then, again, if Andrea could be here, why not?

My heart leaped out of my chest and the tears burned the backs of my eyes as they slipped out and drifted down my cheeks. "Mom?" Disbelief, fear, anxiety, relief, shock, pain, love. All of this swirled around me like some tangible cloud.

"Yes, sweetheart. It's me." She reached out and tenderly caressed my cheek. It felt like a breeze touched me. Gingerly, I reached up and placed my hand over hers where the warmth of her touch penetrated my senses, but I only felt my own hand upon my face. Instantly, happiness was replaced with fear. Pulling away, she remained where she stood just outside of the archway.

Andrea rushed forward to embrace her but she went right through her. Crying out with surprise and catching herself, she spun around to face the deception, asking, "Are you a ghost?"

Instantly, I suspected Ellandra was at her tricks again. Turning from Andrea to the frail vision of my mother, I stepped back cautiously, lifting my hand in front of me to ward off the false vision, "What trick is this?" The pain and hurt of losing my mother came rushing back into my heart. I struggled to keep a mask of strength on my face while the renewed pain was almost enough to put me on the ground.

The wraith in front of me pointed to the fountain and said, "I'm a Spectral, sent here by the Great Spirit."

Devastated, I asked quietly, "So, you're not my mother then?"

The creature had a sad expression on its face and stated, "I'm a memory of your mother. I've been sent here by the Great Spirit to guide you on your journey."

"What's a Spectral," I asked. Andrea made her way to my side and clasped my hand in hers.

"We're a form of spiritual being that can assume the shape or form of whatever will help us achieve our goal." It gave a sly smile. Something about that made me suspicious. The creature continued, "In this instance, I was able to read your innermost thoughts and desires and this is the form that I felt would give me the best opportunity to get close to you."

Again, alarm bells rang in my mind. Secretly, I thought it convenient for the Great Spirit to answer my challenge in such a way. Curiously, I couldn't help but to ask, "Do you always do what the Great Spirit asks you to do?"

The creature that looked like my mother, glanced away and then sheepishly grinned at me, stating matter-of-factly, "No, no, no. Honestly, we were quite surprised that the Great One chose us to do it's bidding." Another sly look.

"What do you mean?" Suspicion and trepidation swirled through my mind.

"Well, we're a cowardly sort and tend to steer clear of any sort of confrontation that may cause us harm. Usually, we only use our peculiar gifts to get close enough to gain an advantage." At my questioning expression, she said, shrugging, "You know, to get food."

The Tree and the Tablet

"But, that's ridiculous," I exclaimed. At its look of shock, I asked, " Forgive me, but if you're a spectral and in essence, others can move through you, how is it possible to harm you?"

Looking slightly uncomfortable at my line of questioning, but fighting with pride, it responded snidely, looking toward Duck. "The dragon knows."

Duck stepped forward and sniffed the air in great snarfing sounds. Then, he stopped momentarily and said, "I know of your kind." His stance was menacing. The spectral flinched.

Shrinking away from Duck, the Spectral pleaded, "Please, I won't harm you. The Great Spirit forbade it. I was sent to help." Duck growled. Flinching, she cried out, "I swear it!"

Raising my hand to sooth Duck, I met the eyes of the spectral. "Best you don't test your luck." Seeing the creature nodding in acceptance, I asked, "If you're going to be with us, I ask that you please change to your original form."

"You wouldn't like my original form." Waving its arms over its body, it queried, "This form does not please you?"

"No!" Again, it flinched. Seeing that I frightened it, I smirked a little and said, "If you can't change to your original form, then change to something less threatening so that Duck doesn't think you're a problem." Duck sensed my purpose and lunged forward growling menacingly and baring his great fangs.

With a whirring blur and a screech, the creature swiftly turned into a beautiful white ermine like the one I'd once seen on a camping trip with my parents as a child. As it scampered up onto the nearest tree limb, I said, giving a short bark of laughter, "This form suits you better. A tricky little weasel."

Looking at the pitiful creature that was peering down at me from the thin perch, I asked, "Do you have a name or am I to give you one like a pet?"

It responded with funny squeaking noises like those of a squirrel or chipmunk. Opening my mind to the possibilities. It was like an echo in my mind and I heard the voice of what sounded like a small child. "*I am Elise.*"

"*Well, then, Elise. We need to find the tablet of power. Did the Great Spirit happen to enlighten you on how to locate it,*" I asked as I waved my hand toward the Glenn and the fountain at the far end.

"*It's located behind the veil of tears within the pool of sorrow.*" Elise scurried down from her perch and carefully avoided being stepped on by Duck as she made her way to the edge of the fountain.

Mentally, I called after her, "*But I can't see it.*"

Removing my hand from Andrea's and giving her a reassuring smile, I started to walk over to the edge of the fountain.

"Are you able to understand it, Maggie? I only hear squeaking." Andrea said.

Glancing back at Andrea, "I hear a voice in my head." Seeing her concerned expression, I smiled reassuringly, "It'll be okay, 'Drea." Turning, I followed Elise to the edge of the pool.

Looking down into the swirling fluid, I whispered, "I am not supposed to touch it, though."

"*But you must enter the pool and tread to the place where the tears formed a waterfall across the rocks.*" Came the small voice in my head.

My head screamed not to do it, but my heart cried out to go into the pool. Looking back over my shoulder at Duck and Andrea, I realized that because neither one could hear what Elise was saying to me, they couldn't know what I was being asked to do. *Well, what's the worst thing that could happen?* Answering myself, *I could end up a raving lunatic or die and not save Kelsey.* My shoulders vaguely lifted in a shrug as I thought, "*I guess if this is how I die, then at least it will be for the ones I love.*"

Duck must have sensed what I was about to do because he stopped mid-conversation with Andrea and started to walk toward me. Too late, with a deep breath, I jumped over the ledge and landed feet first into the goo. Instantly, I felt love. So much love my heart felt like it would burst. Then, sadness. Like nothing I'd ever felt before. The deepest and most desperate sadness, longing, and a sense of loss filled me. Elise yelled in her childlike voice within my head, "Go! Don't stand still! You must hurry!"

Duck was yelling and he and Andrea had crossed the Glenn to stand near the edge of the pool. My mind was filled with so many visions I had no control over and I couldn't hear what they were saying. Facing the small fountain, my feet were suddenly heavy, as if large weights were holding them to the floor of the pool. The effort to move my feet was agonizing. Slowly, I drug my feet across the bottom of the pool, moving closer and closer to my goal. Yet, it still seemed as if I was standing in the same spot.

My mind cried out in agony and I felt as if somewhere deep inside me I just needed someone to pull me out of this agonizing pain and hug me. A fog surrounded my thoughts. Suddenly, the clouds in my brain lifted and Andrea was standing in front of me. Holding me up. She started singing. It was a song we had made up as children.

"As long as I have you, you have me too. We are sisters. Our hearts are one. Under moon and sun. We are forever and we are love."

"Come on, Maggie." She coaxed. "Sing with me." She started singing again.

Holding eye contact with her, I couldn't help but smile. Her beautiful spirit was there with me. Lifting me up when I was lost and I was suddenly transported through space and time to find myself standing next to her, singing our silly little made up sisters' song. We were just kids again. The innocence of youth surrounded us. It looked like us, but it felt different somehow. We were in a pool of clear water. Glancing to the waterfall in front of me I could see my mother and father sitting under a beautiful tree, laughing at our antics as we frolicked in the pool.

Something caught my eye and grasping Andrea's hand I waded over to a waterfall. Leaning over, filled with wonder, there

The Tree and the Tablet

was a beautifully carved stone. Beautiful and white, almost like marble, but glowing from within like a moonstone. It was about the size of a 5x7 portrait, and about an inch thick from what I could see.

My hand slowly reached into the water and pulled it out. Looking at the beautiful monolith, at first, I saw only a smooth slab with nothing written on it. Then, as if sensing my thoughts, beautiful carvings that resembled hieroglyphs appeared on the face of the tablet. Raking drew my fingers across them and mumbling under my breath, I spoke the words that appeared on the stone not knowing how I knew what they meant.

What once was gone or lost in time
Is now within this realm's light
Seek out the soul of one divine
And end the restless lover's plight

Looking up from the glowing white tablet, I was suddenly jolted from my dreamlike state. Suddenly, I was transported through space and time yet again to find that I was standing in the middle of the dark fluid of the pool of sorrow. Andrea stood in front of me, her eyes, large as saucers, an expression of deep emotional agony dancing across her face. Giant tears flowed freely from her eyes. As I grasped her hand tightly in mine, I started to head towards the edge of the pool. Again, I willed us to move to the edge of the pool, but nothing happened. We were

Kathryn O'Brien

walking in place. At this point, it was a sheer battle of my will against whatever force was held in the pool. Barely standing upright, I leaned with all my strength to try and reach the edge.

In my mind, I cried out for help. As if sensing our plight and the futility of our movements, Duck took to the air and lunged forward flapping his huge wings. Hovering over us, the wind from his great wings caused our hair to whip around us violently. He grasped Andrea and I both with his massive talons. Lurching into the air with all his might, he was able to swing us out of the turbulently-churning, purplish-black fluid and onto the soft earth next to the edge of the pool. We both tumbled to a stop.

As I lay on the ground, my prize clutched tightly against my chest, my eyes were closed while I caught my breath, trying to overcome the riotous ride I'd just endured. Duck landed gracefully next to me. Leaning his large snout over me, he sniffed loudly in me spraying droplets of mucus on my face. Coughing and sputtering I opened one eye to stare dubiously at the concerned dragon. Spying his contrite expression, "Oh, mistress, I am so sorry about that." He attempted to remove the droplets of mucus with his extra-large, wet tongue.

Fending off the well-meaning attempt by putting my hand up to ward him off, I laughed. "Enough, Duck!" Sitting up and holding the white marble out in front of me, which was mysteriously devoid of the previous markings, I shouted elatedly, "We did it!"

CHAPTER 24

As I sat there, reveling in my successful retrieval of the tablet, I couldn't control my excitement. Everything in me wanted to share this success with Daniel. Turning to Andrea, I was suddenly thrown into a deep anger at the evident betrayal that was taking place mere feet from where I landed.

Standing over Andrea with its claws unsheathed and perilously close to her neck was the spectral in what I assumed to be its true form. It reminded me of a combination of a viper and a mole. Its fat body was covered in thick brown fur. It had overly large front paws that looked similar to a hand and curled into large claws that looked like knives poised to slice though Andrea on a whim. The head, though, was shaped like a lizard or snake with a large set of slanted eyes and fangs that dripped with a green oozing gelatinous goo.

Giggling and hissing at me, "You foolish Valorian. Did you think that we would allow you to leave this place with such a perfect gift for our mistress?" Its slithering tongue licked at the dripping saliva as it spoke. The once childlike voice that I'd been able to only hear in my head was now gravelly and hoarse. It was also evident by the reactions of Duck and Andrea that they could hear it as well.

"Elise, how could you do this? You slithering snake," I spat at the creature. Andrea whimpered under the reflex of the creature's tightening grip.

"Daughter of Valor, if you wish your sibling to survive this day, you will relinquish the tablet of power to me."

Behind me, I could hear Duck growling low in his throat. Standing close enough to him to feel the heat from his growing rage that built within his belly, I spoke softly, trying to keep him calm, "Easy, Duck."

"Yesssssy, Duck!" Elise repeated. "Easssssy, or elsssssse." She spoke with a slight hiss.

"Why, Elise? I thought you were a friend sent by the Great Spirit to help?" My voice cracked slightly with pent up emotion as I tried to wrap my head around why this creature would go to such great lengths to trick us.

"Sssilly girl! The Great Ssspirit? Ha!" It cackled an evil, twisted sounding laugh that was punctuated by hissing. "You are a fool. I've watched many come and go from this land, trying to

The Tree and the Tablet

gain that which is not theirs to take. I was there on that fateful day." She motioned to the fountain. "I alone, know the truth of what happened."

Duck, hearing this, lunged forward, snarling, claws slicing the air and fangs bared. "I will kill you, vile creature of Doane."

Elise started to close her grip on Andrea's throat causing a small drop of blood to appear under its clawed fingers. "You will call off your dragon or your sister's memory will die with this spirit sprite under my grasp." She made a motion as if she were going to slit Andrea's throat.

My heart leapt out of my chest as I put my hand out, "No, please! Don't!" Turning to face Duck, "Please, Duck, I can't lose her again." A single tear slipped out and glided across my cheek.

Duck placed his head against me and I closed my eyes, feeling his strength course through me. "Mistress, the mind-link is still between us." My eyes flew open. His great big eye was close to mine. Stunned, I'd totally forgotten about the mind link. Not really sure how it worked, I decided that I would ask questions later. Right now, I needed to focus on saving Andrea.

Elise was speaking again, "I have aligned myself with the Ssssorceress of Doane. Her grandmother gave me great power and immortality so I could guide the chosssen one. Mistresssss Ellandra came and gifted me to him for he has alwayssss been my true massster. I waited long to sssserve him. The ssssorceressss promisssed me great rewards if I would help her ssson gain control of the great power ssssource." She giggled, "Look at me, much more powersss than my idiot family. And," Her tongue sliced through the air, moving randomly over Andrea's face. "I am immortal. I can also travel through space and time to be everywhere at every time." Its sickening laugh filled the air.

Pushing my thoughts outward to Duck as I turned toward Elise and spoke, "What do you want, Elise?" In my mind, I asked Duck, *"How can we get Andrea from Elise?"* He had stepped back and was eyeing Elise warily.

"Your sister is only in spirit form. Please do not fall for this ruse. She knows that Andrea is a spirit sprite, a Vardosian, but she does not know that a spirit sprite can only be truly harmed by another spirit sprite. Your sister is truly in no danger."

The soft gasp escaped my lips before I could stop it. Fortunately, Elise hadn't noticed. Suddenly it all made sense. Andrea wasn't really in danger. Elise had counted on my fear of harm to my sister, but she didn't even understand the truth of the situation. It was easy to see that Andrea was frightened, but I suspected that she wasn't aware of how this worked either. Hell, I had a hard time wrapping my head around it all. It was just too crazy. In this strange place, everything seemed topsy-turvy and nothing really made sense. Speaking softly to Andrea, I said, "Andrea, everything will be okay. You need to trust me and remember where you've been prior to this place. What has happened before can happen again." Waiting to see a sign that she understood and receiving no acknowledgment, I explained further, "Everything is fluid and what is easily poured into a cup

The Tree and the Tablet

can be filled again." Andrea's eyes were closed and tears slowly slid down her face. All I could do was pray that she understood my hidden meaning in the riddle.

As I finished speaking her eyes snapped open with a sudden awareness. She kept her expression sullen and shot me a brief nod, "I understand. Do what you have to."

Elise watched us intently. "What are you up to?" She wondered aloud. "Don't try anything funny! Jussst give me the tablet and I will releassse her."

Just then, I gave the mental command for Duck to blast Elise with all his might. *"Now!"*

Letting loose with a horrible roar, white hot flames flew from Duck's mouth and lit Elise on fire. The spectral was engulfed in dragon-fire and screeching with the most intensely painful scream. In the process, it released Andrea. Elise was writhing on the ground as Andrea crawled away from the horrific scene. The ugly spectral, spewed an pained scream, "Nooooooooo, I wouldn't have truly harmed her."

It was laying on the ground wailing in agony and began changing its form from one thing to another. First my mother, then my father, then Daniel, and Kelsey. Each time it shifted into another form, it cried out to me to help it, to ease it's pain or take away it's suffering. Eventually, I couldn't take it and looking to Duck I pleaded, "Please end it. I can't listen anymore."

"As you wish." Turning to the pitiful creature writhing on the ground.

The spectral cried out, "Master, please. Save me." Knowing the end was near, it screeched one last prophetic phrase, "The dark Lord will rule this land one day and"- staring at me intently she screamed, -"they all will die."

Duck shouted at her. "Enough!" Sending a last burst of deep blue at her with all of his rage and might, the Spectral was turned to ash and smoke within a split second. The only thing that lingered was the smell of diesel fuel and earth.

Knowing it was over, I turned to find Andrea standing next to me, unscathed by the fire or the spectral. She smiled and shrugged her shoulders, "Sometimes, I feel so strong, like I'm still..." Her voice trailed off.

Hugging her close, I said, "I wish you were really here. I keep forgetting you aren't really alive, that this is all just a thought in my mind."

Duck looked at me quizzically, "But mistress, how do you not know?"

Glancing over at him, now it was my turn to be skeptical. "What is it that I don't know, Duck?"

"This land is real and you are really here. You are not here in reincarnated form as your sister is. However, she is occupying the form of a spirit sprite called a Vardos. Their power allows them to hold a soul indefinitely in limbo which allows the being to live through them and communicate with their loved ones."

My laughter was purely from disbelief, "No, that's not possible." If that was the case, had I just left Daniel all alone

The Tree and the Tablet

in a cave after almost losing him? Had I always been able to teleport myself? "Duck, there have been times when I was able to speak with Kelsey in my head. Were those also times that I was able to transport myself?"

"It works differently on Earth. There, you can only communicate with those you reach out to in your mind. However, when you wish to return to the land of Nohad, you only need to envision it and it will be done."

As I glanced over at Andrea, I asked, "Do you believe all this?"

Andrea shrugged her shoulders. "Don't look at me, I don't know how all this works." Running her hands over her body, she remarked, "but I feel real." A quirky little smile that reminded me of all the times when she would tease me as a child, settled on her lips.

Turning to Duck, I suddenly felt an urgency to get back to Earth. He sensed my feeling and said, "Whenever you are ready, Mistress Maggie, we can leave this place and transport back to the land of earth and stone. You only have to close your eyes and see it in your mind to wish it so."

Turning back to Andrea, she smiled, "Go, Maggie. Time's running out."

Giving her one last embrace, I was reluctant to release her. Finally, I sighed and stepped back toward Duck, I reached out to him and patted his snout, "See you on the other side." He winked his big eye.

Closing my eyes, I relinquished my hold on the strange land. Spinning and turning through a vortex of earth, clouds, and a myriad of nonsensical objects, I landed with what felt like a thud on my bottom and quickly found myself surrounded by darkness so thick I couldn't see the hand in front of my face.

Remembering where I'd been when this started, I turned to my left and gingerly reached out a hand to find that Daniel was still there, breathing softly and peacefully. Briefly, I wondered how long I'd been gone.

The sound of a rock slide came from my right side and a mist of warmth surrounded me. Duck must have arrived and was now made of stone again. That made me a little sad. It was much more exciting to see him in his true dragon form, all bright and beautiful. Reaching out my thoughts, Duck affirmed my belief with his responding thought. Engulfed by a funny sensation, it kinda felt like a long lost friend hugged me.

A soft ringing sound came from Daniel's pack. It sounded like the ringtone I had set on my phone for Sherri. Looking in his pack, I soon located my cell phone. For a second, I was in shock and wondered how my phone had ended up in his pack and why he hadn't let me know. Standing up to move away and answer the phone, I was surprised when my eyes began to adjust and the return of the strange night vision which illuminated the cave. Startled, I fumbled with the phone and attempting to catch it, I ran into Duck's foreleg. The phone fell to the ground and Duck, attempting to move out of the way, stepped on the phone, smashing it into a hundred tiny pieces of plastic. Moaning, I looked at Duck and said, "Seriously?"

"Oh, I'm sorry. Unfortunately, I'm not that agile," looking down at hisself, "Or light."

"It's alright." Frustrated and wondering why the secrecy and how he got my phone, I sat down next to Daniel again. Starting at the tiny shards that were once my phone, it was unfortunate it was irreparably broken, but I'd gotten used to not having it and it felt good not to be chained to the electronic device. The new vision must have been due to the odd mind-link that Duck and I shared. Lost in thought, I gradually noticed Daniel had been laying on his side watching me intently, and I wondered how he was able to see in the dark. For some odd reason, I decided not to let him know I could see him watching me or that I'd found my phone, and instead made a big deal out of looking for the lost flashlight. Keeping secrets of my own, I kept the tablet hidden beneath my right leg as I fumbled around. He murmured and began to sit up.

"How are you feeling," I asked.

"Better than ever." He responded lightly. "Have you figured out how to get us out of this cave or are we doomed?" Finding the tiny flashlight on the floor of the cave next to his large thigh and clicking the button at the back to see if it worked, it shined into his eyes. He gave an odd sounding laugh and shielded his eyes.

"Sorry," I mumbled as I redirected the light. "I think I have an idea about how we can get out of here." Grabbing my pack, I turned away from Daniel to block his view and pulled out the journal. Sneakily, I tucked the Tablet of Power into the pack while I was still turned away. Taking a moment to close the top of my pack, my attention was soon redirected to the journal.

Talking more to myself than anyone in particular, "I recall seeing a map of the cave on one of these pages." Putting the flashlight in my mouth, it was easier to flip through the pages of the journal.

"Aha!" My voice echoed in the empty space as the flashlight fell to the floor of the cave. Retrieving it, I refocused it to the pages in the book. "Here it is." Duck leaned over and snorted as he looked at the pages in my hand.

"That is at the furthest part of the cave where the water seeps in." He said matter-of-factly.

Positioning myself in his direction, I bumped my nose on his snout since he was so close. Rubbing my nose, I wondered why he was made of stone again and asked, "Is it easy to get to?" Daniel had moved to my other side to see the journal as well. Out of the corner of my eye, I caught him looking toward my pack but refocused his attention to the journal by putting it up in front of his face to show him the location.

Duck apologized for hurting my nose as he pulled away slightly, "Yes, it is, but the doorway shown on the map is under water." His brow was slightly wrinkled in consternation.

"Well, then, we'd best be on our way." As I put the journal

back into the backpack and cinched the top closed securing the hiding place of my new possession, I rose to my feet.

"Daniel, are you able to swim," The question was more due to his injury since I'd seen him in the lake and a way to distract him from my pack as it was soon slung over my shoulders and connected at the waist by the belt.

"So, we'll be diving I presume?" He was putting his pack on and securing it in place. Again, I couldn't help but wonder why he was hiding that he could see in the dark, but I decided to play along and kept my visual acuity to myself as well.

"Duck, my friend, lead the way." Moving aside, I allowed Duck to step out in front of me and made a big deal of trying to find his tail to hold onto. Reaching behind me, I slid my hand down Daniel's arm and grabbed his hand, asking, "Ready?"

"After you, milady." He replied jokingly. The sarcasm dripped from his lips.

Duck started off at an upward angle leading us away from our small hole in the wall. Suggesting to us that we should watch our step, we were suddenly veering to the right and at a steep pitch downward. At one point, the walls seemed remarkably thin or there was some sort of echo as I thought I could hear someone speaking as if through a megaphone. Only it was extremely muffled and I couldn't quite make out the words. At my inquiry, Duck grunted and affirmed that it was Maxwell. "He talks to himself for hours."

Finally, we reached an area where the cave opened up into a

large cavern that had filtered light shining down from a hole in the ceiling. The hole was probably only about five feet in circumference, however, it was almost fifty feet in the air straight above our heads. I could see light shining down through trees and over the top of the hole there was a thin layer of what looked like ivy.

We could clearly hear the sounds of water rushing. It almost sounded like it surrounded us. Probably just acoustics. The walls were slick and curved upward in a dome-like shape. My vision soon adjusted to normal and I could see that we were standing on a ledge high above a pool of water. It appeared to be fed by water that seeped through the walls of the cavern and made the walls look like they were crying. Stalagmites covered the upper ceiling and milky white drops of water dripped from them into the pool giving it the appearance of milk. A soft gasp of appreciation formed in my mouth, taken in by the incredible beauty but also filled me with dread.

"How are we supposed to find an opening in that," I asked incredulously. "Duck, can you fly us up to that hole?"

Stepping back from the ledge fearfully, "No. I can't fly in this form. I tried once and was stuck in a cave-in for months from all the flapping."

It was then that Daniel took advantage of the fact that I'd unclasped my waist clip for my backpack. He quickly pulled the backpack from my shoulders and opened it to find the tablet laying on top. My mouth dropped open. So, he had seen me put

The Tree and the Tablet

it in my backpack in the immense darkness. I'd suspected but wasn't sure.

He turned it over in his hands and holding it up to me, asked angrily with a tinge of awe, "Are you sure this is it? There is no writing on it at all."

Reaching for it, "Of course there…" My words fell short as I grasped the tablet in my hands and it began to glow fiercely. It was blank. Turning it over and over in my hands, confusion dripped from my voice as I stuttered, "But, there were words on it before." Again, I looked at both sides of it and turning to Duck I asked, "Is there anything that you can tell me about this thing?"

Duck looked at me pitifully, "I'm afraid I can't help you."

Feeling totally lost and quite frankly at my breaking point, I dropped to my knees and just stared at the tablet, willing it to show me something, anything, just to help me figure out how to get my niece back. Suddenly, I was exhausted. The events from the pool of Valoria and the Glenn were suddenly like weights holding every fiber of my being down.

Rest. All I needed was to rest. As I crumpled into a pile on the ground with the tablet clutched to my chest, my eyes closed with the weight of a thousand emotional ties pulling them down. Sweet oblivion engulfed me and I knew nothing else existed or mattered at that moment. Like a blanket of peace and tranquility, I was enfolded in a warm cocoon-like embrace of utter exhaustion. There was no time to see that Daniel had slipped away into the darkness again or that Duck was desperately

Kathryn O'Brien

clutching my leg to keep me from toppling over the ledge into the pool.

CHAPTER 25

"*Auntie?*" The voice sounded so familiar. "*Auntie?*" More urgently now. "*Please hurry, Auntie, I'm scared!*"

"*Kelsey?*" My mind responded.

Waking up abruptly to the sound of Duck persistently talking loudly in my ear. "Mistress!?! Mistress MAGGIE!!!! Wake up! Please! I can't hold you any longer." The urgency in his voice was hard to miss.

Opening my eyes, they felt gravelly and dry. Although I was feeling rejuvenated, like I had just woken from the most luxurious nap ever, my eyes struggled to adjust. As my vision started to focus, I realized that I was actually partially hanging off a cliff. The entire left side of my body was dangling at an awkward angle and looking over my shoulder I saw the milky white pool directly below me. Turning back toward Duck's heavy breathing, I felt the pressure of his large clawed foot barely holding onto my right ankle.

Trying desperately to roll to my right side, I didn't have enough upper body strength to counter my body weight. The tablet was still clutched against my chest with my right hand. "Duck, don't let go!" Even though Duck was a large dragon of about eight feet tall at his shoulders and about three foot of head and neck as well as twenty feet long from snout to tail, I knew he couldn't hold me much longer. He was as large as an adolescent elephant, and even though I felt like he would probably grow larger, it didn't help at that moment because I knew that eventually he would lose his battle with gravity.

Deciding on self-preservation over the tablet, I swung my arm out to the right which sent it away from me by a couple of feet to a safe location. That movement caused Duck to lose his grip on my foot, and my body began to shift away from him. As I screeched with fear, he screamed like a frightened child. Spinning in place and rolling to my stomach as my other foot slid over the ledge, I clawed at the earth, breaking my nails against the dry dirt and rock. Duck pounced forward in an attempt to grasp my flailing hands as I was pulled from my precarious position on the ledge by my own weight. The gentle grip he had on me was such an odd sensation. Even though I felt fear that he would crush my wrists under all that weight, I was also surprised by his awareness. The comprehension that he placed the most minimal amount of pressure on my hands with his clawed front feet in order to halt my fall was reassuring.

Kicking my feet toward the ledge, I was shocked when my momentum stopped. My foot had landed on some sort of rock outcropping or a small ledge that was jutting out right below the overhang I was dangling from. Duck was finally able to grasp my hands completely in his massive clawed front feet. He started to pull me up, but I stopped him. "Wait! I think there's something below me."

Duck stopped pulling. As I felt around with my feet to make sure the landing was firm, I ducked my head below the overhang. There it was, in an alcove, a small wooden door, carved into the rock and inset by several feet. It was very elaborately carved around the framework with multiple different hieroglyphics that resembled the Mayan carvings on the amulet and the tablet. The only problem was that the doorway looked like it was only big enough for a dwarf as it was roughly three to four feet tall and about three feet wide. Seeing that the ledge was safely large enough for me to stand on, I looked up above the ledge to Duck who was still holding my hands tightly.

"It's alright, Duck. You can let go." He looked at me doubtfully, blinking his large eyes. "I promise." He slowly released his grip. On seeing that I was still standing in the position without slipping, he released me and grunted in relief.

" I was so scared." He looked like he was going to cry. To see such a beautiful, strong and magnificently built creature almost in tears over me was humbling.

"Sweet, Duck. You are so amazing." Putting my hand toward his large paw and caressing it, "Thank you, my friend." He dropped his head low and licked me. It caused me to giggle. His tongue tickled. It felt like a million tiny smooth round pebbles that had the finest little feathers attached to them.

It was at that moment that I realized Daniel was gone. My heart jumped into my throat and pain filled my soul. "Duck, where's Daniel?"

He simply shook his head and replied, "I do not know, Mistress."

Not understanding why or how he left, I knew at this moment, I needed to put my hurt aside and focus on getting out of the cave to find Kelsey and save her from Mr. Maxwell. "Duck, hand me the tablet please."

His clawed foot hovered over the spot where I'd tossed it, and he gently scooted it across the dirt floor toward me as the size of his claws made it extremely difficult to pick up something so small that was lying flat on the ground. As I grasped it in my hands, it started to glow again. "Don't go anywhere." He nodded.

Dropping to my knees on the small landing, I leaned forward to where the door was. *Hmmm. The journal would be nice to have right now.* The thought flitted through my mind. Within two seconds, my pack was being thrown toward me from above. Smiling to myself, "Thanks, Duck. "Did I think it or speak it?

"You're welcome."

Pulling out the journal, I sat down and started looking

The Tree and the Tablet

through the pages to see if there was anything that would give me a clue about the doorway. Reading through pages about the tablet and it's many powers, there was a small passage about the power to gain access to a myriad of alternate lands, but there was no explanation on how to use it to gain access to the doorway.

Looking at the door, the hieroglyphs suddenly refocused themselves into words. It read - *Entry requires a lover's touch As the light of the One in your hand you clutch.*
"What the heck does that mean?"

I felt Daniel before I heard him. Strange how the connection we had was so strong and electric. It was like a jolt of energy hit me every time he was near. He was above me on the ledge. "Where is she, Dragon?" He sounded menacing and angry.

"She is below." Was all I heard Duck say out loud, but in my mind, it was like I had opened a window and suddenly I heard, "*Do I tell him how to find you?*"

Giving it some serious thought, I decided that maybe Daniel had a good reason for abandoning us without a word. Deciding to trust my choices, I responded mentally, *"Duck, show him how to get down here."*

Soon, Daniel was lowering himself over the upper ledge into the small alcove within the rocks. Facing him as I waited patiently trying not to show any emotion once he came face-to-face with me, he smirked at me, "You look refreshed."

"Where were you?" My words dripped like venom from my lips. There was no hiding it now. I was angry and hurt by his

343

disappearance and I had no idea how long he'd been gone as the light from the cavern had only slightly diminished in the time since I fell into my deep sleep.

He stepped closer to me which caused him to have to stoop and bend over at the waist to get into the small opening near the door. "Did you miss me?" His voice was husky and so sensual it was like a caress against my battered emotions. Ugh. He answered a question with a question. That was one of my pet peeves.

Trying to keep from responding to his nearness, I chided him, "Don't answer a question with a question. And, No, I didn't miss you, but it would have been nice to have your assistance. I was barely hanging onto the ledge. It was all Duck could do to keep me from falling into the pool." As I glared at him, he reached out and gently caressed my face.

"I'm sorry about that." There it was again, a glimpse of humanity and was that true sorrow? "But you are alright, and I knew that you would be."

"Ugh. That's no excuse. **You Left Me Hanging. Literally,**" my hands made a motion to mimic a body hanging over a ledge, "**HANGING!**"

"Maggie, I apologized. One day..." his voice hung suspended with words unspoken.

"Why can't you be more open with me? It's like there's always these secrets between us." My frustration was tangible, and I swallowed hard. *How could I judge him when I was keeping secrets too?*

"You're not being honest either, Maggie." He read me like a book. "Come now, I think the time has passed for these games." He sat next to me which put him closer and less at a disadvantage due to stooping. Pulling me down onto his lap, he asked, "Will you please stop hiding things from me?" Opening my mouth to talk, he shushed me with a light kiss on my lips. My senses were reeling, but I placed my hand on his chest to push him away.

"Daniel, if you want honesty and full disclosure from me, then you have to share as well." My eyes searched his longingly. It felt like all my hopes and dreams were hanging in the balance.

"Maggie, you don't know what you're asking." Looking at me, his face seemed to harden under my scrutiny.

Fine, if that's the way he wanted to play it, then two could play this game. "If you can't bring yourself to let your guard down, then I can't tell you what you want to know." My response was cold but necessary.

His expression was surprised and then became guarded again. "Alright, Maggie. Have it your way." He set me away from him and looking at the door, he asked, "Well? What's next?"

The anger was still coiled around in my belly mixed with the hurt of his refusal to give in, but I needed to save Kelsey and there was no harm in sharing the riddle of the doorway with him. Reciting the riddle, I asked him what he thought.

"Hmmm. Did you find anything in the journal?" He reached for the book in my hands. Turning my body away from him put the journal out of his reach. He dropped his hands in surrender.

"No, only one passage that tells about how to access alternate lands using the tablet but not how to use it." He glanced up at me, his expression seemed sad, but noticing that I was intently watching him, he smiled and focused his attention on the door.

"Anything about this particular door or these carvings other than the riddle?"

Shrugging my shoulder, I ran my hand over the smooth stone that was devoid of writing, "I don't even know anymore." As I held the glowing tablet up next to the door knob, I fumed, "This stupid thing seems useless! It can't even tell me how to open a damned door!" At that moment, it felt as though the tablet had developed a magnet and pulling my hand to the right next to the door knob there was a depression in the wall. Almost like a key card slot only it was a flat indentation that allowed me to still see it. Excited, a small laugh bubbled forth. It couldn't be that simple. I put the tablet into the slot. Stepping back and watching it intently, the tablet glowed even more fiercely. Words began to appear on the surface of the stone which were illuminated in a brighter light. Reading the words, I said, "By the power of the One, I claim entrance to this door."

The glowing became fiercer than it had and the words surrounding the door lit up like fire was shooting from behind them. My hand flew up to shield my eyes, it was so bright. As the door slid open it screeched and growled as if it hadn't been open for a million years. My heart was ready to beat out of my chest.

The Tree and the Tablet

Was it fear, excitement, happiness? I couldn't say, but I knew it meant I was one step closer to getting Kelsey. The door came to a screeching halt and was laying open to view the interior. Swiftly, I grabbed the tablet out of the alcove it was in and put both it and the journal into my pack, slinging it over my shoulder.

Daniel placed his hand on my arm to stop me as I began to pass through the open doorway. "We don't know what's on the other side of the door. We should be cautious."

Laughing and feeling a little cocky, I said, "I'm ready for it. Bring it on." No sooner had I stepped forward than I instantly regretted my rash decision. Standing in front of me was a massive black creature like nothing I'd ever seen before. It resembled a large dog but had two heads and a lion's mane on one. The rest of the body reminded me of a gryphon. Wings stretched out of its sides to span the distance of the room.

Not sure how I knew, but I could understand it's language. Maybe it was speaking English and I just assumed it was speaking a different language. It sounded sort of like an instructor I'd had in college with a thick accent and an annoying voice. The voice was extremely nasally and shrill to the ear. "Go away!" It screeched at me. "You are not welcome in my sanctuary."

Instinctively, I bowed, my voice filled with what I hoped was the utmost respect and calm, I asked, "Oh, lord of the great room, I beg your forgiveness, but one so powerful as yourself could surely assist me to find my way?"

The beast literally glowed under my praise. He lifted his

heads and licked himself as if one of his heads were subservient to the other. "You really think I'm powerful and great?" It asked inquisitively while continuing to preen its own feathers and stretch its wings.

"Oh, definitely." I soothed. Daniel chuckled behind me which caused the bird creature to flinch and growl low. My elbow swiftly found purchase in his ribs and I attempted to calm the beast by cooing softly, "Please, forgive, don't mind him, he is but my lowly servant," At Daniels dark scowl, I glared back at him, silently motioning for him to play along.

Bowing low, Daniel said, "I aim to please." He looked at me sideways and smirked for only me to see.

The creature moved its heads back and forth and wiggled its tail, reminding me of a cat getting ready to pounce. Seeking to calm the creature further, I asked, "If I may, oh great one, my name is Maggie and this is, Daniel." Pulling my pack forward and fishing inside, I soon held up the tablet and asked, "The great spirit has sent us to find our way out of this place and seek a small child, can you help us?"

His eyes snapped together, and one head said to the other in a whisper, "Do not tell her what she wishes. Maybe we can convince her to give us the Tablet of Power." I listened intently to their banter and the other head with the mane said, "But if she is truly sent by the One, then we will offend and it will turn us into something more appalling than this." It visibly shivered. The other head said, "This Maggie is a liar. I can smell it on her." He

The Tree and the Tablet

sniffed the air as if to exaggerate his words. The maned headed one sniffed and replied, "Bah, your sniffer is broken. I say we trust her."

Choosing the break in their discussion to interrupt I asked, "I'm sorry to interrupt such a truly important discussion, but may I ask your names?"

The one with the mane and brown eyes stopped, proudly raised his head and said regally, "I am Phenryr and this,"— he motioned his head toward his companion, who had beautiful blue eyes — "is Falomere." They both bowed.

At that moment, I heard this horrendous noise like a great screech from outside of the doorway and a large splashing sound. I spun on my heel just in time to see a large rocky scaled looking dragon's tail streaking toward the ledge and with a great effort, the end of the tail which was shaped like a grappling hook was caught in the earth. "Help!" Came the cry and forgetting the predicament I was in, I ran past Daniel toward the opening.

CHAPTER 26

As I streaked past Daniel, I couldn't help but think that Duck was face first in the water and drowning while it was taking what felt like forever to get to him. Dropping my head low on my way through the doorway, I reached his tail embedded in the dirt and looking over the edge, I saw Duck, standing upright in the water, looking sheepishly up at me.

The relief I felt was tangible as I leaned over and asked, "What the heck were you thinking?"

Smiling up at me, "Well, I heard the other creature fighting and I thought I could help so I tried to lower myself down, but I lost my grip and fell." He shrugged his massive shoulders and smiling broader said, "Well, at least now we know the water isn't too deep."

Not being able to hold it in, I laughed so hard, I felt like my side would burst. Daniel tapped me on the shoulder, and I turned to see his stern gaze. He motioned his head toward where we had left the odd dog/lion looking creature and said, "Sorry to interrupt, but I think we have more pressing issues to attend to."

Looking past him to the two headed Phenryr and Falomere, I was instantly concerned. They appeared to be arguing again and slowly advancing toward the doorway. Of course, they wouldn't be able to get out of it, but they did make a menacing vision. Turning serious again, I turned back and spoke quickly to Duck and Daniel, "You two wait here!"

Crouching myself down to fit back through the doorway, I entered cautiously and spoke softly, "My friends, it appears that I have a problem and need your assistance."

At that, they stopped bickering or advancing and asked simultaneously, "What is the problem?"

Briefly, I explained that my friend, the dragon, was stuck in the water below the opening to the cavern and that I needed a very strong creature to lift him up. They were very excited to know that there was a dragon close by as they could be considered lucky. After a lengthy back and forth between the two, they agreed to try.

Returning to Daniel, I said, "Well, here goes nothing," as I made a loop and dropped it down to Duck. "Duck, put this in your mouth and hold on." He nodded and took the rope between his teeth. Turning to the boys in the cavern, I said, "Go ahead, you can pull now."

They grunted and groaned but they were not moving Duck at all. As a matter of fact, the rope was actually starting to tear in his mouth due to the sharpness of his teeth. After several minutes, the two stopped and started to argue about who was pulling more, which I thought was actually pretty funny since they shared a body. Finally, I asked, "Do you have any other ideas?"

Phenryr stopped and looked at me with a dawning expression. "But, you have the Tablet of Power. You only need to speak the words and your friend will be shrunk small enough for you to pick him up yourself."

Holding the marbled surface up in front of me, I said, "Oh, great tablet, shrink my dragon into the size of a peach."

Nothing happened. Except divine, shrill laughter. Falomere was guffawing so hard, I thought his head would explode. Cocking my head to the side, I stated, "Oh, that's helpful." Seeing that he wasn't going to stop laughing anytime soon, I looked to Phenryr and asked, "What's so funny?"

However, it was Falomere that answered, "You silly girl-woman."–Falomere was taking great gulps of air in an attempt to stop his uproarious laughter while his blue eyes appeared to be filled with tears,–"You have the most powerful tool in your incompetent hands and know not how to use it." His renewed peals of humor rolled out of him like waves and washed over me sobering my mood quite drastically.

Bristling at the two for having fun at my expense, I

exclaimed, "I've had enough!" As I stomped my foot, the tablet flared to life a brilliant shade of turquoise blue. Noticing the flare of the tablet's power in response to my seemingly unpleasant mood, he stopped laughing. Looking at me speculatively and gauging my anger, he must have decided to take me seriously and asked instead, "How did you come by the tablet?"

Wondering for a moment if I should tell them, I decided on the truth. It didn't matter anymore that Daniel knew. The need to get to Kelsey trumped everything else and this creature held a key of some sort to help me achieve my goal. "I travelled through my thoughts to the land of Valor and fought my way through the pool of the maiden's tears to pull it out from behind the veil."

Glancing over my shoulder at Daniel, his eyes widened but that was his only reaction.

Nodding and cooing as if he suddenly believed me, Falomere asked, "What is your purpose for taking the tablet?"

"My niece, Kelsey, is being held captive by the creature who is the Trickster's henchman. He's taken her and I must bring the tablet to him or he'll hurt her."

"I know the one you speak of. He is very evil and driven mad with his desire for power. He will indeed use her to gain what he desires, but we cannot allow you to give it to him."

Deflated, I sighed. "How am I supposed to do what I need to do, if you won't help me?"

Phenryr spoke up, "Maggie, you obviously know enough about how to use the tablet as you were able to gain entrance to

The Tree and the Tablet

this sanctum." He smiled reassuringly, "Have you not guessed it?" At the slight shaking of my head and pleading look, he stated, "You must wish with your heart and visualize your friend getting smaller for the words to appear on the tablet. Once they appear, you only need to speak the words aloud to have it happen." Smiling, "Go ahead, give it a try."

Holding it firmly in my hands , I closed my eyes and visualized Duck the size of a kitten in my hands. Opening my eyes to the sound of Falomere's whistle, the tablet was now glowing a bright white in my hands. The characters started to appear, and I spoke the words,

A mighty foe so strong and bold
Soon so small that one might hold

Duck screeched outside of the opening and I heard the tiniest voice as he ran into the room the size of a miniature chihuahua grunting, growling, and spitting fire. He was so cute, I picked him up laughing and said, "Awe, now I can take you with me wherever I go." He blew fire on me and singed my fingers. "Ouch! Stop that! Is that any way to treat someone who helped you," I scolded as I set him back on the ground. Daniel laughed from behind him.

He stopped and stood still for a moment. His squeaky voice said, "Thank you mistress, but can you put me back to my prior glory?"

Looking around the room, I gauged his original size to be much too tight for him to fit as the ceiling was only about seven and a half feet tall and from wall to wall was no more than five feet wide. "I'm sorry, Duck, but that won't work. You're much too large for this room. We would all be squashed under you." Making eye contact with Phenryr and Falomere. "How can I thank you?"

They looked at each other and smiled a hopeful smile. "You can release us from our prison."

Slightly surprised, I asked, "But why are you imprisoned here? What did you do and who put you here?"

Falomere, seeming to have let go of his earlier surliness, spoke first, "We were accused of a deed we did not do. We were wronged by the Mistress of Doane, Serena. She sent word to our master that we were the ones who falsely convinced the maiden to go to the Glenn."

At my look of comprehension, Phenryr said, "We were lied to as well. A shapeshifter approached us and told us that we were to find lord Alkard and alert him to the plot. We did what we thought was right." He snorted, "How were we to know?" He moaned, "Our master was frozen because of us. We didn't mean to take our eyes off Valoria. She told us to go get something to eat while she was at the altar."

Falomere grouched, "We were hungry and there were the most amazing foods for us to eat." He sighed, "Alkard's father, Opi-Chee begged the Great Spirit to punish us. We were sent here until a time that we could right the wrong."

"Wow!" It was all beginning to make sense. This was the guard that had told Alkard to go to Valoria and they weren't henchmen but were also tricked. Feeling that there was much more to learn about this duo, I asked, "What can you do to help me get to my niece?"

"Look into the back of this cavern, there is a riddle that you must solve in order to move beyond this area. Once you are out, you will speak the words, *The wrong is right, what was done is undone.*" He smiled, "This will undo our curse and release us to go home."

Well, what was there to lose? Looking at Daniel, he simply shrugged his shoulders and said, "It's up to you."

Squaring my shoulders, I walked toward the back of the cavern. Duck tagged along. Looking down at his cute little miniature stature, I couldn't help but smile. He was just too adorable. He tilted his head sideways at me and indignantly huffed, "Stop it! I can still hear you in my head sometimes."

Lifting my eyebrows at him, I laughed softly, "Sorry."

He swished his tail and let out a puff of smoke that circled around his tiny head. "It's just difficult for me to be this small. I feel so helpless," he grumbled.

"I guess I never thought of it that way." I leaned down and stroked his pebbly exterior, "As soon as it's possible, I'll return you to your glorious self."

He almost was purring like a kitten. "Thank you."

Kathryn O'Brien

As I stood in front of the wall, I could see there were several areas indented into the wall in the shape of a rectangle that I could place the tablet into and each of them had a different symbol inscribed within it. Above them all was a single phrase—*Life is the key.*

That was it. Looking at the tablet that softly glowed in my hands, I stroked it gently, willing it to give me the answer. The color fluctuated from a bright green to a purple and back to white, but no words magically appeared. Sighing heavily, I looked at the wall again. There were eight different options. From top left to right, A bird that looked like a raven, a sun, a tree, a dog, what looked to be a dragon, a man, a woman, and a flying saucer. Well, I wasn't quite sure what the last one was, but it sure looked like a flying saucer and I let loose a small giggle at the thought. Daniel stepped up next to me. I could feel him next to me as an invisible force bounced between us and I shivered. Mistaking me for being cold, he put his jacket around my shoulders, holding me for a minute. He must've sensed that I needed his strength right then.

"Do you have any idea what the right choice is?" He asked gently. His fingers played with the side of my neck as his hand rested gently on my shoulder. It felt so good. As my pulse started to race under his gentle touch, I almost forgot what I was supposed to be doing. Suddenly, as if to remind me, the tablet turned bright pink and started to pulsate. My attention was instantly drawn back to it and the task at hand. Within seconds, my vision blurred, and everything went dark. My last thought was,

The Tree and the Tablet

"Oh, no. Not now!"

Before I knew it, I was standing in a great castle, looking at a frail woman standing next to a throne. She looked as though she had been very beautiful at one time, but now, she appeared worn, like a beautiful rug that had been trampled on for years. The room was void of people and I approached her slowly. It was her and I. She looked up from her musings and I saw that in her hand she had the most luscious, red rose. As she held out her hand to me with the beautiful flower, it transformed into a pink dogwood. She smiled softly and I held out my hand to take it from her. As she released the bloom, she said, "Remember." Then she vanished into thin air. Looking at the beautiful dogwood flower, I suddenly knew the answer that was right in front of my face the entire time. My world turned upside down and I opened my eyes to find Daniel was looking down at me with a slightly worried expression.

Determinedly, I walked to the wall and lifted the tablet to place it in the slot that contained the picture of the tree. The room was so quiet, I could hear a pin drop. It seemed that everyone was holding their breath in anticipation of what may happen. Looking over my shoulder at Daniel, I hoped for some sign that he thought I was right. He shrugged his shoulders, concern creeped into his voice as he gently spoke, "Maggie, please make sure you're right."

"I know this is the right one. I just...." —pausing — "know it," I mumbled as I placed the tablet into the opening and stepped back.

As if my body had a will of its own and I was in a sort of trance, the words left my lips, "The great tree of life open this doorway."

A great rumbling started, and I wondered aloud, "An earthquake?" I could barely stand, and Daniel reached out to me to steady me from falling as everything shook violently. "Oh, no."— I yelled. — "I must've chosen wrong." However, as I looked over my shoulder at Phenryr and Falomere, they were almost giddy with excitement. Duck was trying to keep his footing standing near my feet and Daniel stood with his legs spread wide to prevent himself from falling over with the intensity of the shaking.

The tablet glowed white hot and the wall started to turn red as if it were becoming molten lava. The top of it looked like it was a wax candle. Slowly, it melted and dripped onto the floor below it. It was dissolving and the tablet continued to glow as the rumbling continued and the wall slowly dissolved before us and it was now a pool of cold, hard earth, while the tablet laid on top of the pile of rubble that looked like puddles of hardened wax and rock. The rumbling stopped. Everything was still. There, before my eyes laid an opening that was illuminated by a strange glowing light coming from above it.

Turning to Daniel, I smiled. Duck started running around in circles and screeching in excitement. Not sure what to expect, I stepped forward to go through the opening.

The Tree and the Tablet

Phenryr spoke up, "Maggie?" He sounded unsure. I glanced back at him and Falomere as I stopped mid-stride.

"Oh. Yes, of course." Looking at them I said, "Thank you both."

They bowed low, "Thank you for allowing us to make up for our past."

Smiling gently, I spoke the words, "As a daughter of Valor, I declare, *The wrong is right. What was done is undone.*"

Phenryr and Falomere's forms blurred and swirled in front of my eyes. Magically, there were two very strong seven-foot-tall giant men standing in front of me. They were very muscular and handsome. One with blazing blue eyes and the other with brown eyes. They could have been twins if it weren't for the different colored eyes and their hair. One had short blonde hair with no facial hair and the other had long red hair with a full beard. They were clothed in armor and short tunics with metal covers over their chests. Each had a long sword in their hand. They reminded me of Roman gladiators or Vikings.

As if they were afraid to look at each other, they continued to look straight ahead at me and one of them asked, "Did it work?"

Nodding excitedly and grinning broadly at them, "I think so."

They slowly turned to look at each other and their faces both lit up. They whooped exuberantly as they danced around merrily hugging each other and laughing. One of them ran to me and hugged me excitedly. "Thank you, thank you." He picked me up and swung me around in circles and I giggled. He set me down just long enough for the other to pick me up and repeat the process.

Setting me on my feet, I was out of breath. When one of them reached out to grab me again, Daniel stepped in front of me and stopped the excitement with his droll expression, "You two will break her with your crazy jumping around."

They stopped, looked at each other again, and hugged fiercely. Their happiness was infectious. Stepping around Daniel, placing my hand on his arm, I said, "Stop being such a buzzkill."

The brothers stopped and looked at me. The one with the short hair and blue eyes bowed low and said, "Falomere Longbeard, at your service, Mistress Maggie of Valor."

The other looked at him then looked at me and bowed as well, "Phenryr Longbeard at your service as well."

They both raised up and instantly, I was reminded of the two headed creature as they hugged each other smiling widely. Extending my hand to shake theirs, Phenryr was first to hold out his hand and I took his to shake it. He smiled and pumped my hand up and down.

As he released my hand, Falomere reached out and repeated what he had just witnessed.

"Nice to meet you." I said, as I finished shaking hands with them. Looking at Daniel, I said, "Well, then. We should probably be on our way."

The Tree and the Tablet

They smiled at each other and then at me, "We will go with you."

"Sure! The more the merrier."

Daniel didn't look as keen to have them tag along but didn't say anything. He just frowned and I shrugged.

Reaching down to retrieve the tablet, I heard a sound that just about sent me into a fit. A scream rent the air and my heart dropped to my knees. I'd heard that sound before. My legs wouldn't move fast enough as I stepped into the opening. As I crossed the barrier between rooms, it was like I stepped through a thin curtain. Hard to explain but it was almost like running through one of those banners that they have at football games. Turning back toward the opening, I was confronted with what looked like a wall even though I'd just walked through an opening. Suddenly, I felt a stabbing pain in the back of my head and everything grew dark instantly.

CHAPTER 27

As I came to, my head was pounding. The most awful pain was coursing it's way through my temples and working its way through my head. Gingerly, I tried to move but found that my hands were tied behind my back and there was a disgusting piece of cloth in my mouth. For a brief moment I thought that if I kept getting head injuries, I'd need to be admitted to the looney bin. That thought almost made me laugh. Only no sound came out except a rough moan.

Based on the pressure points, I knew I was laying on my side on the ground. Where was Daniel? Where were the guys? Where was I? All these questions served to cause me more aggravation as I considered that I was probably not going to get an answer anytime soon. My eyes felt gritty and hurt to try and open them. In reality, all I really wanted to do was keep them closed and go to sleep. A sharp pain was soon introduced to my side as a firm booted foot made its way violently into my world from an unseen force.

"Open your eyes!" Was the command given by the little weasel of a man.

Barely squinting my eyes open just enough to let minimal light in. That hurt. Scanning the room, I found he wasn't too far away. He was shorter and uglier than I remembered him. Taking a moment to look around the room, Kelsey was hiding in a corner trying to be brave. I didn't see Peanut. No one else was close by. Recalling what happened when I went through the opening, I'd spun around at the odd sensation and there was a wall behind me. But how could I walk through a wall?

He drew my attention back to him. "Where's the amulet?" He sneered.

Mumbling, I tried to talk around the gag, but couldn't get anything out. He must've realized and decided to remove the gag. As he pulled it down and out of my mouth, I tried to moisten my mouth enough to talk but wound up coughing.

"Water," I rasped. It was all I could get out and was barely audible to my own ears.

Reaching over and grabbing a flask, he opened it and dumped water on my face. The water trickled down over my mouth and I tried to suck it in to quench my thirst. The water stopped. "Talk." He demanded. A deranged expression met my gaze as I peered up at him.

My throat was still dry, and I was barely able to get the words out, "I don't have it."

Another kick. "Liar." He screeched.

"No," I grunted, "Your note didn't tell me to bring it."

Another kick, and another. Groaning under the continued onslaught, I could see Kelsey crying across the room but clearly frightened into staying still. When he stopped kicking me, she started to move toward me and making eye contact with her I shook my head while mouthing silently, "no," at her which kept her still for the moment.

"You stupid woman!" He railed as he paced back and forth. He was still limping. He was talking to himself under his breath. It was mostly incoherent and he turned looking up at the ceiling, "No amulet, but I have the tablet." He held the tablet in the air as if he were showing it to someone. "No!" He seemed frustrated but also fearful. "I swear. I don't know where she came from. One minute there was a wall and the next, she was standing there."

There was a movement out of the corner of my eye. My head was ringing, and my side hurt from being kicked repeatedly. Tears streamed down my face even though I was trying not to cry. Gasping for air was quickly followed by a sharp pain, I was pretty sure that he broke a rib or two. The taste of my own blood was in my mouth. It was really hard to breath and I felt like I was going to throw up. All I could think was, *Focus on something else.*

"No, mistress. I swear it!" He turned his attention back to

me. Spinning on his heel, he marched up to me with his broken gait and leaning over, he whispered menacingly, "You have it!" My response was to shake my head vigorously. He leaned over and ran his disgusting tongue along my face. "You'll tell me where it is." Flinching away from the disgusting smell of his rancid mouth, I continued to shake my head. He sat up and slapped me across the face, "Don't lie!" He screamed as he raised his hand to slap me across the face a second time.

"No, please! I swear I don't have it." As I flinched, his hand swooshed through the air toward me.

"Shut up!" He squealed. *God, what did he want? Talk or shut up?* My head was reeling. His eyes were darting around. He reached down and spun me so that I was mostly on my back, he ripped my shirt open to the waist. Baring my sports bra and the rest of my upper torso as the shreds of my shirt fell to my sides. His eyes narrowed, scanning me for the amulet. Not seeing what he was looking for, he pulled out a knife and leaned in to slit my bra in two.

"Please, don't do this," I begged.

"I said"–he raised his other hand to knock me senseless–"SHUT UP!" He stopped his hand mid-air and his eyes went wide. "I knew it!" Giggling like a giddy schoolgirl, he reached over and plucked something from the ground next to me. My eyes grew wide at what he lifted into view. It was the amulet! *But how?* As he spun around and raised it into the air gleefully, I remembered. Daniel had said that there was an almost identical

The Tree and the Tablet

"fake" amulet in Maxwell's discarded backpack. But how did it end up on the ground next to me?

A little black shadow ran swiftly from one side of the room to the other. It was miniature Duck. That must've been what I'd seen earlier. Something told me that's how the fake amulet magically appeared near me. But where were the Longbeards and Daniel? Dammit, where was Peanut? Looking over to where Kelsey still sat silent and crying, I saw what I'd been looking for. There was Peanut, being held close to Kelsey. Relief flooded me. For now, at least, they were safe and they only looked a little dirty. Now, I just needed to figure out how to escape this crazy man.

As if sensing my grand scheme, Maxwell reached down and dragged me into an upright position. He was almost frantic. Maxwell turned to me, "How did you get here?"

A lie, "I don't know." He started to move toward me as if he were going to kick me. "No, I swear, — Moving away from him and still gasping for air, — "One second I was just sitting in a corner looking at the tablet and thinking about Kelsey and the next, I was looking at a wall."

He studied me, trying to determine if I was telling the truth or not. "I don't know, Mistress." He glanced up at the ceiling. He looked back at me. "Show me how to use it." With a crazy gleam in his eye, he reached out his hands and held the tablet toward me.

"I don't know how to use it." Trying to sound strong, I couldn't hide the small quaver of fear that crept into my voice.

"You lied about the amulet. You're lying about knowing how to use the tablet."

"I can't, I'm tied up." Looking up again, he mumbled something under his breath.

He looked up at the ceiling of the cave again. Shrugging his shoulders, "ok, if you say so." He stopped talking to the ceiling and like lightning, he reached behind me with the knife and quickly sliced through the rope tied around my wrists. Quickly, I reached down and pulled my shirt closed. Imploring with him, "Please, can I have one moment with my niece first?"

Glancing over to Kelsey, he seemed to soften a bit at the sight of her. It was pretty evident that he didn't want to hurt her after all. However, he stared at me with contempt. After looking me over for a second, licking his lips, he looked back at her and replied, "Well, I suppose I don't need her anymore anyway." His eyes roamed over me suspiciously, "Don't try anything funny." Nodding my agreement, he replied, "Okay, then. But only for a minute. Then you have to show me how to work the tablet."

Scrambling over to Kelsey, she ran to me holding Peanut close. We met halfway and hugged fiercely, "Oh, Kelsey. I'm so sorry it took so long." Pulling back to make sure she was alright and taking in every detail of her, I tried to make sure she was okay and reassure her at the same time. "Are you okay?" She nodded, tears falling softly across her precious cheeks.

"That's enough." Maxwell demanded, grasping Kelsey by the hand and pulling her away from me.

The Tree and the Tablet

She clutched at me. Her eyes were wide with fear and she screamed, "NOOOOO!" Followed by sobs of despair, "Please! I promise I'll be good."

"STOP IT!" He exclaimed.

Fearing for her, I quickly kneeled down and made eye contact, "It's going to be okay, honey. I love you so much. We'll be together. Soon." Glancing over her head to Maxwell standing there, then I smiled at her, "Just be a good girl and go back over to the side where you'll be out of the way, sweetie." She was shaking her head and just saying no in a soft voice. "Honey, please. It will be alright, I promise."

"You promise, Auntie?" Her little lip quivered.

"I promise, sweetie." Attempting to smile at her reassuringly, I was trying to figure out how I was going to get out of this one. She finally relinquished her hold on me and walked back over to where she was hiding earlier. My gaze shifted for a moment and then sought her out again to emphasize my pleasure in her actions by giving her another reassuring smile. As I stood, I slowly moved toward her so that she was behind me.

"Okay, show me!" He thrust the tablet at me.

Just then, Daniel came out of the wall behind Maxwell and I grabbed the tablet. "Hello, Weasel!" Daniel said menacingly.

Maxwell jumped. His eyes grew large and he laughed. Turning toward Daniel, he seemed on edge. "Hello, son of Doane. She said you'd be here, but she didn't know how close you were."

371

My heart leapt into my chest. My world was crashing around me and I just couldn't breathe. Swallowing hard, I tried to keep the bile down. My mind raged. *No! I just couldn't believe it. He was playing me all along. No wonder he didn't want to share. I finally understood what Ellandra had meant when she said her son had his hands full with me.* Inside, I was screaming, but outside, I was slowly and calmly moving toward my goal...Kelsey.

Daniel turned a scathing and evil smile toward Maxwell and in that moment, I was afraid of him. "Enough!" He barked. "I'd shut your mouth now if you want to continue to breathe."

Maxwell appeared to jump, but since he was in front of me and facing Daniel, I couldn't determine if he was frightened. However, I could see Daniel's face. He seemed on edge. He looked past Maxwell to where I stood. Frozen, I stopped what I was doing. I'd been slowly motioning behind my back for Kelsey to come to me as I backed away from Maxwell. The next words out of Daniel's mouth almost cut me in two.

A softer expression crossed his face and he gently coaxed me, "Give me the tablet, Maggie." He started to walk toward me.

Just then, Kelsey grabbed my hand and I took a deep gulp of air as I held the tablet out in front of me and yelled, "STOP! Daniel, don't take another step or I'll destroy it."

He had the decency to look unsure and stopped where he was. A spark of doubt crossed his face as he calmly spoke, "Maggie, I know what you're thinking"—

"You have no idea." My voice cracked and speaking over my

shoulder, I whispered to Kelsey, "Hold on, sweetie!" As I quickly glanced over my shoulder at her, I could see she had Peanut in her other arm, and she was nodding slowly.

"Yes, I think I do, but that doesn't matter right now." —He started to move forward again. — "Maggie, please!"

"I'm sorry, Daniel, but this is where we must leave it." The tablet started to pulse. Reaching out with my mind, "*Duck, follow my thoughts.*"

"Yes, Mistress!"

With that, I closed my eyes, and envisioned the land Nohad and the Glenn of the Maiden. As quickly as I thought it, we were whisked away to land on our feet in the Glenn next to the entryway.

Turning to Kelsey, I hugged her close. Peanut wriggled free of Kelsey's grip and started licking my hands and yipping excitedly. Kelsey was in shock and as I checked her over, I knew she was overwhelmed by what she was seeing. She turned away from me sobbing, and cried out, "Mommy?" Before I'd thought of where we would go, I'd forgotten Andrea was there. My only thought had been to get Kelsey out of the cave and away from the danger. Andrea rushed over to hold Kelsey close.

The reunion was bittersweet to watch. They hugged and looked at each other and hugged again. My heart swelled and a tear trickled down my face. I hadn't thought of it before, but bringing Kelsey to this land with me would allow her to be with her mother again. Now, all I needed to do was to find a way to bring Jaxon here.

Looking at the tablet, I wondered if it was possible. Duck arrived and was converted to his beautifully scaled form only still in miniature. Holding the tablet in my hands, I closed my eyes and wished with all my might. *Tablet of power, please convert my dragon friend back to his normal size.* The tablet glowed and words formed on the face.

A mighty foe so strong and bold
No longer small enough to hold

Speaking the words, Duck began to stretch and shimmer. With a puff of smoke, there he was, as large as a full-grown bull elephant.

Looking at him in surprise, I asked, "Did you grow, or did I do that?"

Flexing his superior, now larger, wings, he smiled and said, "I'm not sure which has happened, but it appears that I am definitely larger and magnificent." His voice was actually much deeper, and the end part was in a voice of awe. He was turning this way and that, admiring his new massive wingspan and trying them out which was causing my hair to blow back away from my face. As I laughed at his antics, a thought crossed my mind though.

"Duck?" He continued to flex his wings. "DUCK!" I said loudly to get his attention.

The Tree and the Tablet

He stopped flexing and looked at me quizzically. "Yes, Mistress?"

"Where are Phenryr and Falomere?"

"Once you went through the wall, they disappeared." He gnashed his great fangs together, testing their strength. Slightly distracted with his new and improved self, he continued, "Poof! They were gone."

"Do you think they were transported back in time? Back to where they were when everything happened?"

Stopping his preening, he looked at me earnestly. "I don't know, but it seems likely since they were cursed back in the time of Serena."

"Ahhh, that's a shame. I would've liked to get to know them better."

Kelsey drew Duck's attention with her curiosity, and he was happy to oblige her. He glowed under Kelsey's admiration while Andrea stood by smiling at the pair.

The tablet was emitting a soft green light. A voice came from behind me as if it were an echo from my hurting heart and stirred on the wind, "Maggie."

My heart was playing tricks on me. Looking up at the group that was suddenly silent and looking behind me, my heart stopped. Slowly exhaling, I could feel the blood rush from my face as I turned to face my dreams and nightmares all in one. The sound of my broken heart escaped my lips in the form of an agonized moan. There he stood, bronze and beautiful. Liquid pools of hope stared back at me. Suddenly, my heart hurt as if it were being pulled right out of my chest.

Daniel, the son of Ellandra, the sworn enemy of the house of Valor, stood a short distance away from me. That evil sneak. It was too much. Sitting down right where I'd stood only moments before, my aching ribs, my sore face, my broken heart. My body couldn't take it. My mind reeled and the pain overwhelmed me. A flare shot out from the tablet which began to pulse in rhythm to my heartbeat. It engulfed me in a white-hot light. A strange voice in my head, as if it were all around me but inside me as well, spoke softly, *"Sleep, child."* The last thing I heard was Andrea and Duck talking above me in concerned voices as my body and mind caved into the sweet oblivion that was sleep. Absolutely nothing else mattered as I melted into the soft earth beneath me like a puddle of ice cream on a hot day.

CHAPTER 28

Soft light filtered through billowing curtains greeted my eyes as I awakened to a new day. A gentle breeze swirled around me and I smelled the most delicious scents carried on the air. Like lilacs and roses, lilies and freesias, closely followed by the faint smell of a campfire burning in the distance. It was so lovely. Above me was a canopy of iridescent material that moved with the gentle wind causing the colors to shift. Home. It was all just a horrible nightmare.

Sitting up in my bed, I looked around. Reality crashed into me with the force of a wrecking ball. This wasn't my home. Furthermore, I was in what looked to be some sort of fortress made of the most beautiful white stone. It reminded me of the tablet. Panicked, I looked around quickly and slightly calmed myself when I saw it sitting unassumingly on the bedside table.

Murmuring voices were heard from the doorway and someone shushed the others as I heard a hand upon the doorknob. An elderly woman entered the room. She looked exactly like the one from the vision I'd had in the cave. It was the woman who gave me the rose.

She entered and gently closed the door behind her. Turning, she looked up and smiled at me. "Good. I'm glad you are awake. I was beginning to wonder if you were going to drift in the land of Kerr forever, or if your heart would allow you to rejoin us." Her voice sounded paper thin as she spoke, but very kind and sweet.

As she approached the bed, I felt like I was watching an old movie with the Greek goddesses. She was dressed in a tunic of soft blue and her silver hair flowed gently down her body toward the floor. A rope of silk was tied around her waist. Her hair was so long, it was almost touching her ankles. The softest, kindest, blue eyes smiled down at me. She was just as tall as I remembered. On her head was a small but beautifully carved tiara, set with the most amazing stones of a stunning opalescent blue. Guessing at my thoughts she said, "You are in the Castle Valor." She smiled. "I am the living relic, Shalandria, sworn never to rest until my daughter is avenged."

The air left me in a whoosh as I stared at her with my mouth hanging open. I knew she was old, but how old?

Again, she spoke, waving her hand dismissively, "I am too old to count." She laughed at my look of shock. "I have the

The Tree and the Tablet

ability to read your thoughts before you speak them."

Snidely, I thought, *"What's the point of vocal cords?"* Then I thought, *"Get out of my head. My thoughts are private property."*

Again, she spoke, but this time, it was in my head, without a single movement of her lips. *"Maggie, I know your heart is hurting still, but your mind is sharp, and your body has healed. Your family awaits you outside this very room. You have the ability to right so many wrongs, but you must overcome your hurt pride and your emotional pain."* Her eyes sought mine.

Looking into her eyes. The anger and frustration began to fade and leave my body. The blue in her eyes seemed to have the effect of clouds parting on a sunny day and for some reason, it calmed my spirit. Watching as her frail hand sought to push a stray lock of hair behind my ear, something about it reminded me of my mom. Her soft eyes spoke volumes and she didn't have to project words or a voice into my head. I understood. There was much to be done still. Her presence in my mind retreated and I felt the loss but enjoyed the freedom it afforded me.

"Maggie, this is greater than us and your family. There is much more at stake than you know. Two worlds depend on your ability to close a rift by returning the Great Spirit tree to its rightful place."

Testing the absence, I thought about what she'd said for a moment, but when there was no response, I knew she was respecting my wishes by withdrawing from my mind. My thoughts drifted outward to see if I could read her mind, but it felt like there was a wall in front of me, keeping me from going any further. She smiled knowingly but said nothing. "But how do I return the tree to this land when I don't know how it was taken," I asked out loud.

"I suspect it is much like the way you brought Kelsey and Peanut here, but I have never seen it done with a tree or inanimate object before. However, the Great Spirit tree is not merely a tree but a life source of all the land. It harbors a great power of its own."

She turned and walked to the window. Looking outside, "Even now, the darkness approaches. There are many creatures who will suffer, and our world will die." She bowed her head. Turning to face me, the sorrow was evident in her expression. "Many of our people left and went to other lands, but I remained, hoping to find a way to heal this wound. The darkness will consume our world and enter yours through the rift that was torn if we don't find a way to replace the tree and repair the damage."

Placing my feet on the floor, testing my strength, I found that I felt remarkably strong and fit.

Smiling, she said, "Your dragon friend and the tablet of power healed you. Here are some clothes that you may find more similar to what you are used to." She laid the clothes that she had draped over her arm onto the bed. It looked to be a pair of pants, a shirt, and a jacket. It appeared that my boots were cleaned and sitting on the floor at the end of the bed. My other clothes were

The Tree and the Tablet

on a bench at the end of the bed. The only thing missing was the torn shirt that Maxwell had destroyed. Quickly, I changed my clothes while she was looking out the window.

After lacing my boots, I stood, walking strong and surefooted to the window. Moving aside the gossamer curtains, I was faced with a devastating view. As far as the eye could see, there was darkness. It stopped when it reached a creek of water that had a strange green color to it. It was almost like emeralds, clear and bright. It looked like a fire had ravaged the land and stopped on the other side of the creek. Duck lay sleeping on the soft earth just below my room.

The sight of the devastation meeting the beautiful water filled me with sorrow. Instantly I felt an overwhelming sense of doom and fear. What if I couldn't find a way? What if I failed? Everything in this land would die. It suddenly dawned on me that this wasn't just about the land, but if it was destroyed and everything died, then Kelsey and Andrea wouldn't be able to be together. Andrea would be gone forever.

No. I won't let that happen.

Suddenly, I remembered that right before I'd succumbed to the mind numbing sleep inflicted by the tablet, I'd seen Daniel. Turning to Shalandria, I opened my mouth to ask, when the door opened to usher in Kelsey and Andrea. My heart filled with love for these two precious people. There were many questions in my heart, but the most important thing right now was to fill up my aching heart with the love of the two people who could help me.

I knelt down, tears blurring my vision and opened my arms. "Kells!"

"Auntie!" Kelsey ran across the room and jumped into my outstretched arms. She felt lighter than I remembered, but I was never so glad to have her close to me. Peanut came running into the room just then and nipped my fingers. Laughing we separated. Scooping up Peanut, I cuddled her close.

Shalandria walked toward the door, "If you are well enough, we will be having our meal in the breakfast room shortly."

Looking up from Kelsey and Peanut, I smiled, and replied, "Yes, thank you." She nodded and left the room.

Andrea stepped up and held Kelsey by the shoulders, she looked at me concerned, "Maggie, are you okay?"

"Yes, I think so."

"We were so worried about you." She sighed.

"'Drea," —My heart raced, and I steadied it for the question I had to ask. — "What happened to Daniel?"

"Daniel?" She let Kelsey go to play with Peanut over by the window and looked at me confused. "I'm not sure. Duck said that he showed up in the cave and tried to take the tablet from you but you grabbed Kelsey and Peanut and transported them here." She frowned. "He said he had no idea what was going on, only that you were in a lot of pain. We assumed it was your physical pain." Tears were welling in her eyes, "Maggie, I had no idea what you went through to get Kelsey back." Her voice shook, "I mean, you're so much stronger than I thought. Every time I think about what that man did to you..." A sob escaped her as she stepped forward and took me into her arms. "I'll never doubt you again." She whispered into my ear as she hugged me fiercely.

Stiffening in her arms. "What do you mean?" She pulled back to search my face. "Andrea, Daniel was in the Glenn with us. I saw you and Duck. You looked right at him." Confusion rolled through my head and I pulled away from her. *Why is she hiding things from me?*

"No, Maggie, he wasn't there." Seeing I didn't believe her, she insisted, "We were looking at you." I shook my head. "Maggie, ask Duck. Why would I lie?"

Turning away from her, I took a deep breath, trying to figure out what had happened. "But, I saw him."

"I'm not sure what you saw." She was speaking softly and gently now. "Maggie, Duck sensed something and turned to look at you. His expression was so scary, I couldn't help but look too. Then you moaned and fell to the ground. He said he'd be back and lifted you in his talons. The last time I saw you, he was flying away with you. He brought you here and then came back for me and Kelsey. Shalandria has been the only one allowed to come in and care for you for the past two days." Placing her hands on my shoulders, she slowly turned me toward her. "I swear it." She looked back to the window. "Dragons aren't allowed in the castle, so he's been keeping watch outside your window." She smiled.

Shocked, I said, "But I feel so strong for someone who's been in bed for two days."

"I agree that it's strange, but there are so many strange things that have happened, I don't question it anymore." She smiled reassuringly. "Maggie, let's go get some food and you can talk to Duck."

Glancing over at the window, I could see that Kelsey was laughing and waving at something. As I moved closer, I wasn't surprised to see Duck flapping his great wings and floating just a mere ten feet from the window. "Duck! Look at you flying around," I exclaimed. "I'll be down in a bit to see you."

He was so excited he stopped flapping for a moment which caused him to plummet toward the ground. He flapped his wings once right before he hit the ground which served to stop any damage. He laughed, "I'm okay." he looked up and smiled. "I'm so happy to see you are awake." He turned in a circle like an anxious dog trying to catch his tail. "I'll wait here." He spun once more. "Please hurry, I missed you."

"Okay, calm down." His antics made me laugh. Still so much like a puppy. "I need to get something to eat and then I'll be right out."

"Okay, okay, okay!" He repeated as if he was trying to reassure or calm himself then promptly sat down and a puff of smoke escaped his lips.

Turning, I took Kelsey's outstretched hand and smiling at Andrea, we went down to get some food. Not even sure what time it really was, but I could eat anything right now since I was famished. Peanut followed along and wiggling her little nub, she

The Tree and the Tablet

raced down the grand spiral staircase in front of us.

Someday, I'd explore this place. It was so beautiful with its white stones and flowing design. It reminded me of waterfalls and forests. Columns and open spaces were filled with blooming flowers hanging from grand pots. Brightly colored rugs that looked like moss were spread across many of the open areas. As we entered the breakfast room, which was off the main hall, I was struck by a sense of cozy comfort. There were strange fruits and what looked to be bread and some type of rolls all over the table. Finding a chair, I sat down to eat.

Shalandria was seated at the round table in the seat that was closest to the windows, which were opened and allowed a soft breeze to flow through the room. We all sat and ate quietly. It was delicious. Many of the fruits looked different but tasted the same as what we would eat at home. The breads were light and flaky, like pastry, but had a floral note to them. The Zanta butter-spread was the biggest surprise. Curiously, I looked to Shalandria and asked, "What is a Zanta?"

"It is the large pink two-legged creature that grazes in the fields. We use their milk to make many different things in our diet. It is very delicious and very good for you."

The butter, made from the milk, was so smooth and creamy but slightly salty with caramel flavored. It reminded me of a salted-caramel latte. There were some fruits that looked like mango but tasted like oranges. It was very odd.

As we finished eating, a young boy, about twelve entered the room and started clearing away the dishes. He looked like he had jaundice and his hair was bright orange. His eyes were the oddest things. They looked like marbles that were very large for his face. Like the ones that have swirly colors in them. His ears were similar to those that might be found on an elf with pointy tips but they were cupped out away from his head and turned like a cat where each one could move independently to pick out sounds. His nose was close to his face and when he turned and smiled at me, it reminded me of the Cheshire Cat.

Shalandria noticed my interest and introduced us, "Maggie, this is Eurok. He is a Fellini-child." She looked sad for a moment, "He is the last of his kind here in Nohad."

Returning his smile, I held out my hand, "It's nice to meet you, Eurok."

He swiftly bowed his head down and ran his face along my hand letting out a soft purr. My eyebrows scrunched together in confusion.

Shalandria chuckled, "He does not speak. He is similar to a cross of a cat and a human."

"Oh." Slightly embarrassed by my assumption, I grinned at him. He looked at me and blinked his too large eyes. Reaching over, I rubbed the top of his head. He closed his eyes briefly. His right ear twitched and turning toward the window, he hissed and ran from the room. Duck's snout came through the opening of the window, causing me to giggle, "Duck, I'll be right there, you goof." He apologized and removed his head from the window.

The Tree and the Tablet

Andrea and Kelsey left the table to go clean up. As I stood, making my excuses and thanking my hostess for the lovely meal and the excellent care, I turned and was frozen to the floor. Standing in front of me with a devil-may-care expression, was Daniel. Reaching behind me to grab a knife from the table, I turned back around to find that there was no one there. Deflated and concerned, I promptly sat back down in my chair as the blood drained from my face and the tears slid across my cheeks. *What was happening?*

CHAPTER 29

"What has happened, Maggie?" Shalandria's concerned question pierced my agonized thoughts. She had moved around the table to sit in the chair next to mine as she spoke. Taking my hands in hers, "Please share with me. Maybe I can help." She smiled reassuringly.

"I can't explain why or what is happening, but I keep seeing Daniel, the man who helped me find Kelsey." I was shaken to the core.

Nodding thoughtfully, she said, "Duck shared with me what happened in the caves." At my surprised expression, she raised her brows slightly. A sigh escaped me and she thoughtfully responded, "Maggie, the only explanation is that your destinies are intertwined in some way."

Swallowing the hard lump in my throat, I suddenly felt

devastated by my admission and what it would mean. Looking up at her, I felt my heart thud in my chest. "Yes, we're sworn enemies now." Rolling my eyes, bitterness crept into my voice, "I'm not sure, but I think I've fallen in love with him." Frustrated, I turned to stare out the window at Duck chasing some strange bird, "Maybe it's just lust, but there's definitely a strong connection that I can't overcome." The pain was flowing through me now at his betrayal, "No matter how much I want to hate him for what he's done, I find myself longing to be near him. So much so, that I see him when he isn't here." Glancing back to look into her eyes, I asked, "How do I go on, knowing that everything is a lie between us?" My voice shook as I looked back up to her steady gaze.

"There are many things that I do not know, but the one thing that I do know is that love is a very powerful thing. Some say it is bigger than us and when the great spirit chooses to link two souls together, there is always a greater cause." Her compassion was easy to read in her expression as she explained, "Love is probably the one power that can turn the tides of destiny." She patted my hand. "You will see." She gave me one of those motherly smiles, filled with reassurance and hope. Taking the napkin from the table, she gently wiped my tears away. Staring down at my hands, I took a shaky breath. Placing her hand under my chin, she gently coaxed me to look up into her eyes. "Let us put on our best face and go see Duck before he breaks into my home or kills someone while chasing whatever has fascinated him out there."

We both laughed envisioning the chaos that would cause.

We walked out the arched doorway into the gardens. The beauty was striking against the chaos only miles away. Duck swooped across the small valley, leaving behind his quarry for another day. Landing in front of me, I could swear he'd grown again. He seemed like he was definitely a little larger than a bull elephant now. He had to lean down to sniff my hair. "Mistress!" It was a half sigh, half laugh. He licked me, which made me giggle.

"Duck, we have to go back."

He frowned. "I know, but I don't like it."

Patting him gently and stroking his neck, I felt his anguish. "You're the only one strong enough to carry the tree if I'm not able to transport it."

"But the people who may see me will not understand." He blinked his great eyes. "I don't want to scare them."

I hadn't thought of that. "Duck, I need to try to reach out and communicate with Jaxon. After I speak with him, we'll transport directly to my home."

"Yes, Mistress." A more contrite and obedient puppy, I'd never seen. However, I'd also never had a puppy that could link its mind with mine or speak. A small grin crossed my lips at that thought. He was such a joy to be around. Always concerned and thoughtful but also playful and filled with love. Even now, I could feel the love coursing through me, like a tether that bound us.

Closing my eyes and breathing steadily, I reached out my

thoughts to Jaxon in his beautiful robin form. "Maggie? Is that you?" His thoughts seemed anguished and frail.

There were two visions. One of a cage, and one of a tree. *I don't remember him being in a cage. As a matter of fact, the last time I saw him, I told him to wait outside the waterfall.* "Jaxon? Where are you?"

"Daniel came out of the cave and when I flew to his hand, he grabbed my foot." Occupying his mind, I felt his little heart beating rapidly as he spoke. He was afraid. "He put me in a cage and took me back to your house. But he's upset because Andrea isn't in the tree anymore and it looks like a mole dug a hole next to the tree."

Gasping, my chest constricted with longing and fear. Daniel had Jaxon? Why was he at my house? Did he figure out what was happening?

Quickly, I asked, "Jaxon, where is Daniel now?"

Suddenly, I could see Daniel through one of Jaxon's eyes. "Maggie?" He peered into the other eye. "I know you're in there. You need to come here now. We have things to discuss." He squeezed Jaxon a little and I could feel Jaxon's fear increasing. There was no time to waste. My eyes flew open and sought out Duck. Seeing him standing close by, I placed my hand over my rapidly beating heart.

"Duck, I'm going now! You need to wait and follow me when I reach my thoughts out to you."

"But, Mistress, I don't..."

The Tree and the Tablet

"There's no time to discuss it," I interrupted curtly. "Do as I ask!" Seeing his pained expression, I spoke softer, "Please, Duck." He lowered his head in compliance.

Shalandria was standing by and grasping my upper arm with her frail hand, "Maggie, what is happening?"

"I don't have time to explain. Jaxon's in danger. I must leave now!"

"I understand." She released my arm. "Go with the Great Spirit to watch over you." She nodded solemnly. She reached over to gently place her hand on Duck and he was instantly calmed.

"I am only a thought away." He reminded me.

"Thank you, my friend." My eyes fluttered closed and suddenly, I remembered the tablet was sitting on my bedside table. Better to leave it behind. Just in case. Again, I refocused my thoughts and instantly, I was transported through space and time. With a whoosh and a swirl of colors, I was standing next to the dogwood outside my back deck. Surprised at how quickly it seemed, I thought, "W*ow, I'm getting pretty good at this."* I spied Jaxon in a cage that was hanging from a low branch on the tree.

Strong hands grasped me from behind and turned me around. "Maggie, where's the tablet?" His voice sounded frantic.

My heart did a strange flip in my chest at the electric contact from Daniel, but I remembered that he was holding Jaxon hostage and I needed to take the tree back to Nohad and the Glenn. Reminding myself I was angry at him for his betrayal, I spat out, "Snake! How could you? You knew all along what was going to happen, and you played me like a flute."

His expression turned dark and his eyes penetrated my soul. Those beautiful eyes that I wanted to drown in at one time seemed to be on fire when he first made eye contact with me, but as soon as the words left my lips, they'd hardened, turning a deep jade green, and his lips snarled at me, "A flute?" He laughed, "You have no clue what you're doing. And you have no idea what's at stake." I tried to shake him off, but his grip was like iron. His voice softened slightly, "Give me the tablet, Maggie, and I'll give you Jaxon."

"Let me go." He looked like he was contemplating something, but then released me. "I don't have the tablet."

Watching me carefully, "You're lying." Turning, he walked to the little cage and began to put his hand in. Jaxon started flitting around and squawking fearfully while attempting to keep out of Daniel's reach. Daniel was finally able to grasp Jaxon in his large hand. Jaxon's little head turned this way and that, trying to peck Daniel with his little beak.

I'd started to walk toward him but stopped myself. I pleaded with him, "Daniel, please. Don't do this. I swear I don't have it." To prove myself, I opened my jacket to show him. "I lost it when I left the cave. It just disappeared." The lie came more smoothly this time and I prayed he'd be convinced.

He watched me carefully as he started to gently squeeze Jaxon in his hand. Jaxon started flailing about and screeching

The Tree and the Tablet

wildly. He started to relax his hand, "Maggie, you don't understand. I *NEED* that tablet." He emphasized the word "need".

"Daniel, I'll find it. I have to take the tree and Jaxon though." He looked at the tree and then back to me.

His eyes watched me carefully. He ran his other hand through his hair, and it fell forward, cascading across his troubled brow. Briefly, I wondered what he was thinking. *I don't care. Yes, you do. No! Stop it, Maggie.* I admonished myself for my momentary weakness. He growled low and looked to his right.

He seemed like he was talking to someone else that was standing beside him, but there was no one there, as he said, "Yes, but I'll give her the bird." He looked frustrated. "No, Ellandra! That's not what we agreed on." He released Jaxon who promptly flew to me. As soon as Jaxon reached me, I mentally called out to Duck.

Daniel strode over to me purposefully. "She wants me to kill you, but I think it'll be much more fun to keep you alive." Reaching down he plucked a strand of my hair out of my face. Releasing the air that was burning my lungs, our eyes were locked, and my heart hoped for one moment that he'd change his mind.

As I exhaled, his name danced on my lips, "Daniel." It was a mere whisper. All of my longing and hope was enveloped within that one word. My heart and soul dripped out of my mouth with that one breath.

He grimaced as if he were in the most intense pain. His

395

whisper echoed mine, "Maggie." A deep tenderness crossed his face as he put his hand against my cheek. He was so close I could feel his breath on my lips. There was definitely something there besides lust, but I dared not speak it out loud. I opened my mouth to speak...

Before I had a chance to react, he leaned down and kissed me. It was filled with every single emotion all rolled into one moment. Fire scorched my lips and my soul ached. As I clung to him, my heart ached. A tear trickled down my cheek. *Even now, I can't resist him. Why?* My thoughts spun in circles.

He pulled away. Briefly, he stared at the solitary tear that was dangling precariously on my cheek. Reaching up and wiping it away with his thumb, he turned without a word and strode to the tree. "You leave me no choice." He said as he grasped the tree limb in front of him. "Bring me the tablet and I'll give you the tree."

Regaining my wits, I ran forward, "Daniel, No!"

Just as Duck appeared next to me, Daniel disappeared with the tree. Crumpling to the ground like a puddle of mush next to the churned-up earth where the tree had once been, I cried. The tears flowed freely as I yelled to the sky with anger, pain, and longing mixed, "I'll find you!" Raising my fists, "Do you hear me? I will save them!" With my clenched fist, I punched the dirt next to the hole in the ground. Something caught my eye. A breeze stirred, and my hair flowed around me like a river as I slowly extended my hand toward the glowing white and gold object that

The Tree and the Tablet

was pulsing slowly in the soft earth. Reaching out my hand, I lifted up the one thing that I never thought to see, the amulet.

My mind raced with a million thoughts. Why did he leave the amulet? Suddenly, hope filled my heart and getting to my feet, I turned to Duck who was now stone again and sporting a beautiful robin for a hat. "There's much to do, my friend!" Striding to Duck and placing my hand on his flank, I smiled as I whispered under my breath, "I will find a way! I will fix this and he will be mine!" With that thought, I closed my eyes and allowed the world around me to dissolve as I ventured toward a new world. My journey was just beginning.

The story continues in

The Raven and the Staff
The St. James Chronicles Book 2

***

You can follow the author on Facebook
to find out its release at the link below!

https://www.facebook.com/kathryn.obrien.7330763

ABOUT THE AUTHOR

Dreamer, Spell Weaver, Dragon Lover, Hopeless Romantic.

Kathryn O'Brien lives in a small town outside of Belfair, Washington, with her family and three dogs. When she's not escaping to her fantasy realms, she spends her time taking care of her three young grandchildren and cooking delicious treats for her family and friends. She spends time working on her artistic expression in many ways which includes writing poetry, painting landscapes using oils, and working on finding ways to stay out of trouble. The places she's been in her life are inspirations for all of her stories and her passion for life is evident in every word she writes.

You can visit her online at
https://www.facebook.com/kathryn.obrien.7330763

Made in the USA
Middletown, DE
09 December 2020